DARK
MATTER

Blake Crouch is best known for the 'Wayward Pines' trilogy, which has sold more than a million copies, been translated into thirty languages, and adapted into a prime-time event series on FOX. He lives in Colorado.

BY BLAKE CROUCH

Wayward Pines

Pines • *Wayward* • *The Last Town*

Andrew Z. Thomas/Luther Kite Series

Desert Places • *Locked Doors* • *Break You*
Stirred • *Serial Killers Uncut*

Standalone Novels

Run • *Abandon* • *Snow Bound*
Famous • *Eerie* • *Draculas*

Letty Dobesh Series

The Pain of Others • *Sunset Key* • *Grab*

Other Stories And Novellas

*69 • *Remaking* • *On the Good, Red Road*
Shining Rock • *The Meteorologist*
Unconditional • *Perfect Little Town*
Hunting Season

Story Collections

Fully Loaded • *Thicker Than Blood* • *The Fear Trilogy*

DARK MATTER

A NOVEL

Blake Crouch

PAN BOOKS

First published in the US 2016 by Crown, an imprint of the Crown
Publishing Group, a division of Penguin Random House LLC, New York

First published in the UK 2016 by Macmillan

This edition published 2017 by Pan
an imprint of Pan Macmillan
20 New Wharf Road, London N1 9RR
Associated companies throughout the world
www.panmacmillan.com

ISBN 978-1-4472-9758-1

Grateful acknowledgment is made for the excerpt from "Burnt
Norton" from FOUR QUARTETS by T. S. Eliot. Copyright 1936 by
Houghton Mifflin Harcourt Publishing Company; copyright © renewed
1964 by T. S. Eliot. Reprinted by permission of Houghton Mifflin
Harcourt Publishing Company. All rights reserved.

Pan Macmillan does not have any control over, or any responsibility for,
any author or third-party websites referred to in or on this book.

7 9 8

A CIP catalogue record for this book is available from the British Library.

Typeset by Ellipsis Digital Limited, Glasgow
Printed and bound by CPI Group (UK) Ltd, Croydon, CR0 4YY

Visit www.panmacmillan.com to read more about all our books
and to buy them. You will also find features, author interviews and
news of any author events, and you can sign up for e-newsletters
so that you're always first to hear about our new releases.

*For anyone who has wondered
what their life might look like at the
end of the road not taken.*

Praise for *Dark Matter*

'Brilliant. [...] vented something new'　　　Lee Child, *New York Times* bestselling author of the Jack Reacher series

'Exceptional. It's been a long time since a novel sucked me in and kept me turning pages the way this one did'
Andy Weir, *New York Times*
bestselling author of *The Martian*

'Wow. I gulped down *Dark Matter* in one sitting and put it down awed and amazed by the ride. It's fast, smart, addictive – and the most creative, head-spinning novel I've read in ages. A truly remarkable thriller'
Tess Gerritsen, *New York Times*
bestselling author of the Rizzoli & Isles series

'A mind-bending thriller of the first order, not merely a rollicking entertainment but a provocative investigation into the nature of second chances ... I dare you to put it down, because I sure couldn't'　　　Justin Cronin, *New York Times* bestselling author of the 'Passage' trilogy

'A mind-blowing sci-fi/suspense/love-story mash-up'
Entertainment Weekly

'The kind of book the word "thriller" was coined for – a shoot-ing star through multiple genres, posing fundamental questions about identity and reality before revealing itself as, at its core, a love story. Smart, fast, powerful, and ultimately touching' **Joseph Finder, *New York Times* bestselling author of *Guilty Minds* and *Suspicion***

'An addictive read! You're in for an intelligent, breath-taking ride' **John Lescroart, *New York Times* bestselling author of *The Fall* and *The Oath***

'Blake Crouch yet again proves himself to be a master. Non-stop pacing, fascinating characters and an ingenious concept all come together flawlessly in a crescendo of pursuit, danger and romance all the way to a surprising and satisfying slam-bang conclusion' **Barry Eisler, *New York Times* bestselling author of the John Rain series**

'Excellent characterization and well-crafted tension . . . the rousing and heartfelt ending will leave readers cheering' ***Publishers Weekly***

'Suspenseful, frightening, and sometimes poignant' ***Kirkus***

'Crouch keeps the pace swift and the twists exciting. Readers who liked his *Wayward Pines* trilogy will probably devour this speculative thriller in one sitting [as will] those who enjoy roller-coaster reads in the vein of Harlan Coben' ***Booklist***

What might have been and what has been
Point to one end, which is always present.
Footfalls echo in the memory
Down the passage which we did not take
Towards the door we never opened.

—T. S. ELIOT, "BURNT NORTON"

ONE

I love Thursday nights. They have a feel to them that's outside of time.

It's our tradition, just the three of us—family night.

My son, Charlie, is sitting at the table, drawing on a sketch pad. He's almost fifteen. The kid grew two inches over the summer, and he's as tall as I am now.

I turn away from the onion I'm julienning, ask, "Can I see?"

He holds up the pad, shows me a mountain range that looks like something on another planet.

I say, "Love that. Just for fun?"

"Class project. Due tomorrow."

"Then get back to it, Mr. Last Minute."

Standing happy and slightly drunk in my kitchen, I'm unaware that tonight is the end of all of this. The end of everything I know, everything I love.

No one tells you it's all about to change, to be taken away. There's no proximity alert, no indication that you're standing on the precipice. And maybe that's what makes tragedy so tragic. Not just what happens, but *how* it happens: a sucker punch that comes at you out of nowhere, when you're least expecting it. No time to flinch or brace.

The track lights shine on the surface of my wine, and the onion is beginning to sting my eyes. Thelonious Monk spins on the old turntable in the den. There's a richness to the analog recording I can never get enough of, especially the crackle of static between tracks. The den is filled with stacks and stacks of rare vinyl that I keep telling myself I'll get around to organizing one of these days.

My wife, Daniela, sits on the kitchen island, swirling her almost-empty wineglass in one hand and holding her phone in the other. She feels my stare and grins without looking up from the screen.

"I know," she says. "I'm violating the cardinal rule of family night."

"What's so important?" I ask.

She levels her dark, Spanish eyes on mine. "Nothing."

I walk over to her, take the phone gently out of her hand, and set it on the countertop.

"You could start the pasta," I say.

"I prefer to watch *you* cook."

"Yeah?" Quieter: "Turns you on, huh?"

"No, it's just more fun to drink and do nothing."

Her breath is wine-sweet, and she has one of those smiles that seem architecturally impossible. It still slays me.

I polish off my glass. "We should open more wine, right?"

"It would be stupid not to."

As I liberate the cork from a new bottle, she picks her phone back up and shows me the screen. "I was reading *Chicago Magazine*'s review of Marsha Altman's show."

"Were they kind?"

"Yeah, it's basically a love letter."

"Good for her."

"I always thought . . ." She lets the sentence die, but I know where it was headed. Fifteen years ago, before we met, Daniela was a comer to Chicago's art scene. She had a studio in Bucktown, showed her work in a half-dozen galleries, and had just lined up her first solo exhibition in New York. Then came life. Me. Charlie. A bout of crippling postpartum depression.

Derailment.

Now she teaches private art lessons to middle-grade students.

"It's not that I'm not happy for her. I mean, she's brilliant, she deserves it all."

I say, "If it makes you feel any better, Ryan Holder just won the Pavia Prize."

"What's that?"

"A multidisciplinary award given for achievements in the life and physical sciences. Ryan won for his work in neuroscience."

"Is it a big deal?"

"Million dollars. Accolades. Opens the floodgates to grant money."

"Hotter TAs?"

"Obviously that's the real prize. He invited me to a little informal celebration tonight, but I passed."

"Why?"

"Because it's our night."

"You should go."

"I'd really rather not."

Daniela lifts her empty glass. "So what you're saying is, we both have good reason to drink a lot of wine tonight."

I kiss her, and then pour generously from the newly opened bottle.

"You could've won that prize," Daniela says.

"You could've owned this city's art scene."

"But we did this." She gestures at the high-ceilinged expanse of our brownstone. I bought it pre-Daniela with an inheritance. "And we did that," she says, pointing to Charlie as he sketches with a beautiful intensity that reminds me of Daniela when she's absorbed in a painting.

It's a strange thing, being the parent of a teenager. One thing to raise a little boy, another entirely when a person on the brink of adulthood looks to you for wisdom. I feel like I have little to give. I know there are fathers who see the world a certain way, with clarity and confidence, who know just what to say to their sons and daughters. But I'm not one of them. The older I get, the less I understand. I love my son. He means everything to me. And yet, I can't escape the feeling that I'm failing him. Sending him off to the wolves with nothing but the crumbs of my uncertain perspective.

I move to the cabinet beside the sink, open it, and start hunting for a box of fettuccine.

Daniela turns to Charlie, says, "Your father could have won the Nobel."

I laugh. "That's possibly an exaggeration."

"Charlie, don't be fooled. He's a genius."

"You're sweet," I say. "And a little drunk."

"It's true, and you know it. Science is less advanced because you love your family."

I can only smile. When Daniela drinks, three things

happen: her native accent begins to bleed through, she becomes belligerently kind, and she tends toward hyperbole.

"Your father said to me one night—never forget it—that pure research is life-consuming. He said . . ." For a moment, and to my surprise, emotion overtakes her. Her eyes mist, and she shakes her head like she always does when she's about to cry. At the last second, she rallies, pushes through. "He said, 'Daniela, on my deathbed I would rather have memories of you than of a cold, sterile lab.'"

I look at Charlie, catch him rolling his eyes as he sketches.

Probably embarrassed by our display of parental melodrama.

I stare into the cabinet and wait for the ache in my throat to go away.

When it does, I grab the pasta and close the door.

Daniela drinks her wine.

Charlie draws.

The moment passes.

"Where's Ryan's party?" Daniela asks.

"Village Tap."

"That's your bar, Jason."

"So?"

She comes over, takes the box of pasta out of my hand.

"Go have a drink with your old college buddy. Tell him you're proud of him. Head held high. Tell him I said congrats."

"I will not tell him you said congrats."

"Why?"

"He has a thing for you."

"Stop it."

"It's true. From way back. From our roommate days.

Remember the last Christmas party? He kept trying to trick you into standing under the mistletoe with him?"

She just laughs, says, "Dinner will be on the table by the time you get home."

"Which means I should be back here in . . ."

"Forty-five minutes."

"What would I be without you?"

She kisses me.

"Let's not even think about it."

I grab my keys and wallet from the ceramic dish beside the microwave and move into the dining room, my gaze alighting on the tesseract chandelier above the dinner table. Daniela gave it to me for our tenth wedding anniversary. Best gift ever.

As I reach the front door, Daniela shouts, "Return bearing ice cream!"

"Mint chocolate chip!" Charlie says.

I lift my arm, raise my thumb.

I don't look back.

I don't say goodbye.

And this moment slips past unnoticed.

The end of everything I know, everything I love.

I've lived in Logan Square for twenty years, and it doesn't get any better than the first week of October. It always puts me in mind of that F. Scott Fitzgerald line: *Life starts all over again when it gets crisp in the fall.*

The evening is cool, and the skies are clear enough to see a handful of stars. The bars are more rambunctious than usual, jammed with disappointed Cubs fans.

I stop on the sidewalk in the glow of a gaudy sign that blinks VILLAGE TAP and stare through the open doorway of the ubiquitous corner bar you'll find in any self-respecting Chicago neighborhood. This one happens to be my local watering hole. It's the closest to home—a few blocks from my brownstone.

I pass through the glow of the blue neon sign in the front window and step through the doorway.

Matt, the bartender and owner, nods to me as I move down the bar, threading my way through the crowd that surrounds Ryan Holder.

I say to Ryan, "I was just telling Daniela about you."

He smiles, looking exquisitely groomed for the lecture circuit—fit and tan in a black turtleneck, his facial hair elaborately landscaped.

"Goddamn is it good to see you. I'm moved that you came. Darling?" He touches the bare shoulder of the young woman occupying the stool beside his. "Would you mind letting my dear old friend steal your chair for a minute?"

The woman dutifully abandons her seat, and I climb onto the stool beside Ryan.

He calls the bartender over. "We want you to set us up with a pair of the most expensive pours in the house."

"Ryan, not necessary."

He grabs my arm. "We're drinking the best tonight."

Matt says, "I have Macallan Twenty-Five."

"Doubles. My tab."

When the bartender goes, Ryan punches me in the arm. Hard. You wouldn't peg him as a scientist at first glance. He played lacrosse during his undergrad years, and he still carries the broad-shouldered physique and ease of movement of a natural athlete.

"How's Charlie and the lovely Daniela?"

"They're great."

"You should've brought her down. I haven't seen her since last Christmas."

"She sends along her congrats."

"You got a good woman there, but that's not exactly news."

"What are the chances of you settling down in the near future?"

"Slim. The single life, and its considerable perks, appears to suit me. You're still at Lakemont College?"

"Yeah."

"Decent school. Undergrad physics, right?"

"Exactly."

"So you're teaching . . ."

"Quantum mechanics. Intro stuff mainly. Nothing too terribly sexy."

Matt returns with our drinks, and Ryan takes them out of his hands and sets mine before me.

"So this celebration . . . " I say.

"Just an impromptu thing a few of my postgrads threw together. They love nothing more than to get me drunk and holding court."

"Big year for you, Ryan. I still remember you almost flunking differential equations."

"And you saved my ass. More than once."

For a second, behind the confidence and the polish, I glimpse the goofy, fun-loving grad student with whom I shared a disgusting apartment for a year and a half.

I ask, "Was the Pavia Prize for your work in—"

"Identifying the prefrontal cortex as a consciousness generator."

"Right. Of course. I read your paper on it."

"What'd you think?"

"Dazzling."

He looks genuinely pleased at the compliment.

"If I'm honest, Jason, and there's no false modesty here, I always thought it would be you publishing the seminal papers."

"Really?"

He studies me over the top of his black plastic glass frames.

"Of course. You're smarter than I am. Everyone knew it."

I drink my whisky. I try not to acknowledge how delicious it is.

He says, "Just a question, but do you see yourself more as a research scientist or a teacher these days?"

"I—"

"Because I see myself, first and foremost, as a man pursuing answers to fundamental questions. Now, if the people around me"—he gestures at his students who have begun to crowd in—"are sharp enough to absorb knowledge by sheer proximity to me . . . great. But the passing on of knowledge, as it were, doesn't interest me. All that matters is the science. The research."

I note a flicker of annoyance, or anger, in his voice, and it's building, like he's getting himself worked up toward something.

I try to laugh it off. "Are you upset with me, Ryan? It almost sounds like you think I let you down."

"Look, I've taught at MIT, Harvard, Johns Hopkins, the best schools on the planet. I've met the smartest motherfuckers in the room, and Jason, you would've changed the world if you'd decided to go that path. If you'd stuck with it. Instead, you're teaching undergrad physics to future doctors and patent lawyers."

"We can't all be superstars like you, Ryan."

"Not if you give up."

I finish my whisky.

"Well, I'm so glad I popped in for this." I step down off the barstool.

"Don't be that way, Jason. I was paying you a compliment."

"I'm proud of you, man. I mean that."

"Jason."

"Thanks for the drink."

Back outside, I stalk down the sidewalk. The more distance I put between myself and Ryan, the angrier I become.

And I'm not even sure at whom.

My face is hot.

Lines of sweat trail down my sides.

Without thinking, I step into the street against a crosswalk signal and instantly register the sound of tires locking up, of rubber squealing across pavement.

I turn and stare in disbelief as a yellow cab barrels toward me.

Through the approaching windshield, I see the cabbie so clearly—a mustached man, wide-eyed with naked panic, bracing for impact.

And then my hands are flat against the warm, yellow metal of the hood and the cabbie is leaning out his window, screaming at me, "You dipshit, you almost died! Pull your head out of your ass!"

Horns begin to blare behind the cab.

I retreat to the sidewalk and watch the flow of traffic resume.

The occupants of three separate cars are kind enough to slow down so they can flip me off.

Whole Foods smells like the hippie I dated before Daniela—a tincture of fresh produce, ground coffee, and essential oils.

The scare with the cab has flattened my buzz, and I browse the freezer cases in something of a fog, lethargic and sleepy.

It feels colder when I'm back outside, a brisk wind blowing in off the lake, portending the shitty winter that looms right around the corner.

With my canvas bag filled with ice cream, I take a different route toward home. It adds six blocks, but what I lose in brevity, I gain in solitude, and between the cab and Ryan, I need some extra time to reset.

I pass a construction site, abandoned for the night, and a few blocks later, the playground of the elementary school my son attended, the metal sliding board gleaming under a streetlamp and the swings stirring in the breeze.

There's an energy to these autumn nights that touches something primal inside of me. Something from long ago. From my childhood in western Iowa. I think of high school football games and the stadium lights blazing down on the players. I smell ripening apples, and the sour reek of beer from keg parties in the cornfields. I feel the wind in my face as I ride in the bed of an old pickup truck down a country road at night, dust swirling red in the taillights and the entire span of my life yawning out ahead of me.

It's the beautiful thing about youth.

There's a weightlessness that permeates everything because no damning choices have been made, no paths committed to, and the road forking out ahead is pure, unlimited potential.

I love my life, but I haven't felt that lightness of being in ages. Autumn nights like this are as close as I get.

The cold is beginning to clear my head.

It will be good to be home again. I'm thinking of starting up the gas logs. We've never had a fire before Halloween, but tonight is so unseasonably cold that after walking a mile in this wind, all I want is to sit by the hearth with Daniela and Charlie and a glass of wine.

The street undercuts the El.

I pass beneath the rusting ironwork of the railway.

For me, even more than the skyline, the El personifies the city.

This is my favorite section of the walk home, because it's the darkest and quietest.

At the moment . . .

No trains inbound.

No headlights in either direction.

No audible pub noise.

Nothing but the distant roar of a jet overhead, on final approach into O'Hare.

Wait . . .

There's something coming—footfalls on the sidewalk.

I glance back.

A shadow rushes toward me, the distance between us closing faster than I can process what's happening.

The first thing I see is a face.

Ghost white.

High, arching eyebrows that look drawn.

Red, pursed lips—too thin, too perfect.

And horrifying eyes—big and pitch-black, without pupils or irises.

The second thing I see is the barrel of a gun, four inches from the end of my nose.

The low, raspy voice behind the geisha mask says, "Turn around."

I hesitate, too stunned to move.

He pushes the gun into my face.

I turn around.

Before I can tell him that my wallet is in my front left pocket, he says, "I'm not here for your money. Start walking."

I start walking.

"Faster."

I walk faster.

"What do you want?" I ask.

"Keep your mouth shut."

A train roars past overhead, and we emerge from the darkness under the El, my heart rocketing inside my chest. I absorb my surroundings with a sudden and profound curiosity. Across the street is a gated townhome complex, and this side of the block comprises a collection of businesses that shutter at five.

A nail salon.

A law office.

An appliance repair shop.

A tire store.

This neighborhood is a ghost town, nobody out.

"See that SUV?" he asks. There's a black Lincoln Navigator parked on the curb just ahead. The alarm chirps. "Get in the driver's seat."

"Whatever you're thinking about doing—"

"Or you can bleed to death right here on the sidewalk."

I open the driver's-side door and slide in behind the wheel.

"My grocery bag," I say.

"Bring it." He climbs in behind me. "Start the car."

I pull the door closed and stow the canvas Whole Foods bag in the front passenger floorboard. It's so quiet in the car I can actually hear my pulse—a fast thrumming against my eardrum.

"What are you waiting for?" he asks.

I press the engine-start button.

"Turn on the navigation."

I turn it on.

"Click on 'previous destinations.'"

I've never owned a car with built-in GPS, and it takes me a moment to find the right tab on the touchscreen.

Three locations appear.

One is my home address. One is the university where I work.

"You've been following me?" I ask.

"Choose Pulaski Drive."

I select 1400 Pulaski Drive, Chicago, Illinois 60616, with no idea where that even is. The female voice on the GPS instructs me: *Make a legal U-turn when possible and proceed for point-eight miles.*

Shifting into gear, I turn out into the dark street.

The man behind me says, "Buckle your seat belt."

I strap myself in as he does the same.

"Jason, just so we're clear, if you do anything other than follow these directions to the letter, I'm going to shoot you through the seat. Do you understand what I'm telling you?"

"Yes."

I drive us through my neighborhood, wondering if I'm seeing it all for the last time.

At a red light, I pull to a stop in front of my corner bar. Through the deeply tinted front passenger window, I see the door is still propped open. I glimpse Matt, and through the crowd, Ryan, turned around in his stool now, his back to the bar, his elbows on the scuffed wood, holding court for his postgrads. Probably enthralling them with a horrifying cautionary tale of failure starring his old roommate.

I want to call out to him. To make him understand that I'm in trouble. That I need—

"Green light, Jason."

I accelerate through the intersection.

The GPS navigation guides us east through Logan Square to the Kennedy Expressway, where the indifferent female voice instructs me, *Turn right in one hundred feet and proceed for nineteen-point-eight miles.*

Southbound traffic is light enough for me to peg the speedometer at seventy and keep it there. My hands sweat on the leather steering wheel, and I can't stop wondering, Am I going to die tonight?

It occurs to me that if I do survive, I'll carry a new revelation with me for the rest of my days: we leave this life the same way we enter it—totally alone, bereft. I'm afraid, and there is nothing Daniela or Charlie or anyone can do to help me in this moment when I need them more than ever. They don't even know what I'm experiencing.

The interstate skirts the western edge of downtown. The Willis Tower and its brood of lesser skyscrapers glow with a serene warmth against the night.

Through the writhing panic and fear, my mind races, fighting to puzzle out what's happening.

My address is in the GPS. So this wasn't a random encounter. This man has been following me. Knows me. Ergo, some action of mine has resulted in this outcome.

But which?

I'm not rich.

My life isn't worth anything beyond its value to me and to my loved ones.

I've never been arrested, never committed a crime.

Never slept with another man's wife.

Sure, I flip people off in traffic on occasion, but that's just Chicago.

My last and only physical altercation was in the sixth grade when I punched a classmate in the nose for pouring milk down the back of my shirt.

I haven't wronged anyone in the meaningful sense of the word. In a manner that might have culminated with me driving a Lincoln Navigator with a gun pointed at the back of my head.

I'm an atomic physicist and professor at a small college.

I don't treat my students, even the worst of the bunch, with anything but respect. Those who have failed out of my classes failed because they didn't care in the first place, and certainly none of them could accuse me of ruining their lives. I go *out of my way* to help my students pass.

The skyline dwindles in the side mirror, falling farther and farther away like a familiar and comforting piece of coastline.

I venture, "Did I do something to you in the past? Or someone you work for? I just don't understand what you could possibly want from—"

"The more you talk, the worse it will be for you."

For the first time, I realize there's something familiar in his voice. I can't for the life of me pinpoint when or where, but we've met. I'm sure of it.

I feel the vibration of my phone receiving a text message.

Then another.

And another.

He forgot to take my phone.

I look at the time: 9:05 p.m.

I left my house a little over an hour ago. It's Daniela no doubt, wondering where I am. I'm fifteen minutes late, and I'm never late.

I glance in the rearview mirror, but it's too dark to see anything except a sliver of the ghost-white mask. I risk an experiment. Taking my left hand off the steering wheel, I place it in my lap and count to ten.

He says nothing.

I put my hand back on the wheel.

That computerized voice breaks the silence: *Merge right onto the Eighty-Seventh Street exit in four-point-three miles.*

Again, I take my left hand slowly off the wheel.

This time, I slide it into the pocket of my khaki slacks. My phone is buried deep, and I just barely touch it with my index and pointer fingers, somehow managing to pinch it between them.

Millimeter by millimeter, I tug it out, the rubber case catching on every fold of fabric, and now a sustained vibration rattling between my fingertips—a call coming in.

When I finally work it free, I place my phone faceup in my lap and return my hand to the steering wheel.

As the navigation voice updates the distance from our upcoming turn, I shoot a glance down at the phone.

There's a missed call from "Dani" and three texts:

DANI 2m ago
Dinner's on the table

DANI 2m ago
Hurry home we are STARVING!

DANI 1m ago
You get lost? :)

I refocus my attention on the road, wondering if the glow from my phone is visible from the backseat.

The touchscreen goes dark.

Reaching down, I click the ON/OFF button and swipe the screen. I punch in my four-digit passcode, click the green "Messages" icon. Daniela's thread is at the top, and as I open our conversation, my abductor shifts behind me.

I clutch the wheel with both hands again.

Merge right onto the Eighty-Seventh Street exit in one-point-nine miles.

The screensaver times out, auto-lock kicks in, my phone goes black.

Shit.

Sliding my hand back down, I retype the passcode and begin tapping out the most important text of my life, my index finger clumsy on the touchscreen, each word taking two or three attempts to complete as auto-correct wreaks havoc.

The barrel of the gun digs into the back of my head.

I react, swerving into the fast lane.

"What are you doing, Jason?"

I straighten the wheel with one hand, swinging us back into the slow lane as my other hand lowers toward the phone, closing in on Send.

He lunges between the front seats, his gloved hand reaching around my waist, snatching the phone away.

Merge right onto the Eighty-Seventh Street exit in five hundred feet.

"What's your passcode, Jason?" When I don't respond, he says, "Wait. I bet I know this. Month and year of your birthday backwards? Let's see . . . three-seven-two-one. There we go."

In the rearview mirror, I see the phone illuminate his mask.

He reads the text he stopped me from sending: " '1400 Pulaski call 91 . . .' Bad boy."

I veer onto the interstate off-ramp.

The GPS says, *Turn left onto Eighty-Seventh Street and proceed east for three-point-eight miles.*

We drive into South Chicago, through a neighborhood we have no business setting foot in.

Past rows of factory housing.

Apartment projects.

Empty parks with rusted swing sets and netless basketball hoops.

Storefronts locked up for the night behind security gates.

Gang tagging everywhere.

He asks, "So do you call her Dani or Daniela?"

My throat constricts.

Rage and fear and helplessness burgeoning inside of me.

"Jason, I asked you a question."

"Go to hell."

He leans close, his words hot in my ear. "You do not want to go down this path with me. I will hurt you worse than you've ever been hurt in your life. Pain you didn't even know was possible. What do you call her?"

I grit my teeth. "Daniela."

"Never Dani? Even though that's what's on your phone?"

I'm tempted to flip the car at high speed and just kill us both.

I say, "Rarely. She doesn't like it."

"What's in the grocery bag?"

"Why do you want to know what I call her?"

"What's in the bag?"

"Ice cream."

"It's family night, right?"

"Yeah."

In the rearview mirror, I see him typing on my phone.

"What are you writing?" I ask.

He doesn't respond.

We're out of the ghetto now, riding through a no-man's-land that doesn't even feel like Chicago anymore, with the skyline nothing but a smear of light on the far horizon. The houses are crumbling, lightless, and lifeless. Everything long abandoned.

We cross a river and straight ahead lies Lake Michigan, its black expanse a fitting denouement of this urban wilderness.

As if the world ends right here.

And perhaps mine does.

Turn right and proceed south on Pulaski Drive for point-five miles to destination.

He chuckles to himself. "Wow, are you in trouble with the missus." I strangle the steering wheel. "Who was that man you had whisky with tonight, Jason? I couldn't tell from outside."

It's so dark out here in this borderland between Chicago and Indiana.

We're passing the ruins of railroad yards and factories.

"Jason."

"His name is Ryan Holder. He used to be—"

"Your old roommate."

"How'd you know that?"

"Are you two close? I don't see him in your contacts."

"Not really. How do you—?"

"I know almost everything about you, Jason. You could say I've made your life my specialty."

"Who are you?"

You will arrive at your destination in five hundred feet.

"Who *are* you?"

He doesn't answer, but my attention is beginning to pull away from him as I focus on our increasingly remote surroundings.

The pavement flows under the SUV's headlights.

Empty behind us.

Empty ahead.

There's the lake off to my left, deserted warehouses on my right.

You have arrived at your destination.

I stop the Navigator in the middle of the road.

He says, "The entrance is up ahead on the left."

The headlights graze a teetering stretch of twelve-foot fencing, topped with a tiara of rusted barbed wire. The gate is ajar, and a chain that once locked it shut has been snipped and coiled in the weeds by the roadside.

"Just nudge the gate with the front bumper."

Even from inside the near-soundproof interior of the SUV, the shriek of the gate grinding open is loud. The cones of light illuminate the remnants of a road, the pavement cracked and buckled from years of harsh Chicago winters.

I engage the high beams.

Light washes over a parking lot, where streetlamps have toppled everywhere like spilled matchsticks.

Beyond, a sprawling structure looms.

The brick façade of the time-ravaged building is flanked by huge cylindrical tanks and a pair of hundred-foot smokestacks spearing the sky.

"What is this place?" I ask.

"Put it in PARK and turn it off."

I bring the car to a stop, shift out of gear, and punch off the engine.

It becomes deathly silent.

"What is this place?" I ask again.

"What are your Friday plans?"

"Excuse me?"

A sharp blow to the side of my head sends me slumping into the steering wheel, stunned and wondering for a half second if this is what it feels like to be shot in the head.

But no, he only hit me with his gun.

I touch my hand to the point of impact.

My fingers come away sticky with blood.

"Tomorrow," he says. "What do you have scheduled for tomorrow?"

Tomorrow. It feels like a foreign concept.

"I'm . . . giving a test to my PHYS 3316 class."

"What else?"

"That's it."

"Take off all your clothes."

I look in the rearview mirror.

Why the hell does he want me naked?

He says, "If you wanted to try something, you should've done it while you had control of the car. From this moment forward, you're mine. Now, take off your clothes, and if I have to tell you again, I'm going to make you bleed. A lot."

I unbuckle my seat belt.

As I unzip my gray hoodie and shrug my arms out of the sleeves, I cling to a single shred of hope—he's still wearing a mask, which means he doesn't want me to see his face. If he were planning to kill me, he wouldn't care if I could identify him.

Right?

I unbutton my shirt.

"Shoes too?" I ask.

"*Everything.*"

I slip off my running shoes, my socks.

I slide my slacks and boxer shorts down my legs.

Then my clothes—every last thread—sit in a pile in the front passenger seat.

I feel vulnerable.

Exposed.

Weirdly ashamed.

What if he tries to rape me? Is that what this is all about?

He sets a flashlight on the console between the seats.

"Out of the car, Jason."

I realize that I see the interior of the Navigator as a kind of lifeboat. As long as I stay inside, he can't really hurt me.

He won't make a mess in here.

"Jason."

My chest is heaving, I'm starting to hyperventilate, black spots detonating across my field of vision.

"I know what you're thinking," he says, "and I can hurt you just as easily inside this car."

I'm not getting enough oxygen. I'm starting to freak out.

But I manage to say, breathlessly, "Bullshit. You don't want my blood in here."

When I come to, he's dragging me out of the front seat by my arms. He drops me in the gravel, where I sit dazed, waiting for my head to clear.

It's always colder near the lake, and tonight is no exception. The wind inflicts a raw, serrated bite on my exposed skin, which is covered in gooseflesh.

It's so dark out here I can see five times the number of stars as in the city.

My head is throbbing, and a fresh line of blood runs down the side of my face. But with a full load of adrenaline shotgunning through my system, the pain is muted.

He drops a flashlight in the dirt beside me and shines his at the disintegrating edifice I saw as we drove in. "After you."

I clutch the light in my hand and struggle to my feet. Stumbling toward the building, my bare feet trample sodden newspaper. I dodge crumpled beer cans and chevrons of glass that glitter under the beam.

Approaching the main entrance, I imagine this abandoned parking lot on another night. A night to come. It's early winter, and through a curtain of falling snow, the darkness is ribboned with flashing blues and reds. Detectives and cadaver dogs swarm the ruins, and as they examine my body somewhere inside, naked and decomposed and butchered, a patrol car parks in front of my brownstone in Logan Square. It's two in the morning, and Daniela comes to the door in a nightgown. I've been missing for weeks and she knows in her heart I'm not coming back, thinks she's already made her peace with that brutal fact, but seeing these young police officers with their hard, sober eyes and a dusting of snow on their shoulders and visored caps, which they shelve respectfully under their arms . . . it all finally breaks something inside of her she didn't know was still intact. She feels her knees liquefy, her strength giving way, and as she sinks onto the doormat,

Charlie comes down the creaky staircase behind her, bleary-eyed and wild-haired, asking, "Is it about Dad?"

As we close in on the structure, two words reveal themselves on the faded brick above the entrance. The only letters I can make out spell CAGO POWER.

He forces me through an opening in the brick.

Our light beams sweep across a front office.

Furniture rotted down to the metal frames.

An old water cooler.

The remnants of someone's campfire.

A shredded sleeping bag.

Used condoms on moldy carpet.

We enter a long corridor.

Without the flashlights, this would be can't-see-your-hand-in-front-of-your-face dark.

I stop to shine my light ahead, but it's swallowed by the blackness. There's less debris on the warped linoleum floor beneath my feet, and no sound whatsoever, save for the low, distant moan of wind outside these walls.

I'm growing colder by the second.

He jams the barrel of the gun into my kidney, forcing me on.

At some point, did I fall onto the radar of a psychopath who decided to learn everything about me before he murdered me? I often engage with strangers. Maybe we spoke briefly in that coffee shop near campus. Or on the El. Or over beers at my corner bar.

Does he have plans for Charlie and Daniela?

"Do you want to hear me beg?" I ask, my voice beginning to break. "Because I will. I'll do anything you want."

And the horrible thing is that it's true. I would defile myself. Hurt someone else, do almost anything if he would only take me back to my neighborhood and let this night continue like it was supposed to—with me walking home to my family, bringing them the ice cream I'd promised.

"If what?" he asks. "If I let you go?"

"Yes."

The sound of his laughter ricochets down the corridor. "I'd be afraid to see what-all you'd be willing to do to get yourself out of this."

"Out of what, exactly?"

But he doesn't answer.

I fall to my knees.

My light goes sliding across the floor.

"Please," I beg. "You don't have to do this." I barely recognize my own voice. "You can just walk away. I don't know why you want to hurt me, but just think about it for a minute. I—"

"Jason."

"—love my family. I love my wife. I love—"

"Jason."

"—my son."

"Jason!"

"I will do *anything*."

I'm shivering uncontrollably now—from cold, from fear.

He kicks me in the stomach, and as the breath explodes out of my lungs, I roll over onto my back. Crushing down on top of me, he shoves the barrel of the gun between my lips, into my mouth, all the way to the back of my throat until the taste of old oil and carbon residue is more than I can stomach.

Two seconds before I hurl the night's wine and Scotch across the floor, he withdraws the gun.

Screams, "Get up!"

He grabs my arm, jerks me back onto my feet.

Pointing the gun in my face, he puts my flashlight back into my hands.

I stare into the mask, my light shining on the weapon.

It's my first good look at the gun. I know next to nothing about firearms, only that it's a handgun, has a hammer, a cylinder, and a giant hole at the end of the barrel that looks fully capable of delivering my death. The illumination of my flashlight lends a touch of copper to the point of the bullet aimed at my face. For some reason, I picture this man in a single-room apartment, loading rounds into the cylinder, preparing to do what he's done.

I'm going to die here, maybe right now.

Every moment feels like it could be the end.

"Move," he growls.

I start walking.

We arrive at a junction and turn down a different corridor, this one wider, taller, arched. The air is oppressive with moisture. I hear the distant *drip . . . drip . . . drip* of falling water. The walls are made of concrete, and instead of linoleum, the floor is blanketed with damp moss that grows thicker and wetter with each step.

The taste of the gun lingers in my mouth, laced with the acidic tang of bile.

Patches of my face are growing numb from the cold.

A small voice in my head is screaming at me to do something, try something, anything. Don't just be led like a lamb to slaughter, one foot obediently following the other. Why make it so simple for him?

Easy.

Because I'm afraid.

So afraid I can barely walk upright.

And my thoughts are fractured and teeming.

I understand now why victims don't fight back. I cannot imagine trying to overcome this man. Trying to run.

And here's the most shameful truth: there's a part of me that would rather just have it all be over, because the dead don't feel fear or pain. Does this mean I'm a coward? Is that the final truth I have to face before I die?

No.

I have to do something.

We step out of the tunnel onto a metal surface that's freezing against the soles of my feet. I grasp a rusted iron railing that encircles a platform. It's colder here, and the sense of open space is unmistakable.

As if on a timer, a yellow moon creeps up on Lake Michigan, slowly rising.

Its light streams through the upper windows of an expansive room, and it's bright enough in here for me to take in everything independently of the flashlight.

My stomach churns.

We're standing on the high point of an open staircase that drops fifty feet.

It looks like an oil painting in here, the way the antique light falls on a row of dormant generators below and the latticework of I-beams overhead.

It's as quiet as a cathedral.

"We're going down," he says. "Watch your step."

We descend.

Two steps up from the second-to-highest landing, I spin with the flashlight death-gripped in my right hand, aiming for his head . . .

. . . and hitting nothing, the momentum carrying me right back to where I started and then some.

I'm off balance, falling.

I hit the landing hard, and the flashlight jars out of my hand and disappears over the edge.

A second later, I hear it explode on the floor forty feet below.

My captor stares down at me behind that expressionless mask, head cocked, gun pointed at my face.

Thumbing back the hammer, he steps toward me.

I groan as his knee drives into my sternum, pinning me to the landing.

The gun touches my head.

He says, "I have to admit, I'm proud you tried. It was pathetic. I saw it coming a mile away, but at least you went down swinging."

I recoil against a sharp sting in the side of my neck.

"Don't fight it," he says.

"What did you give me?"

Before he can answer, something plows through my blood-brain barrier like an eighteen-wheeler. I feel impossibly heavy and weightless all at once, the world spinning and turning itself inside out.

And then, as fast as it hit me, it passes.

Another needle stabs into my leg.

As I cry out, he tosses both syringes over the edge. "Let's go."

"What did you give me?"

"Get up!"

I use the railing to pull myself up. My knee is bleeding from the fall. My head is still bleeding. I'm cold, dirty, and wet, my teeth chattering so hard it feels like they might break.

We go down, the flimsy steelwork trembling with our weight. At the bottom, we move off the last step and walk down a row of old generators.

From the floor, this room seems even more immense.

At the midpoint, he stops and shines his flashlight on a duffel bag nestled against one of the generators.

"New clothes. Hurry up."

"New clothes? I don't—"

"You don't have to understand. You just have to get dressed."

Through all the fear, I register a tremor of hope. Is he going to spare me? Why else would he be making me get dressed? Do I have a shot at surviving this?

"Who are you?" I ask.

"Hurry up. You don't have much time left."

I squat by the duffel bag.

"Clean yourself up first."

There's a towel on top, which I use to wipe the mud off my feet, the blood off my knee and face. I pull on a pair of boxer shorts and jeans that fit perfectly. Whatever he injected me with, I think I can feel it in my fingers now—a loss of dexterity as I fumble with the buttons on a plaid shirt. My feet slide effortlessly into a pair of expensive leather slip-ons. They fit as comfortably as the jeans.

I'm not cold anymore. It's like there's a core of heat in the center of my chest, radiating out through my arms and legs.

"The jacket too."

I lift a black leather jacket from the bottom of the bag, push my arms through the sleeves.

"Perfect," he says. "Now, have a seat."

I ease down against the iron base of the generator. It's a massive piece of machinery the size of a locomotive engine.

He sits across from me, the gun trained casually in my direction.

Moonlight is filling this place, refracting off the broken windows high above and sending a scatter of light that strikes—

Tangles of cable.

Gears.

Pipes.

Levers and pulleys.

Instrumentation panels covered with cracked gauges and controls.

Technology from another age.

I ask, "What happens now?"

"We wait."

"For what?"

He waves my question away.

A weird calm settles over me. A misplaced sense of peace.

"Did you bring me here to kill me?" I ask.

"I did not."

I feel so comfortable leaning against the old machine, like I'm sinking into it.

"But you let me believe it."

"There was no other way."

"No other way to what?"

"To get you here."

"And why are we here?"

But he just shakes his head as he snakes his left hand up under the geisha mask and scratches.

I feel strange.

Like I'm simultaneously watching a movie and acting in it.

An irresistible drowsiness lowers onto my shoulders.

My head dips.

"Just let it take you," he says.

But I don't. I fight it, thinking how unsettlingly fast his tenor has changed. He's like a different man, and the disconnect between who he is in this moment and the violence he showed just minutes ago should terrify me. I shouldn't be this calm, but my body is humming too peacefully.

I feel intensely serene and deep and distant.

He says to me, almost like a confession, "It's been a long road. I can't quite believe I'm sitting here actually looking at you. Talking to you. I know you don't understand, but there's so much I want to ask."

"About what?"

"What it's like to be you."

"What do you mean?"

He hesitates, then: "How do you feel about your place in the world, Jason?"

I say slowly, deliberately, "That's an interesting question considering the night you've put me through."

"Are you happy in your life?"

In the shadow of this moment, my life is achingly beautiful.

"I have an amazing family. A fulfilling job. We're comfortable. Nobody's sick."

My tongue feels thick. My words are beginning to sound slurred.

"But?"

I say, "My life is great. It's just not exceptional. And there was a time when it could have been."

"You killed your ambition, didn't you?"

"It died of natural causes. Of neglect."

"And do you know exactly how that happened? Was there a moment when—?"

"My son. I was twenty-seven years old, and Daniela and I had been together a few months. She told me she was pregnant. We were having fun, but it wasn't love. Or maybe it was. I don't know. We definitely weren't looking to start a family."

"But you did."

"When you're a scientist, your late twenties are so critical. If you don't publish something big by thirty, they put you out to pasture."

Maybe it's just the drug, but it feels so good to be talking. An oasis of normal after two of the craziest hours I've ever lived. I know it isn't true, but it feels like as long as we keep conversing, nothing bad can happen. As if the words protect me.

"Did you have something big in the works?" he asks.

Now I'm having to focus on making my eyes stay open.

"Yes."

"And what was it?"

His voice sounds distant.

"I was trying to create the quantum superposition of an object that was visible to the human eye."

"Why did you abandon your research?"

"When Charlie was born, he had major medical issues for the first year of his life. I needed a thousand hours in a clean-room, but I couldn't get there fast enough. Daniela needed me. My son needed me. I lost my funding. Lost my momentum. I was the young, new genius for a minute, but when I faltered, someone else took my place."

"Do you regret your decision to stay with Daniela and make a life with her?"

"No."

"Never?"

I think of Daniela, and the emotion breaks back through, accompanied by the actual horror of the moment. Fear returns, and with it a homesickness that cuts to the bone. I *need* her in this moment more than I've ever needed anything in my life.

"Never."

And then I'm lying on the floor, my face against the cold concrete, and the drug is whisking me away.

He's kneeling beside me now, rolling me onto my back, and I'm looking up at all that moonlight pouring in through the high windows of this forgotten place, the darkness wrinkled with twitches of light and color as swirling, empty voids open and close beside the generators.

"Will I see her again?" I ask.

"I don't know."

I want to ask him for the millionth time what he wants with me, but I can't find the words.

My eyes keep closing, and I try to hold them open, but it's a losing battle.

He pulls off a glove and touches my face with his bare hand.

Strangely.

Delicately.

He says, "Listen to me. You're going to be scared, but you can make it yours. You can have everything you never had. I'm sorry I had to scare you earlier, but I had to get you here. I'm so sorry, Jason. I'm doing this for both of us."

I mouth the words, *Who are you?*

Instead of responding, he reaches into his pocket and takes out a new syringe and a tiny glass ampoule filled with a clear liquid that in the moonlight shines like mercury.

He uncaps the needle and draws the contents of the vial up into the syringe.

As my eyelids slowly lower, I watch him slide the sleeve up his left arm and inject himself.

Then he drops the ampoule and the syringe on the concrete between us, and the last thing I see before my eyes lock shut is that glass ampoule rolling toward my face.

I whisper, "Now what?"

And he says, "You wouldn't believe me if I told you."

TWO

I'm aware of someone gripping my ankles.

As hands slide under my shoulders, a woman says, "How'd he get out of the box?"

A man responds: "No idea. Look, he's coming to."

I open my eyes, but all I see is blurred movement and light.

The man barks, "Let's get him the hell out of here."

I try to speak, but the words fall out of my mouth, garbled and formless.

The woman says, "Dr. Dessen? Can you hear me? We're going to lift you onto a gurney now."

I look toward my feet, and the man's face racks into focus. He's staring at me through the face shield of an aluminized hazmat suit with a self-contained breathing apparatus.

Glancing at the woman behind my head, he says, "One, two, three."

They hoist me onto a gurney and lock padded restraints around my ankles and wrists.

"Only for *your* protection, Dr. Dessen."

I watch the ceiling scroll past, forty or fifty feet above.

Where the hell am I? A hangar?

I catch a glint of memory—a needle puncturing my neck.

I was injected with something. This is some crazy hallucination.

A radio squawks, "Extraction team, report. Over."

The woman says with excitement bleeding through her voice, "We have Dessen. We're en route. Over."

I hear the squeak of wheels rolling.

"Copy that. Initial condition assessment? Over."

She reaches down with a gloved hand and wakes some kind of monitoring device that's been Velcroed to my left arm.

"Pulse rate: one-fifteen. BP: one-forty over ninety-two. Temp: ninety-eight-point-nine. Oh-two sat: ninety-five percent. Gamma: point-eight seven. ETA thirty seconds. Out."

A buzzing sound startles me.

We move through a pair of vaultlike doors that are slowly opening.

Jesus Christ.

Stay calm. This isn't real.

The wheels squeak faster, more urgently.

We're in a corridor lined with plastic, my eyes squinting against the onslaught of light from fluorescent bulbs shining overhead.

The doors behind us slam shut with an ominous clang, like the gates to a keep.

They wheel me into an operating room toward an imposing figure in a positive pressure suit, standing under an array of surgical lights.

He smiles down at me through his face shield and says, as if he knows me, "Welcome back, Jason. Congratulations. You did it."

Back?

I can only see his eyes, but they don't remind me of anyone I've ever met.

"Are you experiencing any pain?" he asks.

I shake my head.

"Do you know how you got the cuts and bruises on your face?"

Shake.

"Do you know who you are?"

I nod.

"Do you know where you are?"

Shake.

"Do you recognize me?"

Shake.

"I'm Leighton Vance, chief executive and medical officer. We're colleagues and friends." He holds up a pair of surgical shears. "I need to get you out of these clothes."

He removes the monitoring device and goes to work on my jeans and boxer shorts, tossing them into a metal tray. As he cuts off my shirt, I gaze up at the lights burning down on me, trying not to panic.

But I'm naked and strapped to a gurney.

No, I remind myself, I'm *hallucinating* that I'm naked and strapped to a gurney. Because none of this is real.

Leighton lifts the tray holding my shoes and clothes and hands it to someone behind my head, outside my line of sight. "Test everything."

Footsteps rush out of the room.

I note the sharp bite of isopropyl alcohol a second before Leighton cleans a swatch of skin on the underside of my arm.

He ties a tourniquet above my elbow.

"Just drawing some blood," he says, taking a large-gauge hypodermic needle from the instrument tray.

He's good. I don't even feel the sting.

When he's finished, Leighton rolls the gurney toward the far side of the OR to a glass door with a touchscreen mounted on the wall beside it.

"Wish I could tell you this is the fun part," he says. "If you're too disoriented to remember what's about to happen, that's probably for the best."

I try to ask what's happening, but words still elude me. Leighton's fingers dance across the touchscreen. The glass door opens, and he pushes me into a chamber that's just large enough to hold the gurney.

"Ninety seconds," he says. "You'll be fine. It never killed any of the test subjects."

There's a pneumatic hiss, and then the glass door glides shut.

Recessed lights in the ceiling glow a chilled blue.

I crane my neck.

The walls on either side of me are covered with elaborate apertures.

A fine, supercooled mist sprays out of the ceiling, coating me head to toe.

My body tenses, the frigid droplets beading on my skin and freezing solid.

As I shiver, the walls of the chamber begin to hum.

A white vapor trickles out of the apertures with a sustained hiss that grows louder and louder.

It gushes.

Then jets.

Opposing streams crash into each other over the gurney, filling the chamber with a dense fog that blots out the overhead light. Where it touches my skin, the frozen droplets explode in bursts of agony.

The fans reverse.

Within five seconds, the gas is sucked out of the chamber, which now holds a peculiar smell, like the air on a summer afternoon moments before a thunderstorm—dry lightning and ozone.

The reaction of the gas and the supercooled liquid on my skin has created a sizzling foam that burns like an acid bath.

I'm grunting, thrashing against the restraints and wondering how much longer this could possibly be allowed to go on. My threshold for pain is high, and this is straddling the line of make-it-stop or kill me.

My thoughts fire at the speed of light.

Is there even a drug capable of this? Creating hallucinations and pain at this level of horrifying clarity?

This is too intense, too real.

What if this is actually happening?

Is this some CIA shit? Am I in a black clinic in the throes of human experimentation? Have I been kidnapped by these people?

Glorious, warm water shoots out of the ceiling with the force of a fire hose, pummeling the excruciating foam away.

When the water shuts off, heated air roars out of the apertures, blasting my skin like a hot desert wind.

The pain vanishes.

I'm wide-awake.

The door behind me opens and the gurney rolls back out.

Leighton looks down at me. "Wasn't so bad, right?" He pushes me through the OR into an adjoining patient room and unlocks the restraints around my ankles and wrists.

With a gloved hand, he pulls me up on the gurney, my head swimming, the room spinning for a moment before the world finally rights itself.

He observes me.

"Better?"

I nod.

There's a bed and a dresser with a change of clothes folded neatly on top. The walls are padded. There are no sharp edges. As I slide to the edge of the stretcher, Leighton takes hold of my arm above the elbow and helps me to stand.

My legs are rubber, worthless.

He leads me over to the bed.

"I'll leave you to get dressed and come back when your lab work is in. It won't take long. Are you all right for me to step out for a minute?"

I finally find my voice: "I don't understand what's happening. I don't know where I—"

"The disorientation will pass. I'll be closely monitoring. We'll get you through this."

He wheels the gurney to the door but stops in the threshold, glancing back at me through his face shield. "It's really good to see you again, brother. Feels like Mission Control when *Apollo Thirteen* returned. We're all real proud of you."

The door closes after him.

Three deadbolts fire into their housings like a trio of gunshots.

I rise from the bed and walk over to the dresser, unstable on my feet.

I'm so weak it takes me several minutes to get the clothes on—good slacks, a linen shirt, no belt.

From just above the door, a surveillance camera watches me.

I return to the bed, sit alone in this sterile, silent room, trying to conjure my last concrete memory. The mere attempt feels like drowning ten feet from shore. There are pieces of memory lying on the beach, and I can see them, I can almost touch them, but my lungs are filling up with water. I can't keep my head above the surface. The more I strain to assemble the pieces, the more energy I expend, the more I flail, the more I panic.

All I have as I sit in this white, padded room is—

Thelonious Monk.

The smell of red wine.

Standing in a kitchen chopping an onion.

A teenager drawing.

Wait.

Not *a* teenager.

My teenager.

My son.

Not *a* kitchen.

My kitchen.

My home.

It was family night. We were cooking together. I can see Daniela's smile. I can hear her voice and the jazz. Smell the onion, the sour sweetness of wine on Daniela's breath. See the glassiness in her eyes. What a safe and perfect place, our kitchen on family night.

But I didn't stay. For some reason, I left. Why?

I'm right there, on the brink of recollection . . .

The deadbolts retract, rapid-fire, and the door to the patient room opens. Leighton has traded the positive pressure suit for a classic lab coat, and he's standing in the door frame grinning, as if he's barely keeping a lid on a wellspring of anticipation. I can now see that he's roughly my age and boarding-school handsome, his face peppered conservatively with five-o'clock shadow.

"Good news," he says. "All clear."

"Clear of what?"

"Radiation exposure, biohazards, infectious disease. We'll have complete results from your blood scan in the morning, but you're cleared from quarantine. Oh. I have this for you."

He hands me a Ziploc bag containing a set of keys and a money clip.

"Jason Dessen" has been scrawled in black Sharpie on a piece of masking tape affixed to the plastic.

"Shall we? They're all waiting for you."

I pocket what are apparently my personal effects and follow Leighton through the OR.

Back in the corridor, a half-dozen workers are busy pulling the plastic down from the walls.

When they see me, they all begin to applaud.

A woman shouts, "You rock, Dessen!"

Glass doors whisk apart as we approach.

My strength and balance are returning.

He leads me into a stairwell, and we ascend, the metal steps clanging under our footfalls.

"You all right on these?" Leighton asks.

"Yeah. Where are we going?"

"Debrief."

"But I don't even—"

"It's better if you just hold your thoughts for the interview. You know—protocol and shit."

Two flights up, he opens a glass door that's an inch thick. We enter another corridor with floor-to-ceiling windows on one side. They look out over a hangar, which the corridors appear to encircle—four levels in all—like an atrium.

I drift toward the windows to get a better look, but Leighton guides me instead through the second door on the left, ushering me into a dimly lit room, where a woman in a black pantsuit is standing behind a table as if awaiting my arrival.

"Hi, Jason," she says.

"Hi."

Her eyes capture my stare for a moment as Leighton straps the monitoring device around my left arm.

"You don't mind, do you?" he asks. "I'd feel better keeping tabs on your vitals a little while longer. We'll be out of the woods soon."

Leighton gently presses his hand into the small of my back and urges me the rest of the way inside.

I hear the door close behind me.

The woman is fortyish. Short, black hair with bangs just skirting striking eyes that somehow manage to be concurrently kind and penetrating.

The lighting is soft and unthreatening, like a movie theater moments before the film begins.

There are two straight-backed wooden chairs, and on the small table a laptop, a pitcher of water, two drinking glasses, a steel carafe, and a steaming mug that fills the room with the aroma of good coffee.

The walls and ceiling are made of smoked glass.

"Jason, if you have a seat, we can get started."

I hesitate for five long seconds, debating just walking out, but something tells me that would be a bad, possibly catastrophic, idea.

So I sit in the chair, reach for the pitcher, and pour myself a glass of water.

The woman says, "If you're hungry, we can have food brought in."

"No thanks."

Finally taking her seat across from me, she pushes her glasses up the bridge of her nose and types something on the laptop.

"It is—" She checks her wristwatch. "—12:07 a.m., October the second. I'm Amanda Lucas, employee ID number nine-five-six-seven, and I'm joined tonight by . . ." She gestures to me.

"Um, Jason Dessen."

"Thank you, Jason. By way of background, and for the record, at approximately 10:59 p.m. on October first, Technician Chad Hodge, during a routine interior locality audit, discovered Dr. Dessen lying unconscious on the floor of the hangar. The extraction team was activated, and Dr. Dessen was removed to quarantine at 11:24 p.m. Following decontamination and primary lab work clearance by Dr. Leighton Vance, Dr. Dessen was escorted to the conference theater on sublevel two, where our first debriefing interview begins."

She looks up at me, smiling now.

"Jason, we are thrilled to have you back. The hour is late, but most of the team rushed in from the city for this. As you might have guessed, they're all looking on behind the glass."

Applause breaks out all around us, accompanied by cheers and several people shouting my name.

The lights come up just enough for me to see through the walls. Theater seating surrounds the glassed-in interview cubicle. Fifteen or twenty people are on their feet, most smiling, a few even wiping their eyes as if I've returned from some heroic mission.

I notice that two of them are armed, the butts of their pistols gleaming under the lights.

These men aren't smiling or clapping.

Amanda scoots her chair back and, rising, begins to clap along with the others.

She seems to be deeply moved as well.

And all I can think is, What the hell has happened to me?

When the applause subsides, Amanda settles back into her seat.

She says, "Pardon our enthusiasm, but so far, you're the only one to return."

I have no idea what she's talking about. Part of me wants to say just that, but part of me suspects that maybe I shouldn't.

The lights dim back down.

I clutch my glass of water in my hands like a lifeline.

"Do you know how long you've been gone?" she asks.

Gone where?

"No."

"Fourteen months."

Jesus.

"Is that a shock to you, Jason?"

"You could say that."

"Well, pins and needles and bated breath and asses on the edges of our seats. We've been waiting for over a year to ask these questions: What did you see? Where did you go? How did you get back? Tell us everything, and please start from the beginning."

I take a sip of water, clinging to my last solid memory like a crumbling handhold on a cliff face—leaving my house on family night.

And then . . .

I walked down the sidewalk through a cool, autumn night. I could hear the noise of the Cubs game in all the bars.

To where?

Where was I going?

"Just take your time, Jason. We're in no rush."

Ryan Holder.

That's who I was going to see.

I walked to Village Tap and had a drink—two drinks, world-class Scotch, to be exact—with my old college roommate, Ryan Holder.

Is he somehow responsible for this?

I wonder again: Is this actually happening?

I raise the glass of water. It looks perfectly real, right down to the way it sweats and the cold wetness of it on my fingertips.

I look into Amanda's eyes.

I examine the walls.

They're not melting.

If this is some drug-induced trip, it's like none I've ever heard of. No visual or auditory distortions. No euphoria. It's not that this place doesn't feel real. I just shouldn't be here. It's somehow *my* presence that's the lie. I'm not even exactly sure what that means, only that I feel it in my core.

No, this is not a hallucination. This is something else entirely.

"Let's try a different approach," Amanda says. "What's the last thing you remember before waking up in the hangar?"

"I was at a bar."

"What were you doing there?"

"Seeing an old friend."

"And where was this bar?" she asks.

"Logan Square."

"So you were still in Chicago."

"Yeah."

"Okay, can you describe . . . ?"

Her voice drops off into silence.

I see the El.

It's dark.

It's quiet.

Too quiet for Chicago.

Someone is coming.

Someone who wants to hurt me.

My heart begins to race.

My hands sweat.

I set the glass down on the table.

"Jason, Leighton is telling me your vitals are becoming elevated."

Her voice is back but still an ocean away.

Is this a trick?

Am I being messed with?

No, do not ask her that. Do not say those words. Be the man they think you are. These people are cool, calm, and *two of them are armed*. Whatever they need to hear you say, say it. Because if they realize you aren't the person they think you are, then what?

Then maybe you never leave this place.

My head is beginning to throb. Reaching up, I touch the back of my skull and graze a knot that's so tender it causes me to wince.

"Jason?"

Was I hurt?

Did someone attack me? What if I was brought here? What if these people, despite how nice they seem, are in league with the person who did this to me?

I touch the side of my head, feel the damage from a second blow.

"Jason."

I see a geisha mask.

I'm naked and helpless.

"Jason."

Just a few hours ago I was home, cooking dinner.

I am not the man they think I am. What happens when they figure that out?

"Leighton, could you come down, please?"

Nothing good.

I need to not be in this room anymore.

I need to get away from these people.

I need to think.

"Amanda." I drag myself back into the moment, try to drive the questions and the fear out of my mind, but it's like shoring up a failing levee. It won't last. It won't hold. "This is embarrassing," I say. "I'm just so exhausted, and to be honest, decontamination was no fun."

"Do you want to break for a minute?"

"Would that be okay? I just need a moment to clear my head." I point at the laptop. "I also want to sound mildly intelligent for this thing."

"Of course." She types something. "We're off the record now."

I get up.

She says, "I can show you to a private room—"

"Not necessary."

I open the door and step out into the corridor.

Leighton Vance is waiting.

"Jason, I'd like you to lie down. Your vitals are headed in the wrong direction."

I rip the device off my arm and hand it to the doctor.

"Appreciate the concern, but what I really need is a bathroom stall."

"Oh. Of course. I'll take you."

We head down the corridor.

Digging his shoulder into the heavy glass door, he leads me back into the stairwell, which at the moment is empty. No sound but the ventilation system pumping heated air through a nearby vent. I grasp the railing and lean out over the core of open space.

Two flights to the bottom, two to the top.

What did Amanda say at the start of the interview? That we're on sublevel two? Does that mean this is all underground?

"Jason? You coming?"

I follow Leighton, climbing, fighting through the weakness in my legs, the pain in my head.

At the top of the stairwell, a sign beside a reinforced-steel door reads GROUND. Leighton swipes a keycard, punches in a code, and holds the door open.

The words VELOCITY LABORATORIES are affixed in block letters across the wall straight ahead.

Left: a bank of elevators.

Right: a security checkpoint, with a hard-looking guard standing between the metal detector and the turnstile, the exit just beyond.

It seems like the security here is outward facing, focused more on preventing people from getting in than getting out.

Leighton directs me past the elevators and down a hallway to a pair of double doors at the far end, which he opens with his keycard.

As we enter, he hits the lights, revealing a well-appointed office, the walls adorned in aviation photographs of commercial airliners and military supersonic jets and the engines that power them.

A framed photo on the desk draws my focus—an older man holding a boy in his arms that looks very much like

Leighton. They're standing in a hangar in front of a massive turbofan in the midst of assembly.

"I thought you'd be more comfortable in my private bathroom." Leighton points toward a door in the far corner. "I'll be right here," he says, sitting down on the edge of his desk and pulling a phone out of his pocket. "Shout if you need anything."

The bathroom is cold and immaculate.

There's a toilet, a urinal, a walk-in shower, and a small window halfway up the back wall.

I take a seat on the toilet.

My chest feels so tight I can barely breathe.

They've been waiting for me to return for fourteen months. There's no way they're letting me walk out of this building. Not tonight. Maybe not for a long time considering I'm not the man they think they're talking to.

Unless this is all some elaborate test or game.

Leighton's voice pushes through the door: "Everything all right in there?"

"Yeah."

"I don't know what you saw inside that thing, but I want you to know I'm here for you, brother. If you're freaking out, you got to tell me, so I can help you."

I rise.

He continues, "I was watching you from the theater, and I have to say, you looked out of it."

If I were to walk back into the lobby with him, could I break away, make a dash through security? I picture that massive guard standing by the metal detector. Probably not.

"Physically, I think you're going to be fine, but I worry about your psychological state."

I have to step onto the lip of the porcelain urinal to reach the window. The glass appears to be locked shut by means of a lever on each side.

It's only two feet by two feet, and I'm not sure if I can fit through.

Leighton's voice echoes through the bathroom, and as I creep back toward the sink, his words become clear again.

". . . worst thing you can do is try to manage this on your own. Let's be honest. You're the kind of guy who thinks he's strong enough to push through anything."

I approach the door.

There's a deadbolt.

With trembling fingers, I slowly turn the lock cylinder.

"But no matter what you're feeling," his voice close now, inches away, "I want you to share it with me, and if we need to push this debriefing until tomorrow or the next—"

He goes silent as the bolt shoots home with a soft *click*.

For a moment, nothing happens.

I take a careful step back.

The door moves imperceptibly, and then rattles ferociously inside its frame.

Leighton says, "Jason. Jason!" And then: "I need a security team to my office right now. Dessen has locked himself inside the bathroom."

The door shudders as Leighton crashes into it, but the lock holds.

I rush for the window, climb up onto the urinal, and flip the levers on either side of the glass.

Leighton is shouting at someone, and although I can't make out the words, I think I hear approaching footsteps.

The window opens.

Night air funnels in.

Even standing on the urinal, I'm not sure if I can make it up there.

Leaping off the edge, I hurl myself toward the open frame, but only manage to get one arm through.

As something bangs into the bathroom door, my shoes scrape across the smooth, vertical surface of the wall. There's no traction or purchase to be had.

I drop to the floor, climb back up onto the urinal.

Leighton screams at someone, "Come on!"

I jump again, and this time, I manage to land both arms across the windowsill. It isn't much of a hold, but it's just enough to keep me from falling.

I wriggle through as the bathroom door breaks down behind me.

Leighton yells my name.

I tumble for a half second through darkness.

Crash face-first into pavement.

Up on my feet, stunned, dazed, ears ringing, blood running down the side of my face.

I'm outside, in a dark alley between two buildings.

Leighton appears in the open window frame above me.

"Jason, don't do this. Let me help you."

I turn and run, no idea where I'm going, just blazing toward the opening at the end of the alley.

I reach it.

Launch down a set of brick steps.

I'm in an office park.

Bland, low-rise buildings cluster around a sad little pond with a lighted fountain in the middle.

Considering the hour, it's no surprise there's no one out.

I fly past benches, trimmed shrubbery, a gazebo, a sign with an arrow under the words TO WALKING PATH.

A quick glance over my shoulder: the building I just escaped is a five-story, nondescript, utterly forgettable piece of architectural mediocrity, and people are streaming out of the entrance like a kicked hornet's nest.

At the end of the pond, I leave the sidewalk and follow a gravel footpath.

Sweat stings my eyes, my lungs are on fire, but I keep pumping my arms and throwing one foot in front of the other.

With each stride, the lights from the office park fall farther and farther away.

Straight ahead, there's nothing but welcoming darkness, and I'm moving toward it, into it, like my life depends upon it.

A strong, reviving wind slams into my face, and I'm starting to wonder where I'm going because shouldn't there be some light in the distance? Like even a speck of it? But I'm running into an immense chasm of black.

I hear waves.

I arrive on a beach.

There's no moon, but the stars are vivid enough to suggest the roiling surface of Lake Michigan.

I look inland toward the office park, catch incoming, wind-cut voices, and glimpse several flashlight beams slashing through the dark.

Turning north, I begin to run, my shoes crunching wave-polished rocks. Miles up the shoreline, I can see the indistinct, nighttime glow of downtown, where the skyscrapers edge up against the water.

I look back, see some lights heading south, away from me, others heading north.

Gaining on me.

I veer away from the water's edge, cross a bike path, and aim for a row of bushes.

The voices are closer.

I wonder if it's dark enough for me to stay unseen.

A three-foot seawall stands in my path, and I scale the concrete, barking my shins on the way over and staying on all fours as I crawl through the hedgerow, branches grabbing my shirt and face, clawing at my eyes.

Out of the bushes, I stumble into the middle of a road that parallels the lakeshore.

From the direction of the office park, I hear an engine revving.

High beams blind me.

I cross the road, hop a chain-link fence, and suddenly I'm running through someone's yard, dodging overturned bicycles and skateboards, then darting alongside the house while a dog goes apoplectic inside, lights popping on as I hit the backyard, jump the fence again, and find myself sprinting across an empty baseball outfield, wondering how much longer I can keep this up.

The answer comes with remarkable speed.

On the edge of the infield, I collapse, sweat pouring off my body, every muscle in agony.

That dog is still barking in the distance, but looking back toward the lake, I see no flashlights, hear no voices.

I lie there I don't know how long, and it seems as if hours pass before I can take a breath without gasping.

I finally manage to sit up.

The night is cool, and the breeze coming off the lake pushes through the surrounding trees, sending a storm of autumn leaves down on the diamond.

I struggle to my feet, thirsty and tired and trying to process the last four hours of my life, but I don't have the mental bandwidth at the moment.

I trek out of the baseball field, into a working-class South Side neighborhood.

The streets are empty.

It's block after block of peaceful, quiet homes.

I walk a mile, maybe more, and then I'm standing at the empty intersection of a business district, watching the traffic lights above me cycle at an accelerated, late-night pace.

The main drag runs two blocks, and there's no sign of life except the shithole bar across the street with three mass-produced beer signs glowing in the windows. As patrons stagger out in a cloud of smoke and overloud conversations, headlights from the first car I've seen in twenty minutes appear in the distance.

A cab with the Off-Duty light illuminated.

I step out into the intersection and stand under the traffic light, waving my arms. The taxi slows down on approach and tries to swerve around me, but I sidestep, keeping its bumper on a collision course, forcing it to stop.

The driver lowers his window, angry.

"What the hell are you doing?"

"I need a ride."

The cabbie is Somali, his razor-thin face splotched with patches of a beard, and he's staring at me through a pair of giant, thick-lensed glasses.

He says, "It's two in the morning. I'm done tonight. No more work."

"Please."

"Can you read? Look at the sign." He slaps the top of his car.

"I need to get home."

The window begins to rise.

I reach into my pocket and pull out the plastic bag containing my personal effects, rip it open, show him the money clip.

"I can pay you more than—"

"Get out of the road."

"I'll double your rate."

The window stops six inches from the top of the door.

"Cash."

"Cash."

I thumb quickly through the wad of bills. It's probably a $75 fare to the North Side neighborhoods, and I've got to cover double that.

"Get in if we go!" he yells.

Some of the bar patrons have noticed the cab stopped in the intersection, and presumably needing rides, they are drifting over, shouting for me to hold the car.

I finish counting my funds—$332 and three expired credit cards.

I climb into the backseat and tell him I'm going to Logan Square.

"That's twenty-five miles!"

"And I'm paying you double."

He glares at me in the rearview mirror.

"Where's the money?"

I peel off $100 and hand it into the front seat. "The rest when we get there."

He snatches the money and accelerates through the intersection, past the drunks.

I examine the money clip. Under the cash and the credit cards, there's an Illinois driver's license with a headshot that's me but that I've never seen, an ID for a gym I've never been to, and a health insurance card from a carrier I've never used.

The cabbie sneaks glances at me in the rearview mirror.

"You have bad night," he says.

"Looks that way, huh?"

"I thought you are drunk, but no. Your clothes are torn. Face bloody."

I probably wouldn't have wanted to pick me up either, standing in the middle of an intersection at two in the morning, looking homeless and deranged.

"You're in trouble," he says.

"Yeah."

"What happened?"

"I'm not exactly sure."

"I take you to hospital."

"No. I want to go home."

THREE

We cruise north toward the city on the vacant interstate, the skyline creeping closer and closer. With each passing mile, I feel some semblance of my sanity returning, if for no other reason than I'll be home soon.

Daniela will help me make sense of whatever's happening.

The cabbie parks across from my brownstone and I pay him the rest of his fare.

I hurry across the street and up the steps, pulling keys out of my pocket that aren't my keys. As I try to find the one that fits the lock, I realize this isn't my door. Well, it is my door. It's my street. My number on the mailbox. But the handle isn't right, the wood is too elegant, and the hinges are these iron, gothic-looking things more suited to a medieval tavern.

I turn the deadbolt.

The door swings inward.

Something is wrong.

Very, very wrong.

I step across the threshold, into the dining room.

This doesn't smell like my house. Doesn't smell like anything but the faintest odor of dust. Like no one has lived here in quite some time. The lights are out, and not just some of them. Every last one.

I close the door and fumble in the darkness until my hand grazes a dimmer switch. A chandelier made of antlers warms the room above a minimalist glass table that isn't mine and chairs that aren't mine.

I call out, "Hello?"

The house is so quiet.

Revoltingly quiet.

In *my* home on the mantel behind the dining-room table there's a large, candid photograph of Daniela, Charlie, and me standing at Inspiration Point in Yellowstone National Park.

In *this* house, there's a deep-contrast black-and-white photograph of the same canyon. More artfully done, but with no one in it.

I move on to the kitchen, and at my entrance, a sensor triggers the recessed lighting.

It's gorgeous.

Expensive.

And lifeless.

In *my* house, there's a Charlie first-grade creation (macaroni art) held by magnets to our white refrigerator. It makes me smile every time I see it. In *this* kitchen, there's not even a blemish on the steel façade of the Gaggenau refrigerator.

"Daniela!"

Even the resonance of my voice is different here.

"Charlie!"

There's less stuff, more echo.

As I walk through the living room, I spot my old turntable sitting next to a state-of-the-art sound system, my library of jazz vinyl lovingly stowed and alphabetized on custom, built-in shelves.

I head up the stairs to the second floor.

The hallway is dark and the light switch isn't where it should be, but it doesn't matter. Much of the lighting system runs on motion sensors, and more recessed bulbs wink on above me.

This isn't my hardwood floor. It's nicer, the planks wider, a little rougher.

Between the hall bath and the guest room, the triptych of my family at the Wisconsin Dells has been replaced with a sketch of Navy Pier. Charcoal on butcher paper. The artist's signature in the bottom right-hand corner catches my eye— Daniela Vargas.

I step into the next room on the left.

My son's room.

Except it's not. There's none of his surrealist artwork. No bed, no manga posters, no desk with homework strewn across it, no lava lamps, no backpack, no clothes scattered all over the floor.

Instead, just a monitor sitting on an expansive desk that's covered in books and loose paper.

I walk in shock to the end of the hallway. Sliding a frosted pocket door into the wall, I enter a master bedroom that is luxurious, cold, and, like everything else in this brownstone, not mine.

The walls are adorned with more charcoal/butcher paper sketches in the style of the one in the hall, but the centerpiece of the room is a glass display case built into an acacia wood stand. Light from the base shines up dramatically to illuminate a certificate in a padded leather folder that leans against a plush velvet pillar. Hanging from a thin chain on the pillar is a gold coin with Julian Pavia's likeness imprinted in the metal.

The certificate reads:

> *The Pavia Prize is awarded to*
> *JASON ASHLEY DESSEN for outstanding achievement*
> *in advancing our knowledge and understanding of the*
> *origin, evolution and properties of the universe by*
> *placing a macroscopic object into a state of*
> *quantum superposition.*

I sit on the end of the bed.

I am not well.

I am so not well.

My home should be my haven, a place of safety and comfort, where I'm surrounded by family. But it's not even mine.

My stomach lurches.

I rush into the master bath, fling open the toilet seat, and empty my guts into the pristine bowl.

I'm racked with thirst.

I turn on the faucet and dip my mouth under the stream.

Splash water in my face.

I wander back into the bedroom.

No idea where my mobile phone is, but there's a landline on the bedside table.

I never actually dial Daniela's cell-phone number, so it takes me a moment to recall, but I finally punch it in.

Four rings.

A male voice answers, deep and groggy.

"Hello?"

"Where's Daniela?"

"I think you misdialed."

I recite Daniela's cell-phone number, and he says, "Yeah, that's the number you called, but it's my number."

"How is that possible?"

He hangs up.

I dial her number again, and this time he answers on the first ring with, "It's three in the morning. Don't call me again, asshole."

My third attempt goes straight to the man's voicemail. I don't leave a message.

Rising from the bed, I return to the bathroom and study myself in the mirror over the sink.

My face is bruised, scraped, bloody, and mud-streaked. I need a shave, my eyes are bloodshot, but I'm still me.

A wave of exhaustion hits me like a haymaker to the jaw.

My knees give out, but I catch myself on the countertop.

And then, down on the first floor—a noise.

A door closing softly?

I straighten.

Alert again.

Back in the bedroom, I move silently to the doorway and stare down the length of the hall.

I hear whispered voices.

The static of a handheld radio.

The hollow *creak* of someone's footfall on a hardwood step.

The voices become clearer, echoing between the walls of the stairwell and spilling out the top and down the corridor.

I can see their shadows on the walls now, preceding them up the staircase like ghosts.

As I take a tentative step into the hallway, a man's voice—calm, measured Leighton—slides out of the stairwell: "Jason?"

Five steps and I reach the hall bath.

"We're not here to hurt you."

Their footfalls are in the hallway now.

Stepping slowly, methodically.

"I know you're feeling confused and disoriented. I wish you'd said something back at the lab. I didn't realize how bad it was for you. I'm sorry I missed that."

I carefully close the door behind me and push in the lock.

"We just want to bring you in so you don't hurt yourself or anyone else."

The bathroom is twice the size of mine, with a granite-walled shower and a double vanity topped with marble.

Across from the toilet, I see what I'm looking for: a large shelf built into the wall with a hatch that opens the laundry chute.

"Jason."

Through the bathroom door, I hear the radio crackling.

"Jason, please. Talk to me." Out of nowhere, his voice hemorrhages frustration. "We have all given up our lives working toward tonight. Come out here! This is fucking insane!"

One rainy Sunday when Charlie was nine or ten, we spent an afternoon pretending we were spelunkers. I would lower him down the laundry chute again and again, as if it were the entrance to a cave. He even wore a little backpack and a make-shift headlamp—a flashlight tied to the top of his head.

I open the hatch, scramble up onto the shelf.

Leighton says, "Take the bedroom."

Footsteps patter down the hall.

The fit down the laundry chute looks tight. Maybe too tight.

I hear the bathroom door begin to shake, the doorknob jiggling, and then a woman's voice: "Hey, this one's locked."

I peer down the chute.

Total darkness.

The bathroom door is thick enough that their first attempt to break through only results in a splintering crack.

I might not even fit down this thing, but as they crash into the door a second time and it explodes off the hinges and thunders down against the tile, I realize I have no other options.

They rush into the bathroom, and in the mirror I catch the fleeting reflection of Leighton Vance and one of those security consultants from the lab, holding what appears to be a Taser.

Leighton and I lock eyes in the glass for a half second, and then the man with the Taser spins, raising his weapon.

I fold my arms into my chest and commit myself to the chute.

As the shouting in the bathroom fades away above me, I slam into an empty laundry hamper, the plastic splitting, sending me tumbling out from between the washer and the dryer.

Their footsteps are already coming, pounding down the staircase.

A needle of pain threads up my right leg from the fall. I scramble to my feet and bolt for the French doors that lead out the back of the brownstone.

The brass door handles are locked.

Footsteps are closing in, the voices louder, radios squeaking as instructions scream over static.

I turn the lock, pull open the doors, and tear across a redwood deck, which boasts a grill that's nicer than mine and a hot tub I have never owned.

Down the steps into the backyard, past a rose garden.

I try the garage door, but it's locked.

With all the movement inside, every light in the house has been triggered. There must be four or five people running around on the first floor trying to find me, shouting at one another.

An eight-foot privacy fence encloses the backyard, and as I flip the hasp on its door, someone barrels onto the deck, shouting my name.

The alley is empty, and I don't stop to think which direction to go.

I just run.

At the next street, I glance back, see two figures chasing me.

In the distance, a car engine roars to life, followed by the screech of tires spinning on pavement.

I hang a left and sprint until I reach the next alley.

Almost every backyard is protected by tall privacy fencing, but the fifth one down is waist-high, wrought-iron construction.

An SUV whips its back end around and accelerates into the alley.

I break for the low fence.

Lacking the strength to hurdle it, I clumsily haul myself over the pointed metal tines and collapse in the backyard. I crawl through the grass to a tiny shed beside the garage, with no padlock on the door.

It creaks open, and I slip inside as someone runs across the backyard.

I shut the door so no one will hear my panting.

I cannot catch my breath.

It's pitch-black inside the shed and redolent of gasoline and old grass clippings. My chest heaves against the back of the door.

Sweat drips off my chin.

I claw a cobweb off my face.

In darkness, my hands palm the plywood walls, fingers grazing various tools—pruning shears, a saw, a rake, the blade of an ax.

I take the ax from the wall and grip the wooden handle, scraping my finger across the head. Can't see a thing, but it feels like it hasn't been sharpened in years—deep chinks in the blade, which no longer holds an edge.

Blinking through the stinging sweat, I carefully open the door.

Not a sound creeps in.

I nudge it open a few more inches, until I can see into the backyard again.

It's empty.

In this sliver of quiet and calm, the principle of Occam's razor whispers to me—all things being equal, the simplest solution tends to be the right one. Does the idea that I was drugged and kidnapped by a secret, experimental group for the purposes of mind control or God-knows-what fit that bill? Hardly. They would've needed to either brainwash me to convince me that my house was not my house, or in the space of several hours, get rid of my family and gut the interior so I didn't recognize anything.

Or—is it more plausible that a tumor in my brain has turned my world upside down?

That it's been growing silently inside my skull for months or years and is finally wreaking havoc on my cognitive processes, skewing my perception of everything.

The idea hits me with the force of conviction.

What else could have crashed through me with such debilitating speed?

What else could make me lose touch with my identity and reality in a matter of hours, calling into question everything I thought I knew?

I wait.

And wait.

And wait.

Finally, I step outside into the grass.

No more voices.

No more footsteps.

No shadows.

No car engines.

The night feels sturdy and real again.

I already know where I'm headed next.

Chicago Mercy is a ten-block trek from my house, and I limp into the harsh light of the ER at 4:05 a.m.

I hate hospitals.

I watched my mother die in one.

Charlie spent the first weeks of his life in a NICU.

The waiting room is practically empty. Aside from me, there's a night construction worker clutching his arm in a bloody bandage, and a distressed-looking family of three, the father holding a red-faced, wailing baby.

The woman at the front desk looks up from her paperwork, surprisingly bright-eyed considering the hour.

Asks through the Plexiglas, "How can I help you?"

I haven't thought of what to say, how to even begin to explain my needs.

When I don't answer right away, she says, "Have you been in an accident?"

"No."

"You have cuts all over your face."

"I'm not well," I say.

"What do you mean?"

"I think I need to talk to someone."

"Are you homeless?"

"No."

"Where's your family?"

"I don't know."

She looks me up and down—a fast, professional appraisal.

"Your name, sir?"

"Jason."

"One moment."

Rising from her chair, she disappears around the corner.

Thirty seconds later, there's a buzzing sound as the door beside her station unlocks and opens.

The nurse smiles. "Come on back."

She leads me to a patient room.

"Someone will be right with you."

As the door closes after her, I take a seat on the examination table and shut my eyes against the glare of the lights. I have never been so tired in my life.

My chin dips.

I straighten.

I almost fell asleep sitting up.

The door opens.

A portly young doctor walks in carrying a clipboard. He's trailed by a different nurse—a bottle blonde in blue scrubs who wears four-in-the-morning exhaustion like a millstone around her neck.

"It's Jason?" the doctor asks without offering his hand or attempting to fake his way through the graveyard-shift indifference.

I nod.

"Last name?"

I'm hesitant to give him my full name, but then again, maybe that's just the brain tumor talking, or whatever has gone wrong inside my head.

"Dessen."

I spell it for him as he scribbles on what I presume to be an intake form.

"I'm Dr. Randolph, attending physician. What brings you into the ER tonight?"

"I think something is wrong with my mind. Like a tumor or something."

"What makes you say that?"

"Things aren't like they should be."

"Okay. Could you elaborate?"

"I . . . all right, this is going to sound crazy. Just know that I realize that."

He glances up from the clipboard.

"My house isn't my house."

"I'm not following."

"It's just what I said. My house isn't my house. My family isn't there. Everything's much . . . nicer. It's all been renovated and—"

"But it's still your address?"

"Right."

"So you're saying the inside is different, but the outside is the same?" He says it like he's speaking to a child.

"Yeah."

"Jason, how did you get the cuts on your face? The mud on your clothes?"

"People were chasing me."

I shouldn't have told him that, but I'm too tired to filter. I must sound absolutely insane.

"Chasing you."

"Yes."

"Who was chasing you?"

"I don't know."

"Do you know *why* they were chasing you?"

"Because . . . it's complicated."

His appraising, skeptical look is far more subtle and trained than the front-desk nurse's. I almost miss it.

"Have you taken any drugs or alcohol tonight?" he asks.

"Some wine earlier, then whisky, but that was hours ago."

"Again, I'm sorry—it's been a very long shift—but what makes you think something is wrong with your mind?"

"Because the last eight hours of my life don't make sense. It all feels real, but it can't possibly be."

"Have you suffered a recent head injury?"

"No. Well. I mean, I think someone hit me in the back of the head. It's painful to the touch."

"Who hit you?"

"I'm not sure. I'm not really sure of anything right now."

"Okay. Do you use drugs? Now or in the past?"

"I smoke weed a couple times a year. But not lately."

The doctor turns to the nurse. "I'm going to have Barbara draw some blood."

He drops the clipboard on a table and plucks a penlight from the front pocket of his lab coat.

"Mind if I examine you?"

"No."

Randolph moves in until our faces are inches apart, close enough for me to smell the stale coffee on his breath, to see the recent razor nick across his chin. He shines the light straight into my right eye. For a moment, there's nothing but a point of brilliance in the center of my field of vision, which momentarily burns away the rest of the world.

"Jason, are you having any thoughts of hurting yourself?"

"I'm not suicidal."

The light hits my left eye.

"Have you had any prior psychiatric hospitalizations?"

"No."

He gently takes my wrist in his soft, cool hands, measures my pulse rate.

"What do you do for a living?" he asks.

"I teach at Lakemont College."

"Married?"

"Yes." I instinctively reach down to touch my wedding band.

Gone.

Jesus.

The nurse begins to roll up the left sleeve of my shirt.

"What's your wife's name?" the doctor asks.

"Daniela."

"You two on good terms?"

"Yes."

"Don't you think she's wondering where you are? I feel like we should call her."

"I tried."

"When?"

"An hour ago, at my house. Someone else answered. It was a wrong number."

"Maybe you misdialed."

"I know my wife's phone number."

The nurse asks, "We okay with needles, Mr. Dessen?"

"Yes."

As she sterilizes the underside of my arm, she says, "Dr. Randolph, look." She touches the needle mark from several hours ago when Leighton drew my blood.

"When did this happen?" he asks.

"I don't know." Probably best not to mention the lab I think I just escaped from.

"You don't remember someone sticking a needle in your arm?"

"No."

Randolph nods to the nurse, and she warns me, "Little pinch coming."

He asks, "Do you have your cell phone with you?"

"I don't know where it is."

He grabs the clipboard. "Give me your wife's name again. And phone number. We'll try to reach her for you."

I spell Daniela's name and rattle off her cell number and our home number as my blood rushes into a plastic vial.

"You're going to scan my head?" I ask. "See what's going on?"

"Absolutely."

They give me a private room on the eighth floor.

I tidy up my face in the bathroom, kick off my shoes, and climb into bed.

Sleep tugs, but the scientist in my brain won't power down.

I can't stop thinking.

Formulating hypotheses and dismantling them.

Struggling to wrap logic around everything that's happened.

In this moment, I have no way of knowing what's real and what isn't. I can't even be sure that I was ever married.

No. Wait.

I raise my left hand and study my ring finger.

The ring is gone, but the proof of its existence lingers as a faint indentation around the base of my finger. It was there. It left a mark. That means someone took it.

I touch the indentation, acknowledging both the horror and the comfort of what it represents—the last vestige of *my* reality.

I wonder—

What will happen when this last physical trace of my marriage is gone?

When there's no anchor?

As the skies above Chicago inch toward dawn—a hopeless, cloud-ridden purple—I lose myself to sleep.

FOUR

Daniela's hands are deep in the warm, soapy water when she hears the front door slam shut. She stops scrubbing the saucepan she's been attacking for the last half minute and looks up from the sink, glancing back over her shoulder as footsteps approach.

Jason appears in the archway between the kitchen and the dining room, grinning—as her mother would say—like a fool.

Turning her attention back to the dishes, Daniela says, "There's a plate for you in the fridge."

In the steamed reflection of the window above the sink, she watches her husband set the canvas grocery bag on the island and move toward her.

His arms slide around her waist.

She says, half jokingly, "If you think a couple pints of ice cream are going to get you out of this, I don't know what to tell you."

He presses up against her and whispers in her ear, his breath fiery with the remnants of whatever whisky he's been drinking, "Life's short. Don't be mad. It's a waste of time."

"How did forty-five minutes turn into almost three hours?"

"The same way one drink turns into two, which turns into three, and on it goes. I feel terrible."

His lips on the back of her neck put a delicate shiver down her spine.

She says, "You're not getting out of this."

Now he kisses the side of her neck. It's been a while since he touched her like this.

His hands glide into the water.

He interlaces their fingers.

"You should eat something," she says. "I'll warm up your plate."

She tries to step past him on her way to the fridge, but he blocks her path.

Facing him now, she stares up into his eyes, and maybe it's because they've both been drinking, but there's an intensity in the air between them, as if every molecule has been charged.

He says, "My God, I've missed you."

"Exactly how much did you drink to—?"

He kisses her out of nowhere, backing her up against the cabinets, the counter digging into her back as he runs his hands over her hips and pulls her shirt out of her jeans, his hands on her skin now, as hot as an oven range.

She pushes him back toward the island.

"Jesus, Jason."

Now she studies him in the low light of the kitchen, trying to figure out this energy he's swaggered back into their home with.

"Something happened while you were out," she says.

"Nothing happened, other than I lost track of time."

"So you didn't chat up some young thing at Ryan's party who made you feel twenty-five again? And now you're back here with a hard-on, pretending—"

He laughs. Beautifully.

"What?" she says.

"That's what you think is going on here?" He takes a step toward her. "When I left the bar, my mind was elsewhere. I wasn't thinking. I stepped out into traffic and this cab nearly splattered me all over the pavement. Scared the hell out of me. I don't know how to explain it, but ever since that moment—in the grocery store, walking home, standing here in our kitchen—I have felt so alive. Like I see my life with force and clarity for once. All the things I have to be grateful for. You. Charlie."

She feels her anger toward him beginning to melt.

He says, "It's like we get so set in our ways, so entrenched in those grooves, we stop seeing our loved ones for who they are. But tonight, right now, I see you again, like the first time we met, when the sound of your voice and your smell was this new country. I'm rambling now."

Daniela goes to him and cups his face in her hands and kisses him.

Then she takes his hand and leads him upstairs.

The hallway is dark, and she can't think of the last time her husband did something to make her heart pound like this.

At Charlie's room, she stops for a moment and leans her ear against the closed door, logs the muffled noise of music blaring through headphones.

"All clear," she whispers.

They move down the creaky hallway as softly as they can.

In their bedroom, Daniela locks the door and opens the top drawer of her dresser, searching for a candle to light, but Jason has no time for it.

He pulls her over to the bed and drags her down onto the mattress, and then he's on top of her, kissing her, his hands moving under her clothes, roaming her body.

She feels wetness on her cheek, her lips.

Tears.

His.

Holding his face between her hands, she asks, "Why are you crying?"

"I felt like I'd lost you."

"You have me, Jason," she says. "I'm right here, baby. You have me."

As he undresses her in the darkness of their bedroom, she has never wanted anyone so desperately. The anger is gone. The wine-sleepiness has vanished. He has taken her back to the first time they made love, in her Bucktown loft with the downtown glowing through the giant windows that she'd cracked open so the crisp October air could trickle in, carrying with it the late-night noise of people stumbling home from bars and distant sirens and the engine of the massive city at rest—not completely shut down, never off, just a comforting, baseline idle.

As she comes, she fights not to cry out in their bedroom, but she can't contain it, and neither can Jason.

Not tonight.

Because something is different; something is better.

They haven't been *unhappy* these last few years, quite the opposite. But it's been a long, long time since she felt that sense of giddy love that effervesces in the pit of your stomach and spectacularly upends the world.

FIVE

"Mr. Dessen?"

I jerk awake.

"Hi. Sorry to startle you."

A doctor is staring down at me—a short, green-eyed redhead in a white lab coat holding a cup of coffee in one hand, a tablet in the other.

I sit up.

It's day outside the window next to my bed, and for five seconds, I have absolutely no idea where I am.

Through the glass: low clouds blanket the city, cutting off the skyline above one thousand feet. From this vantage point, I can see the lake and two miles of Chicago neighborhoods filling the space in between, everything muted under a somber, midwestern gray.

"Mr. Dessen, do you know where you are?"

"Mercy Hospital."

"That's right. You walked into the ER last night, pretty disoriented. One of my colleagues, Dr. Randolph, admitted you, and when he left this morning, he handed your chart over to me. I'm Julianne Springer."

I glance down at the IV in my wrist and trace the line up to the bag hanging over me on a metal stand.

"What are you giving me?" I ask.

"Just old-fashioned H_2O. You were very dehydrated. How are you feeling now?"

I run a quick self-diagnostic.

Queasy.

Head pounding.

Inside of my mouth like cotton.

I point through the window. "Like that," I say. "Weirdly hungover."

Beyond the physical discomfort, I register a crushing sense of emptiness, like it's raining directly on my soul.

Like I've been hollowed out.

"I have your MRI results," she says, waking her tablet. "Your scan came back normal. There was some shallow bruising, but nothing serious. Your tox screen results are far more illuminating. We found traces of alcohol, in line with what you reported to Dr. Randolph, but also something else."

"What?"

"Ketamine."

"Not familiar with it."

"It's a surgical anesthetic. One of its side effects is short-term amnesia. Could explain some of your disorientation. The tox screen also showed something I've never seen before. A psychoactive compound. Really weird cocktail." She sips her coffee. "I have to ask—you didn't take these drugs yourself?"

"Of course not."

"Last night, you gave Dr. Randolph your wife's name and a couple of phone numbers."

"Her cell and our landline."

"I've been trying to track her down all morning, but her

mobile number belongs to a guy named Ralph, and your land-line just keeps going to voicemail."

"Can you read her number back to me?"

Springer reads off Daniela's cell-phone number.

"That's right," I say.

"You're sure about that?"

"Hundred percent." As she looks back at the tablet, I ask, "Could these drugs you found in my system cause long-term altered states?"

"You mean delusions? Hallucinations?"

"Exactly."

"To be honest, I don't know what this psychochemical is, which means I can't say with any certainty what effect it might have had on your nervous system."

"So it could still be affecting me?"

"Again, I don't know what its half-life is, or how long it takes your body to expel it. But you don't strike me as being under the influence of anything at the moment."

Memories of the night before are regenerating.

I see myself walking naked and at gunpoint into an abandoned building.

The injection in my neck.

In my leg.

Pieces of a strange conversation with a man wearing a geisha mask.

A room filled with old generators and moonlight.

And while the thought of last night carries the emotional weight of a real memory, it has the fantasy lining of a dream, or a nightmare.

What was done to me inside that old building?

Springer pulls a chair over and takes a seat beside my bed. In proximity, I can see freckles covering her face like a sprinkling of pale sand.

"Let's talk about what you said to Dr. Randolph. He wrote down . . ." She sighs. "Apologies, his handwriting is atrocious. 'Patient reports: It was my house but it wasn't my house.' You also said that you got the cuts and bruises on your face because people were chasing you, but when asked why they were chasing you, you couldn't provide an answer." She looks up from the screen. "You're a professor?"

"Correct."

"At . . ."

"Lakemont College."

"Here's the thing, Jason. While you were sleeping, and after we couldn't find any trace of your wife—"

"What do you mean you couldn't find any trace of her?"

"Her name is Daniela Dessen, correct?"

"Yes."

"Thirty-nine years old?"

"Yeah."

"We couldn't find anyone with that name and age in all of Chicago."

That levels me. I look away from Springer, back out the window. It's so gray that even the time of day is masked. Morning, noon, evening—it's impossible to determine. Fine droplets of rain cling to the other side of the glass.

At this point, I'm not even sure what to be afraid of—this reality that might actually be true, or the possibility that everything is going to pieces inside my head. I liked it much better when I thought everything was being caused by a brain tumor. That, at least, was an explanation.

"Jason, we took the liberty of looking you up. Your name. Profession. Everything we could find. I want you to answer me very carefully. Do you really believe you're a physics professor at Lakemont College?"

"I don't *believe* it. It's what I am."

"We trawled the faculty webpages for science departments in every university and college in Chicago. Including Lakemont. You weren't listed as a professor on any of them."

"That's impossible. I've been teaching there since—"

"Let me finish, because we did find some information about you." She types something on her tablet. "Jason Ashley Dessen, born 1973 in Denison, Iowa, to Randall and Ellie Dessen. Says here that your mother passed when you were eight. How? If you don't mind my asking."

"She had an underlying heart condition, caught a bad strain of the flu, which turned into pneumonia."

"Sorry to hear that." She continues reading. "Bachelor's degree from University of Chicago, 1995. PhD from same university, 2002. So far so good?"

I nod.

"Awarded the Pavia Prize in 2004, and the same year, *Science* magazine honored your work with a cover story, calling it the 'breakthrough of the year.' Guest lecturer at Harvard, Princeton, UC Berkeley." She looks up, meets my bewildered gaze, and then turns the tablet around so I can see that she's reading from the Wikipedia page of Jason A. Dessen.

My sinus rhythm on the heart monitor I'm attached to has become noticeably faster.

Springer says, "You haven't published any new papers or accepted any teaching positions since 2005, when you took on the role of chief science officer with Velocity Laboratories, a jet propulsion lab. It says finally that a missing-persons report was filed on your behalf eight months ago by your brother, and that you haven't been seen publicly in over a year."

This rocks me so deeply I can barely draw breath.

My blood pressure triggers some kind of alarm on the heart monitor, which begins to emit a grating beep.

A heavyset nurse appears in the doorway.

"We're fine," Springer says. "Could you shut that thing up?"

The nurse walks to the monitor, silences the alarm.

When he's gone, the doctor reaches over the railing and touches my hand.

"I want to help you, Jason. I can see that you're terrified. I don't know what's happened to you, and I get the feeling you don't know either."

The wind coming in off the lake is strong enough to blow the rain sideways. I watch as the droplets streak across the glass and blur the world beyond into an impressionistic cityscape of gray, punctuated by the glow of distant taillights, distant headlights.

Springer says, "I've called the police. They're sending a detective over to take a statement from you and begin trying to get to the bottom of what happened last night. That's the first thing we're doing. Now, I've struck out trying to get in touch with Daniela, but I have been able to locate contact information for your brother, Michael, in Iowa City. I'd like to have your permission to call him and let him know that you're here, and to discuss your condition with him."

I don't know what to say to that. I haven't spoken to my brother in two years.

"I'm not sure if I want you to call him," I say.

"Fair enough, but to be clear, under HIPAA, if in my judgment a patient of mine is unable to agree or object to a disclosure due to incapacity or emergency circumstances, I am authorized to decide whether disclosing your information to a family member or friend is in your best interest. I do believe that your current mental state qualifies as incapacity, and I think consulting with someone who knows you and your history is in your best interest. So I will be calling Michael."

She glances down at the floor, as if she doesn't want to tell me whatever's coming next.

"Third thing, last thing," she says. "We need the guidance of a psychiatrist to get a handle on your condition. I'm having you transferred over to Chicago-Read, which is a mental-health center a little further up on the North Side."

"Look, I admit that I don't have a firm grasp on exactly what's happening, but I'm not crazy. I'd be happy to talk to a psychiatrist. In fact, I'd welcome the opportunity. But I'm not volunteering to be committed, if that's what you're asking."

"It's not what I'm asking. With all due respect, Jason, you don't have a choice in the matter."

"Excuse me?"

"It's called an M1 hold, and by law, if I think you're a threat to yourself or others, I can order a seventy-two-hour involuntary commitment. Look, this is the best thing for you. You're in no condition—"

"I walked into this hospital under my own steam, because I *wanted* to find out what was wrong with me."

"And that was the right choice, and that's exactly what we're going to do: find out why you're having this break with reality, and set you up with the treatment you need to make a full recovery."

I watch my blood pressure rising on the monitor.

I don't want to set off the alarm again.

Closing my eyes, I breathe in.

Let it out.

Take another shot of oxygen.

My levels recede.

I say, "So you're going to put me in a rubber room, no belt, no sharp objects, and medicate me into a stupor?"

"It's not like that. You came into this hospital because you wanted to get better, right? Well, this is the first step. I need you to trust me."

Springer rises from the chair and drags it back across the room under the television. "Just keep resting, Jason. Police will be here soon, and then we'll get you moved over to Chicago-Read this evening."

I watch her go, the threat of unraveling right on top of me, pressing down.

What if all the pieces of belief and memory that comprise who I am—my profession, Daniela, my son—are nothing but a tragic misfiring in that gray matter between my ears? Will I keep fighting to be the man I think I am? Or will I disown him and everything he loves, and step into the skin of the person this world would like for me to be?

And if I have lost my mind, what then?

What if everything I know is wrong?

No. Stop.

I am *not* losing my mind.

There were drugs in my blood from last night and bruises on my body. My key opened the door to that house that wasn't mine. I don't have a brain tumor. There's a mark from a wedding band on my ring finger. I am in this hospital room right now, and all of this is actually happening.

I am not allowed to think I'm crazy.

I am only allowed to solve this problem.

When the elevator doors open to the hospital lobby, I shoulder past two men in cheap suits and wet overcoats. They look like cops, and as they step into the elevator car and our eyes meet, I wonder if they're heading up to see me.

I move past a waiting area, toward the automatic doors. Since I wasn't on a secured ward, slipping out was much easier than I expected. I simply got dressed, waited for the hallway to clear, and cruised past the nurses' station without anyone so much as raising an eyebrow.

As I approach the exit, I keep waiting for alarms to sound, for someone to shout my name, for guards to chase me through the lobby.

Soon I'm outside in the rain, and it feels like early evening, the bustle of traffic supporting something in the neighborhood of six p.m.

I hurry down the steps, hit the sidewalk, and don't slow my pace until I've reached the next block.

I glance over my shoulder.

There's no one following me, at least as far as I can tell.

Just a sea of umbrellas.

I'm getting wet.

I have no idea where I'm going.

At a bank, I step off the sidewalk and take shelter under the entrance overhang. Leaning against a limestone column, I watch people move past as rain drills down on the pavement.

I dig my money clip out of my slacks. Last night's cab fare made a sizeable dent in my measly treasury. I'm down to $182, and my credit cards are worthless.

Home is out of the question, but there's a cheap hotel in my neighborhood a few blocks from my brownstone, and it's just gross enough to make me think I could possibly afford a room there.

I step back out into the rain.

It's getting darker by the minute.

Colder.

Without a coat or jacket, I'm soaked to my skin within two blocks.

The Days Inn occupies the building across the street from Village Tap. Only it doesn't. The canopy is the wrong color, and the entire façade looks bizarrely upmarket. These are luxury apartments. I even see a doorman standing on the curb under an umbrella, trying to hail a cab for a woman in a black trench coat.

Am I on the right street?

I cast a glance back to my corner bar.

VILLAGE TAP should be blinking neon in the front window, but instead there's a heavy wooden panel with brass lettering attached to a pole that's swinging over the entrance, creaking in the wind.

I continue walking, faster now, the rain driving into my eyes.

Past—

Rowdy taverns.

Restaurants poised to receive the dinner rush—sparkling wineglasses and silverware quickly arranged on white linen tablecloths as servers memorize the specials.

A coffee shop I don't recognize bursting with the jangle of an espresso machine grinding fresh beans.

Daniela's and my favorite Italian place looking exactly as it should, and reminding me that I haven't eaten in almost twenty-four hours.

But I keep walking.

Until I'm wet through to my socks.

Until I'm shivering uncontrollably.

Until night has dropped and I'm standing outside a three-story hotel with bars on the windows and an obnoxiously large sign above the entrance:

HOTEL ROYALE

I step inside, dripping a puddle on the cracked checkerboard floor.

It isn't what I expected. Not seedy or dirty in the lurid sense of the word. Just forgotten. Past prime. The way I remember my great-grandparents' living room in their teetering Iowa farmhouse. As if the worn furniture has been here for a thousand years, frozen in time while the rest of the world marched on. The air carries the scent of must, and big-band music plays quietly through a hidden sound system. Something from the 1940s.

At the front desk, the old, tuxedoed clerk doesn't bat an eye at my sodden state. Just takes $95 in damp cash and hands me a key to a room on the third floor.

The elevator car is cramped, and I stare at my distorted features in the bronze doors as the car labors, noisily and with all the grace of a fat man climbing stairs, to the third floor.

Halfway down a dim corridor, scarcely wide enough for two people to walk abreast, I locate my room number and wrestle the old-school lock open with the key.

It isn't much.

A single bed with a flimsy metal frame and a lumpy mattress.

A bathroom the size of a closet.

A dresser.

A cathode-ray television.

And a chair next to a window, where something glows on the other side of the glass.

Stepping around the foot of the bed, I sweep the curtain back and peer outside, finding myself at eye level with the top of the hotel sign and close enough to see the rain falling through the green neon light.

Down on the sidewalk below, I glimpse a man leaning against a streetlamp post, smoke curling up into the rain, the ash of his cigarette glowing and fading in the darkness under his hat.

Is he waiting there for me?

Maybe I'm being paranoid, but I go to the door and check the deadbolt and hook the chain.

Then I kick off my shoes, strip down, and dry myself off with the bathroom's only towel.

The best thing about the room is the ancient cast-iron radiator that stands under the window. I crank it up to high and hold my hands in the jetties of heat.

I drape my wet clothes across the back of the chair and push it close to the radiator.

In the bedside table drawer, I find a Gideon Bible and a sprawling Chicago Metro phone book.

Stretching out across the creaky bed, I thumb to the D's and begin searching for my last name.

I quickly locate my listing.

Jason A. Dessen.

Correct address.

Correct number.

I lift the phone receiver off the bedside table and call my landline.

It rings four times, and then I hear my voice: "Hi, you've reached Jason, well, except not really, because I'm not actually here to take your call. This is a recording. You know what to do."

I hang up before the beep.

That isn't our home voicemail message.

I feel insanity stalking me again, threatening to curl me up fetal and shatter me into a million pieces.

But I shut it down, returning to my new mantra.

I am not allowed to think I'm crazy.

I am only allowed to solve this problem.

Experimental physics—hell, all of science—is about solving problems. However, you can't solve them all at once. There's always a larger, overarching question—the big target. But if you obsess on the sheer enormity of it, you lose focus.

The key is to start small. Focus on solving problems you can answer. Build some dry ground to stand on. And after you've put in the work, and *if* you're lucky, the mystery of the overarching question becomes knowable. Like stepping slowly back from a photomontage to witness the ultimate image revealing itself.

I have to separate myself from the fear, the paranoia, the terror, and simply attack this problem as if I were in a lab—one small question at a time.

Build some dry ground to stand on.

The overarching question that plagues me in this moment: *What has happened to me?* There's no way to answer that. Not yet. I have vague suspicions of course, but suspicion leads to bias, and bias doesn't lead to truth.

Why weren't Daniela and Charlie at our house last night? Why did it seem as though I live alone?

No, that's still too big, too complex. Narrow the field of data.

Where are Daniela and Charlie?

Better but reduce it further. Daniela will know where my son is.

So this is where I'll start: Where is Daniela?

The sketches I saw last night on the walls of the house that isn't my house—they were created by Daniela Vargas. She had signed them using her maiden name. Why?

I hold my ring finger up to the neon light coming in through the window.

The mark of my wedding band is gone.

Was it ever there?

I tear off a piece of loose thread from the curtain and tie it around my ring finger as a physical link to the world and the life I know.

Then I return to the phone book and thumb through to the V's, stopping at the only entry for Daniela Vargas. I rip out the entire page and dial her number.

The familiarity of her voice on the recording moves me, even while the message itself leaves me deeply unsettled.

"You've reached Daniela. I'm away painting. Leave a message. Ciao."

Within an hour, my clothes are warm and nearly dry. I wash up, get dressed, and take the stairwell down to the lobby.

Out on the street, the wind is blowing, but the rain has relented.

The smoking man by the streetlamp is gone.

I'm light-headed with hunger.

I pass a half-dozen restaurants before I find one that won't clean out my funds—a bright, grimy pizza joint that sells enormous, deep-dish slices. There's nowhere to sit inside, so I stand on the sidewalk, stuffing my face and wondering if this pizza is as life-changing as I think it is, or if I'm too ravenous to be discerning.

Daniela's address is in Bucktown. I'm down to $75 and change, so I could hail a cab, but I feel like walking.

The pedestrian and traffic levels point toward Friday night, and the air carries a commensurate energy.

I head east to find my wife.

Daniela's building is yellow-brick with a façade covered in climbing ivy that's turning russet with the recent cold. The buzzer system is an old-fashioned brass panel, and I find her maiden name second up from the bottom of the first column.

I press the buzzer three times, but she doesn't answer.

Through the tall windowpanes that frame the door, I see a woman in an evening gown and overcoat, her stilettoes clicking down the hallway as she approaches. I retreat from the window and turn away as the door swings open.

She's on a cell, and by the whiff of alcohol attendant with her passing, I get the feeling she already has an enthusiastic head start on the evening. She doesn't notice me as she charges down the steps.

I catch the edge of the door before it closes and take the stairwell to the fourth floor.

Daniela's door is at the end of the hall.

I knock and wait.

No answer.

I head back down to the lobby, wondering if I should just wait here for her to return. But what if she's out of town? What would she think if she came back to her apartment to find me loitering outside her building like some stalker?

As I approach the main entrance, my eyes pass over a bulletin board covered in flyers announcing everything from gallery openings to book readings and poetry slams.

The largest notice taped to the center of the board catches my attention. It's a poster actually, advertising a show by Daniela Vargas at a gallery called Oomph.

I stop, scan for the opening date.

Friday, October 2.

Tonight.

*

Back down on the street, it's raining again.

I flag a cab.

The gallery is a dozen blocks away, and I feel the tensile strength of my nerves hit the ceiling as we roll down Damen Avenue, a parking lot of cabs in the crest of the evening's wavelength.

I abandon my ride and join the hipster-heavy crowd marching through the freezing drizzle.

Oomph is an old packing-plant-turned-art-gallery, and the line to get inside runs halfway down the block.

A miserable, shivering forty-five minutes later, I'm finally out of the rain and paying my $15 admission fee and being whisked with a group of ten people into an anteroom with Daniela's first and last name in gigantic, graffiti-style letters on the encircling wall.

During our fifteen years together, I've attended plenty of exhibits and openings with Daniela, but I've never experienced anything like this.

A slim, bearded man emerges from a hidden door in the wall.

The lights dim.

He says, "I'm Steve Konkoly, the producer of what you're about to see." He rips a plastic produce bag off a dispenser by the door. "Phones go in the bag. You get them back on the other side."

The bag of accumulating phones makes the rounds.

"A word about the next ten minutes of your life. The artist asks that you set aside your intellectual processing and make an effort to experience her installation emotionally. Welcome to 'Entanglement.'"

Konkoly takes the bag of phones and opens the door.

I'm the last one through.

For a moment, our group is bunched up in a dark, confined space that turns pitch-black as the echo of the slammed door reveals a vast, warehouse-like room.

My attention is drawn skyward as points of light fade in above us.

Stars.

They look startlingly real, each containing a smoldering quality.

Some are close, some are distant, and every now and then one streaks through the void.

I see what lies ahead.

Someone in our group mutters, "Oh my God."

It's a labyrinth built of Plexiglas, which by some visual effect appears to stretch on infinitely under the universe of stars.

Ripples of light travel through the panels.

Our group shuffles forward.

There are five entrances to the labyrinth, and I stand at the nexus of all of them, watching the others drift ahead on their separate paths.

A low-level sound that has been there all along catches my attention—it's not music so much as white noise, like television static, hissing over a deep, sustained tone.

I choose a path, and as I enter the labyrinth, the transparency vanishes.

The Plexiglas is engulfed in near-blinding light, even under my feet.

One minute in, some of the panels begin to show looped imagery.

Birth—child screaming, mother weeping with joy.

A condemned man kicking and twisting at the end of a noose.

A snowstorm.

The ocean.

A desert landscape scrolling past.

I continue along my path.

Into dead ends.

Around blind curves.

The imagery appearing with greater frequency, on faster loops.

The crumpled remains of a car crash.

A couple in the throes of passionate sex.

The point of view of a patient rolling down a hospital corridor on a gurney with nurses and doctors looking down.

The cross.

The Buddha.

The pentagram.

The peace sign.

A nuclear detonation.

The lights go out.

The stars return.

I can see through the Plexiglas again, only now there's some kind of digital filter overlaid on the transparency—static and swarming insects and falling snow.

It makes the others in the labyrinth look like silhouettes moving through a vast wasteland.

And despite the confusion and fear of the last twenty-four hours, or perhaps precisely *because* of all I've experienced, what I'm witnessing in this moment breaks through and hits me hard.

While I can see the others in the labyrinth, it doesn't feel like we're in the same room, or even the same space.

They seem worlds apart and lost in their own vectors.

I'm struck for a fleeting moment by the overwhelming sense of loss.

Not grief or pain, but something more primal.

A realization and the terror that follows it—terror of the limitless indifference surrounding us.

I don't know if that's the intended takeaway from Daniela's installation, but it's certainly mine.

We're all just wandering through the tundra of our existence, assigning value to worthlessness, when all that we love and hate, all we believe in and fight for and kill for and die for is as meaningless as images projected onto Plexiglas.

At the labyrinth's exit, there's one last loop—*a man and a woman each hold the tiny hand of their child as they run together up a grassy hill under a clear, blue sky*—with the following words slowly materializing on the panel—

Nothing exists.
All is a dream.
God—man—the world—the sun, the moon, the
wilderness of stars—a dream, all a dream; they have
no existence.
Nothing exists save empty space—and you . . .
And you are not you—you have no body, no blood,
no bones, you are but a thought.

MARK TWAIN

I step into another anteroom, where the rest of my group huddles around the plastic bag, retrieving their phones.

On through, into a large, well-lit gallery with glossy hardwood floors, art-adorned walls, a violin trio . . . and a woman in a stunning black dress, standing on a riser, addressing the crowd.

It takes me a full five seconds to realize this is Daniela.

She's radiant, holding a glass of red wine in one hand and gesturing with the other.

"—just the most amazing night, and I'm so grateful to all of you for coming out to support my new project. It means the world."

Daniela raises her wineglass.

"¡Salud!"

The crowd responds in turn, and as everyone drinks, I move toward her.

In proximity, she's electric, so sparkling with life that I have to restrain myself from calling out to her. This is Daniela with an energy like the first time we met fifteen years ago, before years of life—the normalcy, the elation, the depression, the compromise—transformed her into the woman who now shares my bed: amazing mother, amazing wife, but fighting always against the whispers of what might have been.

My Daniela carries a weight and a distance in her eyes that scare me sometimes.

This Daniela is an inch off the ground.

I'm now standing less than ten feet away, my heart thumping, wondering if she'll spot me, and then—

Eye contact.

Hers go wide and her mouth opens, and I can't tell if she's horrified or delighted or just surprised to see my face.

She pushes through the crowd, throws her arms around my neck, and pulls me in tight with, "Oh my God, I can't believe you came. Is everything all right? I'd heard you left the country for a while or were missing or something."

I'm not sure how to respond to that, so I just say, "Well, here I am."

Daniela hasn't worn perfume in years, but she's wearing it tonight, and she smells like Daniela without me, like Daniela before our separate scents merged into *us*.

I don't want to let go—I need her touch—but she pulls away.

I ask, "Where's Charlie?"

"Who?"

"Charlie."

"Who are you talking about?"

Something torques inside of me.

"Jason?"

She doesn't know who our son is.

Do we even have a son?

Does Charlie exist?

Of course he exists. I was at his birth. I held him ten seconds after he came writhing and screaming into the world.

"Everything okay?" she asks.

"Yeah. I just came through the labyrinth."

"What did you think?"

"It almost made me cry."

"It was all you," she says.

"What do you mean?"

"That conversation we had a year and a half ago? When

you came to see me? You inspired me, Jason. I thought of you every day I was building it. I thought of what you said. Didn't you see the dedication?"

"No, where was it?"

"At the entrance to the labyrinth. It's for you. I dedicated it to you, and I've been trying to reach you. I wanted you to be my special guest for tonight, but no one could find you." She smiles. "You're here now. That's all that matters."

My heart is going so fast, the room threatening to spin, and then Ryan Holder is standing next to Daniela with his arm around her. He's wearing a tweed jacket, his hair is graying, and he's paler and less fit than the last time I saw him, which was impossibly at Village Tap last night at his celebration for winning the Pavia Prize.

"Well, well," Ryan says, shaking my hand. "Mr. Pavia. The man himself."

Daniela says, "Guys, I have to go be polite and mingle, but, Jason, I'm having a secret get-together at my apartment after this. You'll come?"

"I'd love to."

As I watch Daniela vanish into the crowd, Ryan says, "Want to get a drink?"

God yes.

The gallery has pulled out all the stops—tuxedoed waiters carrying trays of appetizers and Champagne, and a cash bar on the far side of the room under a triptych of Daniela self-portraits.

As the barkeep pours our whiskies—Macallan 12s—into plastic cups, Ryan says, "I know you're doing just fine, but I got these."

It's so strange—he carries none of the arrogance and swagger of the man I saw holding court last night at my local bar.

We take our Scotches and find a quiet corner away from the mob surrounding Daniela.

As we stand there watching the room fill with more and more people emerging from the labyrinth, I ask, "So what have you been up to? I feel like I lost track of your trajectory."

"I moved over to U Chicago."

"Congrats. So you're teaching?"

"Cellular and molecular neuroscience. I've been pursuing some pretty cool research as well, involving the prefrontal cortex."

"Sounds exciting."

Ryan leans in close. "All seriousness, the rumor mill has been crazy. The whole community's talking. People saying"— he lowers his voice—"that you cracked up and lost your mind. That you're in a rubber room somewhere. That you're dead."

"Here I am. Lucid, warm, and breathing."

"So that compound I built for you . . . it worked out, I assume?"

I just stare at him, no idea what he's talking about, and when I don't provide an immediate answer, he says, "Right, I get it. They've got you buried under a mountain of NDAs."

I sip my drink. I'm still hungry, and the alcohol is traveling too fast to my head. When the next waiter passes within range, I grab three mini-quiches off the silver tray.

Whatever is bugging him, Ryan can't let it go.

"Look, I don't mean to bitch," he says, "but I just feel like I did a lot of work for you and Velocity in the dark. You and I go way back, and I get that you're in a different place in your career, but I don't know . . . I think you got what you wanted from me and . . ."

"What?"

"Forget it."

"No, please."

"You could've shown your old college roommate a little more respect is all I'm saying."

"What compound are you talking about?"

He looks at me with thinly veiled contempt. "Fuck you."

We stand silently on the outskirts as the room grows dense with people.

"So are you two together?" I ask. "You and Daniela?"

"Sort of," he says.

"What does that mean?"

"We've been seeing each other for a little while."

"You always had a thing for her, didn't you?"

He just smirks.

Scanning the crowd, I find Daniela. She's poised and in the moment, surrounded by reporters with notepads flipped open, scribbling furiously as she speaks.

"And how's it going?" I ask, though I'm not sure I really want the answer. "You and my . . . and Daniela."

"Amazing. She's the woman of my dreams."

He smiles enigmatically, and for three seconds, I want to murder him.

At one in the morning, I'm sitting on a sofa at Daniela's place, watching as she sees the last of her guests to the door. These past few hours have been a challenge—trying to hold semi-coherent conversations with Daniela's art friends while biding my time to get an actual moment alone with her. Apparently, that moment will continue to elude me: Ryan Holder, the man who's sleeping with my wife, is still here, and as he collapses into a leather chair across from me, I get the sense that he's settling in, possibly for the night.

From a heavy rocks glass, I sip the dregs of a single malt, not drunk but good and goddamn buzzed, the alcohol serving as a nice buffer between my psyche and this rabbit hole I've fallen down.

This wonderland purporting to be my life.

I wonder if Daniela wants me to leave. If I'm that oblivious, last-remaining guest who doesn't realize when he's outstayed his welcome.

She shuts the door and hooks the chain.

Kicking off her heels, she stumbles over to the sofa and crashes down onto the cushions with, "What a night."

She opens the drawer to the end table beside the couch and pulls out a lighter and a stained-glass pipe.

Daniela quit weed when she became pregnant with Charlie and never took it up again. I watch her take a hit and then offer me the pipe, and because this night can't get any stranger, why not?

Soon we're all stoned and sitting in the softly humming silence of the spacious loft whose walls are covered in a vast, eclectic array of art.

Daniela has the blinds swept back from the huge, south-facing window that serves as the backdrop to the living room, the downtown a twinkling spectacle beyond the glass.

Ryan passes the pipe to Daniela, and as she begins to repack the bowl, my old roommate slumps back in the chair and stares at the ceiling. The way he keeps licking the front of his teeth makes me smile, because it was always his weed tic, even from back in our grad-school days.

I look through that window at all the lights and ask, "How well do you two know me?"

That seems to catch their attention.

Daniela sets the pipe on the table and turns on the sofa so she's facing me, her knees drawn into her chest.

Ryan's eyes snap open.

He straightens in the chair.

"What do you mean?" Daniela asks.

"Do you trust me?"

She reaches over and touches my hand. Pure electricity. "Of course, honey."

Ryan says, "Even when you and I have been on the outs, I've always respected your decency and integrity."

Daniela looks concerned. "Everything okay?"

I shouldn't do this. I *really* shouldn't do this.

But I'm going to.

"A hypothetical," I say. "A man of science, a physics professor, is living here in Chicago. He isn't wildly successful like he always dreamed, but he's happy, mostly content, and married"—I look at Daniela, thinking of how Ryan described it back at the gallery—"to the woman of his dreams. They have a son. They have a good life.

"One night, this man goes to a bar to see an old friend, a college buddy who recently won a prestigious award. On the walk back, something happens. He never makes it home. He's abducted. The events are murky, but when he finally regains his full presence of mind, he's in a lab in South Chicago, and everything has changed. His house is different. He's not a professor anymore. He's no longer married to this woman."

Daniela asks, "Are you saying he *thinks* these things have changed, or that they've actually changed?"

"I'm saying that from his perspective, this isn't his world anymore."

"He has a brain tumor," Ryan suggests.

I look at my old friend. "MRI says no."

"Then maybe people are messing with him. Running an elaborate prank that infiltrates every aspect of his life. I think I saw that in a movie once."

"In less than eight hours, the inside of his house was completely renovated. And not just different pictures on the walls. New appliances. New furniture. Light switches were moved. No prank could possibly be this complex. And what would be the point? This is just a normal guy. Why would anyone want to mess with him at this level?"

"Then he's crazy," Ryan says.

"I'm not crazy."

It becomes very quiet in the loft.

Daniela takes hold of my hand. "What are you trying to tell us, Jason?"

I look at her. "Earlier tonight, you told me that a conversation you and I had inspired your installation."

"It did."

"Can you tell me about this conversation?"

"You don't remember?"

"Not a single word of it."

"How is that possible?"

"Please, Daniela."

There's a long pause while she searches my eyes, maybe to confirm that I'm serious.

She finally says, "It was spring, I think. We hadn't seen each other in a while, and we hadn't really spoken since we went our separate ways all those years ago. I had been following your success, of course. I was always so proud of you.

"Anyway, you showed up at my studio one night. Out of the blue. Said you'd been thinking about me lately, and at first I thought you were just trying to hook up with an old flame, but this was something else. You seriously don't remember *any* of this?"

"It's like I wasn't even there."

"We started talking about your research, how you were involved with this project that was under wraps, and you said—I remember this very clearly—you said you probably wouldn't see me again. And I realized that you hadn't stopped by to catch up. You had come to say goodbye. Then you told me that our existence was all about choices and that you had blown some of them, but none so badly as with me. You said you were sorry for everything. It was very emotional. You left, and I didn't hear from you or see you again until tonight. Now I have a question for you."

"Okay." Between the booze and dope and trying to unpack what she's telling me, I'm reeling.

"When you saw me tonight at the reception, the first thing you asked me was if I knew where 'Charlie' was. Who's that?"

One of the things I love most about Daniela is her honesty. She has a direct link hardwired from her heart to her mouth. No filter, no self-revision. She says what she feels, without a shred of guile or cunning. She works no angles.

So when I look into Daniela's eyes and see that she's utterly sincere, it nearly breaks me.

"It doesn't matter," I say.

"Obviously, it does. We haven't seen each other in a year and a half and that's the first thing you ask me?"

I finish off my drink, crunching the last melting ice cube between my molars.

"Charlie is our son."

The color leaves her face.

"Hold on," Ryan says, his words sharp. "I thought we were just having a stoner conversation. What is this?" He looks at Daniela, back to me. "Is this a joke?"

"No, it's not."

Daniela says, "We don't have a son, and you know it. We haven't been together in fifteen years. You know this, Jason. You *know* this."

I suppose I could try to convince her right now. I know so much about this woman—secrets from her childhood that she only revealed in the last five years of our marriage. But I worry these "revelations" would backfire. That she wouldn't see them as proofs, but sleights of hand. Parlor tricks. I'm betting the best approach to persuade her I'm telling the truth is clear-eyed sincerity.

I say, "Here's what I know, Daniela. You and I live in my brownstone in Logan Square. We have a fourteen-year-old son named Charlie. I'm a middling professor at Lakemont. You're an amazing wife and mother who sacrificed her art career to stay at home. And you, Ryan. You're a famous neuroscientist. *You* won the Pavia Prize. *You've* lectured all over the world. And I know this sounds absolutely crazy, but

I don't have a brain tumor, no one is messing with me, and I haven't lost my mind."

Ryan laughs, but there's an unmistakable twinge of discomfort in it. "Let's assume, for the sake of argument, that everything you just said is true. Or at least that you believe it. The unknown variable in this story is what you've been working on these last few years. This secret project. What can you tell us about it?"

"Nothing."

Ryan struggles onto his feet.

"You're going?" Daniela asks.

"It's late. I've had enough."

I say, "Ryan, it's not that I *won't* tell you. I *can't* tell you. I have no memory of it. I'm a physics professor. I woke up in this lab and everyone thought I belonged there, but I don't."

Ryan takes his hat and heads for the door.

Halfway across the threshold, he turns and faces me, says, "You're not well. Let me take you to the hospital."

"I've already been. I'm not going back."

He looks at Daniela. "Do you want him to leave?"

She turns to me, considering—I'm guessing—whether she wants to be left alone with a madman. What if she decides not to trust me?

She finally shakes her head, says, "It's fine."

"Ryan," I say. "What compound did you make for me?"

He just glares at me, and for a moment I think he's going to answer, the tension draining out of his face, as if he's trying to decide whether I'm crazy or just being a stoned asshole.

And all at once, he arrives at his conclusion.

Hardness returns.

He says with zero warmth in his voice, "Good night, Daniela."

Then turns.

Goes.

Slams the door behind him.

Daniela walks into the guest room wearing yoga pants and a tank top and carrying a cup of tea.

I've had a shower.

I don't feel any better, but at least I'm clean, the hospital stench of sickness and Clorox gone.

Sitting on the edge of the mattress, she hands me the mug. "Chamomile."

I cup my hands around the hot ceramic, say, "You didn't have to do this. I have a place I can go."

"You're staying here with me. End of story."

She crawls across my legs and sits beside me, her back against the headboard.

I sip the tea.

It's warm, soothing, faintly sweet.

Daniela looks over.

"When you went to the hospital, what did they think was wrong with you?"

"They didn't know. They wanted to commit me."

"To a psych ward?"

"Yeah."

"And you wouldn't consent?"

"No, I left."

"So it would have been an involuntary thing."

"That's right."

"Are you sure that's not what's best at this point, Jason? I mean, what would you think if someone were saying to you the things you're saying to me?"

"I'd think he was out of his mind. But I'd be wrong."

"Then tell me," she says. "What do you think is happening to you?"

"I'm not entirely sure."

"But you're a scientist. You have a theory."

"I don't have enough data."

"What does your gut tell you?"

I sip the chamomile tea, savoring the hit of warmth as it slides down my throat.

"We all live day to day completely oblivious to the fact that we're a part of a much larger and stranger reality than we can possibly imagine."

She takes my hand in hers, and even though she isn't Daniela as I know her, I cannot hide from how madly I love this woman, even here and now, sitting in this bed, in this wrong world.

I look over at her, those Spanish eyes glassy and intense. It takes all my willpower to keep my hands off her.

"Are you afraid?" she asks.

I think back to the man who took me at gunpoint. To that lab. To the team that followed me back to my brownstone and tried to apprehend me. I think of the man smoking a cigarette under my hotel room window. On top of all the elements of my identity and this reality that don't align, there are very real people out there, beyond these walls, who want to find me.

Who have hurt me before and possibly want to hurt me again.

A sobering thought crashes over me—could they track me here? Have I put Daniela in danger?

No.

If she isn't my wife, if she's only a girlfriend from fifteen years ago, why would she be on anyone's radar?

"Jason?" And she asks again, "Are you afraid?"

"Very."

She reaches up, gently touches my face, says, "Bruises."

"I don't know how I got them."

"Tell me about him."

"Who?"

"Charlie."

"This must be so weird for you."

"I can't pretend it's not."

"Well, I told you, he's fourteen. Almost fifteen. His birthday is October twenty-first, and he was born premature at Chicago Mercy. A whopping one pound, fifteen ounces. He needed a lot of help his first year, but he was a fighter. Now he's healthy and as tall as I am."

Tears well up in her eyes.

"He has dark hair like you and a wonderful sense of humor. Solid B student. Very right-brained, like his mama. He's into Japanese comics and skateboards. Loves to draw these crazy landscapes. I don't think it's too early to say that he has your eye for it."

"Stop it."

"What?"

She closes her eyes, and the tears squeeze out of the corners and spill down her cheeks.

"We don't have a son."

"You swear to me you have no memory of him?" I ask. "This isn't some game? If you tell me now, I won't—"

"Jason, we broke up fifteen years ago. Well, to be specific, you ended it with me."

"That is not true."

"I had told you the day before that I was pregnant. You needed time to think about it. You came to my loft and said it was the hardest decision you'd ever made, but you were busy with your research, the research that would ultimately win that big award. You said the next year of your life would be in a cleanroom and that I deserved better. That our child deserved better."

I say, "That is not how it happened. I told you it wasn't going to be easy, but that we'd make it work. We got married. You had Charlie. I lost my funding. You quit painting. I became a professor. You became a full-time mother."

"And yet here we are tonight. Not married. No children. You just came from the opening of the installation that's going to make me famous, and you did win that prize. I don't know what's going on in your head. Maybe you do have competing memories, but I know what's real."

I stare down at the steam rising off the surface of the tea.

"Do you think I'm crazy?" I ask.

"I have no idea, but you're not well."

And she looks at me with the compassion that has always defined her.

I touch the ring of thread that's tied around my finger like a talisman.

I say, "Look, maybe you believe what I'm telling you, maybe

you don't, but I need you to know that *I* believe it. I would never lie to you."

This is possibly the most surreal moment I've experienced since coming to consciousness in that lab—sitting in bed in the guest room of the apartment of the woman who is my wife but isn't, talking about the son we apparently never had, about the life that wasn't ours.

I wake alone in bed in the middle of the night, my heart pounding, the darkness spinning, the inside of my mouth sickeningly dry.

For a full terrifying minute, I have no idea where I am.

This isn't the alcohol or the pot.

It's a much deeper level of disorientation.

I wrap the covers tightly around me, but I can't stop shaking, and a full-body ache is growing more painful by the second, my legs restless, my head throbbing.

The next time my eyes open, the room is filled with daylight and Daniela is standing over me, looking worried.

"You're burning up, Jason. I should take you to the ER."

"I'll be fine."

"You don't look fine." She places a freezing washcloth across my forehead. "How does that feel?" she asks.

"Good, but you don't have to do this. I'll grab a cab back to my hotel."

"Just try to leave."

In the early afternoon, my fever breaks.

Daniela cooks me chicken noodle soup from scratch, and

I eat sitting up in bed while she sits in a chair in the corner with a distance in her eyes I know too well.

She's lost in thought, mulling something over, and doesn't notice that I'm watching her. I don't mean to stare, but I can't take my eyes off her. She is still so utterly Daniela, except—

Her hair is shorter.

She's in better shape.

She's wearing makeup, and her clothes—jeans and a form-fitting T—age her down considerably from thirty-nine years.

"Am I happy?" she asks.

"What do you mean?"

"In our life that you say we share together . . . am I happy?"

"I thought you didn't want to talk about it."

"I couldn't sleep last night. It was all I could think about."

"I think you're happy."

"Even without my art?"

"You miss it for sure. You see old friends finding success, and I know you're happy for them, but I also know it stings. Just like it does for me. It's a bonding agent between us."

"You mean we're both losers."

"We are not losers."

"Are *we* happy? Together, I mean."

I set the bowl of soup aside.

"Yeah. There have been rough patches, like with any marriage, but we have a son, a home, a family. You're my best friend."

She looks straight at me and asks with a devious smirk, "How's our sex life?"

I just laugh.

She says, "Oh God, did I actually make you blush?"

"You did."

"But you didn't answer my question."

"I didn't, did I?"

"What's wrong, is it not good?"

She's flirting now.

"No, it's great. You're just embarrassing me."

She gets up and walks over to the bed.

Sits on the edge of the mattress and stares at me with those huge, deep eyes.

"What are you thinking?" I ask.

She shakes her head. "That if you aren't crazy or full of shit, then we just had the strangest conversation in human history."

I sit in bed watching the daylight fade over Chicago.

Whatever storm system brought the rain last night has blown out, and in its wake, the sky is clear and the trees have turned and there's a stunning quality to the light as it moves toward evening—polarized and golden—that I can only describe as loss.

Robert Frost's gold that cannot stay.

Out in the kitchen, pots are banging, cabinets are opening and closing, and the scent of cooking meats drifts back down the hallway into the guest room with a smell that strikes me as suspiciously familiar.

I climb out of bed, stable on my feet for the first time all day, and head for the kitchen.

Bach is playing, red wine is open, and Daniela stands at the island, chopping an onion on the soapstone countertop in an apron and a pair of swimming goggles.

"Smells amazing," I say.

"Would you mind stirring it?"

I walk over to the range and lift the lid off a deep pot.

The steam rising into my face takes me home.

"How are you feeling?" she asks.

"Like a different man."

"So . . . better?"

"Much."

It's a traditional Spanish dish—a bean stew made with an assortment of native legumes and meats. Chorizo, pancetta, black sausage. Daniela cooks it once or twice a year, usually on my birthday, or when the snow flies on a weekend and we just feel like drinking wine and cooking together all day.

I stir the stew, replace the lid.

Daniela says, "It's a bean stew from—"

It slips out before I think to stop myself: "Your mother's recipe. Well, to be specific—*her* mother's mother."

Daniela stops cutting.

She looks back at me.

"Put me to work," I say.

"What else do you know about me?"

"Look, from my perspective, we've been together fifteen years. So I know almost everything."

"And from mine, it was only two and a half months, and that was a lifetime ago. And yet you know this recipe was handed down through my family over several generations."

For a moment, it becomes uncannily quiet in the kitchen.

Like the air between us carries a positive charge, humming on some frequency right at the edge of our perception.

She says finally, "If you want to help, I'm preparing toppings for the stew, and I could tell you what those are, but you probably already know."

"Grated cheddar, cilantro, and sour cream?"

She gives the faintest smile and raises an eyebrow. "Like I said, you already know."

We have dinner at the table beside the huge window with the candlelight reflecting in the glass and the city lights burning beyond—our local constellation.

The food is spectacular, Daniela is beautiful in the firelight, and I'm feeling grounded for the first time since I stumbled out of that lab.

At the end of dinner—our bowls empty, second wine bottle killed—she reaches across the glass table and touches my hand.

"I don't know what's happening to you, Jason, but I'm glad you found your way to me."

I want to kiss her.

She took me in when I was lost.

When the world stopped making sense.

But I don't kiss her. I just squeeze her hand and say, "You have no idea what you've done for me."

We clear the table, load the dishwasher, and tackle the remaining sink full of dishes.

I wash. She dries and puts away. Like an old married couple.

Apropos of nothing, I say, "Ryan Holder, huh?"

She stops wiping down the interior of the stockpot and looks at me.

"Do you have an opinion about that you'd like to share?"

"No, it's just—"

"What? He was your roommate, your friend. You don't approve?"

"He always had a thing for you."

"Are we jealous?"

"Of course."

"Oh, grow up. He's a beautiful man."

She goes back to her drying.

"So how serious is it?" I ask.

"We've been out a few times. Nobody's leaving their toothbrushes at anyone's house yet."

"Well, I think he'd like to. He seems pretty smitten."

Daniela smirks. "How could he not be? I'm amazing."

I lie in bed in the guest room with the window cracked so the city noise can put me under like a sound machine.

Staring out the tall window, I watch the sleeping city.

Last night, I set out to answer a simple question: *Where is Daniela?*

And I found her—a successful artist, living alone.

We've never been married, never had a son.

Unless I'm the victim of the most elaborate prank of all time, the nature of Daniela's existence appears to support the revelation these last forty-eight hours have been building toward . . .

This is not my world.

Even as those five words cross my mind, I'm not exactly certain what they mean, or how to begin to consider their full weight.

So I say it again.

I try it on.

See how it fits.

This is not my world.

A soft knock at my door startles me out of a dream.

"Come in."

Daniela enters, climbs into bed beside me.

I sit up, ask, "Everything okay?"

"I can't sleep."

"What's wrong?"

She kisses me, and it isn't like kissing my wife of fifteen years, it's like kissing my wife fifteen years ago for the first time.

Pure energy and collision.

As I'm on top of her, my hands running up the inside of her thighs, driving the satin chemise over her bare hips, I stop.

She says, breathless, "Why are you stopping?"

And I almost say, *I can't do this, you're not my wife,* but that isn't even true.

This *is* Daniela, the only human being in this insane world who has helped me, and, yes, maybe I am trying to justify it, but I'm so turned around, upside down, terrified, desperate, that I don't just want it, I need this, and I think she does too.

I stare down into her eyes, smoky and glistening in the light stealing through the window.

Eyes you can fall into and keep falling.

She isn't the mother of my son, she isn't my wife, we haven't made a life together, but I love her all the same, and not just the version of Daniela that exists in my head, in my history. I love the physical woman underneath me in this bed here and now, wherever this is, because it's the same arrangement of matter—same eyes, same voice, same smell, same taste . . .

It isn't married-people lovemaking that follows.

We have fumbling, groping, backseat-of-the-car, unprotected-because-who-gives-a-fuck, protons-smashing-together sex.

Moments after, sweaty and shaky, we lie intertwined and gazing out at the lights of our city.

Daniela's heart is banging away in her chest, and I can feel the *bump-bump* of it against my side, decelerating now.

Slower.

Slower.

"Everything okay?" she whispers. "I can hear the wheels turning up there."

"I don't know what I would've done if I hadn't found you."

"Well, you did. And whatever's happening, I'm here for you. You know that, right?"

She runs her fingers across my hands.

They stop at the piece of thread tied around my ring finger.

"What's this?" she asks.

"Proof," I say.

"Proof?"

"That I'm not crazy."

It becomes quiet again.

I'm not sure of the time, but it's definitely past two in the morning.

The bars will be closed now.

The streets as quiet and subdued as they get with the exception of snowstorm nights.

The air creeping through the crack in the window is the coldest of the season.

It trickles across our sweat-glazed bodies.

"I need to get back to my house," I say.

"Your place in Logan Square?"

"Yeah."

"What for?"

"I apparently have a home office. I want to get on the computer, see exactly what I've been working on. Maybe I'll find papers, notes, something that will shed some light on what's happening to me."

"I can drive you over first thing in the morning."

"You probably shouldn't."

"Why?"

"Might not be safe."

"Why wouldn't it—"

Out in the living room, a loud bang rattles the door, like someone pounding on it with their fist. The way I imagine cops knock.

I ask, "Who the hell is that at this hour?"

Daniela climbs out of bed and walks naked out of the room.

It takes me a minute to find my boxer shorts in the twisted-up comforter, and by the time I pull them on, Daniela is emerging from her bedroom in a terrycloth robe.

We head out into the living room.

The pounding on the door continues as Daniela approaches.

"Don't open it," I whisper.

"Obviously."

As she leans into the peephole, the phone rings.

We both startle.

Daniela crosses the living room toward the cordless lying on the coffee table.

I glance through the peephole, see a man standing in the hallway, his back to the door.

He's on a cell phone.

Daniela answers, "Hello?"

The man is dressed in black—Doc Martens, jeans, a leather jacket.

Daniela says into the phone, "Who is this?"

I move toward her and point to the door, mouthing, *It's him?*

She nods.

"What does he want?"

She points at me.

Now I can hear the man's voice coming simultaneously through the door and through the speaker on her cordless.

She says into the phone, "I don't know what you're talking about. It's just me here, and I live alone, and I'm not letting a strange man into my home at two in the—"

The door explodes open, the chain snaps and flies across the room, and the man steps in raising a pistol with a long black tube screwed into the barrel.

He aims it at both of us, and as he kicks the door closed I smell old and recent cigarette smoke wafting into the loft.

"You're here for me," I say. "She has nothing to do with any of this."

He's an inch or two shorter than I am, but sturdier. His head is shaved and his eyes are gray and not so much cold as remote, as if they don't see me as a human being, but rather as information. Ones and zeroes. The way a machine might.

My mouth has gone dry.

There's a strange distance between what's happening and my processing of it. A disconnect. A delay. I should do something, say something, but I feel paralyzed by the suddenness of the man's presence.

"I'll go with you," I say. "Just—"

His aim shifts slightly away from me and up.

Daniela says, "Wait, no—"

She's cut off by a burst of fire and a muted report not quite as loud as a naked gunshot.

A fine, red mist blinds me for half a second, and Daniela sits on the sofa, a hole dead center between her big, dark eyes.

I start toward her, screaming, but every molecule in my body seizes, muscles clenching uncontrollably with stunning agony, and I crash down through the coffee table, shaking and grunting in broken glass and telling myself this isn't happening.

The smoking man lifts my useless arms behind my back and binds my wrists together cruciform with a zip tie.

Then I hear a tearing sound.

He pats a piece of duct tape over my mouth and sits behind me in the leather chair.

I'm screaming through the tape, pleading for this not to be happening, but it is, and there's nothing I can do to change it.

I hear the man's voice behind me—calm and occupying a higher register than I would've imagined.

"Hey, I'm here . . . No, why don't you come around back . . . Exactly. Where the recycling and Dumpsters are. The back gate and rear door to the building are both open . . . Two should be fine. We're in pretty good shape up here, but you know, let's not linger . . . Yep . . . Yep . . . Okay, sounds good."

The excruciating effect of what I assume was a Taser is finally relenting, but I'm too weak to move.

From my vantage point, all I can see is the lower half of Daniela's legs. I watch a line of blood run down her right ankle, across the top of her foot, between her toes, and begin to puddle on the floor.

I hear the man's phone buzz.

He answers, "Hey, baby . . . I know, I just didn't want to wake you . . . Yeah, something came up . . . I don't know, might be morning. How about I take you to breakfast at the Golden Apple whenever I wrap up?" He laughs. "Okay. Love you too. Sweet dreams."

My eyes sheet over with tears.

I shout through the tape, shout until my throat burns, thinking maybe he'll shoot me or knock me unconscious, anything to stop the exquisite pain of this moment.

But it doesn't seem to bother him at all.

He just sits there quietly, letting me rage and scream.

SIX

Daniela sits in the bleachers under the scoreboard, above the ivy-covered outfield wall. It's Saturday afternoon, the last home game of the regular season, and she's with Jason and Charlie, watching the Cubs get their asses kicked in their sold-out ballpark.

The warm autumn day is cloudless.

Windless.

Timeless.

The air redolent of—

Roasted peanuts.

Popcorn.

Plastic cups filled to the brim with beer.

Daniela finds the roar of the crowd strangely comforting, and they're far enough back from home plate to notice a delay between swing and bat-crack—speed of light versus speed of sound—when a player sends a pitch sailing beyond the wall.

They used to come to games when Charlie was a boy, but it's been eons since their last visit to Wrigley Field. When Jason suggested the idea yesterday, she didn't think Charlie would be up for it, but it must be scratching some nostalgic itch in their son's psyche, because he actually wanted to come, and now he seems relaxed and happy. They're all happy, a trio of near-perfect contentment in the sun, eating Chicago-style hot dogs, watching the players run around on the bright grass.

As Daniela sits wedged between the two most important men in her life, buzzed off her lukewarm beer, it occurs to her that the feel of this afternoon is somehow different. Unsure if it's Charlie or Jason or her. Charlie is in the moment, not checking his phone every five seconds. And Jason looks as happy as she's seen him in years. *Weightless* is the word that comes to mind. His smile seems wider, brighter, more freely given.

And he can't keep his hands off her.

Then again, maybe the difference is her.

Maybe it's this beer and the crystalline quality of the autumn light and the communal energy of the crowd.

Which is all to say maybe it's just being alive at a baseball game on a fall day in the heart of her city.

Charlie has plans after the game, so they drop him at a friend's house in Logan Square, stop at the brownstone to change clothes, and then head out into the evening, just the two of them—downtown-bound, no itinerary, no specific destination.

A Saturday-night ramble.

Cruising in heavy evening traffic down Lakeshore Drive, Daniela looks across the center console of the decade-old Suburban, says, "I think I know what I want to do first."

Thirty minutes later, they're in a gondola car on a Ferris wheel strung with lights.

Rising slowly above the spectacle of Navy Pier, Daniela watches the elegant skyline of their city as Jason holds her tight.

At the apex of their single revolution—one hundred and fifty feet above the carnival—Daniela feels Jason touch her chin and turn her face toward his.

They have the car all to themselves.

Even up here, the night air is sweetened with the scent of funnel cakes and cotton candy.

The laughter of children riding on the carousel.

A woman screaming with joy at a hole-in-one on the miniature golf course far below.

Jason's intensity shreds through all of it.

When he kisses her, she can feel his heart through his windbreaker, jackhammering in his chest.

They have dinner in the city at a nicer restaurant than they can afford and spend the entire time talking like they haven't talked in years.

Not about people or remember-whens, but ideas.

They kill a bottle of Tempranillo.

Order another.

Thinking maybe they'll spend the night in the city.

It's been a long time since Daniela has seen her husband this passionate, this sure of himself.

He's a man on fire, in love with his life again.

Halfway through their second bottle of wine, he catches her looking out the window, asks, "What are you thinking about?"

"That's a dangerous question."

"I'm aware."

"I'm thinking about you."

"What about me?"

"It feels like you're trying to sleep with me." She laughs. "What I mean is, it feels like you're trying when you don't have to be trying. We're an old married couple, and I feel like you're, um . . ."

"Romancing you?"

"Exactly. Don't get me wrong, I'm not complaining. At all. It's amazing. I guess I just don't see where it's all coming from. Are you okay? Is something wrong, and you're not telling me?"

"I'm fine."

"So this is all because you almost got hit by a cab two nights ago?"

He says, "I don't know if it was my life flashing before my eyes or what, but when I came home, everything felt different. More real. You especially. Even right now, it's like I'm seeing you for the first time, and I have this nervous ache in my stomach. I think about you every second. I think about all the choices we've made that created this moment. Us sitting here together at this beautiful table. Then I think of all the possible events that could have stopped this moment from ever happening, and it all feels, I don't know . . ."

"What?"

"So fragile." Now he becomes thoughtful for a moment. He says finally, "It's terrifying when you consider that every thought we have, every choice we could possibly make, branches into a new world. After the baseball game today, we went to Navy Pier and then came here for dinner, right? But that's only one version of what happened. In a different reality, instead of the pier, we went to the symphony. In one, we stayed home. In another still, we got into a fatal wreck on Lakeshore Drive and never made it anywhere."

"But those other realities don't really exist."

"Actually, they're just as real as the one you and I are experiencing at this moment."

"How is that possible?"

"It's a mystery. But there are clues. Most astrophysicists believe that the force holding stars and galaxies together—the thing that makes our whole universe *work*—comes from a theoretical substance we can't measure or observe directly. Something they call dark matter. And this dark matter makes up most of the known universe."

"But what is it exactly?"

"No one's really sure. Physicists have been trying to construct new theories to explain its origin and what it is. We know it has gravity, like ordinary matter, but it must be made of something completely new."

"A new form of matter."

"Exactly. Some string theorists think it might be a clue to the existence of the multiverse."

She looks thoughtful for a moment, then asks, "So all these other realities . . . where are they?"

"Imagine you're a fish, swimming in a pond. You can move forward and back, side to side, but never up out of the water. If someone were standing beside the pond, watching you, you'd have no idea they were there. To you, that little pond is an entire universe. Now imagine that someone reaches down and lifts you out of the pond. You see that what you thought was the entire world is only a small pool. You see other ponds. Trees. The sky above. You realize you're a part of a much larger and more mysterious reality than you had ever dreamed of."

Daniela leans back in her chair and takes a sip of wine. "So all these other thousands of ponds are all around us, right at this moment—but we just can't see them?"

"Exactly."

Jason used to talk like this all the time. Would keep her up late into the night positing wild theories, sometimes trying things out, most of the time just trying to impress her.

It worked then.

It's working now.

She looks away for a moment, staring through the window beside their table, watching the water glide past as the light from the surrounding buildings swirls in a kind of perpetual shimmer across the blown-glass surface of the river.

She finally looks back at him over the rim of her wineglass, their eyes connecting, the candlelight quivering between them.

She says, "In one of those ponds out there, do you think there's another version of you that stuck with the research? Who made good on all the plans you had in your twenties, before life got in the way?"

He smiles. "It's crossed my mind."

"And there's maybe a version of me that's a famous artist? That traded all this for that?"

Jason leans forward, pushing their plates out of the way so he can hold both of her hands across the table.

"If there are a million ponds out there, with versions of you and me living similar and different lives, there's none better than right here, right now. I'm more sure of that than anything in the world."

SEVEN

The bare lightbulb in the ceiling rains down a naked and flickering illumination on the tiny cell. I'm strapped to a steel-frame bed, ankles and wrists chained together with restraints and connected, via locking carabiners, to eyebolts in the concrete wall.

Three locks retract in the door, but I'm too sedated to even startle.

It swings open.

Leighton wears a tux.

Wire-rim glasses.

As he approaches, I catch a whiff of cologne, and then alcohol on his breath. Champagne? I wonder where he's just come from. A party? A benefit? There's a pink ribbon still pinned to the satin breast of his jacket.

Leighton eases down onto the edge of the paper-thin mattress.

He looks grave.

And unbelievably sad.

"I'm sure you have some things you want to say, Jason, but I hope you'll let me go first. I take a lot of blame for what happened. You came back, and we weren't prepared for you to be as . . . unwell as you were. As you are. We failed you, and I'm sorry. I don't know what else to say. I just . . . I hate everything that's happened. Your return should have been a celebration."

Even through the heavy sedation, I'm shaking with grief. With rage.

"The man who came to Daniela's apartment—did *you* send him after me?" I ask.

"You left me no choice. Even the possibility you had told her about this place—"

"Did you tell him to kill her?"

"Jason—"

"Did you?"

He doesn't answer, but it is an answer.

I stare into Leighton's eyes, and all I can think about is ripping his face off down to his skull.

"You fucking . . ."

I break down.

Sobbing.

I cannot exile from my brain the image of blood running down Daniela's bare foot.

"I'm so sorry, brother." Leighton reaches out, puts his hand on my arm, and I nearly dislocate my shoulder trying to pull away.

"Don't touch me!"

"You've been in this cell almost twenty-four hours. It gives me no pleasure to keep you restrained and sedated, but as long as you're a danger to yourself or others, this situation can't change. You need to eat and drink something. Are you willing to do that?"

I focus on a crack in the wall.

I imagine using Leighton's head to open another one.

Driving it into the concrete again and again and again until there's nothing left but red paste.

"Jason, it's either you let them feed you, or I run a G-tube into your stomach."

I want to tell him that I'm going to kill him. Him and everyone in this lab. I can feel the words coming up my throat, but better judgment prevails—I'm completely at this man's mercy.

"I know what you saw in that apartment was horrible, and I'm sorry for that. I wish it had never happened, but sometimes, a situation is so far gone . . . Look, please know that I am so, so sorry you had to see that."

Leighton rises, moves toward the door, pulls it open.

Standing in the threshold, he looks back at me, his face half in light, half in shadow.

He says, "Maybe you can't hear this right now, but this place wouldn't exist without you. None of us would be here, but for your work, your brilliance. I'm not going to let anyone forget that, most of all you."

I calm down.

I *pretend* to calm down.

Because staying chained up in this tiny cell isn't accomplishing a goddamn thing.

From the bed, I stare up into the surveillance camera mounted over the door and ask for Leighton.

Five minutes later, he's unlocking my restraints and saying, "I think I'm probably as happy as you are to get you out of these things."

He gives me a hand up.

My wrists have been rubbed raw from the leather bind-ings.

My mouth is dry.

I'm delirious with thirst.

He asks, "You feeling any better?"

It occurs to me that my first inclination when I woke up in this place was the right one. Be the man they think I am. The only way to pull that off is to pretend my memories and my identity have abandoned me. Let them fill in the blanks. Because if I'm not the man they think I am, then they have no use for me.

Then I never leave this lab alive.

I tell him, "I was scared. That's why I ran."

"I totally get it."

"I'm sorry I put you all through this, but you have to understand—I'm lost here. There's just this gaping hole where the last ten years should be."

"And we're going to do everything in our power to help you recover those memories. To get you better. We're firing up the MRI. We're going to screen you for PTSD. Our psychia-trist, Amanda Lucas, will be speaking with you shortly. You have my word—no stone will be left unturned until we fix this. Until we have you fully back."

"Thank you."

"You'd do the same for me. Look, I have no idea what you've been through these last fourteen months, but the man I've known for eleven years, my colleague and friend who built this place with me? He's locked away somewhere in that head of yours, and there is nothing I won't do to find him."

A terrifying thought—what if he's right?

I *think* I know who I am.

But there's a part of me that wonders . . . What if the recollection I have of my real life—husband, father, professor—isn't real?

What if it's a by-product of brain damage I received while working in this lab?

What if I'm actually the man who everyone in this world believes I am?

No.

I know who I am.

Leighton has been sitting on the edge of the mattress.

Now he props his feet up and leans back against the footboard.

"I have to ask," he says. "What were you doing at that woman's apartment?"

Lie.

"I'm not entirely sure."

"How did you know her?"

I fight to hide the tears and rage.

"I dated her a long time ago."

"Let's go back to the beginning. After you escaped through the bathroom window three nights ago, how did you get to your home in Logan Square?"

"A cab."

"Did you tell the driver anything about where you'd just come from?"

"Of course not."

"Okay, and after you managed to elude us at your house, then where'd you go?"

Lie.

"I wandered around all night. I was disoriented, afraid. The next day I saw this poster for Daniela's art show. That's how I found her."

"Did you talk to anyone else besides Daniela?"

Ryan.

"No."

"You're sure about that?"

"Yes. I went back to her apartment, and it was just the two of us until . . ."

"You have to understand—we've dedicated everything to this place. To your work. We're all in. Any one of us would lay down our lives to protect it. Including you."

The gunshot.

The black hole between her eyes.

"It breaks my heart to see you like this, Jason."

He says this with genuine bitterness and regret.

I can see it in his eyes.

"We were friends?" I ask.

He nods, his jaw tight, as if he's holding back a wave of emotion.

I say, "I'm just having a hard time understanding how murdering someone to protect this lab would be acceptable to you or any of these people."

"The Jason Dessen I knew wouldn't have given a second thought to what happened to Daniela Vargas. I'm not saying he would've been happy about it. None of us are. It makes me sick. But he would've been willing."

I shake my head.

He says, "You've forgotten what we built together."

"So show me."

*

They clean me up, give me new clothes, and feed me.

After lunch, Leighton and I ride a service elevator down to sublevel four.

Last time I walked this corridor, it was lined with plastic, and I had no idea where I was.

I haven't been threatened.

Haven't been told specifically that I can't leave.

But I've already noticed that Leighton and I are rarely alone. Two men who carry themselves like cops are always on the periphery. I remember these guards from my first night here.

"It's basically four levels," Leighton says. "Gym, rec room, mess hall, and a few dormitories on one. Labs, cleanrooms, conference rooms on two. Sublevel three is dedicated to fabrication. Four is the infirmary and mission control."

We're moving toward a pair of vaultlike doors that look formidable enough to secure national secrets.

Leighton stops at a touchscreen mounted to the wall beside them.

He pulls a keycard from his pocket and holds it under the scanner.

A computerized female voice says, *Name, please.*

He leans in close. "Leighton Vance."

Passcode.

"One-one-eight-seven."

Voice recognition confirmed. Welcome, Dr. Vance.

The sound of a buzzer startles me, its echo fading down the corridor behind us.

The doors open slowly.

I step into a hangar.

From the rafters high above, lights blaze down, illuminating a twelve-foot cube the color of gunmetal.

My pulse rate kicks up.

I can't believe what I'm looking at.

Leighton must sense my awe, because he says, "Beautiful, isn't it?"

It is exquisitely beautiful.

At first, I think the hum inside the hangar is coming from the lights, but it can't be. It's so deep I can feel it at the base of my spine, like the ultralow-frequency vibration of a massive engine.

I drift toward the box, mesmerized.

I never fathomed I would see it in the flesh at this scale.

Up close, it isn't smooth but an irregular surface that reflects the light in such a way as to make it seem multifaceted, almost translucent.

Leighton gestures to the pristine concrete floor gleaming under the lights. "We found you unconscious right over there."

We walk slowly alongside the box.

I reach out, let my fingers graze the surface.

It's cold to the touch.

Leighton says, "Eleven years ago, after you won the Pavia, we came to you and said we had five billion dollars. We could've built a spaceship, but we gave it all to you. To see what you could accomplish with unlimited resources."

I ask, "Is my work here? My notes?"

"Of course."

We reach the far side of the box.

He leads me around the next corner.

On this side, a door has been cut into the cube.

"What's inside?" I ask.

"See for yourself."

The base of the door frame sits about a foot off the surface of the hangar.

I lower the handle, push it open, start to step inside.

Leighton puts a hand on my shoulder.

"No further," he says. "For your own safety."

"It's dangerous?"

"You were the third person to go inside. Two more went in after you. So far, you're the only one to return."

"What happened to them?"

"We don't know. Recording devices can't be used inside. The only report we can hope for at this point has to come from someone who manages to make it back. Like you did."

The inside of the box is empty, unadorned, and dark.

Walls, floor, and ceiling made of the same material as the exterior.

Leighton says, "It's soundproof, radiation-proof, airtight, and, as you might have guessed, puts out a strong magnetic field."

As I close the door, a deadbolt thunks into place on the other side.

Staring at the box is like seeing a failed dream raised from the dead.

My work in my late twenties involved a box much like this one. Only it was a *one-inch* cube designed to put a macroscopic object into superposition.

Into what we physicists sometimes call, in what passes for humor among scientists, cat state.

As in Schrödinger's cat, the famous thought experiment.

Imagine a cat, a vial of poison, and a radioactive source in a sealed box. If an internal sensor registers radioactivity, like an atom decaying, the vial is broken, releasing a poison that kills the cat. The atom has an equal chance of decaying or not decaying.

It's an ingenious way of linking an outcome in the classical world, our world, to a quantum-level event.

The Copenhagen interpretation of quantum mechanics suggests a crazy thing: before the box is opened, before observation occurs, the atom exists in superposition—an undetermined state of both decaying and not decaying. Which means, in turn, that the cat is both alive and dead.

And only when the box is opened, and an observation made, does the wave function collapse into one of two states.

In other words, we only see one of the possible outcomes.

For instance, a dead cat.

And that becomes our reality.

But then things get really weird.

Is there another world, just as real as the one we know, where we opened the box and found a purring, living cat instead?

The Many-Worlds interpretation of quantum mechanics says yes.

That when we open the box, there's a branch.

One universe where we discover a dead cat.

One where we discover a live one.

And it's the act of our *observing* the cat that kills it—or lets it live.

And then it gets mind-fuckingly weird.

Because those kinds of observations happen *all the time*.

So if the world really splits whenever something is observed, that means there's an unimaginably massive, infinite number of universes—a multiverse—where everything that can happen will happen.

My concept for my tiny cube was to create an environment protected from observation and external stimuli so my macroscopic object—an aluminum nitride disc measuring 40 μm in length and consisting of around a trillion atoms—could be free to exist in that undetermined cat state and not decohere due to interactions with its environment.

I never cracked that problem before my funding evaporated, but apparently some other version of me did. And then scaled the entire concept up to an inconceivable level. Because if what Leighton is saying is true, this box does something that, according to everything I know about physics, is impossible.

I feel shamed, like I lost a race to a better opponent. A man of epic vision built this box.

A smarter, better me.

I look at Leighton.

"Does it work?"

He says, "The fact that you're standing here beside me would appear to suggest that it does."

"I don't get it. If you wanted to put a particle in a quantum state in a lab, you'd create a deprivation chamber. Remove all light, suck out the air, turn down the temperature to a fraction of a degree above absolute zero. It would kill a human being. And the larger you go, the more fragile it all becomes. Even though we're underground, there are all sorts of particles—neutrinos, cosmic rays—passing through that cube that could disturb a quantum state. The challenge seems insurmountable."

"I don't know what to tell you . . . You surmounted it."

"How?"

Leighton smiles. "Look, it made sense when you explained it to me, but I can't exactly explain it back. You should read your notes. What I can tell you is that box creates and sustains an environment where everyday objects can exist in a quantum superposition."

"Including us?"

"Including us."

Okay.

Though everything I know tells me it's impossible, I apparently figured out a way to create a fertile quantum environment at the macro scale, perhaps utilizing the magnetic field to couple objects on the inside to the atomic-scale quantum system.

But what about the occupant inside the box?

Occupants are observers too.

We live in a state of decoherence, in one reality, because we're constantly observing our environment and collapsing our own wave function.

There has to be something else at work.

"Come on," Leighton says. "I want to show you something."

He leads me toward a bank of windows on the side of the hangar that faces the door to the box.

Swiping his keycard at another secured door, he shows me into a room that resembles a com center or mission control.

At the moment, only one of the workstations is occupied,

by a woman with her feet kicked up on a desk, jamming out to a pair of headphones, oblivious to our entry.

"That station is manned twenty-four hours a day, seven days a week. We all take turns waiting for someone to return."

Leighton slides in behind a computer terminal, inputs a series of passcodes, and dives through several folders until he finds what he's looking for.

He opens a video file.

It's HD, shot from a camera facing the door of the box, probably positioned right above these windows in mission control.

Across the bottom of the screen, I see a timestamp from fourteen months ago, the clock keeping time down to a hundredth of a second.

A man moves into frame and approaches the box.

He wears a backpack over a streamlined space suit, the helmet for which he carries under his left arm.

At the door, he turns the lever and pushes it open. Before stepping inside, he looks back over his shoulder, straight into the camera.

It's me.

I wave, step into the box, and shut myself inside.

Leighton accelerates the playback speed.

I watch the box sit motionless as fifty minutes races by.

He slows the video back down when someone new emerges into frame.

A woman with long brown hair walks toward the box and opens the door.

The camera feed switches to a head-mounted GoPro.

It pans the interior of the box, a light shining across the

naked walls and floor, glinting off the uneven surface of the metal.

"And poof," Leighton says. "You're gone. Until . . ." He fires up another file. "Three and a half days ago."

I see myself stagger out of the box and crash to the floor, almost like I was pushed out.

More time elapses, and then I watch the hazmat team appear and hoist me onto a gurney.

I can't get over how entirely surreal it feels to be viewing a playback of the exact moment when the nightmare that is now my life began.

My first seconds in this brave, new, fucked-up world.

One of the sleeping quarters on sublevel one has been prepared for me, and it's a welcome upgrade from the cell.

Luxurious bed.

Full bath.

A desk with a vase of fresh-cut flowers that have perfumed the entire space.

Leighton says, "I hope you'll be more comfortable here. I'm just going to say it: please don't try to kill yourself, because we're all on the lookout for it. There will be people right outside this door to stop you, and then you'll have to live in a straitjacket in that disgusting cell downstairs. If you start feeling desperate, just pick up the phone and tell whoever answers to come find me. Don't suffer in silence."

He touches the laptop sitting on the desk.

"It's loaded with your work product from the last fifteen years. Even goes back to your pre-Velocity Laboratories research. There's no password. Feel free to explore. Maybe it'll jog something loose." On his way out the door, he glances back, says, "By the way, this is going to stay locked." He smiles. "But only for your safety."

I sit in bed with the laptop, attempting to wrap my head around the sheer volume of information contained in the tens of thousands of folders.

The organization is by year, and it goes back to before I won the Pavia, to my grad-school days, when the first intimation of my life's ambition began to present itself.

The early folders contain work familiar to me—drafts of a paper that would ultimately become my first published work, abstracts from related articles, everything building toward my stint in that University of Chicago lab and the construction of the first tiny cube.

The cleanroom data is meticulously sorted.

I read the files on the laptop until I start seeing double, and even then I push on, watching my work advance beyond where I know it stopped in *my* version of my life.

It's like forgetting everything about yourself and then reading your own biography.

I worked every day.

My notes became better, more thorough, more specific.

But still I struggled to find a way to create the superposition of my macroscopic disc, the frustration and despair bleeding into my notes.

I can't keep my eyes open any longer.

Killing the light on the bedside table, I pull up the blankets.

It's pitch-black in here.

The sole point of light in the room is a green dot high up the wall that faces my bed.

It's a camera, filming in night vision.

Someone is watching my every move, my every breath.

I close my eyes, try to tune it out.

But I see the same thing that haunts me every time I shut my eyes: the blood running down her ankle, across her bare foot.

The black hole between her eyes.

It would be so easy to crack.

To fly apart.

In the darkness, I touch the piece of thread on my ring finger and remind myself that my other life is real, that it's still out there somewhere.

Like standing on a beach as the tide sucks the sand beneath my feet back out to sea, I can feel my native world, and the reality that supports it, pulling away.

I wonder: If I don't fight hard enough against it, will this reality slowly click in and carry me off?

I slam awake.

Someone is knocking on the door.

I hit the light and stumble out of bed, disoriented, no idea how long I've been sleeping.

The knocking gets louder.

I say, "I'm coming!"

I try to open the door, but it's locked from the outside.

I hear a deadbolt turn.

The door opens.

It takes me a moment to realize when and where I've seen

this woman in a black wrap dress, standing in the hallway holding two cups of coffee and a notebook under one arm. Then it hits me—here. She ran, or tried to run, that bizarre debriefing on the night I came to consciousness outside the box.

"Jason, hi. Amanda Lucas."

"Right, yes."

"Sorry, I didn't want to just barge in."

"No, it's fine."

"Do you have some time to speak with me?"

"Um, sure."

I let her in and close the door.

I pull out the chair from the desk for her.

She holds up a paper cup. "I brought you coffee if you're interested."

"Please," I say, taking it. "Thank you."

I sit on the end of the bed.

The coffee warms my hands.

She says, "They had this chocolate-hazelnut nonsense, but you like straight-up regular, right?"

I take a sip. "Yeah, this is perfect."

She sips her coffee, says, "So this must be strange for you."

"You could say that."

"Leighton said he mentioned that I might come talk with you?"

"He did."

"Good. I'm the lab psychiatrist. I've been here almost nine years. I'm board-certified and all that. Ran a private practice before I joined Velocity Laboratories. Do you mind if I ask you some questions?"

"Okay."

"You reported to Leighton . . ." She opens her notebook. "Quote, 'There's just this gaping hole where the last ten years should be.' Is that accurate?"

"It is."

She scribbles something with a pencil onto the page.

"Jason, have you recently experienced or witnessed a life-threatening event that caused intense fear, helplessness, or horror?"

"I saw Daniela Vargas shot in the head right in front of me."

"What are you talking about?"

"You people murdered my . . . this woman I was with. Right before I was brought here." Amanda looks legitimately stunned. "Wait. You didn't know about that?"

Swallowing, she recovers her composure.

"That must have been horrifying, Jason." She says it like she doesn't believe me.

"Do you think I'm making it up?"

"I'm curious if you remember anything from the box itself, or your travels during the last fourteen months."

"Like I said, I have no memory of it."

She makes another note, says, "Interestingly, and maybe you don't recall this . . . but during that very short debriefing, you did say your last memory was of being in a bar in Logan Square."

"I don't remember saying that. I was pretty out of it at the time."

"Of course. So no memories from the box. All right, these next few are yes-or-no questions. Any problems sleeping?"

"No."

"Increased irritability or anger?"

"Not really."

"Problems concentrating?"

"I don't think so."

"Do you feel on guard?"

"Yes."

"Okay. Have you noticed that you have an exaggerated startle response?"

"I'm . . . not sure."

"Sometimes, an extreme stress situation can trigger what's called psychogenic amnesia, which is abnormal memory functioning in the absence of structural brain damage. I have a feeling we're going to rule out any structural damage with the MRI today. Which means your memories from the last fourteen months are still there. They're just buried deep in your mind. It'll be my job to help you recover them."

I sip the coffee. "How exactly?"

"There are a number of treatment options we can explore. Psychotherapy, cognitive therapy, creative therapy. Even clinical hypnosis. I just want you to know that nothing is more important to me than helping you through this."

Amanda stares into my eyes with a sudden, unnerving intensity, searching them as if the mysteries of our existence have been written on my corneas.

"You really don't know me?" she asks.

"No."

Rising from the chair, she takes her things.

"Leighton will be up soon to take you down for the MRI. I just want to help you, Jason, however I can. If you don't remember me, that's okay. Just know that I'm your friend. Everyone in this place is your friend. We're here because of you. We're all taking it for granted that you know that, so please hear me: we're in awe of you and your mind and this thing you built."

At the door she stops, looks back at me.

"What's the woman's name again? The one you think you saw murdered."

"I don't *think* I saw. I saw. And her name is Daniela Vargas."

I spend the rest of the morning at the desk, eating breakfast and scrolling through files that chronicle scientific achievements of which I have no memory.

Despite my present circumstances, it's exhilarating to read my notes, see them progressing toward my breakthrough with the miniature cube.

The solution to creating the superposition of my disc?

Superconducting qubits integrated with an array of resonators capable of registering simultaneous states as vibrations. Sounds incomprehensibly boring, but it's groundbreaking.

It won me the Pavia.

It apparently landed me here.

Ten years ago, my first day on the job at Velocity Laboratories, I wrote an intriguing mission statement to the entire team, essentially bringing them up to speed on the concepts of quantum mechanics and the multiverse.

One section in particular, a discussion about dimensionality, catches my eye.

I wrote . . .

We perceive our environment in three dimensions, but we don't actually live in a 3-D world. 3-D is static. A snapshot. We have to add a fourth dimension to begin to describe the nature of our existence.

The 4-D tesseract doesn't add a spatial dimension. It adds a temporal one.

It adds time, a stream of 3-D cubes, representing space as it moves along time's arrow.

This is best illustrated by looking up into the night sky at stars whose brilliance took fifty light-years to reach our eyes. Or five hundred. Or five billion. We're not just looking into space, we're looking back through time.

Our path through this 4-D spacetime is our worldline (reality), beginning with our birth and ending with our death. Four coordinates (x, y, z, and t [time]) locate a point within the tesseract.

And we think it stops there, but that's only true if every outcome is inevitable, if free will is an illusion, and our worldline is solitary.

What if our worldline is just one of an infinite number of worldlines, some only slightly altered from the life we know, others drastically different?

The Many-Worlds interpretation of quantum mechanics posits that all possible realities exist. That everything which has a probability of happening is happening. Everything that might have occurred in our past did occur, only in another universe.

What if that's true?

What if we live in a fifth-dimensional probability space?

What if we actually inhabit the multiverse, but our brains have evolved in such a way as to equip us with a firewall that limits what we perceive to a single universe? One worldline. The one we choose, moment to moment. It makes sense if you think about it. We couldn't possibly contend with simultaneously observing all possible realities at once.

So how do we access this 5-D probability space?

And if we could, where would it take us?

Leighton finally comes for me in the early evening.

We take the stairwell this time, but instead of heading all the way down to the infirmary, we get off on sublevel two.

"Slight change of plan," he tells me.

"No MRI?"

"Not just yet."

He shows me into a place I've been before—the conference room where Amanda Lucas tried to debrief me the night I woke up outside the box.

The lights have been dimmed.

I ask, "What's going on?"

"Have a seat, Jason."

"I don't under—"

"Have a seat."

I pull out the chair.

Leighton sits across from me.

He says, "I hear you've been going through your old files."

I nod.

"Ringing any bells?"

"Not really."

"That's too bad. I was hoping a trip down memory lane might spark something."

He straightens.

His chair creaks.

It's so quiet I can hear the lightbulbs humming above me.

From across the table, he watches me.

Something feels off.

Wrong.

Leighton says, "My father founded Velocity forty-five years ago. In my old man's time, things were different. We built jet engines and turbofans, and it was more about keeping the big government and corporate contracts than doing cutting-edge scientific exploration. There's just twenty-three of us now, but one thing hasn't changed. This company has always been a family, and our lifeblood is complete and total trust."

He turns away from me and gives a nod.

The lights kick on.

I can see beyond the smoked-glass enclosure into the small theater, and it's filled, just like on that first night, with fifteen or twenty people.

Except no one is standing and applauding.

No one is smiling.

They're all staring down at me.

Grim.

Tense.

I note the first twinge of panic looming on my horizon.

"Why are they all here?" I ask.

"I told you. We're a family. We clean up our messes together."

"I'm not following—"

"You're lying, Jason. You're not who you say you are. You're not one of us."

"I explained—"

"I know, you don't remember anything about the box. The last ten years are a black hole."

"Exactly."

"Sure you want to stick with that?"

Leighton opens the laptop on the table and types something.

He stands it up, types something on the touchscreen.

"What is this?" I ask. "What's happening?"

"We're going to finish what we started the night you returned. I'm going to ask questions, and this time, you're going to answer them."

I rise from the chair, move to the door, try to pull it open.

Locked.

"Sit!"

Leighton's voice is as loud as a gunshot.

"I want to leave."

"And I want you to start telling the truth."

"I told you the truth."

"No, you told Daniela Vargas the truth."

On the other side of the glass, a door opens and a man staggers into the theater, led by one of the guards clutching the back of his neck.

The first man's face is crushed up against the glass.

Jesus Christ.

Ryan's nose looks misshapen, and one eye is completely shut.

His bruised and swollen face streaks blood across the glass.

"You told Ryan Holder the truth," Leighton says.

I rush over to Ryan and say his name.

He tries to respond, but I can't hear him through the barrier.

I glare down at Leighton.

He says, "Sit, or I will have someone come in here and strap you to that chair."

The rage from earlier comes flooding back. This man is responsible for Daniela's death. Now this. I wonder how much damage I could inflict before they pulled me off of him.

But I sit.

I ask, "You tracked him down?"

"No, Ryan came to me, disturbed by the things you told him at Daniela's apartment. It's those particular things I want to hear about right now."

As I watch the guards force Ryan into a chair in the front row, it hits me—Ryan created the missing piece that makes the box function, this "compound" he mentioned at Daniela's art installation. If our brain is wired to prevent us from perceiving our own quantum state, then perhaps there's a drug that can disable this mechanism—the "firewall" I wrote about in that mission statement.

The Ryan from my world had been studying the prefrontal cortex and its role in generating consciousness. It's not that far of a leap to think this Ryan might have created a drug that changes the way our brain perceives reality. That stops us from decohering our environment and collapsing our wave functions.

I crash back into the moment.

"Why did you hurt him?" I ask.

"You told Ryan you're a professor at Lakemont College, that you have a son, and that Daniela Vargas was actually your wife. You told him you were abducted one night while walking home, after which you woke up here. You told him this isn't your world. Do you admit to saying these things?"

I wonder again how much damage I could do before someone hauled me away. Break his nose? Knock out teeth? Kill him?

My voice comes like a growl. "You murdered a woman I love, because she *talked* to me. You've beaten my friend. You're holding me here against my will. And you want me to answer your questions? Fuck you." I stare through the glass. "Fuck all of you."

Leighton says, "Maybe you're not the Jason I know and love. Maybe you're just a shadow of that man with a fraction of his ambition and intellect, but certainly you can grasp this question: What if the box works? That means we're sitting on the greatest scientific breakthrough of all time, with applications we can't even begin to fathom, and you're quibbling that we go to extremes to protect it?"

"I want to leave."

"You want to leave. Huh. Keep in mind everything I just said, and now consider that you're the only person who's successfully flown that thing. You're in possession of critical knowledge that we've spent billions and a decade of our lives trying to acquire. I'm not saying this to scare you, only to appeal to your logical reasoning—do you think there's anything we won't do to extract that information from you?"

He lets the question hang.

In the brutal silence, I glance across the theater.

I look at Ryan.

I look at Amanda. She won't make eye contact. Tears glisten in her eyes, but her jaw is tense and rigid, like she's fighting with everything she has to hold herself together.

"I want you to listen very closely," Leighton says. "Right here, right now, in this room—this is as easy as it's ever going to be for you. I want you to try very hard to make the most of this moment. Now, look at me."

I look at him.

"Did you build the box?"

I say nothing.

"*Did you* build the box?"

Still nothing.

"Where did you come from?"

My thoughts run rampant, playing out all possible scenarios—tell them everything I know, tell them nothing, tell them something. But *if* something, what specifically?

"Is this your world, Jason?"

The dynamics of my situation haven't materially changed. My safety still depends on my usefulness. As long as they want something from me, I have leverage. The moment I tell them everything I know, all my power goes away.

I look up from the table and meet Leighton's eyes.

I say, "I'm not going to talk to you right now."

He lets out a sigh.

Cracks his neck.

Then says to no one in particular, "I guess we're done here."

The door behind me opens.

I turn, but before I can see who's there, I'm lifted out of my chair and slammed against the floor.

Someone sits on my back, their knees driving into my spine.

They hold my head in place as a needle slides into my neck.

I regain consciousness on a hard, thin mattress that feels depressingly familiar.

Whatever drug they injected me with kicks out a nasty hangover—feels like a rift has opened down the center of my skull.

A voice is whispering into my ear.

I start to sit up, but the slightest movement takes the pounding in my head to a whole new level of agony.

"Jason?"

I know this voice.

"Ryan."

"Hey."

"What happened?" I ask.

"They carried you in here a little while ago."

I force my eyes to open.

I'm back in that cell on the steel-frame cot, and Ryan is kneeling beside me.

Up close, he looks even worse.

"Jason, I'm so sorry."

"None of this is your fault."

"No, what Leighton said is true. After I left you and Daniela that night, I called him. Told him I'd seen you. Told him where." Ryan closes his one functional eye, his face breaking as he says, "I had no idea they would hurt her."

"How'd you end up in the lab?"

"I guess you weren't giving them the information they wanted, so they came for me in the middle of the night. Were you with her when she died?"

"Happened right in front of me. A man just broke into her apartment and shot her between the eyes."

"Oh God."

Climbing onto the cot, he sits beside me, both of us leaning back against the concrete wall.

He says, "I thought if I told them what you said to me and Daniela, that maybe they'd finally bring me in on the research. Reward me somehow. Instead, they just beat me. Accused me of not telling them everything."

"I'm sorry."

"You kept me in the dark. I never even knew what this place was. I did all that work for you and Leighton, but you—"

"*I* didn't keep you in the dark about anything, Ryan. That wasn't me."

He looks over at me, as if trying to process the magnitude of that statement.

"So the stuff you said at Daniela's—that was all true?"

Leaning in close, I whisper, "Every word. Keep your voice low. They're probably listening."

"How did you get here?" Ryan whispers. "Into this world?"

"Right outside this cell, there's a hangar, and in that hangar, a metal box, which another version of me built."

"And this box does what exactly?"

"As far as I can tell, it's a gateway to the multiverse."

He looks at me like I'm crazy. "How is that possible?"

"I just need you to listen. The night after I escaped from

this place, I went to a hospital. They ran a tox screen that returned traces of a mysterious psychoactive compound. When I saw you at Daniela's art reception, you asked me if the 'compound' had worked out. What exactly were you working on for me?"

"You asked me to build a drug that would temporarily alter the functioning of brain chemistry in three Brodmann areas of the prefrontal cortex. It took me four years. At least you paid me well."

"Alter how?"

"Put them to sleep for a little while. I had no idea what the application was."

"You understand the concept behind Schrödinger's cat?"

"Sure."

"And how observation determines reality?"

"Yes."

"This other version of me was trying to put a human being into superposition. Theoretically impossible, considering our consciousness and force of observation would never allow it. But if there was a mechanism in the brain that was responsible for the observer effect . . ."

"You wanted to turn it off."

"Exactly."

"So my drug stops us from decohering?"

"I think so."

"But it doesn't stop others from decohering us. It doesn't stop their observer effect from determining our reality."

"That's where the box comes in."

"Holy shit. So you figured out a way to turn a human being into a living and dead cat? That's . . . terrifying."

The cell door unlocks and opens.

We both look up, see Leighton standing in the threshold, flanked by his guards—two middle-aged men with too-tight polo shirts tucked into their jeans and slightly past-prime physiques.

They strike me as men for whom violence is just work.

Leighton says, "Ryan, would you come with us, please?"

Ryan hesitates.

"Drag him out of there."

"I'm coming."

Ryan rises and limps to the door.

The guards each take an arm and haul him away, but Leighton stays behind.

He looks at me.

"This is not who I am, Jason. I hate this. I hate that you're forcing me to be this monster. What's about to happen? It's not my choice. It's yours."

I lunge off the bed and charge Leighton, but he slams the door in my face.

They kill the lights to my cell.

All I can see is the glowing green dot from the surveillance camera that watches me over the door.

I sit in the corner in the dark, thinking how I've been on a collision course with this moment since I first heard those footsteps rushing up behind me in my neighborhood, in my world, five impossible days ago.

Since I saw a geisha mask and a gun, and fear and confusion became the only stars in my sky.

In this moment, there is no logic.

No problem-solving.

No scientific method.

I am simply devastated, broken, terrified, and on the brink of just wanting it all to end.

I watched as the love of my life was murdered right in front of me.

My old friend is likely being tortured as I sit here.

And these people will undoubtedly make me suffer before my end comes.

I am so afraid.

I miss Charlie.

I miss Daniela.

I miss my run-down brownstone that I never had the money to properly remodel.

I miss our rusty Suburban.

I miss my office on campus.

My students.

I miss the life that's mine.

And there in the darkness, like the filaments of a lightbulb warming to life, the truth finds me.

I hear the voice of my abductor, somehow familiar, asking questions about my life.

My job.

My wife.

If I ever called her "Dani."

He knew who Ryan Holder was.

Jesus.

He took me to an abandoned power plant.

Drugged me.

Asked me questions about my life.

Took my phone, my clothes.

Holy fuck.

It's staring me in the face now.

My heart shuddering with rage.

He did these things so he could step into my shoes.

So he could have the life that's mine.

The woman I love.

My son.

My job.

My house.

Because that man was me.

This other Jason, the one who built the box—*he did this to me.*

As the green light of the surveillance camera goes dark, I realize that on some level, I've known since I first laid eyes on the box.

Just haven't been willing to look it in the eye.

And why would I?

It's one thing to be lost in a world that's not your own.

Another thing entirely to know you've been replaced in yours.

That a better version of you has stepped into your life.

He's smarter than I am, no question.

Is he also a better father to Charlie?

A better husband to Daniela?

A better lover?

He did this to me.

No.

It's way more fucked up than that.

I did this to me.

When I hear the locks in the door retract, I instinctively scoot back against the wall.

This is it.

They've come for me.

The door opens slowly, revealing a single person standing in the threshold, profiled against the light beyond.

They step inside, close the door after them.

I can't see a thing.

But I can smell her—trace of perfume, body wash.

"Amanda?"

She whispers, "Keep your voice down."

"Where's Ryan?"

"He's gone."

"What do you mean, 'gone'?"

She sounds on the verge of tears, of breaking down. "They killed him. I'm so sorry, Jason. I thought they were just going to scare him, but . . ."

"He's dead?"

"They're coming for you any minute now."

"Why are you—?"

"Because I didn't sign up for this shit. What they did to Daniela. To Holder. What they're about to do to you. They crossed lines that shouldn't be crossed. Not for science. Not for anything."

"Can you get me out of this lab?"

"No, and it wouldn't do you any good with your face all over the news."

"What are you talking about? Why am I on the news?"

"The police are looking for you. They think you killed Daniela."

"You people framed me?"

"I am so sorry. Look, I can't get you out of this lab, but I can get you into the hangar."

"Do you know how the box works?" I ask.

I feel her stare, even though I can't see it.

"No idea. But it's your one way out."

"From everything I've heard, stepping inside that thing is like jumping out of an airplane and not knowing if your chute is going to open."

"If the plane's going down anyway, does it really matter?"

"What about the camera?"

"The one in here? I turned it off."

I hear Amanda move toward the door.

A vertical line of light appears and widens.

When the cell door is open all the way, I see that she's shouldering a backpack. Stepping out into the corridor, she adjusts her red pencil skirt and looks back at me.

"You coming?"

I use the bed frame to drag myself onto my feet.

Must have been hours in the dark, because the light in the corridor is almost too much to bear. My eyes burn against the sudden brilliance.

For the moment, we have it all to ourselves.

Amanda is already moving away from me toward the vault doors at the far end.

She glances back, whispers, "Let's go!"

I quietly follow, the panels of fluorescent lighting streaming past overhead.

Aside from the echoes of our footfalls, the corridor is soundless.

By the time I reach the touchscreen, Amanda is holding her keycard under the scanner.

"Won't there be someone in mission control?" I ask. "I thought there was always someone monitoring—"

"I'm on duty tonight. I got you covered."

"They'll know you helped me."

"By the time they realize, I'll be out of here."

The computerized female voice says, *Name, please.*

"Amanda Lucas."

Passcode.

"Two-two-three-seven."

Access denied.

"Oh shit."

"What's happening?" I ask.

"Someone must have seen us on the corridor cams and frozen my clearance. Leighton will know in a matter of seconds."

"Give it another shot."

She scans her card again.

Name, please.

"Amanda Lucas."

Passcode.

She speaks slowly this time, overenunciating her words: "Two-two-three-seven."

Access denied.

"Goddammit."

A door at the opposite end of the corridor opens.

When Leighton's men step out, Amanda's face pales with fear, and a sharp, metallic taste coats the roof of my mouth.

I ask, "Do the employees create their own passcodes or are they assigned?"

"We create them."

"Give me your card."

"Why?"

"Because maybe no one thought to freeze my clearance."

As she hands it over, Leighton emerges from the same door.

He shouts my name.

I look back down the corridor as Leighton and his men start toward us.

I scan the card.

Name, please.

"Jason Dessen."

Passcode.

Of course. This guy is me.

Month and year of my birthday backwards.

"Three-seven-two-one."

Voice recognition confirmed. Welcome, Dr. Dessen.

The buzzer rakes my nerves.

As the doors begin to inch apart, I watch helplessly as the men rush toward us—red-faced, arms pumping.

Four or five seconds away.

The moment there's enough space between the vault doors, Amanda squeezes through.

I follow her into the hangar, racing across the smooth concrete toward the box.

Mission control is empty, the lights beating down from high above, and it's dawning on me that there is no possible scenario where we make it out of this.

We're closing in on the box, Amanda yelling, "We just have to get inside!"

I glance back as the first man explodes through the wide-open vault doors, a gun or Taser in his right hand, a smear of what I assume is Ryan's blood across his face.

He clocks me, raises his weapon, but I round the corner of the box before he can fire.

Amanda is pushing open the door, and as an alarm blares through the hangar, she disappears inside.

I'm right on her heels, launching myself over the threshold, into the box.

She shoves me out of the way and digs her shoulder back into the door.

I hear voices and approaching footsteps.

Amanda is struggling, so I throw my weight into the door alongside her.

It must weigh a ton.

At last, it begins to move, swinging back.

Fingers appear across the door frame, but we've got inertia working in our favor.

The door thunders home, and a massive bolt fires into its housing.

It's quiet.

And pitch-black—the darkness so instantly pure and unbroken it creates the sensation of spinning.

I stagger toward the nearest wall and put my hands on the metal, just needing to tether myself to something solid as I try to wrap my mind around the idea that I'm actually inside this thing.

"Can they get through the door?" I ask.

"I'm not sure. It's supposed to stay locked for ten minutes. Kind of like a built-in safeguard."

"Safeguard against what?"

"I don't know. People chasing you? Getting out of dangerous situations? You designed it. Seems to be working."

I hear a rustling in the dark.

A battery-powered Coleman lantern glows to life, illuminating the interior of the box with a bluish light.

It's strange, frightening, but also undeniably exhilarating to finally be in here, enclosed by these thick, nearly indestructible walls.

The first thing I notice in the new light are four fingers at the foot of the door, severed at the second knuckle.

Amanda is kneeling over an open backpack, her arm thrust in to her shoulder, and considering how everything just exploded in her face, she seems remarkably composed, calmly triaging the situation.

She pulls out a small leather bag.

It's filled with syringes, needles, and tiny ampoules of a clear liquid that I'm guessing contains Ryan's compound.

I say, "So you're doing this with me?"

"As opposed to what? Walking back out there and explaining to Leighton how I betrayed him and everything we've been working toward?"

"I have no idea how the box works."

"Well, that makes two of us, so I guess we can look forward to some fun times ahead." She checks her watch. "I set a timer when the door locked. They come through in eight minutes, fifty-six seconds. If there were no time pressure, we could just drink one of these ampoules or do an intramuscular injection, but now we have to find a vein. Ever inject yourself?"

"No."

"Pull up your sleeve."

She ties a rubber band above my elbow, grabs my arm, and holds it in the light of the lantern.

"See this vein that's anterior to your elbow? That's your antecubital. That's the one you want to hit."

"Shouldn't you be doing this?"

"You'll be fine."

She hands me a packet containing an alcohol wipe.

I rip it open, wipe down a large swath of skin.

Next, she gives me a 3ml syringe, two needles, and a single ampoule.

"This is a filtered needle," she says, touching one of them. "Use that one to draw up the liquid so you don't catch a glass shard. Then switch to the other needle to inject yourself. Got it?"

"I think so." I insert the filtered needle into the syringe, pull off the cap, and then snap the neck of the glass vial. "All of it?" I ask.

She's tying a rubber band around her arm now and cleaning her injection site.

"Yep."

I carefully draw the contents of the ampoule up into the syringe and swap needles.

Amanda says, "Make sure you always tap the syringe and push out a tiny bit of liquid through the needle. You don't want to be injecting air bubbles into your vascular system."

She shows me her watch again: 7:39 . . .

7:38.

7:37.

I thump the syringe and squeeze a drop of Ryan's chemical compound through the needle.

I say, "So I just . . ."

"Stick it in the vein at a forty-five-degree angle, with the hole in the end of the needle facing up. I know this is a lot to think about. You're doing great."

There's so much adrenaline raging through my system I barely even feel the penetration.

"Now what?"

"Make sure you're in the vein."

"How do I—?"

"Pull back a little on the plunger."

I pull it back.

"See blood?"

"Yeah."

"Good job. You hit it. Now untie the tourniquet and slowly inject."

As I depress the plunger, I ask, "So how long until it takes effect?"

"Pretty close to instantaneous, if I had to . . ."

I don't even register the end of her sentence.

The drug crashes into me.

I slump back against the wall and lose time until Amanda is in my face again, saying words that I'm trying and failing to comprehend.

Looking down, I watch her pull the needle out of my arm and press an alcohol pad against the tiny puncture wound.

I finally realize what she's saying: "Keep pressure on it."

Now I watch Amanda extend her arm under the glow of the lantern, and as she sticks a needle into her vein and loosens the tourniquet, my focus lands on her watch face and the numbers counting down toward zero.

Soon Amanda is lying stretched out on the floor like a junkie who just shot up, and the time is still running out, but that doesn't matter anymore.

I can't believe what I'm seeing.

EIGHT

I sit up.

Clearheaded and alert.

Amanda isn't lying on the floor anymore. She's standing several feet away with her back to me.

I call out to her, ask if she's okay, but she doesn't answer.

I struggle onto my feet.

Amanda is holding the lantern, and as I move toward her, I see that the light isn't striking the wall of the box, which should be straight ahead of us.

I walk past her.

She follows with the lantern.

The light reveals another door, identical to the one we just came through from the hangar.

I continue walking.

Another twelve feet brings us to another door.

And then another.

And another.

The lantern only exudes the brilliance of a single, sixty-watt bulb, and beyond seventy or eighty feet, the light dwindles off into haunting shreds of illumination, glinting off the cold surface of the metal walls on one side, the perfectly spaced doors on the other.

Beyond our sphere of light—absolute darkness.

I stop, awestruck and speechless.

I think of the thousands of articles and books I've read in my lifetime. Tests taken. Classes taught. Theories memorized. Equations scribbled on blackboards. I think of the months I spent in that cleanroom trying to build something that was a pale imitation of this place.

For students of physics and cosmology, the closest one can ever get to the tangible implications of research are ancient galaxies seen through telescopes. Data readouts following particle collisions we know occurred but can never see.

There's always a boundary, a barrier between the equations and the reality they represent.

But no more. Not for me at least.

I can't stop thinking, I am here. I am actually in this place. It exists.

At least for a moment, fear has left me.

I'm filled with wonder.

I say, " 'The most beautiful thing we can experience is the mysterious.' "

Amanda looks at me.

"Einstein's words, not mine."

"Is this place even real?" she asks.

"What do you mean by 'real'?"

"Are we standing in a physical location?"

"I think it's a manifestation of the mind as it attempts to visually explain something our brains haven't evolved to comprehend."

"Which is?"

"Superposition."

"So we're experiencing a quantum state right now?"

I glance back down the corridor. Then into the darkness ahead. Even in the low light, there's a recursive quality to the space, like two mirrors facing each other.

"Yeah. It looks like a corridor, but I think it's actually the box repeating itself across all possible realities that share the same point in space and time."

"Like a cross-section?"

"Exactly. In some presentations of quantum mechanics, the thing that contains all the information for the system—before it collapses due to an observation—is called a wave function. I'm thinking this corridor is our minds' way of visualizing the content of the wave function, of all possible outcomes, for our superposed quantum state."

"So where does this corridor lead?" she asks. "If we just kept walking, where would we end up?"

As I say the words, the wonder recedes and the horror creeps in: "There is no end."

We keep walking to see what happens, if anything will change, if *we* will change.

But it's just door after door after door after door.

When we've been going a while, I say, "I've been counting them since we started down the corridor, and this is the four hundred and fortieth door. Each box repetition is twelve feet, which means we've already gone a full mile."

Amanda stops and lets the backpack slide off her shoulders.

She sits against the wall, and I take a seat beside her, with the lantern between us.

I say, "What if Leighton decides to take the drug and come charging in here after us?"

"He'd never do that."

"Why?"

"Because he's terrified of the box. We all are. Except for you, no one who went inside ever came out again. That's why Leighton was willing to do anything to make you tell him how to fly it."

"What happened to your test pilots?"

"The first one to enter the box was this guy named Matthew Snell. We had no idea what we were dealing with, so Snell was given clear and simple instructions. Enter the box. Close the door. Sit. Inject himself with the drug. No matter what happened, no matter what he saw, he was to sit in the same place, wait for the drug to wear off, and walk right back out into the hangar. Even if he had seen all this, he wouldn't have left his box. He wouldn't have moved."

"So what happened?"

"An hour passed. He was overdue. We wanted to open the door, but we were afraid of interfering with whatever he was experiencing on the inside. Twenty-four hours later, we finally opened it."

"And the box was empty."

"Yep." Amanda looks exhausted in the blue light. "Stepping into the box and taking the drug is like walking through a one-way door. There's no coming back, and no one's going to risk following us. We're on our own here. So what do you want to do?"

"Like any good scientist, experiment. Try a door, see what happens."

"And just to be clear, you have no idea what's behind any of these doors?"

"None."

I give Amanda a hand up. As I hoist the backpack onto my shoulders, I note the first mild twinge of thirst and wonder if she brought along any water.

We head down the corridor, and the truth is I'm hesitant to make a choice. If there is an endless possibility of doors, then from a statistical perspective, the choice itself means everything *and* nothing. Every choice is right. Every choice is wrong.

I finally stop and say, "This one?"

She shrugs. "Sure."

Grasping the cold, metal handle, I ask, "We have the ampoules, right? Because that would be—"

"I checked the pack when we stopped a minute ago."

I crank the lever down, hear the latch bolt slide, and pull back.

The door swings inward, clearing the frame.

She whispers, "What do you see out there?"

"Nothing yet. It's too dark. Here, let me have that." As I take the lantern from her, I notice that we're standing in a single box again. "Look," I say. "The corridor collapsed."

"That surprises you?"

"Actually, it makes perfect sense. The environment outside the door is interacting with the interior of the box. It destabilized the quantum state."

I turn back to the open door and hold the lantern out in front of me. All I can see is the ground directly ahead.

Cracked pavement.

Oil stains.

When I step down, glass crunches under my feet.

I help Amanda out, and as we venture the first few steps, the light diffuses, hits a concrete column.

A van.

A convertible.

A sedan.

It's a parking garage.

We move up a slight incline with cars on either side of us, following the remnants of a white paint stripe that divides the left and right lanes.

The box is a ways behind us now and out of sight, tucked away in the pitch-black.

We pass a sign with an arrow pointing left beside the words—

EXIT TO STREET

Turning a corner, we begin to climb the next ramp.

All along the right side, chunks have fallen out of the ceiling and crushed the windshields, hoods, and roofs of the vehicles. The farther we go, the worse it gets, until we're scrambling over concrete boulders and weaving around knifelike projections of rusted rebar.

Halfway up the next level, we're stopped in our tracks by an impassable wall of debris.

"Maybe we should just go back," I say.

"Look . . ." She grabs the lantern and I follow her over to a stairwell entry.

The door is cracked open, and Amanda forces it back the rest of the way.

Total darkness.

We ascend to the door at the top of the stairs.

It takes both of us to drag it open.

Wind blows through the lobby straight ahead.

There's some semblance of ambient light coming through the empty steel frames of what used to be immense, two-story windows.

At first, I think it's snow on the floor, but it isn't cold.

I kneel, grasp a handful. It's dry and a foot deep over the marble flooring. It slides through my fingers.

We trudge past a long reception desk with the name of a hotel still attached in artful block letters across the façade.

At the entrance, we pass between a pair of giant planters holding trees withered down to gnarled branches and brittle leaf shards twittering in the breeze.

Amanda turns off the lantern.

We step through the glassless revolving doors.

Even though it isn't nearly cold enough, it looks like a raging snowstorm outside.

I walk out into the street and stare up between the dark buildings at a sky tinged with the faintest suggestion of red. It glows the way a city does when the clouds are low and all the lights from the buildings are reflecting off the moisture in the sky.

But there are no lights.

Not a single one as far as I can see.

Though they fall like snow, in torrent-like curtains, the particles that strike my face carry no sting.

"It's ash," Amanda says.

A blizzard of ash.

Out here in the street, it's knee-deep, and the air smells like a cold fireplace the morning after, before the ashes have been carried off.

A dead, burnt stench.

The ash is falling hard enough to obscure the upper stories of the skyscrapers, and there's no sound but the wind blowing between the buildings and through the buildings and the whoosh of the ash as it piles into gray drifts against long-abandoned cars and buses.

I can't believe what I'm seeing.

That I'm actually standing in a world that isn't mine.

We walk up the middle of the street, our backs to the wind.

I can't shake the feeling that the blackness of the skyscrapers is all wrong. They're skeletons, nothing but ominous profiles in the pouring ash. Closer to a range of improbable mountains than anything man-made. Some are leaning, and some have toppled, and in the hardest gusts, high above us, I can hear the groan of steel framework torquing past its tensile strength.

I note a sudden tightening in the space behind my eyes.

It comes and goes in less than a second, like something turning off.

Amanda asks, "Did you just feel that too?"

"That pressure behind your eyes?"

"Exactly."

"I did. I bet it's the drug wearing off."

After several blocks, the buildings end. We arrive at a guardrail that runs along the top of a seawall. The lake yawns out for miles under the radioactive sky, and it doesn't even resemble Lake Michigan anymore, but instead a vast gray desert, the ash accumulating on the surface of the water and undulating like a waterbed as black foam waves crash against the seawall.

The walk back is into the wind.

Ash streaming into our eyes and mouths.

Our tracks already covered.

When we're a block from the hotel, a sound like sustained thunder begins in the near distance.

The ground trembles beneath our feet.

Another building falls to its knees.

The box is waiting where we left it, in a remote corner on the parking garage's lowest level.

We're both covered in ash, and we take a moment at the door to brush it off our clothes, out of our hair.

Back inside, the lock shoots home after us.

We're in a simple, finite box again.

Four walls.

A door.

A lantern.

A backpack.

And two bewildered human beings.

Amanda sits hugging her knees into her chest.

"What do you think happened up there?" she asks.

"Supervolcano. Asteroid strike. Nuclear war. No telling."

"Are we in the future?"

"No, the box would only connect us to alternate realities at the same point in space and time. But I suppose some worlds might seem like the future if they've made technological advancements that ours never figured out."

"What if they're all destroyed like this one?"

I say, "We should take the drug again. I don't think we're exactly safe under this crumbling skyscraper."

Amanda pulls off her flats and shakes the ash out of them.

I say, "What you did for me back at the lab . . . You saved my life."

She looks at me, her bottom lip threatening to quiver. "I used to dream about those first pilots who went into the box. Nightmares. I can't believe this is happening."

I unzip the backpack and start pulling out the contents to catalog them.

I find the leather bag containing the ampoules and injection kits.

Three notebooks sealed in plastic.

Box of pens.

A knife in a nylon sheath.

First-aid kit.

Space blanket.

Rain poncho.

Toiletry kit.

Two rolls of cash.

Geiger counter.

Compass.

Two one-liter water bottles, both full.

Six MREs.

"You packed all this?" I ask.

"No, I just grabbed it from the stockroom. It's standard

issue, what everyone takes into the box. We should be wearing space suits, but I didn't have time to grab any."

"No kidding. A world like that? Radiation levels could be off the charts, or the atmospheric makeup drastically altered. If the pressure is off—too low, for instance—our blood and all the liquids in our bodies will boil."

The water bottles are calling out to me. I haven't had anything to drink in hours, since lunch. My thirst is blaring.

I open the leather bag. It looks custom-made for the ampoules, each glass vial held in its own miniature sleeve.

I begin to count them.

"Fifty," Amanda says. "Well, forty-eight now. I would've grabbed two backpacks, but . . ."

"You weren't planning to come with me."

"How fucked are we?" she asks. "Be honest."

"I don't know. But this is our spaceship. We'd better learn to fly it."

As I begin to cram everything back into the pack, Amanda reaches for the injection kits.

This time, we break the necks of the ampoules and drink the drug, the liquid sliding across my tongue with a sweet, borderline unpleasant sting.

Forty-six ampoules remaining.

I start the timer on Amanda's watch and ask, "How many times can we take this stuff and not fry our brains?"

"We did some testing a while back."

"Pulled some homeless guy off the street?"

She almost smiles. "Nobody died. We learned that repeated use definitely strains neurological functioning and builds up a tolerance. The good news is the half-life is really short, so as long as we're not slamming one ampoule right after another, we should be all right." She slides her feet back into her flats, looks at me. "Are you impressed with yourself?"

"What do you mean?"

"You built this thing."

"Yeah, but I still don't know how. I understand the theory, but creating a stable quantum state for human beings is . . ."

"An impossible breakthrough?"

Of course. The hair on the back of my neck stands up as the improbability of it all makes sense.

I say, "It's a one in a billion chance, but we're dealing with the multiverse. With infinity. Maybe there are a million worlds like yours, where I never figured it out. But all it takes is one where I did."

At the thirty-minute mark, I note the first sensation of the drug taking effect—the flickering of a shining, bright euphoria.

A beautiful disengagement.

Though not quite as intense as in the Velocity Laboratories box.

I look at Amanda.

I say, "I think I feel it."

She says, "Me too."

And we're back in the corridor.

I ask, "Is your watch still running?"

Amanda tugs back the sleeve of her sweater and illuminates the watch face into tritium green.

31:15.

31:16.

31:17.

I say, "So a little over thirty-one minutes since we took the drug. Do you know how long it's supposed to alter our brain chemistry?"

"I've heard about an hour."

"Let's clock it to be sure."

I move back toward the door to the parking garage and pull it open.

Now I'm staring into a forest.

Except there's no trace of green.

No trace of life.

Just scorched trunks as far as I can see.

The trees look haunted, their spindly branches like black spiderwebs against a charcoal sky.

I close the door.

It automatically locks.

Vertigo hits me as I watch the box push out away from me again, smearing off into infinity.

I unlock the door, drag it back open.

The corridor collapses again.

The dead forest is still there.

I say, "Okay, so now we know that the connections between the doors and these worlds only hold during a given session on the drug. That's why none of your pilots ever made it back to the lab."

"So when the drug kicks in, the corridor resets?"

"I think so."

"Then how do we ever find our way home?"

Amanda begins to walk.

Faster and faster.

Until she's jogging.

Then running.

Into a darkness that never changes.

Never ends.

The backstage of the multiverse.

The exertion is making me sweat and ratcheting my thirst to an unbearable level, but I say nothing, thinking maybe she needs this. Needs to burn through some energy. Needs to see that no matter how far she goes, this corridor will never end.

I suppose we're both just trying to come to terms with how horrifying infinity really is.

Eventually, she burns out.

Slows down.

There's nothing but the sound of our footfalls echoing into the darkness ahead of us.

I'm light-headed with hunger and thirst, and I can't stop thinking about those two liters of water in our backpack, wanting them, but knowing we should save them.

Now we move methodically down the corridor.

I hold the lantern so I can inspect every wall of every box.

I don't know what I'm looking for exactly.

A break in the uniformity, perhaps.

Anything that might let us exert some measure of control over where we end up.

All the while, my thoughts race in the dark—

What will happen when the water's gone?

When the food is gone?

When the batteries that power this lantern—our only source of light—fail?

How will I ever find my way home?

I wonder how many hours have passed since we first entered the box back at the Velocity Laboratories hangar.

I've lost all sense of time.

I'm faltering.

Exhaustion bears down so hard on me that sleep seems sexier than water.

I glance over at Amanda, her features cold but beautiful in the blue light.

She looks terrified.

"Hungry yet?" she asks.

"Getting there."

"I'm really thirsty, but we should save the water, right?"

"I think that's the smart thing to do."

She says, "I feel so disoriented, and it's getting worse by the moment. I grew up in North Dakota, and we used to get these wild blizzards. Whiteouts. You'd be driving out on the plains, and the snow would start blowing so hard you'd lose all sense of direction. Blowing so hard it'd make you dizzy just looking at it through the windshield. You'd have to pull over on the side of the road, wait it out. And sitting in the cold car, it was like the world was gone. That's how I feel right now."

"I'm scared too. But I'm working this problem."

"How?"

"Well, first, we have to find out exactly how much corridor time this drug will give us. Down to the minute."

"How far do you want to wind out the clock?"

"If you're saying we have about an hour, then our deadline is ninety minutes on your watch. That accounts for thirty minutes for the drug to kick in, plus the sixty minutes we're under its influence."

"I weigh less than you. What if it affects me for longer?"

"It doesn't matter. The moment it stops working on one of us, that person will decohere the quantum state and collapse the corridor. Just to be safe, let's start opening doors at the eighty-five-minute mark."

"And hope for what exactly?"

"A world that doesn't eat us alive."

She stops and looks at me. "I know you didn't actually build this box, but you must have some idea of how all this works."

"Look, this is light-years beyond anything I could've—"

"So is that a 'No, I don't have any idea'?"

"What are you asking me, Amanda?"

"Are we lost?"

"We're gathering information. We're working a problem."

"But the problem is that we're lost. Right?"

"We're exploring."

"Jesus Christ."

"What?"

"I don't want to spend the rest of my life wandering down this never-ending tunnel."

"I won't let that happen."

"How?"

"I don't know yet."

"But you're working on it?"

"Yes. I'm working on it."

"And we're not lost."

We are so fucking lost. Literally adrift in the nothing space between universes.

"We're not lost."

"Good." She smiles. "Then I'll postpone freaking out."

We move along in silence for a while.

The metal walls are smooth and featureless, nothing to distinguish one from the next and the next and the next.

Amanda asks, "What worlds do you think we actually have access to?"

"I've been trying to puzzle that out. Let's assume the multiverse began with a single event—the Big Bang. That's the starting point, the base of the trunk of the most immense, elaborate tree you could fathom. As time unfolded and matter began to organize into stars and planets in all possible permutations, this tree sprouted branches, and those branches sprouted branches, and on and on, until somewhere, fourteen billion years down the line, my birth triggered a new branch. And from that moment, every choice I made or didn't make, and the actions of others that affected me—those all gave rise to more branches, to an infinite number of Jason Dessens living in parallel worlds, some very similar to the one I call home, some mind-bogglingly different.

"Everything that can happen will happen. *Everything.* I mean, somewhere along this corridor, there's a version of you and me that never made it into the box when you tried to help me escape. And now we're being tortured or already dead."

"Thanks for the morale boost."

"Could be worse. I don't think we have access to the entire breadth of the multiverse. I mean, if there's a world where the sun burned out just as prokaryotes—the first life-forms—

were appearing on Earth, I don't think any of these doors open into that world."

"So we can only walk into worlds that . . ."

"If I had to guess, worlds that are adjacent to ours somehow. Worlds that split off at some point in the recent past, which are next door to ours. That we exist in, or *existed* in at some point. How far back they branched, I don't know, but my suspicion is there's some form of conditional selection at work. This is just my working hypothesis."

"But we're still talking about an infinite number of worlds, right?"

"Well, yeah."

I lift her wrist and press the light feature on her watch.

The tiny square of luminous green shows . . .

84:50.

84:51.

I say, "The drug should wear off in the next five minutes. I guess it's time."

I move toward the next door, hand Amanda the lantern, and grip the handle.

Turning the lever, I pull the door open one inch.

I see a concrete floor.

Two inches.

A familiar glass window straight ahead.

Three.

Amanda says, "It's the hangar."

"What do you want to do?"

She pushes past me and steps out of the box.

I follow, the lights shining down on us.

Mission control is empty.

The hangar quiet.

We stop at the corner of the box and peer around the edge toward the vault doors.

I say, "This isn't safe." My words carry through the expanse of the hangar like whispers in a cathedral.

"And the box is?"

With a thunderous clang, the vault doors disengage and begin to part.

Panicked voices bleeding through the opening.

I say, "Let's go. Right now."

A woman is fighting to squeeze through the space between the doors.

Amanda says, "Oh my God."

The vault doors are only fifty feet away, and I know we should go back into the box, but I can't stop watching.

The woman pushes through the doors into the hangar, and then reaches back and gives a hand to the man behind her.

The woman is Amanda.

The man's face is so swollen and battered I wouldn't have known right away that he was me except he's wearing clothes identical to mine.

As they begin running toward us, I start to involuntarily retreat to the door of the box.

But they only make it ten feet before Leighton's men rush through the doors behind them.

A gunshot stops Jason and Amanda in their tracks.

My Amanda starts toward them, but I pull her back.

"We have to help them," she whispers.

"We can't."

Peeking around the corner of the box, we watch our doppelgängers turn slowly to face Leighton's men.

We should leave.

I know this.

Part of me is screaming to go.

But I can't tear myself away.

My first thought is that we've gone back in time, but of course that's impossible. There's no time travel in the box. This is simply a world where Amanda and I escaped several hours later.

Or failed to.

Leighton's men have their guns drawn, and they're moving deliberately into the hangar toward Jason and Amanda.

As Leighton steps in after them, I hear this other version of myself say, "It's not her fault. I threatened her. I made her do this."

Leighton looks at Amanda.

He asks, "Is this true? He *made* you? Because I've known you for more than a decade, and I've never seen anyone *make* you do anything."

Amanda looks scared, but also defiant.

Her voice trembles as she says, "I won't stand by and let you keep hurting people. I'm done."

"Oh. Well, in that case . . ."

Leighton places his hand on the thick shoulder of the man to his right.

The gunshot is deafening.

The muzzle flash is blinding.

Amanda drops like someone flipped a power switch, and next to me, my Amanda lets slip a stifled shriek.

As this other Jason rushes Leighton, the second guard executes a lightning-fast Taser draw and brings him down screaming and twitching on the floor of the hangar.

My Amanda's shriek has given us away.

Leighton is staring right at us with a look of pure confusion.

He shouts, "Hey!"

They start after us.

I grab Amanda by the arm and drag her back through the door of the box and slam it home.

The door locks, the corridor reconstitutes, but the drug will be wearing off any moment now.

Amanda is quaking, and I want to tell her everything is fine, but it isn't. She just witnessed her own murder.

"That isn't you out there," I tell her. "You're standing right here beside me. Alive and well. That is not you."

Even in the bad light I can tell she's crying.

Tears streak down through the grime on her face like running eyeliner.

"It's some part of me," she says. "Or was."

Gently, I reach down and lift her arm, turning it so I can see the watch. We're forty-five seconds shy of the ninety-minute mark.

I say, "We have to go."

I start down the corridor.

"Amanda, come on!"

When she catches up, I open a door.

Total darkness.

No sound, no smell. Just a void.

I slam it shut.

Trying not to panic, but I need to be opening more doors, giving us a shot at finding someplace to rest and reset.

I open the next door.

Ten feet away, standing in weeds in front of a teetering chain-link fence, a wolf glares at me through large amber eyes. Lowering its head, it growls.

As it starts toward me, I shove the door closed.

Amanda grabs hold of my hand.

We keep walking.

I should be opening more doors, but the truth is I'm terrified. I've lost faith we'll find a world that's safe.

I blink and we're confined to a single box again.

The drug has worn off for one of us.

This time, she opens the door.

Snow streams into the box.

A shot of bitter cold hits my face.

Through a curtain of falling snow, I glimpse the silhouettes of trees nearby and houses in the distance.

"What do you think?" I ask.

"I think I don't want to be in this box for another fucking second."

Amanda steps down into the snow and sinks to her knees in the soft powder.

She immediately begins to shiver.

I feel the drug wink out for me, and this time the sensation is like an ice pick through my left eye.

Intense but fleeting.

I follow Amanda out of the box, and we head in the general direction of the neighborhood.

Beyond the initial layer of powder, I can feel myself

continuing to sink—the weight of each step slowly breaking through a deeper, older crust of compacted snow.

I catch up with Amanda.

We trudge through a clearing toward a neighborhood, which seems to be slowly vanishing before my eyes.

While I'm marginally protected from the cold in my pair of jeans and hoodie, Amanda is suffering in her red skirt, black sweater, and flats.

I've lived most of my life in the Midwest, and I've never known cold like this. My ears and cheekbones are rocketing toward frostbite, and I'm already beginning to lose the fine-motor control in my hands.

A driving wind blasts us straight-on, and as the snow intensifies, the world ahead takes on the appearance of a furiously shaken snow globe.

We push on through the snow, moving as quickly as we can, but it's getting deeper and nearly impossible to navigate with anything approaching efficiency.

Amanda's cheeks have gone blue.

She's violently shivering.

Her hair is matted with snow.

"We should go back," I say through chattering teeth.

The wind has grown deafening.

Amanda looks at me, confused, then nods.

I glance back, but the box is gone.

My fear spikes.

The snow is blowing sideways, and the houses in the distance have vanished.

In every direction, it all looks the same.

Amanda's head is nodding up and down, and I keep

squeezing my hands into fists, trying to force warm blood through to my fingertips, but it's a losing battle. My ring of thread is encrusted with ice.

My thought processes are beginning to spin out.

I'm shaking with cold.

We fucked up.

It isn't just cold. It's way-below-zero cold.

Lethally cold.

I have no idea how far we've come from the box.

Does it even matter anymore, when we're functionally blind?

This cold will kill us in a matter of minutes.

Keep moving.

Amanda has a faraway look in her eyes, and I wonder if it's the shock setting in.

Her bare legs are in direct contact with the snow.

"It hurts," she says.

Bending down, I lift her in my arms and stagger into the storm, holding Amanda tightly against me as her entire body shakes.

We're standing in a vortex of wind and snow and killing cold, and it all looks exactly the same. If I don't stare down at my legs, the motion of it all induces vertigo.

It occurs to me: we're going to die.

But I keep going.

One foot in front of the other, my face now on fire from the cold, my arms aching from holding Amanda, my feet in agony as the snow works down into my shoes.

Minutes pass and the snow falls harder and the cold keeps biting.

Amanda is mumbling, delirious.

I can't keep doing this.

Can't keep walking.

Can't keep holding her.

Soon—so soon—I will have to stop. Will sit in the snow and hold this woman I barely know, and we will freeze to death together in this awful world that isn't even ours.

I think about my family.

Think about not ever seeing them again, and I try to process what that means as my control over the fear finally slips—

There's a house in front of us.

Or rather, the second story of a house, because its first floor has been completely buried in snow that's drifted all the way up to a trio of dormer windows.

"Amanda."

Her eyes are closed.

"Amanda!"

She opens them. Barely.

"Stay with me."

I set her down in the snow against the roof, stumble toward the middle dormer, and put my foot through the window.

When I've kicked out all the sharpest jags of glass, I take hold of Amanda by her arms and pull her down into a child's bedroom—a little girl's, by the looks of it.

Stuffed animals.

A wooden dollhouse.

Princess paraphernalia.

A Barbie flashlight on the bedside table.

I drag Amanda far enough into the room that the snow pouring through the window can't reach her. Then I grab the Barbie flashlight and move through the doorway into an upstairs hall.

I call out, "Hello?"

The house swallows my voice, gives nothing back.

All the bedrooms on the second floor stand empty. In most of them, the furniture has been removed.

Turning on the flashlight, I head down the staircase.

The batteries are low. The bulb emits a weak beam.

Moving off the stairs, I pass the front door into what used to be a dining room. Boards have been nailed across the window frames to support the glass against the pressure of the snow, which fills the frames entirely. An ax leans on the remnants of a dining-room table that's been chopped down into burnable pieces of kindling.

I step through a doorway that opens into a smaller room.

The tepid light beam strikes a couch.

A pair of chairs almost completely stripped of their leather.

A television mounted above a fireplace overflowing with ashes.

A box of candles.

A stack of books.

Sleeping bags, blankets, and pillows have been spread across the floor in the vicinity of the fireplace, and there are people inside them.

A man.

A woman.

Two teenage boys.

A young girl.

Eyes closed.

Not moving.

Their faces blue and emaciated.

A framed photograph of the family at the Lincoln Park Conservatory, in a better time, rests on the woman's chest, her blackened fingers still clutched around it.

Along the hearth, I see matchboxes, stacks of newspaper, a pile of wood shavings harvested from a cutlery block.

A second doorway out of the family room brings me into the kitchen. The refrigerator is open and barren, and the cabinets too. The countertops are covered with empty metal cans.

Creamed corn.

Kidney beans.

Black beans.

Whole, peeled tomatoes.

Soups.

Peaches.

The stuff that lives in the backs of cabinets and usually just expires from neglect.

Even the condiment jars have been scraped clean—mustards, mayonnaise, jellies.

Behind the overflowing trash can, I see a frozen puddle of blood and a skeleton—small, feline—stripped to the bone.

These people didn't freeze to death.

They starved.

Firelight glows on the walls of the family room. I'm naked in a sleeping bag that's inside of a sleeping bag that's covered in blankets.

Amanda thaws out beside me in two sleeping bags of her own.

Our wet clothes are drying on the brick hearth, and we're lying close enough to the fire that I can feel the warmth of it lapping at my face.

Outside, the storm rages on, the entire framework of the house creaking in the strongest gusts of wind.

Amanda's eyes are open.

She's been awake a little while, and we've already killed the two bottles of water, which are now packed with snow and standing on the hearth near the fire.

"What do you think happened to whoever lived here?" she asks.

Truth: I dragged their bodies into an office so she wouldn't see them.

But I say, "I don't know. Maybe they went somewhere warm?"

She smiles. "Liar. We're not doing so hot with our space-ship."

"I think this is what they call a steep learning curve."

She draws in a long, deep breath, lets it out.

Says, "I'm forty-one. It wasn't the most amazing life, but it was mine. I had a career. An apartment. A dog. Friends. TV shows I liked to watch. This guy, John, I'd seen three times. Wine." She looks at me. "I'm never going to see any of that again, am I?"

I'm not certain how to respond.

She continues, "At least you have a destination. A world you want to get back to. I can't return to mine, so where does that leave me?"

She stares at me.

Tense.

Unblinking.

I have no answer.

The next time I come to consciousness, the fire has reduced itself to a pile of glowing embers, and the snow near the tops of the windows is backlit and sparkling as threads of sunlight attempt to sneak through.

Even inside the house, it is inconceivably cold.

Reaching a hand out of the sleeping bag, I touch our clothes on the hearth, relieved to find them dry. I pull my hand back inside and turn toward Amanda. She has the sleeping bag pulled over her face, and I can see her breath pushing through the down in puffs of steam that have formed a structure of ice crystals on the surface of the bag.

I put on my clothes and build a new fire and hold my hands in the heat just in time to keep my fingers from going numb.

Leaving Amanda to sleep, I walk through the dining room, where the sun cutting through the snow at the top of the windows casts just enough illumination to light my way.

Up the dark staircase.

Down the hall.

Back into the girl's room, where snow has blown in and covered most of the floor.

I climb through the window frame and squint against the painful light, the glare coming off the ice so intense that for five seconds I can't see a thing.

The snow is waist-deep.

The sky a perfect blue.

No sound of birds.

No sound of life.

There's not even a whisper of wind and no trace of our tracks. Everything smoothed-over and drifted.

The temperature must be miles below zero, because even in the direct sun, I'm not anywhere close to warm.

Beyond this neighborhood, the skyline of Chicago looms, the towers snow-blown and ice-encrusted and glittering in the sun.

A white city.

A world of ice.

Across the street, I survey the open field where we nearly froze to death yesterday.

There's no sign of the box.

Back inside, I find Amanda awake, sitting up at the edge of the hearth with the sleeping bags and blankets wrapped around her.

I head into the kitchen, locate some silverware.

Then I open the backpack and dig out a couple of MREs.

They're cold but rich.

We eat ravenously.

Amanda asks, "Did you see the box?"

"No, I think it's buried under the snow."

"Fantastic." She looks at me, then back into the flames, says, "I don't know whether to be mad at you or grateful."

"What are you talking about?"

"While you were upstairs, I had to use the bathroom. I stumbled into the office."

"So you saw them."

"They starved, didn't they? Before they ran out of fuel for the fire."

"Looks like it."

As I stare into the flames, I feel something needling the back of my brain.

An inkling.

It started when I was outside a moment ago, looking at the field, thinking about us almost dying in that whiteout.

I say, "Remember what you said about the corridor? How it reminded you of being trapped in a whiteout?"

She stops eating, looks at me.

"The doors in the corridor are the connections to an infinite array of parallel worlds, right? But what if *we're* defining these connections?"

"How?"

"What if it's like dream-building, where we're somehow choosing these specific worlds?"

"You're saying that, out of an infinite number of realities, I intentionally picked *this* shithole?"

"Not intentionally. Maybe it's a reflection of what you were feeling at the moment you opened the door."

She takes the last bite of food and tosses her empty MRE packet into the fire.

I say, "Think about the first world we saw—that ruined Chicago, with the buildings crumbling all around us. What was our emotional state as we walked into that parking garage?"

"Fear. Terror. Despair. Oh my God. Jason."

"What?"

"Before we opened the door to the hangar and saw the

other versions of you and me getting caught, you had mentioned that very thing happening."

"Did I?"

"You were talking about the idea of the multiverse, and everything that can happen will happen, and you said that somewhere there was a version of you and me that never made it into the box. Moments later, you opened a door and we watched that exact scenario play out."

I feel the spine-tingling rush of a revelation sweeping over me.

I say, "This whole time, we've been wondering where the controls are—"

"But we're the controls."

"Yep. And if that's the case, then we have the ability to go wherever we want. Including home."

Early the next morning, we stand in the midst of this silent neighborhood, waist-deep in snow and shivering, even though we're wearing layer upon layer of that poor family's winter clothes, which we raided from the coat closet.

In the field ahead of us, there's no sign of our tracks. No sign of the box. Nothing but smooth, unbroken snow.

The field is huge and the box is tiny.

The chances of us stumbling upon it through blind luck are minuscule.

With the sun just creeping above the trees, the cold is unreal.

"What are we supposed to do, Jason? Take a guess? Start digging?"

I glance back at the half-buried house, wondering for a

terrifying moment how long we could survive there. How long before the firewood ran out? Before our food ran out? Before we gave up and perished like all the others?

I can feel a dark pressure mounting in my chest—fear pushing in.

I draw a deep breath into my lungs, and the air is so cold it makes me cough.

Panic stalks me from all sides.

Finding the box is impossible.

It's too cold out here.

There won't be enough time, and when the next storm comes, and the next, the box is going to be buried so deep we'll never have a chance of reaching it.

Unless . . .

I let the backpack slide off my shoulders into the snow and unzip it with trembling fingers.

"What are you doing?" Amanda asks.

"Throwing a Hail Mary."

It takes me a moment to find what I'm looking for.

Grasping the compass, I leave Amanda and the pack and wade into the field.

She follows, shouting for me to wait up.

Fifty feet out, I stop to let her catch up to me.

"Look at this," I say, touching the face of the compass. "We're in South Chicago, right?" I point toward the distant skyline. "So magnetic north is that way. But this compass says otherwise. See how the needle is pointing east toward the lake?"

Her face lights up. "Of course. It's the box's magnetic field, pushing the compass needle away from it."

We posthole through the deep powder.

In the middle of the field, the needle swings from east to west.

"We're right on top of it."

I begin to dig, my bare hands aching from the snow, but I don't stop.

Four feet down, I hit the edge of the box, and I keep digging, faster now, my sleeves pulled forward to protect my hands, which are passing from a cold-driven agony into numbness.

When my half-frozen fingers finally graze the top of the open door, I let out a shout that echoes through the frozen world.

Ten minutes later, we're back inside the box, drinking ampoule forty-six and ampoule forty-five.

Amanda starts the timer on her watch, kills the lantern to preserve the batteries, and as we sit beside each other in the frigid dark, waiting for the drug to hit, she says, "Never thought I'd be glad to see our shitty little lifeboat again."

"Right?"

She leans her head against my shoulder.

"Thank you, Jason."

"For what?"

"Not letting me freeze to death out there."

"Does this mean we're even?"

She laughs. "Not even close. I mean, let's not forget, this is still all your fault."

It's a strange exercise in sensory deprivation to sit in the total darkness and silence of the box. The only physical sensations are the chill of the metal bleeding through my clothes and the pressure of Amanda's head against my shoulder.

"You're different than him," she says.

"Who?"

"My Jason."

"How so?"

"Softer. He had a real hard edge when you got down to it. *The* most driven human being I've ever met."

"Were you his therapist?"

"Sometimes."

"Was he happy?"

I sense her pondering my question in the dark.

"What?" I ask. "Am I putting you in a doctor-patient confidentiality quandary?"

"Technically, you two are the same person. It's new territory for sure. But no. I wouldn't say he was happy. He lived an intellectually stimulating but ultimately one-dimensional life. All he did was work. In the last five years, he didn't have a life outside the lab. He practically lived there."

"You know your Jason is the one who did this to me. I'm here right now because several nights ago, someone abducted me at gunpoint while I was walking home. He took me to an abandoned power plant, drugged me, asked me a bunch of questions about my life and the choices I'd made. If I was happy. If I would've done things differently. The memories are back now. Then I woke up in your lab. In your world. I think your Jason did this to me."

"You're suggesting that he went into the box, somehow found your world, your life, and switched places with you?"

"Do you think he was capable?"

"I don't know. That's crazy."

"Who else would've done this to me?"

Amanda is quiet for a moment.

She says finally, "Jason was obsessed with the path not taken. He talked about it all the time."

Now I feel the anger coming back.

I say, "There's still a part of me that doesn't want to believe it. I mean, if he wanted my life, he could've just killed me. But he went to the trouble of injecting me, not only with an ampoule, but ketamine, which rendered me unconscious and blurred my memories of the box and what he'd done. Then he actually brought me back to his world. Why?"

"It actually makes a lot of sense."

"You think?"

"He wasn't a monster. If he did this to you, he would have rationalized it somehow. That's how decent people justify bad behavior. In your world, are you a renowned physicist?"

"No, I teach at a second-rate college."

"Are you wealthy?"

"Professionally and financially speaking, I can't hold a candle to your Jason."

"There you go. He tells himself he's giving you the chance of a lifetime. *He* wants a shot at the path not taken. Why wouldn't you? I'm not saying it's right. I'm saying that's how a good man works himself up to do a terrible thing. It's Human Behavior 101."

She must sense my rage building, because she says, "Jason, you don't have the luxury of freaking out right now. In a minute, we're going back into that corridor. We're the controls. Your words. Right?"

"Yeah."

"If that's the truth, if it's our emotional state that's somehow selecting these worlds, to what kind of a place is your rage and jealousy going to take us? You can't hold on to this energy as you open a new door. You have to find a way to let it go."

I can feel the drug coming.

My muscles relax.

For a moment, the anger vanishes into a river of peace and calm I would give anything to make last, to have carry me through.

When Amanda turns on the lantern, the walls perpendicular to the door are gone.

I look down at the leather bag that holds the remaining ampoules, thinking, If the asshole who did this to me figured out how to navigate the box, then I will too.

In the blue light, Amanda watches me.

I say, "We have forty-four ampoules left. Twenty-two chances to get this right. How many did the other Jason take with him into the box?"

"A hundred."

Shit.

I feel a glimmer of panic course through me, but I smile in spite of it.

"I guess it's lucky for us I'm way smarter than him, right?"

Amanda laughs, rises to her feet, and offers me her hand.

"We have one hour," she says. "You up for this?"

"Absolutely."

NINE

He gets up earlier.

He drinks less.

Drives faster.

Reads more.

Has started exercising.

Holds his fork differently.

Laughs more easily.

Texts less.

He takes longer showers, and instead of just running a bar of soap over his entire body, he lathers up a washcloth now.

He shaves once every two days instead of four, and at the bathroom sink instead of in the shower.

Puts his shoes on immediately after dressing, not at the front door before leaving the house.

He flosses regularly, and she actually saw him plucking his eyebrows three days ago.

He hasn't worn his favorite sleeping shirt—a faded U2 T-shirt from a concert they saw a decade ago at the United Center—in almost two weeks.

He does the dishes differently—instead of building an unwieldy tower in the drying rack, he sets the wet plates and glassware on towels that he's spread across the countertop.

He drinks one cup of coffee with breakfast instead of two, and he makes it weaker than he used to, so weak in fact that she's been making an effort to beat him down to the kitchen each morning to brew the coffee herself.

Lately, their family dinner conversations have centered around ideas, books, and articles Jason is reading, and Charlie's studies, instead of a mundane recounting of the day's events.

Speaking of Charlie, Jason is also different with their son.

More lenient, less paternal.

As if he's forgotten how to be a father to a teenager.

He's stopped staying up until two every morning watching Netflix on his iPad.

He never calls her Dani anymore.

He wants her constantly, and it's like their first time every time.

He looks at her with a smoldering intensity that reminds her of the way new lovers stare into each other's eyes when there's still so much mystery and uncharted territory to discover.

These thoughts, all these tiny realizations, accumulate in the back of her mind as Daniela stands in front of the mirror next to Jason.

It's morning, and they're getting ready for their respective days.

She's brushing her teeth, he's brushing his, and when he catches her staring at him, he gives a toothpaste-foamy grin and winks.

She wonders—

Does he have cancer and isn't telling me?

Is he taking a new antidepressant and isn't telling me?

Lost his job and isn't telling me?

A sick, hot feeling erupts in the pit of her stomach: is he having an affair with one of his students and it's her that's making him feel and act like this brand-new man?

No. None of that feels right.

The thing is, nothing is obviously wrong.

On paper, they're actually better. He's paying her more attention than he ever has. They haven't talked and laughed this much since the beginning of their relationship.

It's just that he's . . . different.

Different in a thousand tiny ways that might mean nothing and might mean everything.

Jason leans over and spits into the sink.

He turns off the faucet and steps around behind her and puts his hands on her hips and pushes up gently against her.

She watches his reflection in the mirror.

Thinking, *What secrets are you keeping?*

Wanting to say those words.

Those exact words.

But she keeps brushing, because what if the price tag on that answer is this amazing status quo?

He says, "I could just watch you do this all day."

"Brush my teeth?" She garbles the words, the toothbrush still in her mouth.

"Uh-huh." He kisses the back of her neck, and the shiver goes down her spine and into her knees, and for a split second it all falls away—the fear, the questions, the doubt.

He says, "Ryan Holder is giving a lecture tonight at six. You want to come with me?"

Daniela leans over, spits, rinses.

"I'd love to, but I have a lesson at five thirty."

"Then can I take you to dinner when I get home?"

"I'd love that."

She turns around and kisses him.

He even kisses differently now.

Like it's an event, every time.

As he starts to pull away, she says, "Hey."

"Yeah?"

She should ask.

She should bring up all these things she's noticed.

Throw it all down and clear the air.

Part of her wants to know so badly.

Part of her never wants to know.

And so she tells herself that now isn't the time as she plays with his collar and fixes his hair and sends him off into the day with one last kiss.

TEN

Amanda glances up from the notebook, asks, "You're sure writing it down is the best way to go?"

"When you write something, you focus your full attention on it. It's almost impossible to write one thing while thinking about another. The act of putting it on paper keeps your thoughts and intentions aligned."

"How much should I write?" she asks.

"Maybe keep it simple to start? One short paragraph?"

She finishes the sentence she's been working on, closes the notebook, and rises to her feet.

"You've got it all in the forefront of your mind?" I ask.

"I think so."

I shoulder our backpack. Amanda crosses to the door, turns the handle, pulls it open. Morning sunlight enters the corridor, so blinding that for a moment I can't see a thing outside.

As my eyes adjust to the brilliance, the surroundings fade into focus.

We're standing in the doorway of the box, at the top of a hill overlooking a park.

To the east, emerald grass slopes for several hundred

yards, down to the shore of Lake Michigan. And in the distance rises a skyline like none I've ever seen—the buildings slim, constructions of glass and steel so reflective they border on invisible, creating an effect almost like a mirage.

The sky is filled with moving objects, most crisscrossing the airspace above what I assume is Chicago, a few accelerating vertically, straight up into the deep blue with no sign of stopping.

Amanda looks over at me and smirks, tapping the notebook.

I open it to the first page.

She wrote . . .

I want to go to a good place, to a good time to be alive. A world I'd want to live in. It isn't the future, but it feels like it . . .

I say, "Not bad."

"Is this place actually real?" she asks.

"Yes. And you brought us here."

"Let's explore. We should give ourselves a break from the drug anyway."

She starts down the grassy slope away from the box. We pass a playground and then hit a walking path that runs through the park.

The morning is cold and flawless. My breath steams.

The grass is blanched with frost where the sun has yet to touch it, and the hardwoods that border the park are turning.

The lake stands as still as glass.

A quarter mile ahead, a series of elegant Y-shaped structures cut across the park at intervals of fifty meters.

Only as we draw near do I realize what they are.

We ride a lift up to the northbound platform and wait under the heated overhang, now forty feet above the greenway. A digital, interactive map emblazoned with Chicago Transit Authority identifies this route as the Red Line Express, linking South Chicago to Downtown.

An urgent female voice blares through a speaker overhead.

Stand clear. A train is arriving. Stand clear. A train is arriving in five . . . four . . . three . . .

I glance up and down the line, but I don't see anything approaching.

Two . . .

A blur of incoming movement rockets out of the tree line.

One.

A sleek, three-car train decelerates into the station, and as the doors open, that computerized female voice says, *Please wait to board on green.*

The handful of passengers who detrain and move past us are wearing workout clothes. The panel of red light above each of the open doors turns to green.

You may board now for Downtown Station.

Amanda and I share a glance, shrug, and then step into the first car. It's nearly full with commuters.

This isn't the El I know. It's free. No one is standing. Everyone is strapped into chairs that look like they should be bolted to a rocket sled.

The word VACANT hovers helpfully above each empty seat.

As Amanda and I move up the aisle, the automated attendant says, *Please find a seat. The train cannot depart the station until everyone is safely seated.*

We slide into a couple of seats at the front of the car. As I lean back, padded restraints emerge from the chair and gently secure my shoulders and waist.

Head back against your seat, please. The train is departing in three . . . two . . . one.

The acceleration is smooth but intense. It shoves me deep into the cushioned seat for two seconds, and then we're floating along a single rail at an inconceivable speed, no sense of friction beneath us as a cityscape blurs past on the other side of the glass, too fast for me to actually process what I'm seeing.

In the distance, that fantastical skyline inches closer. The buildings don't even make sense. In the sharp morning light, it looks as if someone shattered a mirror and stood all the shards of glass upright in formation. They're too beautifully random and irregular to be man-made. Perfect in their imperfection and asymmetry, like a range of mountains. Or the shape of a river.

The track drops.

My stomach lifts.

We scream through a tunnel—darkness interspersed with bursts of light that only serve to amplify the sense of disorientation and velocity.

We break out of the darkness and I grip the sides of my chair, forced forward into the restraints as the train slams to a stop.

The attendant announces, *Downtown Station.*

Is this your stop? appears as a hologram six inches from my face above *Y?* and *N?*

Amanda says, "Let's get off here."

I swipe the *Y.* She does the same.

Our restraints release and disappear into the seats. Rising, we exit the car with the other passengers onto the platform of a magnificent station that dwarfs New York's Grand Central. It's a soaring terminal topped with a ceiling that resembles beveled glass in the way the sunlight passes through and diffuses into the hall as scattered brilliance, projecting twittering chevrons of light onto the marble walls.

The space is brimming with people.

The long, croaking notes of a saxophone hang in the air.

At the opposite side of the hall, we climb a daunting waterfall of steps.

Everyone around us is talking to themselves—phone calls, I'm sure, though I don't see any mobile devices.

At the top of the stairs, we pass through one of a dozen turnstiles.

The street is crushed with pedestrians—no cars, no traffic lights. We're standing at the base of the tallest building I've ever seen. Even in proximity, it doesn't look real. With no differentiation from floor to floor, it resembles a piece of solid ice or crystal.

Pulled along by naked curiosity, we cross the street, enter the lobby of the tower, and follow the signs to the queue for the observation deck.

The elevator is astonishingly fast.

I have to keep swallowing to clear my ears against the constant change in pressure.

After two minutes, the car comes to a stop.

The attendant informs us that we have ten minutes to enjoy the top.

As the doors part, we're met with a chilling blast of wind. Moving out of the car, we pass a hologram that reads: *You are now 7,082 feet above street level.*

The elevator shaft occupies the center of the tiny observation deck, and the pinnacle of the tower is a mere fifty feet above us, the apex of the glass structure twisted into a flame-like point.

Another hologram materializes as we walk toward the edge: *The Glass Tower is the tallest building in the Midwest and the third tallest in America.*

It's freezing up here, the breeze steadily coming off the lake. The air feels thinner sliding into my lungs, and I register a twinge of light-headedness, but whether from the lack of oxygen or from vertigo, I'm not sure.

We reach the anti-suicide railing.

My head swims. My stomach churns.

It's almost too much to take in—the sparkling sprawl of the city and the profusion of neighboring towers and the vast expanse of the lake, which I can see clear across into southern Michigan.

To the west and south, beyond the suburbs, the prairie glows in the morning light, a hundred miles away.

The tower sways.

Four states—Illinois, Indiana, Michigan, and Wisconsin— are visible on a clear day.

Standing on this work of art and imagination, I feel small in the best kind of way.

It's enthralling to breathe the air of a world that could build something as beautiful as this.

Amanda is beside me, and we're staring down the gorgeously feminine curve of the building. It's serene and nearly silent up here.

The only sound is the lonely whisper of wind.

The noise of the streets below doesn't reach us.

"Was all of this in your head?" I ask.

"Not consciously, but it all feels right somehow. Like a half-remembered dream."

I gaze toward the northern neighborhoods, where Logan Square should be.

It doesn't look anything like my home.

A few feet away, I see an old man standing behind his old wife, his gnarled hands on her shoulders as she peers through a telescope, which is pointed down at the most extraordinary Ferris wheel I've ever seen. A thousand feet tall, it looms over the lakeshore, right where Navy Pier should be.

I think of Daniela.

Of what this other Jason—Jason2—might be doing at this moment.

What he might be doing to my wife.

Anger, fear, and homesickness envelop me like an illness.

This world, for all its grandeur, isn't my home.

It isn't even close.

AMPOULES REMAINING: 42

Down the dark corridor through this in-between place again, our footfalls echoing into infinity.

I'm holding the lantern and considering what I should write in the notebook when Amanda stops walking.

"What's wrong?" I ask.

"Listen."

It becomes so quiet I can hear the escalated beating of my heart.

And then—something impossible.

A sound.

Far, far down the corridor.

Amanda looks at me.

She whispers, "What the fuck?"

I stare into the darkness.

There's nothing to see but the dwindling light of the lantern refracting off the repeating walls.

The sound becomes louder from moment to moment.

It's the shuffling of footsteps.

I say, "Someone's coming."

"How is that possible?"

Movement edges into the periphery of illumination.

A figure coming toward us.

I take a step back, and as they draw closer, I'm tempted to run, but where would I go?

Might as well face it.

It's a man.

He's naked.

His skin covered in mud or dirt or . . .

Blood.

Definitely blood.

He reeks of it.

As if he rolled around in a pool.

His hair is matted, face smeared and caked so heavily it makes the whites of his eyes stand out.

His hands are trembling and his fingers curled in tightly, like they've been clawing desperately at something.

Only when he's ten feet away do I realize this man is me.

I step out of his way, backing up against the nearest wall to give him the widest possible berth.

As he staggers past, his eyes fix on mine.

I'm not even sure he sees me.

He looks shell-shocked.

Hollowed out.

Like he just stepped out of hell.

Across his back and shoulders, chunks of flesh have been ripped out.

I say, "What happened to you?"

He stops and stares at me, and then opens his mouth and makes the most terrifying sound I've ever heard—a throat-scarring scream.

As his voice echoes, Amanda grabs my arm and pulls me away.

He doesn't follow.

Just watches us go, and then shuffles on down the corridor.

Into that endless dark.

Thirty minutes later, I'm sitting in front of a door that's identical to all the rest, trying to wipe my mind and emotional register of what I just saw in the corridor.

Taking a notebook from the backpack, I open it, the pen poised in my hand.

I don't even have to think.

I simply write the words:

I want to go home.

I wonder, Is this what God feels? The rush that comes from having literally spoken a world into existence? And yes, this world already existed, but I connected us to it. Out of all the possible worlds, I found this one, and it's exactly, at least from the doorway of the box, what I wanted.

I step down, glass crunching on the concrete beneath my shoes as afternoon light pours through the windows high above, striking a row of iron generators from another era.

Although I've never seen it in daylight, I know this room.

The last time I was here a harvest moon was on the rise over Lake Michigan, and I was slumped back against one of these ancient contraptions, drugged out of my mind, staring at a man in a geisha mask who had forced me at gunpoint into the depths of this abandoned power plant.

Staring—though I had no idea at the time—at myself.

I couldn't have imagined the journey.

The hell that actually awaited me.

The box is situated in a far corner of the generator room, hidden away behind the stairs.

"Well?" Amanda asks.

"I think I did it. This is the last place I saw before waking up in your world."

We make our way back through the derelict power plant.

Outside, the sun is shining.

Descending.

It's late afternoon, and the only sound is the lonely cry of gulls flying out over the lake.

We hike west into the neighborhoods of South Chicago, walking along the shoulder like a pair of drifters.

The distant skyline is familiar.

It's the one I know and love.

The sun keeps dropping, and we've been walking twenty minutes before it dawns on me that we haven't seen a single car on the road.

"Kind of quiet, isn't it?" I ask.

Amanda looks at me.

The silence wasn't so noticeable out in the industrial wasteland near the lake.

Here it's startling.

There are no cars out.

No people.

It's so quiet I can hear the current running through the power lines above us.

The Eighty-Seventh Street CTA station is closed—no buses or trains running.

The only other sign of life is a stray black cat with a corkscrew tail, slinking across the road, a rat in its jaws.

Amanda says, "Maybe we should go back to the box."

"I want to see my home."

"The vibe here is wrong, Jason. Can't you feel it?"

"We're not going to learn anything about flying the box if we don't explore where it takes us."

"Where's home?"

"Logan Square."

"Not exactly walking distance."

"So we'll borrow a car."

We cross Eighty-Seventh and walk a residential block of downtrodden row houses. No street sweeper has been by in weeks. There's trash everywhere. Disgusting, splitting bags of it in huge piles up and down the sidewalk.

Many of the windows have been boarded up.

Some are covered in sheets of plastic.

From most hang pieces of clothing.

Some red.

Some black.

The drone of radios and televisions creeps out of a few houses.

The cry of a child.

But otherwise, the neighborhood stands ominously silent.

Halfway down the sixth block, Amanda calls out, "Found one!"

I cross the street toward a mid-'90s Oldsmobile Cutlass Ciera.

White. Rusting around the edges. No hubcaps on the wheels.

Through the dirty glass, I glimpse a pair of keys dangling from the ignition.

Pulling open the driver's-side door, I slide in behind the steering wheel.

"So we're really doing this?" Amanda asks.

I crank the engine as she climbs into the passenger side.

There's a quarter tank of gas remaining.

Should be enough.

The windshield is so filthy, it takes ten seconds of pummeling with wiper fluid to scrape away the grime and the dirt and the plastered-on leaves.

The interstate is desolate.

I've never seen anything like it.

Empty in both directions as far as I can see.

It's early evening now, the sun glinting off the Willis Tower.

I speed north, and with each passing mile, the knot in my stomach tightens.

Amanda says, "Let's go back. Seriously. Something is obviously very wrong."

"If my family's here, my place is with them."

"How do you even know this is your Chicago?"

She turns on the radio and scrolls through static on the FM dial until the familiar warning pings of the Emergency Alert System screech through the speakers.

The following message is transmitted at the request of the Illinois State Police Department. The mandatory twenty-four-hour curfew remains in effect for Cook County. All residents are ordered to stay in their homes until further notice. The National Guard continues to monitor the safety of all neighborhoods, deliver food rations, and provide transport to CDC Quarantine Zones.

In the southbound lanes, a convoy of four camouflaged Humvees speeds by.

The threat of contagion remains high. Initial symptoms include fever, severe headache, and muscle pain. If you believe that you or anyone in your home is infected, display a red piece of cloth in a street-facing window. If anyone in your *home is deceased, display a black piece of cloth in a street-facing window.*

CDC personnel will assist as soon as they are able.

Stay tuned for further details.

Amanda looks at me.

"Why aren't you turning around?"

There's nowhere to park on my block, so I leave the car in the middle of the street with the engine running.

"You're out of your fucking mind," Amanda says.

I point toward the brownstone with a red skirt and black sweater hanging from the window of the master bedroom.

"That's my home, Amanda."

"Just hurry. And be safe, please."

I step out of the car.

It's so very quiet, the streets blue in the dusk.

One block up, I glimpse pale figures dragging themselves down the middle of the road.

I reach the curb.

The power lines are silent, the light emanating from inside the houses softer than it should be.

Candlelight.

There's no power in my neighborhood.

Climbing the steps to the front door, I peer through the large window that looks in on the dining room.

It's darkness and gloom inside.

I knock.

After a long time, a shadow emerges from the kitchen, trudging slowly past the dining-room table toward the front door.

My mouth runs dry.

I shouldn't be here.

This isn't even my home.

The chandelier is wrong.

So is the Van Gogh print above the hearth.

I hear three locks click back.

The door cracks open less than an inch, and a waft from inside creeps out that doesn't smell anything like my home.

All sickness and death.

Daniela holds a candle that trembles in her grasp.

Even in the low light, I can see that every square inch of her exposed skin is blanketed with bumps.

Her eyes look black.

They're hemorrhaging.

Only slivers of white remain.

She says, "Jason?" Her voice is soft and wet. Tears run from her eyes. "Oh my God. Is it you?"

She pulls the door open and staggers toward me, unsteady on her feet.

It's a heart-crushing thing to feel revulsion for the one you love.

I take a step back.

Sensing my horror, she stops herself.

"How is this possible?" she rasps. "You died."

"What are you talking about?"

"A week ago, they carried you out of here in a body bag full of blood."

"Where's Charlie?" I ask.

She shakes her head, and as the tears stream, coughs a bloody sob into the bend of her elbow.

"Dead?" I ask.

"No one's come to get him. He's still up in his room. He's rotting up there, Jason."

For a moment, she loses her balance, then catches herself on the door frame.

"Are you real?" she asks.

Am I real?

What a question.

I can't speak.

My throat aches with grief.

Tears begin to fill my eyes.

As much as I pity her, the awful truth is that I'm scared of her, my self-preservation recoiling in horror.

Amanda calls from the car, "Someone's coming!"

I glance up the street, see a pair of headlights rolling down through the darkness.

"Jason, I will fucking leave you!" Amanda shouts.

"Who is that?" Daniela asks.

The rumble of the approaching engine sounds like a diesel.

Amanda was right. I should have turned around the moment I realized how dangerous this place might be.

This isn't my world.

And still, my heart feels tethered to the second floor of this house in a bedroom where some version of my son lies dead.

I want to rush up there and carry him out, but it would be my death.

I move back down the steps toward the street as a Humvee pulls to a stop in the road, ten feet from the bumper of the car we boosted in the South Side.

It's covered in various insignia—Red Cross, National Guard, CDC.

Amanda is leaning out her window.

"What the hell, Jason?"

I wipe my eyes.

"My son is dead in there. Daniela is dying."

The front passenger door of the Humvee opens, and a figure in a black biohazard suit and gas mask steps out and sights me down with an assault rifle.

The voice projected through the mask belongs to a woman.

She says, "Stop right there."

I instinctively raise my hands.

Next, she swings the rifle toward the windshield of the Cutlass Ciera and walks toward the car.

Says to Amanda, "Shut that engine off."

Amanda reaches across the center console and kills the ignition as the driver of the Humvee climbs out.

I motion to Daniela, who's standing on the porch, wavering on her feet.

"My wife is very ill. My son is dead upstairs."

The driver stares up through his mask at the façade of the brownstone.

"You've got the colors properly displayed. Someone will be along to—"

"She needs medical attention right now."

"Is this your car?"

"Yes."

"Where were you planning to go?"

"I just wanted to get my wife to some people who could help her. Aren't there any hospitals or—"

"Wait here."

"Please."

"Wait," he snaps.

The driver steps onto the sidewalk and climbs the stairs to where Daniela is now sitting on the highest step, leaning against the railing.

He kneels in front of her, and though I hear his voice, I can't make out the words.

The woman with the assault rifle covers me and Amanda.

Across the street, I see firelight flickering through a window as one of our neighbors looks down on whatever is unfolding in front of my house.

The driver returns.

He says, "Look, the CDC camps are at capacity. Have been for two weeks. And it wouldn't matter if you got her into one anyway. Once the eyes hemorrhage, the end is very close. I don't know about you, but I'd rather pass in my own bed than a cot in a FEMA tent filled with dead and dying people." He looks over his shoulder. "Nadia, would you grab this gentleman some auto-injectors? And a mask while you're at it."

She says, "Mike."

"Just fucking do it."

Nadia goes to the back of the Humvee and opens the cargo doors.

"So she's going to die?"

"I'm sorry."

"How long?"

"I'd be surprised if she makes it to the morning."

Daniela groans in the darkness behind me.

Nadia returns, slaps five auto-injectors into my hand along with a face mask.

The driver says, "Wear the mask at all times, and I know it's hard, but try not to touch her."

"What is this stuff?" I ask.

"Morphine. If you give her all five at once, she'll slip away. I wouldn't wait. The last eight hours are ugly."

"She has no chance?"

"No."

"Where's the cure?"

"There won't be one in time to save the city."

"They're just letting people die in their homes?"

He studies me through his mask.

The face shield is tinted.

I can't even see his eyes.

"If you try to leave and hit the wrong roadblock, they'll kill you. Especially after dark."

He turns away.

I watch as they climb back into the Humvee, fire up the engine, and drive off down the block.

The sun has gone below the horizon.

The street is getting dark.

Amanda says, "We should go right now."

"Just give me a second."

"She's contagious."

"I'm aware."

"Jason—"

"That's my wife up there."

"No, it's a *version* of your wife, and if you catch whatever she has you'll never see your real wife again."

I strap on the mask and climb the steps to the front porch.

Daniela looks up as I approach.

Her ruined face breaks me.

She's vomited blood and black bile all over herself.

"They won't take me?" she asks.

I shake my head.

I want to hold her and comfort her.

I want to run away from her.

"It's okay," she says. "You don't have to pretend it's going to be all right. I'm ready."

"They gave me these," I say, setting the auto-injectors down.

"What are they?"

"A way to make it end."

"I watched you die in our bed," she says. "I watched my son die in his. I don't ever want to go back in that house. Of all the ways I thought my life would go, I never imagined this."

"This isn't how your life turned out. Only how it ended. Your life was beautiful."

The candle falls out of her hand and extinguishes on the concrete, the wick smoking.

I say, "If I give you all of these at once, this can be over. Is that what you want?"

She nods, tears and blood running down her cheeks.

I pull a purple cap off one of the auto-injectors, hold the end against her thigh, and press the button on the opposite end.

Daniela barely even flinches as the spring-loaded syringe fires a dose of morphine into her system.

I set up the next four and administer them all in quick succession.

The effect is nearly instantaneous.

She falls back against the wrought-iron railing, and her black eyes glass over as the drug takes hold.

"Better?" I ask.

She almost smiles, then says, her words thickening, "I know I'm just hallucinating this, but you're my angel. You came back to me. I was so afraid to die alone in that house."

The dusk deepens.

The first stars appear in the eerily black skies above Chicago.

"I'm so . . . light-headed," she says.

I think of all the evenings we've sat on this porch. Drinking. Laughing. Bullshitting with the neighbors passing by as the streetlamps up and down the block winked on.

In this moment, my world seems so safe and perfect. I see now—I took all that comfort for granted. It was so good, and there were so many ways it could've all gone to pieces.

Daniela says, "I wish you could touch me, Jason."

Her voice has become hoarse and brittle, little more than a whisper.

Her eyes close.

Each cycle of her respiration becomes longer by a second or two.

Until she stops breathing altogether.

I don't want to leave her out here, but I know I shouldn't touch her.

Rising, I move to the door and step inside. The house is silent and dark, and the presence of death clings to my skin.

I pass the candlelit walls of the dining room, move through the kitchen, and into the study. The hardwood floor creaks under my footsteps—the only sound in the house.

At the foot of the stairs, I stop and stare up into the darkness of the second floor, where my son lies rotting in his bed.

I feel the pull to go up there like the irresistible gravity of a black hole.

But I resist.

I grab the blanket draped over the couch, take it outside, and cover Daniela's body.

Then I close the door to my house and walk down the steps and away from the horror.

I get in the car, start the engine.

Look over at Amanda.

"Thanks for not leaving me."

"I should have."

I drive away.

Some parts of the city have power.

Some are in the black.

My eyes keep welling up.

I can hardly see to drive.

Amanda says, "Jason, this isn't your world. That wasn't your wife. You can still go home and find them."

Intellectually, I know she's right, but emotionally, that just ripped my guts out.

I am hardwired to love and protect that woman.

We're passing through Bucktown.

In the distance, an entire city block is hurling hundred-foot flames at the sky.

The interstate is dark and empty.

Amanda reaches over and pulls the mask off my face.

The smell of death from inside my home lingers in my nose.

I can't shake it.

I keep thinking of Daniela, lying dead under a blanket on our front porch.

As we pass to the west of downtown, I glance out my window.

There's just enough starlight to profile the towers.

They're black, lifeless.

Amanda says, "Jason?"

"What?"

"There's a car following us."

I look in the rearview mirror.

With no lights, it looks like a phantom riding my bumper.

Blinding high beams and red-and-blues kick on, sending splinters of light through the interior of the car.

A voice booms through a megaphone behind us: *Pull your vehicle onto the shoulder.*

Panic swells.

We have nothing to defend ourselves with.

We can't outrun anything in this piece of shit.

I take my foot off the gas, watch the speedometer needle swing counterclockwise.

Amanda says, "You're stopping?"

"Yes."

"Why?"

I ease down on the brake pedal, and as our speed falls, I veer onto the shoulder and bring the car to a stop.

"Jason." Amanda grabs my arm. "What are you doing?"

In the side mirror, I watch a black SUV pull to a stop behind us.

Turn off your vehicle and drop the keys out the window.

"Jason!"

"Just trust me."

This is your last warning. Turn off the car and drop the keys out the window. Any attempt to flee will be met with lethal force.

A mile or so back, more headlights appear.

I shift the car into PARK and kill the lights. Then I lower my window several inches, stick my arm through, and pretend to drop a set of keys outside.

The driver's-side door to the SUV opens, and a man in a gas mask steps out with his weapon already drawn.

I throw the car back into gear, hit the lights, and floor the accelerator.

I hear a gunshot over the roar of the engine.

A bullet hole stars the windshield.

Then another.

One rips into the cassette deck.

Looking back, I see the SUV now several hundred yards down the shoulder.

The speedometer is at sixty and climbing.

"How far are we from our exit?" Amanda asks.

"A mile or two."

"There's a bunch of them coming."

"I see them."

"Jason, if they catch us—"

"I know."

I'm doing a little over ninety now, the engine straining to maintain speed, the RPMs inching into the red.

We blow past a sign giving notice that our exit is a quarter mile ahead on the right.

At this speed, we reach it in a matter of seconds.

I hit the exit at seventy-five and brake hard.

Neither of us are buckled in.

The inertia slams Amanda into the glove box and shoves me forward into the steering wheel.

At the end of the ramp, I take a brutal left turn through a stop sign—tires squealing, rubber burning. It slings Amanda against her door and nearly sends me flying into her seat.

As I drive across the overpass, I count five sets of flashing lights on the interstate, the closest SUV now speeding onto the exit ramp with two Humvees in tow.

We tear through the vacated streets of South Chicago.

Amanda leans forward, stares out the windshield.

"What is it?" I ask.

She's looking at the sky.

"I see lights up there."

"Like a helicopter?"

"Exactly."

I scream through empty intersections, past the shuttered El station, and then we're clear of the ghetto, speeding alongside abandoned warehouses and train yards.

In the boondocks of the city.

"They're getting close," Amanda says.

A round thunks into the trunk of the car.

Followed by three more in fast succession, like someone taking a hammer to metal.

She says, "That's a machine gun."

"Get down on the floorboard."

I can hear the anthem of sirens drawing near.

This antiquated sedan is no match for what's coming.

Two more rounds pierce the back window and the windshield.

One rips through the middle of Amanda's seat.

Through the bullet-riddled glass, I see the lake straight ahead.

I say, "Hang on, we're almost there."

I make a hard right onto Pulaski Drive, and as a trio of bullets peppers the rear passenger door, I cut the lights.

The first few seconds of driving without headlights feels like we're flying through total darkness.

Then my eyes begin to adjust.

I can see the pavement ahead, the black silhouettes of structures all around us.

It's as dark as the countryside out here.

I take my foot off the gas, but I don't touch the brake.

Glancing back, I see two SUVs make aggressive turns onto Pulaski.

Up ahead, I can just make out the pair of familiar smokestacks spearing the starlit sky.

Our speed is under twenty miles per hour, and though the SUVs are gaining fast, I don't think their high beams have touched us yet.

I see the fence.

Our speed keeps dropping.

I steer across the road, and the grille smashes into the locked gate, splitting the doors apart.

We roll slowly into the parking lot, and as I maneuver around the toppled light poles, I look back toward the road.

The sirens are getting louder.

Three SUVs streak past the gate, trailed by two Humvees with machine-gun turrets mounted to their roofs.

I kill the engine.

In the new silence, I listen to the sirens fading away.

Amanda climbs up from the floorboard as I grab our pack from the backseat.

The slams of our doors bounce off the brick building straight ahead.

We move toward the crumbling structure and all that's left of the original signage: CAGO POWER.

A helicopter buzzes overhead, a brilliant spotlight scraping across the parking lot.

Now I hear a revving engine.

A black SUV skids sideways across Pulaski.

Headlights blind us.

As we run toward the building, a man's voice through a megaphone orders us to stop.

I step through the hole in the brick façade, give Amanda a hand inside.

It's pitch-black.

Ripping open the pack, I quickly dig out the lantern.

The light reveals the destroyed front office, and the sight of this place in the dark takes me back to that night with Jason2, when he walked me naked and at gunpoint into another version of this old building.

We move out of the first room, the lantern piercing the darkness.

Down a hallway.

Faster and faster.

Our footsteps pounding the rotten floor.

Sweat runs down my face, stings my eyes.

My heart beats so hard it rattles my chest.

I'm gasping for breath.

Voices call after us.

I look back, see lasers cutting through the black and splotches of green from what I assume are night-vision goggles.

I hear the noise of radios and whispered voices and the rotors of the helicopter bleeding through the walls.

A torrent of gunfire fills the hallway, and we flatten ourselves against the ground until the shooting stops.

Struggling back onto our feet, we push on with even more urgency.

At a junction, I take us down a different hall, mostly sure it's the right way though it's impossible to be certain in the dark.

We finally emerge onto the metal platform at the top of the open stairs that lead down into the generator room.

We descend.

Our pursuers are so close I can pick out three distinct voices reverberating through the last hallway.

Two men, one woman.

I move off the last step, Amanda right on my heels as heavy footfalls clang on the stairs above us.

Two red dots crisscross my path.

I sidestep and keep running, straight into the darkness ahead, where I know the box has to be.

Gunshots ring out above us as two figures in full biohazard gear launch off the bottom of the stairs, hurtling toward us.

The box stands fifty feet ahead, the door open and the metallic surface gently diffusing the light of our incoming lantern.

Gunshot.

I feel something zip by my right ear like a passing hornet.

A bullet strikes the door with a spark of fire.

My ear burns.

A man behind us screams, "There's nowhere to go!"

Amanda is first into the box.

Then I cross the threshold, turn, dig my shoulder into the door.

The soldiers are twenty feet away, so close I can hear them panting through their gas masks.

They open fire, and the blinding muzzle flashes and the bullets chinking into the metal of the box are the last I see and hear of that nightmare world.

We shoot up immediately and start walking down the corridor.

After a while, Amanda wants to stop, but I can't.

I need to keep moving.

I walk for a full hour.

Through an entire cycle of the drug.

My ear bleeding all over my clothes.

Until the corridor collapses back into a single box.

I throw off the pack.

Cold.

Coated in dried sweat.

Amanda is standing in the center of the box, her skirt dirty and ripped, sweater torn off completely from our run through the abandoned power plant.

As she sets the lantern on the floor, something inside of me releases.

The strength, the tension, the anger, the fear.

Everything flooding out at once in a stream of tears and uncontrollable sobbing.

Amanda turns off the lantern.

I crumple down against the cold wall, and she pulls me over into her lap.

Runs her fingers through my hair.

AMPOULES REMAINING: 40

I come to consciousness in the pitch-black, lying on my side on the floor of the box, my back to the wall. Amanda is pressed up close against me, our bodies contoured together, her head resting in the crook of my arm.

I'm hungry and thirsty.

I wonder how long I've slept.

At least my ear has stopped bleeding.

It's impossible to deny the reality of our helplessness.

Aside from each other, this box is the only constant we have.

A very tiny boat in the middle of a very large ocean.

It's our shelter.

Our prison.

Our home.

Carefully, I untangle us.

Pulling off my hoodie, I fold it into a pillow and slide it under Amanda's head.

She stirs but doesn't wake.

I feel my way around to the door, knowing I shouldn't take the risk of breaking the seal. But I have to know what's out there, and the claustrophobia of the box is wearing on me.

Turning the handle, I drag it slowly open.

First sensation: the smell of evergreens.

Shafts of sunlight slant down through a forest of closely spaced pine trees.

In the near distance, a deer stands motionless, staring through its dark, wet eyes at the box.

When I step outside, the deer bounds off soundlessly through the pines.

The forest is startlingly quiet.

Mist hovers over the pine-needle floor.

I walk out a little ways from the box and sit on a piece of ground in direct morning sun that feels warm and bright against my face.

A breeze pushes through the tops of the trees.

I catch a hint of woodsmoke in the wind.

From an open fire?

A chimney?

I wonder, Who lives here?

What sort of a world is this?

I hear footsteps.

Glancing back, I see Amanda coming toward me through the trees and register a pang of guilt—I almost got her killed in that last world. She isn't just here because of me. She's here because she saved me. Because she did a brave, risky thing.

She sits beside me and turns her face to the sun.

"How'd you sleep?" she asks.

"Hard. Awful crick in my neck. You?"

"Sore all over."

She leans in close and studies my ear.

"Bad?" I ask.

"No, the bullet just trimmed off part of your earlobe. I'll clean it up for you."

She hands me a liter of water we refilled in that futuristic Chicago, and I take a long sip that I wish would never end.

"You doing okay?" she asks.

"I can't stop thinking about her. Lying dead on our porch. And Charlie up in his room. We are so lost."

Amanda says, "I know it's hard, but the question you should be thinking about—we should both be thinking about—is why did you bring us to that world?"

"All I wrote was, 'I want to go home.'"

"Exactly. That's what you wrote, but you carried baggage through the door."

"What do you mean?"

"Isn't it obvious?"

"Obviously not."

"Your worst fear."

"That type of scenario isn't everyone's?"

"Maybe. But it's so perfectly yours I'm surprised you don't see it."

"How is it perfectly mine?"

"Not just losing your family, but losing them to illness. The same way you lost your mother when you were eight years old."

I look over at Amanda.

"How'd you know that?"

"How do you think?"

Of course. She was Jason2's therapist.

She says, "Watching his mother die was the defining event of his life. It played a critical part in why he never married, never had kids. Why he sunk himself into work."

I believe it. There were moments, early on, when I considered running from Daniela. Not because I wasn't crazy about her, but because on some level, I was afraid of losing her. And I felt the same fear all over again when I found out she was pregnant with Charlie.

"Why would I seek out a world like that?"

"Why do people marry versions of their controlling mothers? Or absent fathers? To have a shot at righting old wrongs. Fixing things as an adult that hurt you as a child. Maybe it doesn't make sense at a surface level, but the subconscious marches to its own beat. I happen to think that world taught us a lot about how the box works."

Passing the water back to her, I say, "Forty."

"Forty what?"

"Forty ampoules left. Half are yours. That gives us each twenty chances to get this right. What do you want to do?"

"I'm not sure. All I know at this point is that I'm not going back to my world."

"So do you want to stay together, or is this goodbye?"

"I don't know how you feel, but I think we still need each other. I think maybe I can help you get home."

I lean back against the trunk of a pine tree, a notebook resting on my knees, my thoughts teeming.

What a strange thing to consider imagining a world into being with nothing but words, intention, and desire.

It's a troubling paradox—I have total control, but only to the extent I have control over myself.

My emotions.

My inner storm.

The secret engines that drive me.

If there are infinite worlds, how do I find the one that is uniquely, specifically mine?

I stare at the page and begin to write down every detail of my Chicago that comes to mind. I paint my life with words.

The sounds of the children in my neighborhood walking to school together, their voices like a stream flowing over rocks—high and burbling.

Graffiti on the faded white brick of a building three blocks from my house that was so artfully done it was never painted over.

I meditate on the intricacies of my home.

The fourth step on the staircase that always creaks.

The downstairs bathroom with the leaky faucet.

The way my kitchen smells as coffee brews first thing in the morning.

All the tiny, seemingly insignificant details upon which my world hangs.

ELEVEN

AMPOULES REMAINING: 32

There's a theory in the field of aesthetics called the uncanny valley. It holds that when something looks *almost* like a human being—a mannequin or humanlike robot—it creates revulsion in the observer, because the appearance is so close to human, yet just off enough to evoke a feeling of uncanniness, of something that is both familiar and alien.

It's a similar psychological effect as I walk the streets of this Chicago that's *almost* mine. I would take an apocalyptic nightmare any day. Crumbled buildings and gray wasteland don't hold a candle to standing on a corner I've passed a thousand times and realizing that the street names are wrong. Or the coffee place where I always stop to grab my morning triple-shot Americano with soy is a boutique wine shop instead. Or my house at 44 Eleanor Street is a brownstone inhabited by strangers.

This is the fourth Chicago we've connected to since escaping that world of sickness and death. Each has been like this one—*almost* home.

Night is imminent, and since we've taken four hits of the

drug in fairly rapid succession with no recovery period, we decide for the first time not to return to the box.

It's the same hotel in Logan Square where I stayed in Amanda's world.

The neon sign is red instead of green but the name is the same—HOTEL ROYALE—and it's just as quirky, just as frozen in time, but in a thousand insignificantly different ways.

Our room has two double beds, and just like the last room I had here, it looks out onto the street.

I set our plastic bags containing toiletries and thrift-store clothes on the dresser beside the television.

Any other time, I might have balked at this dated room that smells like cleaning product failing to cover up mildew and worse.

Tonight it feels like luxury.

Pulling off my hoodie and undershirt, I say, "I'm too gross to even have an opinion about this place."

I toss them into the waste bin.

Amanda laughs. "You don't want to get into a who's-more-disgusting competition with me."

"I'm surprised they rented us a room at any price."

"That might tell you something about the quality of establishment we're dealing with."

I go to the window, part the curtains.

It's early evening.

Raining.

The exterior hotel sign bleeds red neon light into the room.

I couldn't begin to guess the day or date.

I say, "Bathroom's all yours."

Amanda grabs her things from the plastic bag.

Soon, I can hear the bright sound of running water echoing off the tile.

She calls out, "Oh my God, you have to take a bath, Jason! You have no idea!"

I'm too dirty to lie down on the bed, so I sit on the carpet next to the radiator, letting waves of heat wash over me and watching the sky darken through the window.

I take Amanda's advice and draw a bath.

Condensation runs down the walls.

The heat works wonders on my lower back, which has been out for days from sleeping in the box.

As I shave my beard, the questions of identity keep haunting me.

There's no Jason Dessen employed as a physics professor at Lakemont College or any of the local schools, but I can't help wondering if I'm out there somewhere.

In another city.

Another country.

Perhaps living under a different name, with a different woman, a different job.

If I am, if I spend my days under broken-down cars in a mechanic's shop or drilling cavities instead of teaching physics to college students, am I still the same man at the most fundamental level?

And what is that level?

If you strip away all the trappings of personality and lifestyle, what are the core components that make me me?

After an hour, I emerge, clean for the first time in days,

wearing jeans, a plaid button-down, and an old pair of Timberlands. They're a half size too big, but I've doubled up on wool socks to compensate.

Amanda studies me appraisingly, says, "Works."

"Not so bad yourself."

Her thrift-store score consists of black jeans, boots, a white T-shirt, and a black leather jacket that still reeks of the prior owner's smoking habit.

She's lying in bed, watching a TV show I don't recognize.

She looks up at me. "Know what I'm thinking?"

"What?"

"Bottle of wine. Ridiculous amount of food. Every dessert on the menu. I mean, I haven't been this skinny since college."

"The multiverse diet."

She laughs, and it's a good thing to hear.

We walk for twenty minutes in the rain, because I want to see if one of my favorite restaurants exists in this world.

It does, and it's like running into a friend in a foreign city.

This cozy, hipster place is a riff on an old Chicago neighborhood inn.

There's a long wait for a table, so we stalk the bar until a pair of stools opens up, sliding in at the far end beside a rain-streaked window.

We order cocktails.

Then wine.

A thousand small plates that just keep coming.

We catch a hard, beautiful glow off the booze, and our conversation stays very much in the moment.

How the food is.

How good it feels to be inside and warm.

Neither of us mentions the box even once.

Amanda says I look like a lumberjack.

I tell her she looks like a biker chick.

We both laugh too hard, too loud, but we need it.

As she gets up to go to the bathroom, she says, "You'll be right here?"

"I will not move from this spot."

But she keeps looking back.

I watch her walk down the bar and disappear around the corner.

On my own, the ordinariness of the moment is almost too much to stand. I glance around the restaurant, taking in the faces of the waiters, the customers. Two dozen noisy conversations mixing into a kind of meaningless roar.

I think, What if you people knew what I knew?

The walk back is colder and wetter.

Near the hotel, I see the sign for my local bar, Village Tap, blinking across the street.

I say, "Feel like a nightcap?"

It's late enough that the bulk of the evening crowd has thinned out.

We grab seats at the bar, and I watch as the bartender finishes updating someone's ticket at the touchscreen.

He finally turns and comes over, looks at Amanda first, then me.

It's Matt. He has probably served me a thousand drinks in

my lifetime. He served me and Ryan Holder my last night in my world.

But there's no hint of recognition.

Just blank, disinterested courtesy.

"What can I get you guys?"

Amanda orders a wine.

I ask for a beer.

As he pulls the tap, I lean over and whisper to Amanda, "I know the bartender. He doesn't recognize me."

"What do you mean you know him?"

"This is my local bar."

"No. It's not. And of course he doesn't recognize you. What'd you expect?"

"It's just weird. This place looks exactly like it should."

Matt brings our drinks over.

"Want to start a tab?"

I have no credit card, no identification, nothing but a roll of cash in the inner pocket of my Members Only jacket right next to our remaining ampoules.

"I'll just settle up now." As I reach for the money, I say, "I'm Jason, by the way."

"Matt."

"I like this place. Yours?"

"Yep."

He seems not to give a single fuck what I think of his bar, and it puts a sad, hollow feeling in the pit of my stomach. Amanda senses. When Matt leaves us, she lifts her wineglass and clinks it against my pint.

Says, "To a good meal, a warm bed, and not being dead yet."

*

Back in the hotel room, we kill the lights and get undressed in the dark. I know I've lost all objectivity with regard to our accommodations, because the bed feels wonderful.

Amanda asks from her side of the room, "You locked the door?"

"I did."

I close my eyes. I can hear the rain ticking against the window. The occasional car moving past on the wet street below.

"It was a nice night," Amanda says.

"It was. I don't miss the box, but it's strange being away from it."

"I don't know about you, but my old world is feeling more and more like a ghost. You know how a dream feels the farther you get from it? It loses its color and intensity and logic. Your emotional connection to it fades."

I ask, "You think you'd ever forget it entirely? Your world?"

"I don't know. I could see it getting to the point where it didn't feel real anymore. Because it isn't. The only thing that's real in this moment is this city. This room. This bed. You and me."

In the middle of the night, I realize Amanda is beside me.

It's nothing totally new. We've slept like this in the box many times. Holding each other in darkness, as lost as two people have ever been.

The only difference now is that we're wearing nothing but our underwear and her skin is distractingly soft against mine.

Shivers of neon light slip through the curtains.

Reaching over in the dark, she takes hold of my hand and puts it around her.

Then she turns over, faces me.

"You're a better man than he ever was."

"Who?"

"The Jason I knew."

"I hope so. Jesus." I smile to flag the joke. She just stares at me with these midnight eyes. We've looked at each other a lot lately, but there's something different in the way she's looking at me now.

There's a connection here, and it's getting stronger every day.

If I moved even an inch closer in her direction, we would do this.

No question in my mind.

And if I did kiss her, if we slept together, maybe I'd feel guilty and regret it, or maybe I'd realize that she could make me happy.

Some version of me certainly kissed her in this moment.

Some version knows the answer.

But it won't be me.

She says, "If you want me to go back over there, just say it."

I say, "I don't want you to, but I need you to."

AMPOULES REMAINING: 24

Yesterday, I saw myself on the Lakemont campus in a world where Daniela had died—according to an obituary I found online at the public library—at thirty-three from brain cancer.

Today, it's a gorgeous afternoon in a Chicago where Jason Dessen died two years ago in a car accident.

I step into an art gallery in Bucktown, trying not to look at the woman behind the counter, whose nose is in a book. Instead, I focus on the walls, which are covered in oil paintings whose subject appears to be exclusively Lake Michigan.

In every season.

Every color.

Every time of day.

The woman says without looking up, "Let me know if there's anything I can help you with."

"Are you the artist?"

She sets the book aside and steps out from behind the register.

Walks over.

It's the closest I've been to Daniela since the night I helped her die. She's stunning—form-fitting jeans and a black T-shirt splattered with acrylic paint.

"I am, yes. Daniela Vargas."

She clearly doesn't know me, doesn't recognize me. I guess in this world, we never met.

"Jason Dessen."

She offers her hand, and I take it. It feels just like hers—rough and strong and adept—the hand of an artist. Paint is stuck to her fingernails. I can still feel them running down my back.

"These are amazing," I say.

"Thank you."

"I love the focus on one subject."

"I started painting the lake three years ago. It's so different season to season." She points to the one we're standing in front of. "This was one of my first attempts. That's from Juneway Beach in August. On clear days in late summer, the water turns this luminescent, greenish blue. Almost tropical." She moves down the wall. "Then you get a day like this in October, all clouded over, and it paints the water gray. I love these because there's almost no distinction between the water and the sky."

"You have a favorite season?" I ask.

"Winter."

"Really?"

"It's the most diverse, and the sunrises are spectacular. When the lake froze over last year, those were some of my best paintings."

"How do you work? *En plein air,* or—"

"From photographs mainly. I occasionally set up my easel on the shore in the summer, but I love my studio so much I rarely paint elsewhere."

The conversation stalls.

She glances back at the register.

Wanting to get back to her book probably.

Having most likely made an appraisal of my faded, thrift-store jeans and hand-me-down button-down and realized I'm unlikely to buy anything.

"Is this your gallery?" I ask, though I know the answer.

Just wanting to hear her talk.

To make this moment last as long as it possibly can.

"It's actually a co-op, but since my work is hanging this month, I'm on deck to hold down the fort."

She smiles.

Only politely.

Begins to drift away.

"If there's anything else I can—"

"I just think you're so talented."

"Oh, that's really nice of you to say. Thank you."

"My wife is an artist."

"Local?"

"Yep."

"What's her name?"

"It's um, well, you probably wouldn't know it, and we're not really together anymore, so . . ."

"Sorry to hear that."

I reach down and touch the frayed thread that's still, against all odds, tied around my ring finger.

"It's not that we're not together. It's just . . ."

I don't finish the thought, because I want her to *ask* me to finish it. To show a shred of interest, stop looking at me like a stranger, because we are not strangers.

We've made a life together.

We have a son.

I've kissed every inch of your body.

I've cried with you and laughed with you.

How can something so powerful in one world not bleed through into this one?

I stare into Daniela's eyes, but there's no love or recognition or familiarity coming back.

She just looks mildly uncomfortable.

Like she's hoping I'll leave.

"Do you want to get a cup of coffee?" I ask.

She smiles.

Now severely uncomfortable.

"I mean after you get off, whenever that is."

If she says yes, Amanda will kill me. I'm already late meeting her back at the hotel. We're supposed to return to the box this afternoon.

But Daniela isn't going to say yes.

She's biting her lip like she always does when she's nervous, no doubt trying to come up with some reason beyond a blanket, ego-destroying "no," but I can see she's drawing a blank, that she's working up the nerve to drop the hammer on my foundering ass.

"You know what?" I say. "Never mind. I'm sorry. I've put you on the spot."

Fuck.

I'm dying.

It's one thing to get shot down by a total stranger.

Another entirely to crash and burn with the mother of your child.

"I'm just going to go now."

I head for the door.

She doesn't try to stop me.

AMPOULES REMAINING: 16

Every Chicago we've stepped into this last week, the trees are looking more and more skeletal, their leaves stripped and rain-pasted to the pavement. I sit on the bench across the street from my brownstone, bundled up against the bitter morning cold in a thrift-store coat I bought yesterday for $12 with currency from another world. It smells like an old man's closet—mothballs and analgesic cream.

Back at the hotel, I left Amanda scribbling away in a notebook of her own.

I lied, told her I was going out for a walk to clear my head and get a cup of coffee.

I see myself step out the front door and move quickly down the steps and onto the sidewalk, heading for the El station, where I'll take the Purple Line to the Lakemont campus in Evanston. I'm wearing noise-canceling headphones, probably listening to a podcast—some science lecture or an episode of *This American Life.*

It's October 30 according to the front page of the *Tribune,* a little less than a month since the night I was taken at gunpoint and ripped out of my world.

Feels like I've been traveling in the box for years.

I don't know how many Chicagos we've connected to so far.

They're all beginning to blend.

This one is the closest yet, but it still isn't mine. Charlie attends a charter school, and Daniela works out of the house as a graphic designer.

Sitting here, I realize I've always looked at Charlie's birth and my choice to make a life with Daniela as the threshold event that caused the trajectory of our lives to swing away from success in our careers.

But that's an oversimplification.

Yes, Jason2 walked away from Daniela and Charlie and subsequently had the breakthrough. But there are a million Jasons who walked away and didn't invent the box.

Worlds where I left Daniela and our careers still amounted to nothing.

Or where I left and we both found moderate levels of success, but failed to set the world on fire.

And inversely, there are worlds where I stayed and we had Charlie, which branched into less-than-perfect timelines.

Where our relationship deteriorated.

Where I decided to leave our marriage.

Or Daniela did.

Or we struggled and suffered along in a loveless and broken state, toughing it out for the sake of our son.

If I represent the pinnacle of family success for all the Jason Dessens, Jason2 represents the professional and creative apex. We're opposite poles of the same man, and I suppose it isn't a coincidence that Jason2 sought out my life from the infinite possibilities available.

Though he'd experienced complete professional success, total fulfillment as a family man was as foreign to him as his life was to me.

It all points to the fact that my identity isn't binary.

It's multifaceted.

And maybe I can let go of the sting and resentment of the path not taken, because the path not taken isn't just the inverse of who I am. It's an infinitely branching system that represents all the permutations of my life between the extremes of me and Jason2.

Reaching into my pocket, I take out the prepaid mobile phone that cost $50, money that could have fed Amanda and me for a day, or put us up in a cheap motel for another night.

With my fingerless gloves, I uncrumple the torn-out sheet of yellow paper from the D section of the Chicago Metro phone book and dial the circled number.

There's something horribly lonely about a place that's almost home.

From where I sit, I can see the room on the second floor that I assume serves as Daniela's in-home office. The blinds are open and she's seated with her back to me, facing a giant monitor.

I see her lift a cordless handset and stare at the display.

Not recognizing the number.

Please answer.

She shelves the phone.

My voice: "You've reached the Dessens. We can't take your call, but if you—"

I hang up before the beep.

Call again.

This time, she picks up and answers before the second ring, "Hello?"

For a moment, I don't say anything.

Because I can't find my voice.

"Hello?"

"Hi."

"Jason?"

"Yeah."

"What number are you calling from?"

I suspected she would ask this right off the bat.

I say, "My phone's dead, so I borrowed one off this woman on the train."

"Is everything okay?"

"How's your morning going?" I ask.

"Fine. I just saw you, silly."

"I know."

She spins around on the swivel chair at her desk, says, "So you just wanted to talk to me so badly that you borrowed a stranger's phone?"

"I did, actually."

"You're sweet."

I just sit there, absorbing her voice.

"Daniela?"

"Yes?"

"I really miss you."

"What's wrong, Jason?"

"Nothing."

"You sound weird. Talk to me."

"I was walking to the El, and it just hit me."

"What did?"

"I take so many moments with you for granted. I walk out the door to work, and I'm already thinking about my day, about the lecture I have to give, whatever, and I just ... I had a moment of clarity getting on the train about how much I love you. How much you mean to me. Because you never know."

"Never know what?"

"When it could all be taken away. Anyway, I tried to call you, but my phone was dead."

For a long moment, there's just silence on the other end of the line.

"Daniela?"

"I'm here. And I feel the same way about you. You know that, right?"

I close my eyes against the emotion.

Thinking, I could cross the street right now and come inside and tell you everything.

I am so lost, my love.

Daniela steps down off her chair and walks over to the window. She's wearing a long, cream-colored sweater over yoga pants. Her hair is up, and she's holding a mug of what I suspect is tea from a local shop.

She cradles her belly, which is rounded with child.

Charlie is going to be a big brother.

I smile through the tears, wondering what he thinks of that.

It's something my Charlie missed.

"Jason, are you sure everything's okay?"

"Positive."

"Well, look, I'm on a deadline for this client, so . . ."

"You have to go."

"I do."

I don't want her to. I need to keep hearing her voice.

"Jason?"

"Yes?"

"I love you very much."

"I love you too. You have no idea."

"I'll see you tonight."

No, you'll see a very lucky version of me who has no clue how good he has it.

She hangs up.

Goes back to her desk.

I return the phone to my pocket, shivering, my thoughts running in mad directions, toward dark fantasies.

I see the train I'm riding into work derailing.

My body mangled beyond recognition.

Or never found.

I see myself stepping into this life.

It isn't mine exactly, but maybe it's close enough.

In the evening, I'm still sitting on the bench on Eleanor Street across from the brownstone that isn't mine, watching our neighbors arrive home from work and school.

What a miracle it is to have people to come home to every day.

To be loved.

To be expected.

I thought I appreciated every moment, but sitting here in the cold, I know I took it all for granted. And how could I not? Until everything topples, we have no idea what we actually have, how precariously and perfectly it all hangs together.

The sky darkens.

Up and down the block, the houses light up.

Jason comes home.

I'm in a bad way.

Haven't eaten all day.

Water hasn't touched my lips since morning.

Amanda must be losing her mind wondering where I am, but I can't drag myself away. My life, or at least a devastating approximation of it, is unfolding right across the street.

It's long after midnight when I unlock the door to our hotel room.

The lights are on, the television blaring.

Amanda climbs out of bed, wearing a T-shirt and pajama bottoms.

I close the door softly behind me.

I say, "I'm sorry."

"You asshole."

"I had a bad day."

"*You* had a bad day."

"Amanda—"

Charging toward me, she shoves me with both hands as hard as she can, sending me crashing back into the door.

She says, "I thought you'd left me. Then I thought something had happened to you. I had no way to get in touch with you. I started calling hospitals, giving them your physical description."

"I would never just leave you."

"How am I supposed to know that? You scared me!"

"I'm sorry, Amanda."

"Where have you been?"

She has me boxed in against the door.

"I just sat on this bench across the street from my house all day."

"All day? Why?"

"I don't know."

"That isn't your house, Jason. That isn't your family."

"I know that."

"Do you?"

"I also followed Daniela and Jason on a date."

"What do you mean you followed them?"

"I stood outside the restaurant where they ate."

The shame hits me as I say the words.

I push past Amanda into the room, take a seat on the end of my bed.

She comes over and stands in front of me.

I say, "They went to a movie after. I followed them inside. Sat behind them in the theater."

"Oh, Jason."

"I did something else stupid."

"What?"

"I used some of our money to buy a phone."

"Why did you need a phone?"

"So I could call Daniela and pretend to be her Jason."

I brace for Amanda to lose it again, but instead she steps toward me and cradles my neck and kisses the top of my head.

"Stand," she says.

"Why?"

"Just do what you're told."

I rise.

She unzips my jacket and helps slide my arms out of the sleeves. Then she pushes me back onto the bed and kneels.

Unlaces my boots.

Pries them off my feet and tosses them into the corner.

I say, "For the first time, I think I understand how the Jason you knew might have done what he did to me. I'm having some fucked-up thoughts."

"Our minds aren't built to handle this. Seeing all these different versions of your wife—I can't even imagine."

"He must have followed me for weeks. To work. On date nights with Daniela. He probably sat on that same bench and watched us moving through our house at night, imagining me out of the picture. Do you know what I almost did tonight?"

"What?" She looks scared to hear.

"I figure they probably keep their spare key in the same place we keep it. I left the movie early. I was going to find the key and let myself inside the house. I wanted to hide in a closet and watch their life. Watch them sleep. It's sick, I know. And I know your Jason was probably in my house multiple times before the night he finally worked up the nerve to steal my life."

"But you didn't do it."

"No."

"Because you're a decent man."

"I don't feel very decent right now."

I fall back onto the mattress and stare up at the ceiling of this hotel room that, in all its inconsequential permutations, has become our home away from the box.

Amanda crawls onto the bed beside me.

"This isn't working, Jason."

"What do you mean?"

"We're just spinning our wheels."

"I don't agree. Look where we started. Remember that first world we stepped into, with the buildings crashing down all around us?"

"I've lost count of how many Chicagos we've been to."

"We're getting closer to my—"

"We're *not* getting closer, Jason. The world you're looking for is a grain of sand on an infinite beach."

"That's not true."

"You've seen your wife murdered. Die of a horrible disease. You've seen her not recognize you. Married to other men. Married to multiple versions of you. How much more of this can you take before you suffer a psychotic break? It's not that far off from your current mental state."

"It's not about what I can or can't take. It's about finding my Daniela."

"Really? That's what you were doing sitting on a bench all day? Looking for your wife? Look at me. We have sixteen ampoules left. We're running out of chances."

My head is pounding.

Spinning.

"Jason." I feel her hands on my face now. "You know what the definition of insanity is?"

"What?"

"Doing the same thing again and again and expecting different results."

"Next time—"

"What? Next time we'll find your home? How? You going to fill another notebook tonight? Would it make a difference if you did?" She lays her hand on my chest. "Your heart is going crazy. You have to calm down."

Rolling over, she turns off the lamp on the table between the beds.

Lies down beside me, but there's nothing sexual about her touch.

My head feels better with the lights off.

The only illumination in the room is the blue neon light from the sign outside the window, and it's late enough that the passing cars on the street below are few and far between.

Sleep is riding in. Mercifully.

I shut my eyes, thinking of the five notebooks stacked on my bedside table. Almost every page is filled with my increasingly manic scrawl. I keep thinking if I write enough, if I'm specific enough, that I'll capture a full-enough picture of my world to finally take me home.

But it's not happening.

Amanda isn't wrong.

I'm looking for a grain of sand on an infinite beach.

TWELVE

In the morning, Amanda is no longer beside me. I lie on my side, watching the sunlight push through the blinds, listening to the noise of traffic humming through the walls. The clock is behind me on the bedside table. I can't see the time, but it feels late. We've slept in.

I sit up, throw back the covers, look over at Amanda's bed. It's empty.

"Amanda?"

I start quickly toward the bathroom to see if she's in there, but what I see on top of the dresser makes me stop.

Some cash.

A few coins.

Eight ampoules.

And a piece of paper ripped out of a notebook, covered in Amanda's handwriting.

Jason. After last night, it was clear to me that you've made a decision to go down a path I can't follow. I struggled with this all night. As your friend, as a therapist, I want to help you. I want to fix you. But I can't. And I can't keep watching you fall down. Especially if I'm part of the reason you keep falling down. To what extent is our collective subconscious driving our connections to these worlds? It's not that I don't want you to get back to your wife. I want nothing more. But we've been together now for weeks. It's hard not to get attached, especially under these circumstances, when you're all I have.

I read your notebooks yesterday, when I was wondering if you'd left me, and honey, you're missing the point. You're writing down all these things about your Chicago, but not what you feel.

I've left you the backpack, half the ampoules, and half the money (a whopping $161 and change). I don't know where I'll end up. I'm curious and scared, but excited too. There's a part of me that really wants to stay, but you need to choose your own next door to open. So do I.

Jason, I wish you nothing but happiness. Be safe.

Amanda

AMPOULES REMAINING: 7

By myself, the full horror of the corridor sinks in.

I have never felt so alone.

There's no Daniela in this world.

Chicago feels wrong without her.

I hate everything about it.

The color of the sky seems off.

The familiar buildings mock me.

Even the air tastes like a lie.

Because it isn't my city.

It's ours.

AMPOULES REMAINING: 6

I'm striking out.

All night, I walk the streets alone.

Dazed.

Afraid.

Letting my system purge the drug.

I eat at an all-night diner and ride the train back to the South Side at dawn.

On my way to the abandoned power plant, three teenagers see me.

They're on the other side of the road, but at this hour, the streets are empty.

They call out to me.

Taunts and slurs.

I ignore them.

Walk faster.

But I know I'm in trouble when they start across the street, purposefully moving in my direction.

For a moment, I consider running, but they're young and no doubt faster. Besides, it occurs to me as my mouth runs dry and the fight-or-flight response kicks an initial dump of adrenaline into my system that I may need my strength.

On the outskirts of a neighborhood, where the row houses end and a train yard begins, they catch up to me.

There's no one else out at this hour.

No help in sight.

They're even younger than I first thought, and the smell of malt liquor wafts off them like malicious cologne. The ragged energy they carry in their eyes suggests they've been out all night, perhaps searching for this exact opportunity.

The beating begins in earnest.

They don't even bother talking shit.

I'm too tired, too broken to fight back.

Before I even know what's happening, I'm down on the pavement getting kicked in the stomach, the back, the face.

I black out for a moment, and when I come to, I can feel their hands running up and down my body, searching—I assume—for a wallet that isn't there.

They finally rip my backpack away, and as I bleed on the pavement, take off laughing and running down the street.

I lie there for a long time, listening to the volume of traffic steadily increase.

The day grows brighter.

People walk past me on the sidewalk without stopping.

Each breath drives a wedge of pain between my bruised ribs, and my left eye is swollen shut.

After a while, I manage to sit up.

Shit.

The ampoules.

Using a chain-link fence, I drag myself onto my feet.

Please.

I snake my hand up the inside of my shirt, my fingers grazing the piece of duct tape that's affixed to my side.

It hurts like hell to peel it slowly back, but everything hurts like hell.

The ampoules are still there.

Three crushed.

Three intact.

*

I stumble back into the box and shut myself inside.

My money is gone.

My notebooks are gone.

My syringes and needles.

I have nothing but my broken body and three more chances to get this right.

AMPOULES REMAINING: 2

I spend the first half of the day begging on a South Side street corner for enough money to catch a train into the city.

I spend the rest of it four blocks from my brownstone, sitting on the pavement behind a cardboard sign that reads:

HOMELESS. DESPERATE. ANYTHING HELPS.

The condition of my battered face must go a long way toward garnering sympathy, because I collect $28.15 by the time the sun goes down.

I'm hungry, thirsty, and sore.

I choose a diner that looks shitty enough to have me, and as I pay for my meal, the exhaustion hits.

I have nowhere to go.

No money for a motel room.

Outside, the night has turned cold and rainy.

I walk to my house and head around the block to the alley, thinking of a place where I might sleep undisturbed, undetected.

There's a space between my garage and the neighbor's that's hidden behind the trash can and recycling bin. I crawl between them, taking with me a flattened box, which I lean against the wall of my garage.

Underneath it, I listen to the rain pattering on the cardboard above my head, hoping my makeshift shelter will last the night.

From my vantage point, I can see over the high fence that encircles my backyard, through a window, into the second floor of my house.

It's the master bedroom.

Jason walks past.

It isn't Jason2. I know for a fact this isn't my world. The stores and restaurants down the block from my house are wrong. These Dessens own different cars than my family. And he's heavier than I've ever been.

Daniela appears for a moment in the window, reaches up, pulls the blinds closed.

Good night, my love.

The rain intensifies.

The box sags.

I begin to shiver.

My eighth day on the streets of Logan Square, Jason Dessen himself drops a $5 bill into my collection box.

There's no danger.

I'm unrecognizable.

Sunburned and bearded and reeking of abject poverty.

The people in my neighborhood are generous. Every day, I make enough to eat a cheap meal each evening and pocket a few dollars.

Every night, I sleep in the alley behind 44 Eleanor Street.

It becomes a kind of game. When the lights in the master bedroom cut out, I close my eyes and imagine I'm him.

With her.

Some days, I feel my sanity slipping.

Amanda once said that her old world had begun to feel like a ghost, and I think I know what she means. We associate reality with the tangible—everything we can experience with our senses. And though I keep telling myself there's a box on the South Side of Chicago that can take me to a world where I have everything I want and need, I no longer believe that place exists. My reality—more and more every day—is *this* world. Where I have nothing. Where I'm a homeless, filthy creature whose existence evokes only compassion, pity, and disgust.

Nearby, another homeless man is standing in the middle of the sidewalk, having a full-volume conversation with nobody.

I think, Am I so different? Aren't we both lost in worlds that, for reasons beyond our control, no longer align with our identity?

The most frightening moments are those that seem to be arriving with increasing frequency. Moments where the idea of a magic box, even to me, sounds like the ravings of a crazy person.

One night, I pass a liquor store and realize I have enough money for a bottle of something.

I drink an entire pint of J&B.

Find myself standing in the master bedroom of 44 Eleanor

Street, staring down at Jason and Daniela, asleep in their bed under a tangle of blankets.

The bedside-table clock shows 3:38 a.m., and though the house is dead silent, I'm so drunk I can feel my pulse beating against my eardrum.

I can't piece together the thought process that brought me here.

All I can think is that I had this.

Once upon a time.

This beautiful dream of a life.

And in this moment, with the room spinning and tears streaking down my face, I actually don't know if that life of mine was real or imagined.

I take a step toward Jason's side of the bed, my eyes beginning to adjust in the darkness.

He sleeps peacefully.

I want what's his so badly I can taste it.

I'd do anything to have his life. To step into his shoes.

I imagine killing him. Choking the life out of him or shooting a bullet into his brain.

I see myself trying to be him.

Trying to accept this version of Daniela as my wife. This Charlie as my son.

Would this house ever feel like mine?

Could I sleep at night?

Could I ever look Daniela in the eyes and not think about the fear in her real husband's face two seconds before I took his life?

No.

No.

Clarity comes crashing—painful, shameful, but in the exact moment when it's so desperately needed.

The guilt and all the tiny differences would transform my life here into hell. Into a reminder not just of what I'd done, but of what I still didn't have.

This would never feel like my world.

I'm not capable of this.

I don't *want* this.

I am not this man.

I shouldn't be here.

As I stumble out of the bedroom and down the hall, I realize that to have even considered this was to give up on finding my Daniela.

To say I'm letting her go.

That she isn't attainable.

And maybe that's true. Maybe I don't have a prayer of ever finding my way back to her and Charlie and my perfect world. To that single grain of sand on an infinite beach.

But I still have two ampoules left, and I won't stop fighting until they're gone.

I go to a thrift store and buy new clothes—jeans, flannel shirt, a black peacoat.

Then toiletries at a drugstore, along with a notebook, pack of pens, and a flashlight.

I check into a motel, throw my old clothes away, and take the longest shower of my life.

The water running off my body is gray.

Standing in front of the mirror, I look almost like myself

again, though my cheekbones stand out with more prominence from malnutrition.

I sleep into the afternoon and then train down to the South Side.

The power plant is quiet, sunlight slanting through the windows of the generator room.

Sitting in the doorway of the box, I open the notebook.

I've been thinking ever since I woke up about what Amanda said in her goodbye note, how I haven't really written about what I feel.

Here goes . . .

I'm twenty-seven years old. I've worked all morning at the lab, and things are going so well I almost shrug off the party. I've been doing that a lot lately—neglecting friends and social engagements to steal just a few more hours in the cleanroom.

I first notice you in the far corner of the small backyard as I stand on the deck, sipping a Corona-and-lime, my thoughts still back at the lab. I think it's the way you're standing that catches my attention—boxed in by a tall, lanky guy in tight black jeans who I recognize from this circle of friends. He's an artist or something. I don't even know his name, only that my friend Kyle has said to me recently, Oh, that guy fucks everyone.

I can't explain it, even to this day, but as I watch him chatting up this dark-haired, dark-eyed woman in a cobalt-blue dress—you—a flash of jealousy consumes me.

Inexplicably, insanely, I want to hit him. Something in your body language suggests discomfort. You aren't smiling, your arms are crossed, and it occurs to me that you're trapped in a bad conversation, and that for some reason, I care. You hold an empty wineglass, streaked with the dregs of a red. Part of me urges, Go talk to her, save her. *The other half screams,* You know nothing about this woman, not even her name. You are not that guy.

I find myself moving toward you through the grass, carrying a new glass of wine, and when your eyes avert to mine, it feels like some piece of machinery has just seized in my chest. Like worlds colliding. As I draw near, you take the glass out of my hand as if you had previously sent me off to get it and smile with an easy familiarity, like we've known each other forever. You try to introduce me to Dillon, but the skinny-jeaned artist, now effectively cockblocked, makes his excuses and bails.

Then it's just the two of us standing in the shade of the hedgerow, and my heart is going like mad. I say, "I'm sorry to interrupt, but it looked like you might need rescuing," and you say, "Good instincts. He's pretty, but insufferable." I introduce myself. You tell me your name. Daniela. Daniela.

I only remember pieces of what was said in our first moments together. Mainly how you laugh when I tell you I'm an atomic physicist, but not derisively. As if the revelation truly delights you. I remember how the wine had stained your lips. I've always known, on a purely intellectual level, that our separateness and isolation are an illusion. We're all made of the same thing—the blown-out pieces of matter formed in the fires of dead stars. I've just never felt that knowledge in my bones until that moment, there, with you. And it's because of you.

Yes, maybe I just want to get laid, but I also wonder if this sense of entanglement might be evidence of something deeper. This line of thinking I wisely keep to myself. I remember the pleasant buzz from the beer and the warmth of the sun, and then, as it begins to drop, realizing how badly I want to leave this party with you but not having the balls to ask. And then you say, "I have a friend whose gallery opening is tonight. Want to come?"

And I think: I will go anywhere with you.

AMPOULES REMAINING: I

I walk the infinite corridor, the beam of my flashlight glancing off the walls.

After a while, I stop in front of a door like all the rest.

One in a trillion, trillion, trillion.

My heart is racing, my palms sweating.

There is nothing else I want.

Just my Daniela.

I want her in a way I can't explain.

That I don't ever want to be able to explain, because the mystery of it is a perfect thing.

I want the woman I saw at that backyard party all those years ago.

The one I chose to make a life with, even though it meant giving up some other things I loved.

I want her.
Nothing more.
I draw in a breath.
I let it out.
And I open the door.

THIRTEEN

Snow from a recent storm has dusted the concrete and coated the generators beneath those glassless upper windows.

Even now, flurries blow in off the lake, drifting down like cold confetti.

I wander away from the box, trying to temper my hope.

This could be an abandoned power plant in South Chicago in any number of worlds.

As I move slowly down the row of generators, a glint on the floor catches my eye.

I approach.

Resting in a crack in the concrete six inches from the base of the generator: an empty ampoule with its neck snapped off. In all the abandoned power plants I've passed through during the last month, I've never seen this.

Perhaps the one Jason2 injected himself with seconds before I lost consciousness, on the night he stole my life.

I hike out of the industrial ghost town.

Hungry, thirsty, exhausted.

The skyline looms to the north, and even though it's decapitated by the low winter clouds, it's unmistakably the one I know.

*

I board the northbound Red Line at Eighty-Seventh Street as dusk is falling.

There are no seat belts, no holograms on this El.

Just a slow, rickety ride through South Chicago.

Then the urban sprawl of downtown.

I switch trains.

The Blue Line carries me into the gentrified northern neighborhoods.

Over the last month, I've been in Chicagos that looked similar, but there's something different about this one. It isn't just that empty ampoule. It's something deeper that I can't explain other than to say it feels like a place where I belong. It feels like mine.

As we cruise past gridlocked rush-hour traffic on the expressway, the snow intensifies.

I wonder—

Is Daniela, *my* Daniela, alive and well under the snow-laden clouds?

Is my Charlie breathing the air of this world?

I exit the train onto the El platform in Logan Square and thrust my hands deep into the pockets of my coat. Snow is sticking to the familiar streets of my neighborhood. To the sidewalks. To the cars parked along the curbs. The headlight beams from rush-hour traffic slash through the profusion of snowflakes.

Up and down my block, the houses stand glowing and lovely in the storm.

A fragile half inch has already collected on the steps to my porch, where a single set of footprints leads to the door.

Through the front window of the brownstone, I see the

lights on inside, and from where I stand on the sidewalk, this looks exactly like home.

I keep expecting to discover that some minor detail is off—the wrong front door, the wrong street number, a piece of furniture on the stoop I don't recognize.

But the door is right.

The street number is right.

There's even a tesseract chandelier hanging above the dinner table in the front room, and I'm close enough to see the large photograph on the mantel—Daniela, Charlie, and me at Inspiration Point in Yellowstone National Park.

Through the open doorway that leads from the dining room into the kitchen, I glimpse Jason standing at the island, holding a bottle of wine. Reaching across, he pours into someone's wineglass.

Elation hits, but it doesn't last.

From my vantage point, all I can see is a beautiful hand holding the stem of the glass, and it crashes down on me again what this man did to me.

All that he took.

Everything he stole.

I can't hear anything out here in the snow, but I see him laugh and take a sip of wine.

What are they talking about?

When was the last time they fucked?

Is Daniela happier now than she was a month ago, with me?

Can I stand to know the answer to that question?

The sane, even voice in my head is wisely suggesting that I move away from the house right now.

I'm not ready to do this. I have no plan.

Only rage and jealousy.

And I shouldn't get ahead of myself. I still need more confirmation that this is my world.

A little ways down the block, I see the familiar back end of our Suburban. Walking over, I brush off the snow that's clinging to the Illinois tag.

The license plate number is mine.

The paint is the right color.

I clear the back windshield.

The purple Lakemont Lions decal looks perfect, inasmuch as it's half ripped off. I instantly regretted putting the sticker on the glass the moment I did it. Tried to tear it off, but only managed to remove the top half of the lion's face, so all that's left is a growling mouth.

But that was three years ago.

I need something more recent, more definitive.

Several weeks before I was abducted, I accidentally backed the Suburban into a parking meter near campus. It didn't do much damage beyond cracking the right rear taillight and denting in the bumper.

I wipe the snow off the red plastic of the taillight and then the bumper.

I touch the crack.

I touch the dent.

No other Suburban in the countless Chicagos I've visited has borne these markings.

Rising, I glance across the street toward that bench where I once spent an entire day watching another version of my life unfold. It's empty at the moment, the snow piling up silently on the seat.

Shit.

A few feet behind the bench, a figure watches me through the snowy darkness.

I begin walking quickly down the sidewalk, thinking it probably looked as if I were stealing the license plate off the Suburban.

I have to be more careful.

The blue neon sign in the front window of Village Tap blinks through the storm, like a signal from a lighthouse, telling me I'm close to home.

There is no Hotel Royale in this world, so I check into the sad Days Inn across from my local bar.

Two nights is all I can afford, and it brings my cash reserves down to $120 and change.

The business center is a tiny room down the hallway on the first floor, with a borderline-obsolete desktop, fax machine, and printer.

Online, I confirm three pieces of information.

Jason Dessen is a professor in the Lakemont physics department.

Ryan Holder just won the Pavia award for his research contributions in the field of neuroscience.

Daniela Vargas-Dessen isn't a renowned Chicago artist, and she doesn't run a graphic-design business. Her charmingly amateurish website displays several pieces of her best work and advertises her services as an art instructor.

As I trudge up the stairwell to my third-floor room, I finally begin to let myself believe.

This is my world.

I sit by the window of my hotel room, staring down at the blinking neon sign of Village Tap.

I am not a violent person.

I've never hit a man.

Never even tried to.

But if I want my family back, there's simply no way around it.

I have to do a terrible thing.

Have to do what Jason2 did to me, only without the conscience-protecting option of simply putting him back into the box. Even though I have one ampoule left, I wouldn't repeat his mistake.

He should've killed me when he had the chance.

I feel the physicist side of my brain creeping in, trying to take over the controls.

I'm a scientist, after all. A process-minded thinker.

So I think of this like a lab experiment.

There's a result I want to achieve.

What are the steps it will take for me to arrive at that result?

First, define the desired result.

Kill the Jason Dessen who's living in my home and put him in a place where no one will ever find him again.

What tools do I need to accomplish that?

A car.

A gun.

Some method of restraining him.

A shovel.

A safe place to dispose of his body.

I hate these thoughts.

Yes, he took my wife, my son, my life, but the idea of the preparation and the violence is so ugly.

There's a forest preserve an hour south of Chicago. Kankakee River State Park. I've been there several times with Charlie and Daniela, usually in the fall when the leaves are turning and we're antsy for wilderness and solitude and a day out of the city.

I could drive Jason2 there at night, or make *him* drive, just like he did to me.

Lead him down one of the trails I know on the north side of the river.

I will have been there a day or two prior, so his grave will already be dug in some quiet, secluded place. I'll have researched how deep to make it so animals can't smell the rot. Make him think he's going to dig his own grave, so he thinks he has more time to figure out an escape or to convince me not to do this. Then, when we're within twenty feet of the hole, I'll drop the shovel and say that it's time to start digging.

As he bends down to pick it up, I'll do the thing I can't imagine.

I will fire a bullet into the back of his head.

Then I'll drag him over to the hole and roll him into it and cover him up with dirt.

The good news is that no one will be looking for him.

I'll slide back into his life the same way he slid into mine.

Maybe years down the road, I'll tell Daniela the truth.

Maybe I'll never tell her.

*

The sporting-goods store is three blocks away and still an hour shy of closing. I used to come in here once a year to buy cleats and balls when Charlie was into soccer during middle school.

Even then, the gun counter always held a fascination for me.

A mystique.

I could never imagine what would drive someone to want to own one.

I've only fired a gun two or three times in my life, while I was in high school in Iowa. Even then, shooting at rusted oil drums on my best friend's farm, I didn't experience the same thrill as the other kids. It scared me too much. As I would stand facing the target, aiming the heavy pistol, I couldn't escape the thought that I was holding death.

The store is called Field and Glove, and I'm one of three customers at this late hour.

Wandering past racks of windbreakers and a wall of running shoes, I make my way toward the counter at the back of the store.

Shotguns and rifles hang on the wall over boxes of ammunition.

Handguns gleam under glass at the counter.

Black ones.

Chrome ones.

Ones with cylinders.

Ones without.

Ones that look like they should only be carried by vigilante cops in 1970s action movies.

A woman walks over wearing a black T-shirt and faded blue jeans. She's got a distinct Annie Oakley vibe with her frizzy red hair and a tattoo that wraps around her freckled right arm and reads: . . . *the right of the people to keep and bear Arms, shall not be infringed.*

"Help you with something?" she asks.

"Yeah, I was looking to buy a handgun, but to be honest, I don't know the first thing about them."

"Why do you want one?"

"Home defense."

She pulls a set of keys out of her pocket and unlocks the cabinet I'm standing in front of. I watch her arm reach under the glass and lift out a black pistol.

"So this is a Glock 23. Forty caliber. Austrian-made. Solid knockdown power. I could also set you up in a subcompact version if you wanted something smaller for a concealed-carry permit."

"And this will stop an intruder?"

"Oh yeah. This'll put 'em down, and they won't be getting back up."

She pulls the slide, checks to make sure the tube is clear, and then locks it back and ejects the magazine.

"How many bullets does it hold?"

"Thirteen rounds."

She offers me the gun.

I'm not exactly sure what I'm supposed to do with it. Aim it? Feel the weight?

I hold it awkwardly in my hand, and even though it isn't loaded, I register that same *I'm-holding-death* unease.

The price tag hanging from the trigger guard reads $599.99.

I need to figure out my money situation. I could probably

walk into the bank and tap Charlie's savings account. It had a balance of around $4,000 the last time I looked. Charlie never accesses that account. No one does. If I withdrew a couple thousand dollars, I doubt it would be missed. At least, not right away. Of course, I'd need to somehow get my hands on a driver's license first.

"What do you think of it?" she asks.

"Yeah. I mean, it feels like a gun."

"I could show you a few others. I have a really nice Smith and Wesson .357 if you were thinking more along the lines of a revolver."

"No, this would do fine. I just need to scrape together some cash. What's the background-check process?"

"Do you have a FOID card?"

"What's that?"

"A firearm owners' identification card that's issued by the Illinois State Police. You have to apply for it."

"How long does that take?"

She doesn't answer.

Just stares at me strangely, then reaches out and takes the Glock from my hand and returns it to its resting place under the glass.

I ask, "Did I say something wrong?"

"You're Jason, right?"

"How do you know my name?"

"I've been standing here trying to put it all together, to make sure I wasn't crazy. You don't know *my* name?"

"No."

"See, I think you're messing with me, and it's not a wise—"

"I've never spoken to you before. In fact, I haven't been in this store in probably four years."

She locks the cabinet and returns the key ring to her pocket.

"I think you should leave now, Jason."

"I don't understand—"

"If this isn't some game, then you have a head injury or Alzheimer's or you're just plain crazy."

"What are you talking about?"

"You really don't know?"

"No."

She leans her elbows on the counter. "Two days ago, you walked in here, said you wanted to buy a handgun. I showed you the same Glock. You said it was for home defense."

What does this mean? Is Jason2 generally preparing in case I possibly return, or is he actually expecting me?

"Did you sell me a gun?" I ask.

"No, you didn't have a FOID card. You said you needed to get cash. I don't think you even had a driver's license."

Now a prickling sensation trails down my spine.

My knees go weak.

She says, "And it wasn't just two days ago. I got a weird vibe from you, so yesterday, I asked Gary, who also works the gun counter, if he'd ever seen you in here before. He had. Three other times in the last week. And now, here you are again."

I brace myself against the counter.

"So, Jason, I don't ever want to see you in this store again. Not even to buy a jockstrap. If I do, I'll call the police. Do you understand what I'm telling you?"

She looks scared and resolute, and I would not want to cross her in a dark alley where she took me for a threat.

I say, "I understand."

"Get out of my store."

I step out into the pouring snow, the flakes blasting my face, my head spinning.

I glance down the street, see a cab approaching. When I raise my arm, it veers toward me, easing to a stop alongside the curb. Pulling open the rear passenger door, I hop in.

"Where to?" the cabbie asks.

Where to.

Great question.

"A hotel, please."

"Which one?"

"I don't know. Something within ten blocks. Something cheap. I want you to pick it."

He looks back through the Plexiglas separating the front and backseats.

"You want *me* to pick it?"

"Yes."

For a moment, I think he isn't going to do it. Maybe it's too weird a request. Maybe he's going to order me out. But instead, he starts the meter running and pulls back out into traffic.

I stare through the window at the snow falling through headlights, taillights, streetlights, flashing lights.

My heart stomping inside my chest, my thoughts racing.

I need to calm down.

Approach this logically, rationally.

The cab pulls over in front of a seedy-looking hotel called the End o' Days.

The cabbie glances back, asks, "This work for you?"

I pay the fare and head for the front office.

There's a Bulls game on the radio and a heavy hotel clerk behind the desk eating Chinese food from a fleet of white cartons.

Brushing the snow off my shoulders, I check in under the name of my mother's father—Jess McCrae.

I pay for a single night.

It leaves me with $14.76.

I head up to the fourth floor and lock myself inside the room behind the deadbolt and the chain.

It's utterly without life.

A bed with a depressing floral-print comforter.

Formica table.

Dressers built of particleboard.

At least it's warm.

I move to the curtains and peek outside.

It's snowing hard enough that the streets are beginning to empty and the pavement is frosting over, showing the tire tracks of passing cars.

I undress and stow my last ampoule in the Gideon Bible in the bottom drawer of the bedside table.

Then I jump in the shower.

I need to think.

I ride the elevator down to the first floor and use my keycard to access the business center.

I have an idea.

Bringing up the free email service I use in this world, I type in the first idea for a username that comes to mind.

My name spelled out in Pig Latin: *asonjayessenday*.

Not surprisingly, it's already taken.

The password is obvious.

The one I've used for almost everything the last twenty years—the make, model, and year of my first car: *jeepwrangler89*.

I attempt to log in.

It works.

I find myself in a newly created email account whose inbox contains several introductory emails from the provider and one recent email from "Jason" that has already been opened.

The subject heading: Welcome Home The Real Jason Dessen

I open it.

There's no message in the email.

Just a hyperlink.

The new page loads and an alert pops up on the screen:

Welcome to UberChat!
There are currently three active participants.
Are you a new user?

I click *Yes*.

Your username is Jason9.

I have to create a password before logging in.

A large window displays the entire history of a conversation.

A selection of emoticons.

A small field in which to type and send public messages to the board and private messages to individual participants.

I scroll to the top of the conversation, which started approximately eighteen hours ago. The most recent message is forty minutes old.

JasonADMIN: I've seen some of you around the house. I know there's more of you out there.

Jason3: Is this seriously happening?

Jason4: Is this seriously happening?

Jason6: Unreal.

Jason3: So how many of you went to field & glove?

JasonADMIN: Three days ago.

Jason4: Two.

Jason6: I bought one in South Chicago.

Jason5: You have a gun?

Jason6: Yes.

JasonADMIN: Who all thought about Kankakee?

Jason3: Guilty.

Jason4: Guilty.

Jason6: I actually drove out there and dug a hole last night. Was all ready to go. Had a car lined up. Shovel. Rope. Everything planned out perfectly. This evening, I went to the house to wait for the Jason who did this to all of us to leave. But then I saw myself behind the Suburban.

Jason8: Why'd you call it off, jason6?

Jason6: What's the point of going forward with it? If I got rid of him, one of you would just show up and do the same thing to me.

Jason3: Did everyone run through the game-theory scenarios?

Jason4: Yes.

Jason6: Yes.

Jason8: Yes.

JasonADMIN: Yes.

Jason3: So we all know there's no way this ends well.

Jason4: You could all just kill yourselves and let me have her.

JasonADMIN: I opened this chat room and have administrator controls. Five more Jasons are lurking right now, just FYI.

Jason3: Why don't we all join forces and conquer the world? Can you imagine what would happen with this many versions of us actually working together? (Only half-kidding)

Jason6: Can I imagine what would happen? Totally. They'd put us in a government lab and test us until the end of time.

Jason4: Can I just say what we're all thinking? This is fucking weird.

Jason5: I have a gun too. None of you fought as hard as I did to get home. None of you saw what I saw.

Jason7: You have no idea what the rest of us went through.

Jason5: I saw hell. Literally. Hell. Where are you right now,

Jason7: I've already killed two of us.

Another alert flashes across the screen:

You have a private message from Jason7.

I open the message, my head pounding, exploding.

I know this situation is totally insane, but do you want to partner with me? Two minds are stronger than one. We could work together to get rid of the others, and when all the smoke has cleared, I'm sure we can figure something out. Time is critical. What do you say?

What do I say?

I can hardly breathe.

I leave the business center.

Sweat runs down my sides, but I feel so cold.

The first-floor hallway is empty, quiet.

I hurry to the elevator and ride up to the fourth floor.

Stepping off onto the beige carpeting, I move quickly down the hall and lock myself back in my room.

Spiraling.

How did I not anticipate this happening?

In hindsight, it was inevitable.

Though I wasn't branching into alternate realities in the corridor, I certainly was in every world I stepped into. Which means other versions of me were split off in those worlds of ash and ice and plague.

The infinite nature of the corridor precluded me from running into more versions of myself, but I did see one—the Jason with his back flayed open.

Undoubtedly most of those Jasons were killed or lost forever in other worlds, but some, like me, made the right choices. Or got lucky. Their paths might have altered from mine, through different doors, different worlds, but they eventually found their respective ways back to this Chicago.

We all want the same thing—to get our life back.

Jesus.

Our life.

Our family.

What if most of these other Jasons are exactly like me? Decent men who want back what was taken from them. And if that's the case, what right do I have to Daniela and Charlie over the rest of them?

This isn't just a game of chess. It's a game of chess against myself.

I don't want to see it this way, but I can't help it. The other Jasons want the thing in the world that is most precious to me—my family. That makes them my enemy. I ask myself what I would be willing to do to regain my life. Would I kill another version of me if it meant I could spend the rest of my days with Daniela? Would they?

I picture these other versions of me sitting in their lonely hotel rooms, or walking the snowy streets, or watching my brownstone, wrestling with this exact line of thinking.

Asking themselves these same questions.

Attempting to forecast their doppelgängers' next moves.

There can be no sharing. It's strictly competitive, a zero-sum game, where only one of us can win.

If anyone is reckless, if things get out of hand and Daniela or Charlie is injured or killed, then no one wins. That must be why things seemed normal when I looked inside the front window of my house several hours ago.

No one knows which move to make, so no one has made a play against Jason2.

It's a classic setup, pure game theory.

A terrifying spin on the Prisoner's Dilemma that asks, Is it possible to outthink yourself?

I'm not safe.

My family isn't safe.

But what can I do?

If every possible move I think of is doomed to be anticipated or made before I even get a chance, where does that leave me?

I feel like crawling out of my skin.

The worst days in the box—volcanic ash raining down on my face, almost freezing to death, seeing Daniela in a world where she had never said my name—none of it compares to the storm that's roiling inside of me in this moment.

I've never felt farther from home.

The phone rings, snapping me back into the present.

I walk over to the table, lift the receiver on the third ring. "Hello?"

No response, only soft breathing.

I hang up the phone.

Move to the window.

Part the curtains.

Four floors below, the street is empty, the snow still pouring down.

The phone rings again, but only once this time.

Weird.

As I ease back down onto the bed, the phone call keeps needling me.

What if another version of me is trying to confirm that I'm in my room?

First, how the hell would he find me at this hotel?

The answer comes fast, and it's terrifying.

At this very moment, there must be numerous versions of me in Logan Square doing exactly what he's doing—calling every motel and hotel in my neighborhood to find other Jasons. It isn't luck that he found me. It's a statistical probability. Even a handful of Jasons, making a dozen phone calls each, could cover all the hotels within a few miles of my house.

But would the clerk give out my room number?

Maybe not intentionally, but it's possible the man downstairs listening to the Bulls game and stuffing his face with Chinese food could be duped.

How would *I* dupe him?

If it were anyone other than me looking for me, the name I checked in under would probably keep me undetected. But all these other versions know my mother's father's name. I screwed that up. If using that name was my first impulse, it would have also been another Jason's first impulse. So assuming I knew the name I might have checked in under, what would I do next?

The front desk wouldn't just give out my room number.

I'd have to pretend to know that I was staying here.

I would call the hotel and ask to be connected to Jess McCrae's room.

When I heard my voice pick up on the other end of the line, I would know I was here and hang up right away.

Then I would call back thirty seconds later and say to the clerk, "Sorry to bother you again, but I just called a second ago and was accidentally disconnected. Could you please reconnect me to . . . Oh shit, what room number was that?"

And if I got lucky, and the front-desk clerk was an absent-minded idiot, there'd be a decent chance he would just blurt out my room number before reconnecting me.

Thus the first call to confirm it was me who answered.

Thus the second, where the caller hung up right after learning which room I'm staying in.

I rise from the bed.

The thought is absurd, but I can't ignore it.

Am I coming up here right now to kill me?

I slide my arms into the sleeves of my wool coat and head for the door.

I feel dizzy with fear, even as I second-guess myself, thinking maybe I'm crazy. Maybe I'm rushing to some outlandish explanation of a mundane thing—the phone ringing twice in my room.

Perhaps.

But after that chat room, nothing would surprise me.

What if I'm right and don't listen to my gut?

Go.

Right now.

I slowly open the door.

Step out into the hall.

It's empty.

Silent save for the low-register hum of the fluorescent lights above me.

Stairs or elevator?

At the far end of the hallway, the elevator dings.

I hear the doors begin to part, and then a man in a wet jacket steps out of the elevator car.

For a moment, I can't move.

Can't tear my eyes away.

It's me walking toward me.

Our eyes meet.

He isn't smiling.

Wears no emotion on his face but a chilling intensity.

He raises a gun, and I'm suddenly running in the opposite direction, sprinting down the hallway toward the door at the far end that I'm praying isn't locked.

I crash through under the glowing Exit sign, glancing back as I enter the stairwell.

My doppelgänger runs toward me.

Down the steps, my hand sliding along the guardrail to steady my balance, thinking, *Don't fall, don't fall, don't fall.*

As I reach the third-floor landing, I hear the door bang open above me, the echo of his footsteps filling the stairwell.

I keep descending.

Hit the second floor.

Then the first, where one door with a window in the center leads into the lobby and another without a window leads elsewhere.

I choose elsewhere, smashing through . . .

Into a wall of freezing, snow-filled air.

I stumble down some steps into several inches of fresh powder, my shoes slipping on the frosted pavement.

Just as I right myself, a figure emerges out of the shadows of the alley between two Dumpsters.

Wearing a coat like mine.

His hair dusted with snow.

It's me.

The blade in his hand throws a glint of light from the nearby streetlamp, and he advances on me, a knife spearing toward my abdomen—the knife that came standard-issue with the Velocity Laboratories backpack.

I sidestep at the last conceivable moment, grabbing his arm and slinging him with all my power into the steps that lead up to the hotel.

He crashes into the stairs as the door busts open above us, and two seconds before I run for my life, I commit the most impossible image to memory: one version of myself stepping out of the stairwell with a gun, the other version picking himself up off the stairs, his hands frantically searching for his knife, which has disappeared in the snow.

Are they a pair?

Working together to murder every Jason they can find?

I race between the buildings, snow plastering my face, my lungs burning.

Turning out onto the sidewalk of the next street, I look back down the alley, see two shadows moving toward me.

I head through the blowing snow.

No one out.

The streets empty.

Several doors down, I hear an explosion of noise—people cheering.

I rush toward it, pushing through a scuffed, wooden door into a dive bar with standing room only, everyone turned facing the row of flatscreens above the bar, where the Bulls are locked in a fourth-quarter death match with the visiting team.

I force my way into the crowd, letting it swallow me.

There's nowhere to sit, barely anyplace to stand, but I finally carve out a cramped square foot of legroom underneath a dartboard.

Everyone is glued to the game, but I'm watching the door.

The Bulls' point guard drains a three-point shot, and the room erupts in a roar of pure joy, strangers high-fiving and embracing.

The door to the bar swings open.

I see myself standing in the threshold, covered in snow.

He takes a step inside.

I lose him for a moment, then see him again as the crowd undulates.

What has this version of Jason Dessen experienced? What worlds did he see? What hell did he fight through to arrive back in this Chicago?

He scans the crowd.

Behind him, I can see the snow falling outside.

His eyes look hard and cold, but I wonder if he would say the same about me.

As his gaze tracks toward where I'm standing in the back of the room, I squat beneath the dartboard, hidden in a forest of legs.

I let a full minute pass.

When the crowd roars again, I slowly stand.

The door to the bar is closed now.

My doppelgänger gone.

The Bulls win.

People linger, happy and drunk.

It takes an hour for a spot to open up at the bar, and since I have no place to go, I climb onto a stool and order a light beer that brings my balance down to less than $10.

I'm starving, but this place doesn't serve food, so I devour several bowls of Chex mix as I nurse my beer.

An inebriated man attempts to engage me in a conversation about the Bulls' postseason chances, but I just stare down into my beer until he insults me and starts bothering two women standing behind us.

He's loud, belligerent.

A bouncer appears and hauls him outside.

The crowd thins.

As I sit at the bar, trying to tune out the noise, I keep landing on a single concept: I need to get Daniela and Charlie away from our brownstone on 44 Eleanor Street. As long as they're home, the threat of these Jasons doing something crazy persists.

But how?

Jason2 is presumably with them right now.

It's the middle of the night.

Going anywhere near our house entails way too much risk.

I need Daniela to leave, to come to me.

But for every idea I have, another Jason is having the same, or already has, or soon will.

There's no way for me to win.

As the door to the bar swings open, I look over.

A version of me—backpack, peacoat, boots—steps through the doorway, and when our eyes meet, he betrays surprise and raises both arms in a show of deference.

Good. Maybe he's not here for me.

If there are as many Jasons running around Logan Square as I suspect, chances are he just stumbled in out of the cold, seeking shelter and safety. Like I did.

He crosses to the bar and climbs onto the empty stool beside mine, his bare hands trembling with cold.

Or fear.

The bartender drifts over and looks at both of us with curiosity—as if she *wants* to ask—but all she says to the new arrival is, "What can I get you?"

"Whatever he's drinking."

We watch her pull a pint from the tap and bring over the glass, foam spilling down the sides.

Jason lifts his beer.

I lift mine.

We stare at each other.

He has a fading wound across the right side of his face, like someone slashed him with a knife.

The thread tied around his ring finger is identical to mine.

We drink.

"When did you get—?"

"When did you get—?"

We can't help but smile.

I say, "This afternoon. You?"

"Yesterday."

"I have a feeling it's going to be kind of hard—"

"—not finishing each other's sentences?"

"You know what I'm thinking right now?"

"I can't read your mind."

It's strange—I'm talking to myself, but his voice doesn't sound like what I think I sound like.

I say, "I'm wondering how far back you and I branched. Did you see the world of falling ash?"

"Yes. And then the ice. I barely escaped that one."

"What about Amanda?" I ask.

"We were separated in the storm."

I feel a pang of loss like a small detonation in my gut.

I say, "We stayed together in mine. Took shelter in a house."

"The one that was buried to the dormer windows?"

"Exactly."

"I found that house too. With the dead family inside."

"So then where—?"

"So then where—?"

"You go," he says.

As he sips his beer, I ask, "Where did you go after the ice world?"

"I walked out of the box into this guy's basement. He freaked out. He had a gun, tied me up. Probably would have killed me except he took one of the ampoules and decided to have a look at the corridor for himself."

"So he went in and never came out."

"Exactly."

"And then?"

His eyes go distant for a moment.

He takes another long pull from his beer.

"Then I saw some bad ones. Really bad. Dark worlds. Evil places. What about you?"

I share my story, and though it feels good to unload, it's undeniably strange to unload on him.

This man and I were the same person up until a month ago. Which means ninety-nine-point-nine percent of our history is shared.

We've said the same things. Made identical choices. Experienced the same fears.

The same love.

As he buys our second round of beers, I can't take my eyes off him.

I'm sitting next to me.

There's something about him that doesn't seem quite real.

Perhaps because I'm watching from an impossible vantage point—looking at myself from outside of myself.

He looks strong, but also tired, damaged, and afraid.

It's like talking to a friend who knows everything about you, but there's an added layer of excruciating familiarity. Aside from the last month, there are no secrets between us. He knows every bad thing I've done. Every thought I've entertained. My weaknesses. My secret fears.

"We call him Jason2," I say, "which implies that we think of ourselves as Jason1. As the original. But we can't both be Jason1. And there are others out there who think *they're* the original."

"None of us are."

"No. We're pieces of a composite."

"Facets," he says. "Some very close to being the same man, like I assume you and I are. Some worlds apart."

I say, "It makes you think about yourself in a different light, doesn't it?"

"Makes me wonder, who is the ideal Jason? Does he even exist?"

"All you can do is live the best version of yourself, right?"

"Took the words."

The bartender announces last call.

I say, "Not many people can say they've done this."

"What? Share a beer with themselves?"

"Yeah."

He finishes his beer.

I finish mine.

Sliding off his stool, he says, "I'll leave first."

"Which way are you heading?"

He hesitates. "North."

"I'm not going to follow you. Can I expect the same?"

"Yes."

"We can't both have them."

He says, "Who deserves them is the question, and there may be no answer. But if it comes down to you and me, I won't let you stop me from being with Daniela and Charlie. I won't like it, but I'll kill you if it comes to that."

"Thanks for the beer, Jason."

I watch him go.

Wait five minutes.

I'm the last one to leave.

It's still snowing.

There's a half foot of fresh powder on the streets, and the snowplows are out.

Stepping down onto the sidewalk, I take a moment to absorb my surroundings.

Several customers from the bar are staggering away, but I see no one else out on the streets.

I don't know where to go.

I *have* nowhere to go.

Two valid hotel keycards in my pocket, but it wouldn't be safe to use either of them. Other Jasons could have easily obtained copies. They could be inside my room at this moment, waiting for me to return.

It dawns on me—my last ampoule is back at that second hotel.

Gone now.

I start walking down the sidewalk.

It's two in the morning, and I'm running on fumes.

How many other Jasons are wandering these streets at this very moment, facing the same fears, the same questions?

How many have been killed?

How many are out hunting?

I can't escape the feeling that I'm not safe in Logan Square, even in the middle of the night. Every alley I pass, every shadowy doorway, I'm looking for movement, for someone coming after me.

A half mile brings me to Humboldt Park.

I track through the snow.

Out into a silent field.

I'm beyond tired.

My legs aching.

My stomach rumbling with hunger.

I can't keep going.

A large evergreen towers in the distance, its branches sagging with snow.

The lowest limbs are four feet off the ground, but they offer some semblance of shelter from the storm.

Close to the trunk, there's only a dusting of snow, and I brush it away and sit in the dirt against the tree on the leeward side.

It's so quiet.

I can hear the distant mumble of snowplows moving through the city.

The sky is neon pink from all the lights reflecting off the low clouds.

I draw my coat in close and ball my hands into fists to preserve some core heat.

From where I sit, my view is of an open field, interspersed with trees.

The snow falls through the streetlamps along a distant walking path, making coronas of brilliant flakes near the light.

Nothing moves out there.

It's cold, but not as bad as it might be if the skies were calm and clear.

I don't think I'm going to freeze to death.

But I don't think I'm going to sleep either.

As I shut my eyes, an idea strikes me.

Randomness.

How do you beat an opponent who is inherently wired to predict any and all moves you might make?

You do something completely random.

Unplanned.

You make a move you haven't considered, to which you've given little or no prior thought.

Maybe it's a bad move that blows up in your face and costs you the game.

But perhaps it's a play the other you never saw coming, which gives you an unanticipated strategic advantage.

So how do I apply that line of thinking to my situation?

How do I do something utterly random that defies anticipation?

*

Somehow I sleep.

Wake up shivering to a world of gray and white.

The snow and the wind have stopped, and through the leafless trees I can see pieces of the skyline in the distance, the highest buildings just touching the cloud deck that overhangs the city.

The open field is white and still.

It's dawn.

The streetlamps wink out.

I sit up, unbelievably stiff.

There's the faintest dusting of snow on my coat.

My breath plumes in the cold.

Of all the versions of Chicago I've seen, none can touch the serenity of this morning.

Where the empty streets keep everything hushed.

Where the sky is white and the ground is white and the buildings and the trees stand starkly against it all.

I think of the seven million people still in bed under the covers or standing at their windows, looking out between the curtains at what the storm left behind.

Something so safe and comforting in the imagining of it.

I struggle onto my feet.

I woke up with a crazy idea.

Something that happened in the bar last night, right before the other Jason showed up, inspired it. It's nothing I would have ever thought of on my own, which makes me almost trust it.

Heading back across the park, I walk north toward Logan Square.

Toward home.

*

At the first convenience store I come to, I go inside and buy a single Swisher Sweets cigar and a mini BIC lighter.

$8.21 remaining.

My coat is damp from the snow.

I hang it at the rack by the entrance and make my way down the counter.

This place feels gloriously authentic, as if it's always been here. The 1950s-era vibe isn't from the red-vinyl upholstering on the booths and stools or the framed photographs of regulars on the walls down through the decades. It comes, I think, from never changing. The smell of the place is all bacon grease and brewing coffee and the indelible remnants of a time when I would've been moving through clouds of cigarette smoke en route to a table.

Aside from a few customers at the counter, I spot two cops in one booth, three nurses just off-shift in another, and an old man in a black suit staring with a kind of bored intensity into his cup of coffee.

I sit at the counter just to be near the heat radiating off the open grill.

An ancient waitress comes over.

I know I must look homeless and strung-out, but she doesn't let on, doesn't judge, just takes my order with a worn-out midwestern courtesy.

It feels good to be indoors.

The windows are fogging up.

The cold is leaving my bones.

This all-night diner is only eight blocks from my house, but I've never eaten here.

When the coffee arrives, I wrap my dirty fingers around the ceramic mug and soak in the warmth.

I had to do the math in advance.

All I can afford is this cup of coffee, two eggs, and some toast.

I try to eat slowly, to make it last, but I'm famished.

The waitress takes pity on me and brings more toast at no extra charge.

She's kind.

It makes me feel even lousier about what's going to happen.

I check the time on my drug-dealer flip phone, the one I bought to call Daniela in another Chicago. It won't make calls in this world—I guess minutes aren't transferable across the multiverse.

8:15 a.m.

Jason2 probably left for work twenty minutes ago in order to catch the train to his 9:30 lecture.

Or maybe he hasn't left at all. Maybe he's sick, or staying home today for some reason I've not anticipated. That would be a disaster, but it's too risky for me to go anywhere near my house to confirm that he's not there.

I pull the $8.21 out of my pocket and set it on the counter.

It just barely covers my breakfast plus a cheap-ass tip.

I take one last sip of coffee.

Then I reach into the patch pocket of my flannel button-down and pull out the cigar and the lighter.

I glance around.

The diner is now packed.

The two cops who were here when I first arrived are gone,

but there's another one sitting in the corner booth at the far end.

My hands shake imperceptibly as I tear open the packaging.

True to its name, the end of the cigar tastes faintly sweet.

It takes me three tries to strike a flame.

I fire the tobacco at the end of the cigar, draw in a mouthful of smoke, and blow a stream toward the back of the short-order cook who's flipping hotcakes on the griddle.

For ten seconds, no one notices.

Then the older woman sitting next to me in a cat-hair-covered jacket turns and says, "You can't do that in here."

And I respond with something I would never in a million years even dream of saying: "But there's nothing like a cigar after a meal."

She looks at me through her plate-glass lenses like I've lost my mind.

The waitress walks over holding a carafe of steaming coffee and looking massively disappointed.

Shaking her head, she says with the voice of a scolding mother, "You know you can't smoke that in here."

"But it's delicious."

"Do I need to call the manager over?"

I take another puff.

Exhale.

The short-order cook—a wide, muscled guy with ink-covered arms—turns around and glares at me.

I say to the waitress, "That's a great idea. You should go get the manager right now, because I am not putting this out."

As the waitress leaves, the old woman sitting beside me, whose meal I've ruined, mutters, "What a rude young man."

And she throws down her fork, climbs off the stool, and heads for the door.

Some of the other customers in my vicinity have begun to take notice.

But I keep smoking, until a rail of a man emerges from the back of the restaurant with the waitress in tow. He wears black jeans and a white oxford with sweat stains down the sides and a solid-color tie whose knot is unraveling.

By the general dishevelment of his appearance, I'm guessing he's worked all night.

Stopping behind me, he says, "I'm Nick, the manager on duty. You can't smoke that inside. You're disturbing the customers."

I turn slightly in my stool and meet his eyes. He looks tired and annoyed, and I feel like such a jerk putting him through this, but I can't stop now.

I glance around, all eyes on me now, a hotcake burning on the griddle.

I ask, "Are you all disturbed by my fine cigar?"

Yesses abound.

Someone calls me an asshole.

Movement at the far end of the diner catches my eye.

Finally.

The police officer slides out of the corner booth, and as he heads my way down the length of the aisle, I hear his radio crackle.

He's young.

Late twenties if I had to guess.

Short and stocky.

A Marine-like hardness in his eyes and an intelligence too.

The manager takes a step back, relieved.

Now the officer stands beside me, says, "We have a clean indoor air ordinance in the city, which you're violating right now."

I take another puff from the cigar.

The cop says, "Look, I've been up most of the night. A lot of these other customers have as well. Why do you want to ruin everyone's breakfast?"

"Why do you want to ruin my cigar?"

A flicker of anger passes over the cop's face.

His pupils dilate.

"Put that cigar out right now. Last warning."

"Or what?"

He sighs.

"That was not the response I was hoping for. Get up."

"Why?"

"Because you're going to jail. If that cigar isn't out in five seconds, I'm going to assume you're resisting arrest, which means I get to be a lot less gentle."

I drop my cigar in my coffee cup, and as I step down off the stool, the officer deftly whips the handcuffs off his belt and locks the bracelets around my wrists.

"Carrying any weapons or needles? Anything that could hurt me or that I should know about?"

"No, sir."

"Are you on any drugs or medication right now?"

"No, sir."

He pats me down, then takes me by the arm.

As we walk toward the entrance, the other customers applaud.

His cruiser is parked right out front.

He opens the rear door and tells me to watch my head.

It's almost impossible to gracefully duck into the back of a police car with your hands cuffed behind you. The officer climbs in behind the wheel.

Buckling his seat belt, he cranks the engine and pulls out into the snowy street.

The backseat seems to have been constructed especially for discomfort. There's no legroom whatsoever, my knees are crushed into the cage, and the seats themselves are made of a hard plastic composite that feels like I'm sitting on concrete.

As I stare through the bars that protect the window, I watch the familiar buildings of my neighborhood scroll past, wondering if this has any hope in hell of working.

We pull into the parking garage of the 14th District Police Station.

Officer Hammond hauls me out of the backseat and escorts me through a pair of steel doors into a booking room.

There's a row of desks, with chairs for prisoners on one side and a Plexiglas partition that separates them from a workstation on the other.

The room smells like vomit and desperation badly covered over with Lysol.

At this hour of the morning, there's only one other prisoner aside from me—a woman at the far end of the room, chained to a desk. She's rocking manically back and forth, scratching herself, tweaking.

Hammond searches me again, and then tells me to have a seat.

He unlocks the bracelet on my left wrist, cuffs it to an eyebolt in the desk, and says, "I need to see your driver's license."

"I lost it."

He makes a note of this on his paperwork and then goes around to the other side of the desk and logs in to the computer.

He takes my name.

Social Security number.

Address.

Employer.

I ask, "What exactly am I being charged with?"

"Disorderly conduct and disturbing the peace."

Hammond begins to fill out the arrest report.

After a few minutes, he stops typing and looks at me through the scratched-up Plexi. "You don't strike me as a crazy person or an asshole. You don't have a sheet. You've never been in trouble before. So what happened back there? It's almost like . . . you were *trying* to get arrested. Anything you want to tell me?"

"No. I am sorry I messed up your breakfast."

He shrugs. "There'll be others."

I'm fingerprinted.

Photographed.

They take my shoes and give me a pair of slippers and a blanket.

When he's finished booking me into the system, I ask, "When do I get my phone call?"

"You can have it right now." He lifts the receiver from a landline. "Who would you like to call?"

"My wife."

I give him the number and watch him dial.

When it starts to ring, he hands me the receiver across the partition.

My heart is pounding.

Pick up, honey. Come on.

Voicemail.

I hear my voice, but it's not my message. Did Jason2 re-record it as a subtle marking of his territory?

I say to Officer Hammond, "She's not answering. Would you hang up, please?"

He kills the call a second before the beep.

"Daniela probably didn't recognize the number. Would you mind trying one more time?"

He dials again.

It rings again.

I'm wondering—if she doesn't answer, should I risk just leaving a message?

No.

What if Jason2 heard it? If she doesn't answer this time, I'll have to figure out some other way to—

"Hello?"

"Daniela."

"Jason?"

Tears sting my eyes at the sound of her voice. "Yeah, it's me."

"Where are you calling from? It says Chicago Police on the

caller ID. I thought it was one of those fraternal order charity things, so I didn't—"

"I just need you to listen for a minute."

"Is everything okay?"

"Something happened on my way to work. I'll explain everything when—"

"Are you okay?"

"I'm fine, but I'm in jail."

For a moment, it gets so quiet on the other end of the line that I can hear the NPR show she's listening to in the background.

She says finally, "You got arrested?"

"Yeah."

"For what?"

"I need you to come bail me out."

"Jesus. What did you do?"

"Look, I don't have all the time in the world right now to explain. This is kind of like my one phone call."

"Should I call a lawyer?"

"No, just get down here as soon as you can. I'm at the Fourteenth District Precinct on . . ." I look to Hammond for the street address.

"North California Avenue."

"North California. And bring your checkbook. Has Charlie already left for school?"

"Yeah."

"I want you to pick him up and bring him with you when you come to get me. This is very—"

"Absolutely not."

"Daniela—"

"I am not bringing my son to get his father out of jail. What the hell happened, Jason?"

Officer Hammond raps his knuckles on the Plexiglas and moves a finger across his throat.

I say, "My time's up. Please get here as soon as you can."

"Okay."

"Honey."

"What?"

"I love you so much."

She hangs up.

My lonely holding cell consists of a paper-thin mattress on a concrete base.

Toilet.

Sink.

Camera over the door, watching me.

I lie in bed with the jail-issue blanket draped over me and stare at a patch of ceiling that I'm guessing has been studied by all manner of people in the throes of despair and hopelessness and poor decision-making.

What runs through my mind are the innumerable things that might go wrong, that could so easily stop Daniela from coming to me.

She could call Jason2 on his cell phone.

He could call her between classes just to say hi.

One of the other Jasons could decide to make his move.

If any one of those things happens, this entire plan will blow up spectacularly in my face.

My stomach hurts.

My heart is racing.

I try to calm myself down, but there's no stopping the fear.

I wonder if any of my doppelgängers have anticipated this move. I try to take comfort in the idea that they couldn't have. If I hadn't seen that belligerent drunk at the bar last night, obnoxiously hitting on those women and getting thrown out by the bouncer, it would never have occurred to me to get myself arrested as a ploy to make Daniela and Charlie come to me in a safe environment.

What led to this decision was a unique experience that was mine alone.

Then again, I could be wrong.

I could be wrong about everything.

I get up, pace back and forth between the toilet and the bed, but there's not much ground to cover in this six-by-eight-foot cell, and the more I pace, the more the walls seem to inch in closer until I can actually feel the claustrophobia of this room as a tightening in my chest.

It's getting harder to breathe.

I move finally to the tiny window at eye level in the door.

Peer through into a sterile white hallway.

The sound of a woman crying in one of the neighboring cells echoes off the cinder-block walls.

She sounds so far beyond hope.

I wonder if it's the same woman I saw in the booking room when I first arrived.

A guard walks by, holding another inmate by his arm above the elbow.

Returning to the bed, I curl up under the blanket and face the wall and try not to think, but it's impossible.

It feels like hours have passed.

Why could it possibly be taking this long?

I can only think of one explanation.

Something happened.

She isn't coming.

The door to my cell unlocks with a mechanized jolt that spikes my heart rate.

I sit up.

The baby-faced guard standing in the doorway says, "You get to go home, Mr. Dessen. Your wife just posted bail."

He leads me back to the booking room, where I sign some papers I don't even bother to read.

They return my shoes and escort me through a series of corridors.

As I push through the doors at the end of the last hallway, my breath catches in my throat and my eyes sheet over with tears.

Of all the places I imagined our reunion finally happening, the lobby of the 14th District Precinct wasn't one of them.

Daniela rises from her chair.

Not a Daniela who doesn't know me, or is married to another man, or another version of me.

My Daniela.

The one, the only.

She's wearing the shirt she sometimes paints in—a faded blue button-down spattered with oil and acrylic—and when she sees me her face screws up with confusion and disbelief.

I rush to her across the lobby, wrapping my arms around

her, and she's saying my name, saying it like something isn't adding up, but I don't let go, because I *can't* let go. Thinking— the worlds I've come through, the things I've done, endured, suffered, to get back into the arms of this woman.

I can't believe how good it feels to touch her.

To breathe the same air.

To smell her.

Feel the voltage of my skin against hers.

I frame her face in my hands.

I kiss her mouth.

Those lips—so maddeningly soft.

But she pulls away.

And then pushes me away, her hands against my chest, her brow deeply furrowed.

"They told me you were arrested for smoking a cigar in a restaurant, and that you wouldn't . . ." Her train of thought derails. She studies my face like there's something wrong with it, her fingers running through two weeks' worth of stubble. Of course there's something wrong with it—it's not the face she woke up to today. "You didn't have a beard this morning, Jason." She looks me up and down. "You're so thin." She touches my ragged, filthy shirt. "These aren't the clothes you left the house in."

I can see her trying to process it all and coming up blank.

"Did you bring Charlie?" I ask.

"No. I told you I wasn't going to. Am I losing my mind or—?"

"You're not losing your mind."

Gently, I take her by the arm and pull her over to a couple of straight-backed chairs in a small waiting area.

I say, "Let's sit for a minute."

"I don't want to sit, I want you to—"

"Please, Daniela."

We sit.

"Do you trust me?" I ask.

"I don't know. This is all . . . scaring me."

"I'll explain everything, but first I need you to call a cab."

"My car is parked two blocks—"

"We're not walking to your car."

"Why?"

"It's not safe out there for us."

"What are you talking about?"

"Daniela, will you please just trust me on this?"

I think she's going to balk, but instead she takes out her phone, opens an app, and orders a car.

Looking up at me finally, she says, "Done. It's three minutes out."

I glance around the lobby.

The officer who escorted me here from the booking room is gone, and at the moment, we're the only occupants aside from the woman at the welcome window. But she's sitting behind a thick wall of protective glass, so I feel reasonably sure she can't hear us.

I look at Daniela.

I say, "What I'm about to tell you is going to sound crazy. You're going to think I've lost my mind, but I haven't. Remember the night of Ryan's celebration at Village Tap? For winning that prize?"

"Yeah. That was over a month ago."

"When I walked out the door of our house that night,

that's the last time I saw you, until five minutes ago when I came through those doors."

"Jason, I've seen you every day since that night."

"That man isn't me."

Her face becomes dark.

"What are you talking about?"

"He's another version of me."

She just stares into my eyes, blinking.

"Is this some kind of trick? Or a game you're playing? Because—"

"Not a trick. Not a game."

I take her phone out of her hand and check the time. "It's 12:18. I have office hours right now."

I type in the number to my direct line on campus and hand Daniela the phone.

It rings twice, and then I hear my voice answer with, "Hi, beautiful. I was just thinking about you."

Daniela's mouth opens slowly.

She looks ill.

I put it on speaker and mouth, *"Say something."*

She says, "Hey. How's your day going so far?"

"Great. Finished my morning lecture, and now I'm seeing a few students over the lunch hour. Everything okay?"

"Um, yeah. I just . . . wanted to hear your voice."

I grab the phone from her and mute it.

Jason says, "I can't stop thinking about you."

I look at Daniela, say, "Tell him you've been thinking, and that since we had such an amazing time in the Keys last Christmas, you want to go back."

"We didn't go to the Keys last Christmas."

"I know that, but he doesn't. I want to prove to you he's not the man you think he is."

My doppelgänger says, "Daniela? Did I lose you?"

She unmutes the phone. "No, I'm right here. So, the real reason for my call—"

"Wasn't just to hear the dulcet tones of my voice?"

"I was thinking about when we went to the Keys for Christmas last year, and how much fun we all had. I know money's tight, but what if we went back?"

Jason doesn't miss a beat.

"Absolutely. Whatever you want, my love."

Daniela stares into my eyes as she says into the phone, "Do you think we can get the same house we had? The pink-and-white one that was right on the beach? It was so perfect."

Her voice breaks on the last word, and I think she's right on the verge of losing her composure, but she somehow manages to hold the scaffolding together.

"We'll make it work," he says.

The phone begins to shake in her hand.

I want to tear him slowly apart.

Jason says, "Honey, someone's waiting out in the hall to see me, so I better jump off."

"Okay."

"I'll see you tonight."

No you won't.

"See you tonight, Jason."

She ends the call.

Reaching down, I squeeze her hand and say, "Look at me."

She looks lost, addled.

I say, "I know your head is spinning right now."

"How can you be at Lakemont and also sitting here right in front of me at the same moment?"

Her phone beeps.

A message appears on the touchscreen, advising that our car is arriving.

I say, "I'll explain everything, but right now we need to get in this car and pick our son up from school."

"Is Charlie in danger?"

"We all are."

That seems to wrench her back into the moment.

Rising, I give her a hand up out of the chair.

We move across the lobby toward the precinct entrance.

A black Escalade is parked at the curb, twenty feet ahead.

Pushing through the doors, I pull Daniela along the sidewalk toward the idling SUV.

There's no trace of last night's storm, at least not in the sky. A fierce north wind has raked away the clouds and left in its wake a brilliant winter day.

I open the rear passenger door and climb in after Daniela, who gives the black-suited driver the address to Charlie's school.

"Please get there as quickly as you can," she says.

The windows are deeply tinted, and as we accelerate away from the precinct, I look over at Daniela and say, "You should text Charlie, let him know we're coming, to be ready."

She turns her phone over, but her hands are still shaking too badly to compose a text.

"Here, let me."

I take her phone and open the messaging app, find the last thread between her and Charlie.

I type:

Dad and I are coming to pick you up from school right now. There's no time to sign you out, so you'll just have to excuse yourself to the bathroom and head out front. We'll be in the black Escalade. See you in 10.

Our driver pulls out of the parking lot and into a street that's been plowed clean of snow, the pavement drying out under the bright winter sun.

A couple blocks down, we pass Daniela's navy Honda.

Two cars ahead of hers, I see a man who looks exactly like me sitting behind the wheel of a white van.

I glance through the rear window.

There's a car behind us, but it's too far back for me to see who's driving.

"What is it?" Daniela asks.

"I want to make sure no one's following us."

"Who would be following us?"

Her phone vibrates as a new text arrives, saving me from having to answer that question.

CHARLIE now
Everything ok?

I respond with:

All good. Explain when we see you.

Putting my arm around Daniela, I pull her in close.

She says, "I feel like I'm caught in a nightmare and I can't wake myself up. What's happening?"

"We'll go someplace safe," I whisper. "Where we can talk in private. Then I'll tell you and Charlie everything."

Charlie's school is a sprawling brick complex that looks like a mental institution crossed with a steampunk castle.

He's sitting out on the front steps when we pull into the pickup lane, looking at his phone.

I tell Daniela to wait, and then I step out of the car and walk toward my son.

He stands, bewildered at my approach.

At my appearance.

I crash into him and squeeze him tight and say, "God, I've missed you," before I even think to stop myself.

"What are you doing here?" he asks. "What's with the car?"

"Come on, we have to go."

"Where?"

But I just grab hold of his arm and pull him toward the open passenger door of the Escalade.

He climbs in first and I follow, shutting the door after us.

The driver glances back and asks with a heavy Russian accent, "Where to now?"

I thought about it on the drive over from the police station—someplace big and bustling, where even if one of the other Jasons followed us, we could easily blend into a crowd. Now I second-guess that choice. I think of three alternates— Lincoln Park Conservatory, the observation deck of the Willis

Tower, and the Rosehill Cemetery. Rosehill feels like the safest option, the most unexpected. And I'm similarly drawn to Willis and Lincoln Park. So I go against my instinct and swing back to my first choice.

I tell him, "Water Tower Place."

We ride in silence into the city.

As the buildings of downtown edge closer, Daniela's cell phone vibrates.

She looks at the screen and then hands it over so I can see the text she just received.

It's a 773 number I don't recognize.

Daniela, it's Jason. I'm texting you from a strange number, but I'll explain everything when I see you. You're in danger. You and Charlie both. Where are you? Please call me back ASAP. I love you so much.

Daniela looks scared out of her mind.

The air inside the car is prickling with electricity.

Our driver turns onto Michigan Avenue, which is clogged with lunch-hour traffic.

The yellowed limestone of the Chicago Water Tower looms in the distance, dwarfed by the surrounding skyscrapers that line the expansive avenue of the Magnificent Mile.

The Escalade pulls to a stop at the main entrance, but I ask the driver to drop us underground instead.

From Chestnut Street, we descend into the darkness of a parking garage.

Four levels down, I tell him to stop at the next bank of elevators.

As far as I can see, no other cars have followed us in.

Our door slams echo off the concrete walls and columns as the SUV pulls away.

Water Tower Place is a vertical mall, with eight floors of boutique and luxury stores built around a chrome-and-glass atrium.

We ride up to the mezzanine level, which houses all the restaurants, and step off the glass elevator.

The snowy weather has brought the crowds indoors.

For the moment at least, I feel perfectly anonymous.

We find a bench off in a quiet corner, out of the flow of foot traffic.

Sitting between Daniela and Charlie, I think of all the other Jasons in Chicago at this moment willing to do anything, willing to kill, just to be where I'm sitting.

I take a breath.

Where to even begin?

I look Daniela in the eye and brush a wisp of hair behind her ear.

I look into Charlie's eyes.

I tell them how much I love them.

That I've come through hell to be sitting here between them.

I start with my abduction on a crisp October night when I was forced to drive at gunpoint to an abandoned power plant in South Chicago.

I tell them about my fear, how I thought I was going to be murdered, about waking up instead in the hangar of a mysterious science lab, where people I'd never seen appeared not only to know me, but to have been anticipating my return.

They listen intently to the details of my escape from Velocity Laboratories on that first night, and my return to our house on Eleanor Street, to a home that wasn't my home, where I lived alone as a man who had chosen to dedicate his life to his research.

A world where Daniela and I had never been married and Charlie had never been born.

I tell Daniela about meeting her doppelgänger at the art installation in Bucktown.

My capture and imprisonment in the lab.

My escape with Amanda into the box.

I describe the multiverse.

Every door I walked through.

Every ruined world.

Every Chicago that wasn't quite right, but which brought me one step closer to home.

There are things I leave out.

Things I can't yet bring myself to say.

The two nights I spent with Daniela after the installation opening.

The two times I watched her die.

I'll share these moments eventually, when the time is right.

I try to imagine what it must feel like for Daniela and Charlie to hear this story.

When the tears begin to slide down Daniela's face, I ask, "Do you believe me?"

"Of course I believe you."

"Charlie?"

My son nods, but the look in his eyes is miles away. He's

staring vacantly at the shoppers strolling past, and I wonder how much of what I've said has actually landed.

How does someone even begin to process such a thing?

Daniela wipes her eyes and says, "I just want to be sure I understand exactly what you're telling me. So on the night you went out to Ryan Holder's celebration, this other Jason stole your life? He took you into the box and stranded you in his world so he could live in this one? With me?"

"That's what I'm telling you."

"That means the man I've been living with is a stranger."

"Not completely. I think he and I were the same person up until fifteen years ago."

"What happened fifteen years ago?"

"You told me you were pregnant with Charlie. The multiverse exists because every choice we make creates a fork in the road, which leads into a parallel world. That night you told me you were pregnant didn't just happen the way you and I remember it. It unfolded in a multitude of permutations. In one world, the one we live in now, you and I decided to make a life together. We got married. Had Charlie. Made a home. In another, I decided that becoming a father in my late twenties wasn't the path for me. I worried my work would be lost, that my ambition would die.

"So there's a version of our life where we didn't keep the baby. Charlie. You pursued your art. I pursued my science. And eventually, we parted ways. That man, the version of me you've been living with for the last month—*he* built the box."

"Which is a large version of that thing you were working on when we first met—the cube?"

"Exactly. And somewhere along the way, he realized

everything he'd given up by letting his work be the thing that defined him. He looked back at the choice he made fifteen years ago with regret. But the box can't take you back or forward in time. It only connects all possible worlds at the same moment, in the present. So he searched until he found my world. And he traded my life for his."

The look on Daniela's face is pure shock and disgust.

She rises from the bench and runs toward the restrooms.

Charlie starts after her, but I put my hand on his shoulder and say, "Just give her a minute."

"I knew something wasn't right."

"What do you mean?" I ask.

"You—well, not you, *him*—he had this different, like, energy about him. We talked more, especially at dinner. He was just, I don't know . . ."

"What?"

"Different."

There are things I want to ask my son, questions blazing through my mind.

Was he more fun?

A better father?

A better husband?

Was life more exciting with the imposter?

But I'm afraid the answers to those questions might shatter me.

Daniela returns.

So pale.

As she sits back down, I ask, "You all right?"

"I have a question for you."

"What?"

"This morning, when you got yourself arrested—was that to get me to come to you?"

"Yes."

"Why? Why not just come to the house after . . . Jesus, I don't even know what to call him."

"Jason2."

"After Jason2 left?"

I say, "Here's where things get really crazy."

Charlie asks, "Things aren't already crazy?"

"I wasn't the only . . ." It sounds insane to even be saying the words.

But I have to tell them.

"What?" Daniela asks.

"I wasn't the only version of me to make it back into this world."

"What does that mean?" she asks.

"Other Jasons made it back as well."

"What other Jasons?"

"Versions of me who escaped into the box in that lab, but took different paths through the multiverse."

"How many?" Charlie asks.

"I don't know. A lot, maybe."

I explain what happened at the sporting-goods store and in the chat room. I tell them about the Jason who tracked me to my room and the one who attacked me with a knife.

My family's confusion takes a turn toward outright fear.

I say, "This is why I got myself arrested. For all I know, many Jasons have been watching you, following you, tracking your every move as they try to figure out what to do. I needed you to come to me in a safe place. That's why I had you call the car service. I know at least one version of me followed you to the police station. I saw him as we drove past your Honda. This is why I wanted you to bring Charlie with you. But it doesn't matter. We're here together, and safe, and now you both know the truth."

It takes Daniela a moment to find her voice.

She says softly, "These other . . . Jasons . . . what are they like?"

"What are you asking?"

"Do they all share your history? Are they basically you?"

"Yes. Up until the moment I stepped into the multiverse. Then we all took different paths, had different experiences."

"But some are just like you? Versions of my husband who have fought like hell to get back to this world. Who want nothing more than to be with me again. With Charlie."

"Yeah."

Her eyes narrow.

What must this be like for her?

I can see her trying to wrap her mind around the impossibility of it all.

"Dani, look at me."

I stare into her shimmering eyes.

I say, "I love you."

"I love you too. But so do the others, right? Just as much as you do."

It rips my guts out to hear those words.

I have no response to them.

I look up at the people in our immediate vicinity, wondering if we're being watched.

The mezzanine level has become more crowded since we sat.

I see a woman pushing a stroller.

Young lovers meandering slowly through the mall, holding hands and ice-cream cones, lost in their bliss.

An old man shuffling along behind his wife, with a look on his face that says, *Take me home, please.*

We're not safe here.

We're not safe anywhere in this city.

I ask, "Are you with me?"

She hesitates, looks at Charlie.

Then back at me.

"Yeah," she says. "I'm with you."

"Good."

"So what do we do now?"

FOURTEEN

We leave with nothing but the clothes on our backs and a bank envelope filled with cash from our emptied checking and savings accounts. Daniela puts the rental car on our credit card, but every transaction going forward will be cash-only to make us harder to track.

By midafternoon, we're cruising through Wisconsin.

Rolling pasture

Minor hills.

Red barns.

Silos form a rustic skyline.

Smoke trickles out of farmhouse chimneys.

Everything sparkling under a fresh blanket of snow and the sky a brilliant winter blue.

It's slow-going, but I keep off the highways.

Stick to the country roads.

Take random, unplanned turns with no destination in mind.

When we stop for gas, Daniela shows me her phone. There's a stream of missed calls and new texts, all from 773, 847, and 312 Chicago-area phone numbers.

I open the messaging app.

Dani—It's Jason, pls call me back at this number
immediately.

Daniela, this is Jason. First of all, I love you. There's so
much I have to tell you. Pls call me as soon as you get this.

Daniela, you're going to be hearing from a bunch of other
Jasons if you haven't already. Your head must be spinning.
I am yours. You are mine. I love you forever. Call me the
moment you get this.

Daniela the Jason you're with is an imposter. Call me.

Daniela you and Charlie are not safe. The Jason you're
with isn't who you think he is. Call me right away.

None of them love you like I do. Call me, Daniela. Pls.
Begging you. Love you.

I will kill them all for you and fix this. Say the word. I will
do anything for you.

I stop reading, put a block on each number, and delete the
messages.

But one text in particular calls out to me.

It's not from an unknown number.

It's from *Jason*.

My cell number. He's had my phone all this time. Since the
night he grabbed me off the street.

You're not home, not answering your cell. You must
know. All I can say is that I love you. That's why. My time

with you has been the best of my life. Pls call me. Hear me out.

I power off her phone and tell Charlie to turn his off as well. "We have to leave them off," I say. "From here on out. Any one of them could track us if they're transmitting."

As the afternoon turns toward evening and the sun begins to slip, we drive into the vast Northwoods.

The road is empty.

Ours alone.

We've taken numerous summer vacations to Wisconsin but never ventured this far north. And never in winter. We go miles without seeing any signs of civilization, and each town we pass through seems smaller than the one before— crossroads in the middle of nowhere.

A hard silence has taken hold inside the Jeep Cherokee, and I'm not sure how to break it.

Or rather, that I have the courage to.

All your life you're told you're unique. An individual. That no one on the planet is just like you.

It's humanity's anthem.

But that isn't true for me anymore.

How can Daniela love me more than the other Jasons?

I look at her in the front passenger seat, wondering what she thinks of me now, what she feels toward me.

Hell, what *I* think of me is up for debate.

She sits quietly beside me, just watching the forest rushing by outside the window.

I reach across the console and hold her hand.

She looks over at me, and then back out the window.

At dusk, I drive into a town called Ice River, which feels appropriately remote.

We grab some fast food and then stop at a grocery store to stock up on food and basic necessities.

Chicago goes on forever.

There's no breathing space even in the suburbs.

But Ice River just ends.

One second we're in town, passing an abandoned strip mall with boarded-up storefronts. The next, the buildings and the lights are dwindling away in the side mirror, and we're cruising through forest and darkness, the headlights firing a cone of brilliance through a narrow corridor of tall pines that edge up close on either side of the road.

Pavement streams under the lights.

We pass no cars.

I take the third turnoff, 1.2 miles north of town, down a one-lane, snowy drive that winds through spruce and birch trees to the end of a small peninsula.

After several hundred yards, the headlights strike the front of a log house that seems to be exactly what I'm looking for.

Like most lakefront residences in this part of the state, it's dark and appears uninhabited.

Shuttered for the season.

I pull the Cherokee to a stop in the circular drive and kill the engine.

It's very dark, very quiet.

I look over at Daniela.

I say, "I know you don't love the idea, but breaking in is less risky than actually creating a paper trail by renting some place."

The whole way up from Chicago—six hours—she's barely spoken.

As if in shock.

She says, "I get it. We're way past breaking-and-entering at this point anyway, right?"

Opening the door, I step down into a foot of fresh snow.

The cold is sharp.

The air is still.

One of the bedroom windows isn't latched, so I don't even have to break glass.

We carry the plastic grocery bags up onto the covered porch.

It's freezing inside.

I hit the lights.

Straight ahead, a staircase ascends into the darkness of the second floor.

Charlie says, "This place is gross."

It isn't gross so much as redolent of must and neglect.

A vacation home in the off-season.

We carry our bags into the kitchen and drop them on the counter and wander through the house.

The interior décor straddles the line of cozy and dated.

The appliances are old and white.

The linoleum floor in the kitchen is cracking, and the hardwood floors are scuffed and creaky.

In the living room, a largemouth bass is mounted over the brick hearth, and the walls are covered with fishing lures in frames—at least a hundred of them.

There's a master bedroom downstairs and two bedrooms

on the second floor, one of them crammed tight with triple bunk beds.

We eat Dairy Queen out of greasy paper bags.

The light above us throws a harsh, naked glare on the surface of the kitchen table, but the rest of the house stands dark.

The central heating struggles to warm the interior to a livable temperature.

Charlie looks cold.

Daniela is quiet, distant.

Like she's caught in a slow free fall into some dark place.

She barely touches her food.

After dinner, Charlie and I bring in armloads of wood from the front porch, and I use our fast-food bags and an old newspaper to get the fire going.

The wood is dry and gray, several seasons old, and it quickly takes the flame.

Soon the walls of the living room are aglow.

Shadows flickering across the ceiling.

We fold down the sleeper sofa for Charlie and pull it close to the hearth.

Daniela goes to prepare our room.

I sit next to Charlie on the end of the mattress, letting the heat from the fire wash over me.

I say, "If you wake up in the night, throw an extra log on the fire. Maybe we can keep it going until morning, warm this place up."

He kicks off his Chuck Taylors and pulls his arms out of the sleeves of his hoodie. As he crawls under the covers, it hits me that he's fifteen years old now.

His birthday was October 21.

"Hey," I say. He looks at me. "Happy birthday."

"What are you talking about?"

"I missed it."

"Oh. Yeah."

"How was it?"

"Fine, I guess."

"What'd you do?"

"We went to the movies and out to dinner. Then I hung out with Joel and Angela."

"Who's Angela?"

"Friend."

"Girlfriend?" He blushes in the firelight. "So I'm dying to know—did you pass your driving test?"

He gives up a small smile. "I am the proud owner of a learner's permit."

"That's great. So did he take you?"

Charlie nods.

Fuck. That hurts.

I pull the sheets and blankets up to Charlie's shoulders and kiss him on the forehead. It's been years since I actually tucked my son into bed, and I try to savor the moment, to slow it down. But like all good things, it goes by so fast.

Charlie stares up at me in the firelight, asks, "Are you okay, Dad?"

"No. Not really. But I'm with you guys now. That's all that matters. This other version of me . . . you liked him?"

"He's not my father."

"I know, but did you—?"

"He's not my father."

Rising from the sleeper sofa, I toss another log on the fire and trudge back through the kitchen toward the other end of the house, the hardwood floor cracking under my weight.

It's almost too cold to be sleeping in this room, but Daniela has stripped the beds upstairs and raided the closets for extra blankets.

The walls are wood-paneled.

A space heater glows in the corner, filling the air with the smell of scorched dust.

A sound is coming from inside the bathroom.

Sobbing.

I knock on the hollow-core door.

"Daniela?"

I hear her catch her breath.

"What?"

"Can I come in?"

She's quiet for a moment.

Then the lock punches out.

I find Daniela huddled in the corner against an old claw-foot tub, her knees drawn into her chest, eyes red and swollen.

I've never seen her like this—physically shaking, breaking right in front of me.

She says, "I can't. I just . . . I can't."

"Can't what?"

"You're right here in front of me, and I love you so much, but then I think about all those other versions of you, and—"

"They aren't here, Daniela."

"They want to be."

"But they're not."

"I don't know how to think or feel about this. And then I wonder . . ."

She loses what little composure she had left.

It's like watching ice crack.

"What do you wonder?" I ask.

"I mean . . . are you even you?"

"What are you talking about?"

"How do I know you're *my* Jason? You say you stepped out our door in early October, and that you didn't see me again until this morning in the police station. But how do I know you're the man I love?"

I move down onto the floor.

"Look in my eyes, Daniela."

She does.

Through tears.

"Can't you see it's me? Can't you tell?"

She says, "I can't stop thinking about the last month with him. It makes me sick."

"What was it like?"

"Jason, don't do that to me. Don't do it to you."

"Every day I was in that corridor, in the box, trying to find my way home—I thought about the two of you. I tried not to, but put yourself in my place."

Daniela opens her knees, and as I crawl between them, she pulls me in close against her chest and runs her fingers through my hair.

She asks, "Do you really want to know?"

No.

But I have to.

I say, "I'll always wonder."

I rest my head against her.

Feel the rise and fall of her chest.

She says, "To be honest, it was amazing at first. The reason I remember that night you went to Ryan's party so vividly is because of how you—*he*—acted when you got home. At first, I thought you were drunk, but it wasn't that. It was like . . . like you were looking at me in this new way.

"I still remember, all those years ago, the first time we made love in my loft. I was lying in bed, naked, waiting for you. And you just stood at the end of the bed for a minute and stared at me. It felt like it was the first time you had really seen me. Maybe the first time anyone had ever really seen me. It was the hottest thing.

"This other Jason looked at me like that, and there was this new energy between us. Kind of like how it feels when you come home after a weekend at one of your conferences, but way more intense."

I ask, "So with him, it must've been like the first time we were together?"

She doesn't answer right away.

Just breathes for a while.

Then says finally, "I'm so sorry."

"It's not your fault."

"After a couple weeks, it hit me that this wasn't a one-night, or even one-weekend, kind of thing. I realized that something in you had changed."

"What was different?"

"A million little things. The way you dressed. The way you got ready in the morning. The things you talked about at dinner."

"The way I fucked you?"

"Jason."

"Please don't lie to me. That, I can't take."

"Yes. It was different."

"Better."

"Like it was the first time again. You did things you never did. Or hadn't in a long time. It was like I was something, not that you wanted, but that you needed. Like I was your oxygen."

"Do you want this other Jason?"

"No. I want the man I've made a life with. The man I made Charlie with. But I need to know you're that man."

I sit up and look at her in this cramped, windowless bathroom in the middle of nowhere that smells faintly of mildew.

She looks at me.

So tired.

Struggling onto my feet, I give her a hand up.

We move into the bedroom.

Daniela climbs into bed, and I hit the lights and crawl in beside her under the freezing sheets.

The frame is creaky, and the slightest movement bangs the headboard against the wall, which rattles the picture frames.

She's wearing underwear and a white T-shirt, and she smells like she's been riding in the car all day without a shower—fading deodorant tinged with funk.

I love it.

She whispers in the dark, "How do we fix this, Jason?"

"I'm working on it."

"What does that mean?"

"It means ask me again in the morning."

Her breath in my face is sweet and warm.

The essence of everything I associate with home.

She's asleep within a moment, breathing deeply in and out.

I think I'm right behind her, but when I close my eyes, my thoughts run rampant. I see versions of me stepping out of elevators. In parked cars. Sitting on the bench across the street from our brownstone.

I see me everywhere.

The room is dark except for the coils of the space heater glowing in the corner.

The house lies silent.

I can't sleep.

I need to fix this.

Quietly, I slide out from under the covers. At the door, I stop and glance back at Daniela, safe under a mountain of blankets.

I head down the noisy hardwood floor of the hallway, the house getting warmer the closer I get to the living room.

The fire is already low.

I add several logs.

For a long time, I sit just staring into the flames, watching the wood slowly crumble into the radiant bed of embers as my son snores softly behind me.

The idea first occurred to me on the drive north today, and I've been mulling it over ever since.

It seemed insane at first.

But the more I pressure-check it, the more it seems like my only option.

In the living room beside the entertainment center, there's a desk with a ten-year-old Mac and a dinosaur printer. I power the computer on. If there's a password required or no Internet connection, this will have to wait until tomorrow, when I can find an Internet café or coffee shop in town.

I'm in luck. There's a guest login option.

I open the web browser and access that *asonjayessenday* email account.

The hyperlink still works.

> Welcome to UberChat!
> There are currently seventy-two active participants.
> Are you a new user?

I click *No* and log in with my username and password.

> Welcome back Jason9!
> Logging you into UberChat now!

The conversation is much longer, with so many participants I break out in a cold sweat.

I scan everything, down through the most recent message, which is less than a minute old.

> Jason42: The house has been empty since at least midafternoon.
>
> Jason28: So which of you did this?
>
> Jason4: I followed Daniela from 44 Eleanor St. to the police station on North California.
>
> Jason14: What was she doing there?
>
> Jason25: What was she doing there?

Jason10: What was she doing there?

Jason4: No idea. She went inside, never came out. Her Honda is still there.

Jason66: Does this mean she knows? Is she still in the police station?

Jason4: I don't know. Something is up.

Jason49: I was nearly killed last night by one of us. He got a key to my hotel room and came in with a knife in the middle of the night.

I start typing . . .

Jason9: DANIELA AND CHARLIE ARE WITH ME.

Jason92: Safe?

Jason42: Safe?

Jason14: How?

Jason28: Prove it.

Jason4: Safe?

Jason25: How?

Jason10: You fucker.

Jason9: How doesn't matter, but yes, they're safe. They're also very scared. I've been giving this a lot of thought. I assume we all share the same basic desire, that no matter what, Daniela and Charlie can't be harmed?

Jason92: Yes.

Jason49: Yes.

Jason66: Yes.

Jason10: Yes.

Jason25: Yes.

Jason4: Yes.

Jason28: Yes.

Jason14: Yes.

Jason103: Yes.

Jason5: Yes.

Jason16: Yes.

Jason82: Yes.

Jason9: I would rather die than see anything happen to them. So here's what I'm proposing. Two days from now, at midnight, we all meet up at the power plant and conduct a peaceful lottery. The winner gets to live in this world with Daniela and Charlie. Also, we destroy the box, so no other Jasons find their way here.

Jason8: No.

Jason100: No way.

Jason21: How would this work?

Jason38: Never.

Jason28: Prove you have them or fuck off.

Jason8: Why chance? Why not fight it out? Let merit decide.

Jason109: And what happens to the losers? Suicide?
JasonADMIN: For the sake of this conversation *not* becoming incomprehensible, I've temporarily frozen all accounts from participating except me and Jason9. Everyone else can still watch this conversation. Jason9, continue please.

Jason9: I realize there are many ways this could all go wrong. I could decide to not show up. You'd never know. Any number of Jasons could choose not to participate, to essentially wait in the wings for the smoke to clear and then do to one of us what Jason2 did. Except that I know I'll keep my word, and maybe this is naïve on my part, but I think that means all of you will too. Because you wouldn't be keeping your word for us. You'd be keeping it for Daniela and Charlie. The other alternative is for me to take them and disappear forever. New identities. A life always on the run. Always looking over our shoulder. As much as I want to be with them, I don't want that life for my wife and son. And I don't have the right to keep them for myself. I feel so strongly about it, I'm willing to submit myself to this lottery, where, judging by the sheer number of us involved, I'm almost certain to lose. I have to talk to Daniela first, but in the meantime, spread the word. I'll be back online tomorrow night with more details, including proof, jason28.

JasonADMIN: I think someone already asked, but what happens to the losers?

Jason9: I don't know yet. All that matters is our wife and son living out the rest of their lives in peace and safety. If you feel otherwise, you don't deserve them.

Light coming through the curtain wakes me.

Daniela is in my arms.

For the longest time, I just lie there.

Holding her.

This extraordinary woman.

After a while, I disentangle myself and grab my pile of clothes off the floor.

I dress by the remains of the fire—nothing but a bed of coals—and throw on the last two logs.

We've slept in.

The clock on the stove reads 9:30, and through the window above the sink, I see sunlight angling down through the evergreens and birches, making pools of light and shadow across the floor of the forest as far as I can see.

I head outside into the morning chill and step down off the porch.

Past the back of the cabin, the property slopes gently to the edge of a lake.

I walk out to the end of a snowcapped pier.

There's a rim of ice a few feet out from the shore, but it's too early in the season, even with the recent storm, for the rest of the lake to have frozen.

I brush the snow off a bench, take a seat, and watch the sun creep up behind the pine trees.

The cold is invigorating. Like an espresso shot.

Mist rises from the surface of the water.

I register footsteps squeaking in the snow behind me.

Turning, I see Daniela coming down the pier, following in my footprints.

She's carrying two steaming mugs of coffee, her hair is a gorgeous wreck, and she has several blankets thrown around her shoulders like a shawl.

As I watch her approach, it occurs to me that in all likelihood, this is the last morning I'll ever get to spend with her. I'll be returning to Chicago first thing tomorrow. Alone.

Handing me both mugs, she takes one of her blankets and wraps it around me. Then she sits on the bench and we drink our coffees and stare out across the lake.

I say, "I always thought we'd end up in a place like this."

"I didn't know you wanted to move to Wisconsin."

"When we're older. Find a cabin to fix up."

"*Can* you fix things up?" She laughs. "I'm kidding. I know what you mean."

"Maybe spend summers here with the grandchildren. You could paint by the lakeshore."

"What would you do?"

"I don't know. Finally catch up on my *New Yorker* subscription. Just be with you."

She reaches down and touches the piece of thread that's still tied around my ring finger. "What's this?"

"Jason2 took my wedding ring, and there was a point early on where I was beginning to lose my grasp on what was real. On who I was. If I'd ever been married to you. So I tied this string around my finger as a reminder that you, *this* version of you, existed."

She kisses me.

For a long time.

I say, "I have to tell you something."

"What?"

"In that first Chicago I woke up in—the one where I found you at this art installation about the multiverse—"

"What?" She smiles. "Did you fuck me?"

"Yeah."

The smile dies.

She just stares at me for a moment, and there's almost no emotion in her voice when she asks, "Why?"

"I didn't know where I was or what was happening to me. Everyone thought I was crazy. I was starting to think so too. Then I found you—the only familiar thing in a world that was completely wrong. I wanted so badly for that Daniela to be you, but she wasn't. She couldn't be. Just like the other Jason isn't me."

"So you were just fucking your way across the multiverse then?"

"That was the only time, and I didn't realize where I was when it happened. I didn't know if I was losing my mind or what."

"And how was she? How was I?"

"Maybe we shouldn't—"

"I told you."

"Fair enough. It was just the way you described this other Jason coming home that first night. It was like being with you before I knew I loved you. Like experiencing that incredible connection all over again for the first time. What are you thinking right now?"

"I'm figuring out how mad I should be at you."

"Why should you be mad at all?"

"Oh, is that your argument? It isn't cheating if it's another version of me?"

"I mean, it's original at least."

This makes her laugh.

That it makes her laugh says everything about why I love her.

"What was she like?" Daniela asks.

"She was you without me. Without Charlie. She was sort of dating Ryan Holder."

"Shut up. And I was this successful artist?"

"You were."

"Did you like my installation?"

"It was brilliant. You were brilliant. Do you want to hear about it?"

"I'd love to."

I tell her about the Plexiglas labyrinth, what it felt like to walk through it. The startling imagery. The spectacular design.

It makes her eyes light up.

And it makes her sad.

"Do you think I was happy?" she asks.

"What do you mean?"

"With everything I'd given up to be this woman."

"I don't know. I was with this woman for forty-eight hours. I think, like you, like me, like everyone, she had regrets. I think sometimes she woke up in the night wondering if the path she took was the right one. Afraid it wasn't. Wondering what a life with me might have been like."

"I wonder those things sometimes."

"I've seen so many versions of you. With me. Without me. Artist. Teacher. Graphic designer. But it's all, in the end, just life. We see it macro, like one big story, but when you're in it, it's all just day-to-day, right? And isn't that what you have to make your peace with?"

Out in the middle of the lake, a fish jumps, its splash sending perfect, concentric ripples across the glasslike water.

I say, "Last night, you asked me how we fix this."

"Any bright ideas?"

My first instinct is to protect her from the knowledge of what I'm contemplating, but our marriage isn't built on keeping secrets. We talk about everything. The hardest things. It's embedded in our identity as a couple.

And so I tell her what I proposed to the chat room last night and watch the expression on her face move through flashes of anger, horror, shock, and fear.

She says finally, "You want to raffle me off? Like a fucking fruit basket?"

"Daniela—"

"I don't need you doing something heroic."

"No matter what happens, you're going to have me back."

"But some other version of you. That's what you're saying, right? And what if he's like this asshole who ruined our lives? What if he isn't good like you?"

I look away from her, out across the lake, and blink through the tears.

She asks, "Why would you sacrifice yourself so someone else can be with me?"

"We all have to sacrifice ourselves, Daniela. That's the only way it works out for you and Charlie. Please. Just let me make your lives in Chicago safe again."

When we walk back inside, Charlie is at the stovetop flipping pancakes.

"Smells great," I say.

He asks, "Will you make your fruit thing?"

"Sure."

It takes me a moment to locate the cutting board and a knife.

I stand next to my son, peeling the apples and dicing them and adding the pieces to a saucepan filled with simmering maple syrup.

Through the windows, the sun climbs higher and the forest fills with light.

We eat together and talk comfortably, and there are moments where it feels almost normal, where the fact that this is likely the last breakfast I'll ever share with them isn't at the forefront of my mind.

In the early afternoon, we head to town on foot, walking down the middle of the faded country road, the pavement dry in the sun, snow-packed in the shadows.

We buy clothes at a thrift shop and then go to a matinee in a little downtown cinema showing a movie that came out six months ago.

It's a stupid romantic comedy.

It's just what we need.

We stay through the credits, until the lights come up, and as we step out of the theater, the sky is already growing dark.

At the edge of town, we take a shot with the only restaurant that's open—the Ice River Roadhouse.

We sit at the bar.

Daniela orders a glass of pinot noir. I order a beer for me, a Coke for Charlie.

The place is crowded, the only thing going on on a weeknight in Ice River, Wisconsin.

We order food.

I drink a second beer, and then a third.

Before long, Daniela and I are buzzed and the noise of the roadhouse growing.

She puts her hand on my leg.

Her eyes are glassy from the wine, and it feels so good to

be close to her again. I'm trying not to think about how every little thing that happens is my last experience of it, but the knowledge weighs so heavy.

The roadhouse keeps filling up.

It's wonderfully noisy.

A band begins to set up on a small stage in the back.

I'm drunk.

Not belligerent or sloppy.

Just perfectly lit up.

If I think about anything other than the moment, I tear up, so I don't think about anything other than the moment.

The band is a country-and-western four-piece, and soon Daniela and I are slow-dancing in a mass of people on a tiny dance floor.

Her body is pressed against mine, my hand cupping the small of her back, and between the steel guitar and the way she's looking at me, I want nothing more than to take her back to our creaky bed with the loose headboard and knock all the picture frames off the walls.

Daniela and I are laughing, and I'm not even sure why.

Charlie says, "You guys are wasted."

It might be an overstatement, but not by much.

I say, "There was steam to blow off."

He says to Daniela, "Hasn't felt like this in the last month, has it?"

She looks at me.

"No, it hasn't."

We stagger up the highway in the dark, no headlights behind us or ahead.

The woods utterly silent.

Not even a breath of wind.

As still as a painting.

I lock the door to our room.

Daniela helps me lift the mattress off the bed.

We set it on the floorboards and kill the lights and take off all our clothes.

It's chilly in the room, even with the space heater running.

We climb naked and shivering under the blankets.

Her skin is smooth and cool against mine, her mouth soft and warm.

I kiss her.

She says that she needs me inside of her so much it hurts.

Being with Daniela isn't like being home.

It defines home.

I remember thinking that the first time I made love to her fifteen years ago. Thinking that I'd found something I didn't even know I'd been searching for.

It holds even more true tonight as the hardwood floor groans softly beneath us and the moonlight steals between the break in the curtains just enough to light her face as her mouth opens and her head tilts back and she whispers, so urgently, my name.

We're sweaty, our hearts racing in the silence.

Daniela runs her fingers through my hair, and she's staring at me in the dark the way I love.

"What is it?" I ask.

"Charlie was right."

"About?"

"What he said on the walk home. It *hasn't* been like this since Jason2 came here. You aren't replaceable. Not even by you. I keep thinking about how we met. At that point in our lives, we could've crashed into anyone. But *you* showed up at that backyard party and saved me from that asshole. I know part of our story is the electricity of our connection, but the other part is equally miraculous. It's the simple fact that you walked into my life at the exact moment you did. You instead of someone else. In some ways, isn't that even more incredible than the connection itself? That we found each other at all?"

"It's remarkable."

"What I realized is that the same thing happened yesterday. Of all the versions of Jason, it was you who pulled that crazy stunt at the diner, which landed you in jail, which brought us safely together."

"So you're saying it's fate."

She smiles. "I think I'm saying we found each other, for a second time."

We make love again and fall asleep.

In the dead of night, she wakes me, whispers in my ear, "I don't want you to leave."

I turn over onto my side and face her.

Her eyes are wide open in the dark.

My head hurts.

My mouth is dry.

I'm caught in that disorienting transition between inebriation and hangover, when the pleasure slowly morphs into pain.

"What if we just kept driving?" she says.

"To where?"

"I don't know."

"What are we supposed to tell Charlie? He has friends. Maybe a girlfriend. We just tell him to forget all that? He's finally happy at school."

"I know," she says, "and I hate it, but yes, that's what we tell him."

"Where we live, our friends, our jobs—those things define us."

"They're not *all* that defines us. As long as I'm with you, I know exactly who I am."

"Daniela, I want nothing more than to be with you, but if I don't do this thing tomorrow, you and Charlie will never be safe. And no matter what happens, you will still have me."

"I don't want some other version of you. I want you."

I wake in the dark to my pulse pounding in my head and my mouth bone-dry.

Pulling on my jeans and shirt, I stagger down the hall.

With no fire tonight, the sole source of illumination on the entire ground level is a timid nightlight plugged into an outlet above the kitchen counter.

I take a glass from the cabinet and fill it at the tap.

Drink it down.

Fill it again.

The central heating cuts off.

I stand at the sink, sipping the cold well water.

The cabin so quiet I can hear the floor popping as the wood fibers expand and contract in distant corners of the house.

Through the window over the kitchen sink, I stare into the woods.

I love that Daniela wants me, but I don't know where we go from here. I don't know how to keep them safe.

My head is spinning.

A little ways beyond the Jeep, something catches my attention.

A shadow moving across the snow.

Adrenaline surges.

I set the glass down, head to the front door, and step into my boots.

On the porch, I button my shirt and walk into the trodden snow between the steps and the car.

Then out past the Jeep.

There.

I see what caught my eye from the kitchen.

As I approach, it's still moving.

Larger than I first thought.

The size of a man.

No.

Jesus.

It is a man.

The path along which he's dragged himself is plain to see by the streaks of blood that look black in the starlight.

He's groaning as he crawls in the direction of the front porch. He's never going to make it.

I reach him, kneel beside him.

It's me, right down to the coat and the Velocity Laboratories backpack and the ring of thread.

He's holding his stomach with one hand, which is covered

in steaming blood, and he looks up at me with the most desperate eyes I've ever seen.

I ask, "Who did this to you?"

"One of us."

"How'd you find me here?"

He coughs up a mist of blood. "Help me."

"How many of us are here?"

"I think I'm dying."

I look around. It only takes me a second to lock on the pair of blood-tinged footprints moving away from this Jason toward the Jeep, and then on around the side of the cabin.

The dying Jason is saying my name.

Our name.

Begging for my help.

And I want to help him, but all I can think is—they found us.

Somehow, they found us.

He says, "Don't let them hurt her."

I look back at the car.

I didn't notice at first, but now I see that all the tires have been slashed.

Somewhere in the near distance, I hear footsteps in the snow.

I scan the woods for movement, but the starlight doesn't penetrate the denser forest farther out from the cabin.

He says, "I'm not ready for this."

I look down into his eyes as my own panic builds. "If this is the end, be brave."

A gunshot shreds the silence.

It came from behind the cabin, near the lake.

I race back through the snow, past the Jeep, sprinting toward the front porch, trying to process what's happening.

From inside the cabin, Daniela calls my name.

I climb the steps.

Crash through the front door.

Daniela is coming down the hallway, wrapped in a blanket and backlit by the light spilling out of the master bedroom.

My son approaches from the kitchen.

I lock the front door behind me as Daniela and Charlie converge in the foyer.

She asks, "Was that a gunshot?"

"Yeah."

"What's happening?"

"They found us."

"Who?"

"I did."

"How is that possible?"

"We have to leave right now. Both of you head to our bedroom, get dressed, start getting our things together. I'm going to make sure the back door is locked, then I'll join you."

They head down the hallway.

The front door is secure.

The only other way into the house is through the French doors that lead from the screened-in porch into the living room.

I move through the kitchen.

Daniela and Charlie will be looking to me to tell them what's next.

And I have no idea.

We can't take the car.

We'll have to leave on foot.

As I reach the living room, my thoughts come in a raging stream of consciousness.

What do we need to bring with us?

Phones.

Money.

Where's our money?

In an envelope in the bottom dresser drawer of our bedroom.

What else do we need?

What can we not forget?

How many versions of me tracked us here?

Am I going to die tonight?

By my own hand?

I feel my way through the darkness, past the sleeper sofa, to the French doors. As I reach down to test the handles, I realize—it shouldn't be this cold in here.

Unless these doors were recently opened.

As in a few seconds ago.

They're locked now, and I don't remember locking them.

Through the glass panes, I can see something on the patio, but it's too dark to make out any detail. I think it's moving.

I need to get back to my family.

As I turn away from the French doors, a shadow rises from behind the sofa.

My heart stops.

A lamp blinks on.

I see myself standing ten feet away, one hand on the light switch, the other pointing a gun at me.

He's wearing nothing but a pair of boxer shorts.

His hands are covered in blood.

Coming around the sofa with the gun aimed at my face, he says quietly, "Take your clothes off."

The slash across his face identifies him.

I glance behind me through the French doors.

The lamplight illuminates just enough of the patio for me to see a pile of clothes—Timberlands and a peacoat—and another Jason lying on his side, his head in a pool of blood, throat laid open.

He says, "I won't tell you again."

I start undoing the buttons of my shirt.

"We know each other," I say.

"Obviously."

"No, that cut on your face. We had beers together two nights ago."

I watch that piece of information land, but it doesn't derail him like I'd hoped.

He says, "That doesn't change what has to happen. This is the end, brother. You'd do the same and you know it."

"I wouldn't, actually. I thought so at first, but I wouldn't."

I slide my arms out of the sleeves, toss him the shirt.

I know what he's planning: dress himself in my clothes. Go to Daniela pretending to be me. He'll have to reopen the slash across his face to make it look like a fresh wound.

I say, "I had a plan to protect her."

"Yeah, I read it. I'm not sacrificing myself so someone else can be with my wife and son. Jeans too."

I unbutton them, thinking, I misjudged. We're not all the same.

"How many of us have you murdered tonight?" I ask.

"Four. I'll kill a thousand of you if that's what it takes."

As I pull off the jeans, one leg at a time, I say, "Something happened to you in the box, in those worlds you mentioned. What turned you into this?"

"Maybe you don't want them back badly enough. And if that's the case, you don't deserve them any—"

I throw the jeans at his face and rush him.

Wrapping my arms around Jason's thighs, I lift with everything I've got and run him straight into the wall, crushing the air out of his lungs.

The gun hits the floor.

I kick it into the kitchen as Jason crumples and drive my knee into his face.

I hear bone crunch.

Grabbing his head, I bring my knee back for another blow, but he sweeps my left leg out from under me.

I slam into the hardwood floor, the back of my head hitting so hard I see bursts of light, and then he's on top of me, blood dripping off his ruined face, one hand squeezing my throat.

When he hits me, I feel my cheek fracture in a supernova of pain below my left eye.

He hits me again.

I blink through a sheet of tears and blood, and the next time I can see clearly, he's holding a knife in the hand he was hitting me with.

Gunshot.

My ears ringing.

A small black hole through his sternum and blood spilling out of it and down the center of his chest. The knife drops from his hands onto the floor beside me. I watch him put a finger in the hole and try to plug it, but the blood won't be stopped.

He takes a wet, ragged breath and looks up at the man who shot him.

I crane my neck too, just enough to see another Jason aiming a gun at him. This one is clean-shaven, and he's wearing the black leather jacket that Daniela gave me ten years ago for our anniversary.

On his left hand, a gold wedding band gleams.

My ring.

Jason2 pulls the trigger again, and the next bullet shears off the side of my attacker's skull.

He topples.

I turn over and sit up slowly.

Spitting blood.

My face on fire.

Jason2 aims the gun at me.

He's going to pull the trigger.

I actually see my death coming, and I have no words, just a fleeting image of me as a child on my grandparents' farm in western Iowa. A warm spring day. A massive sky. Cornfields. I'm dribbling a soccer ball through the backyard toward my brother, who's guarding the "goal"—a space between two maple trees.

I think, Why this last memory on the brink of my death? Was I the most happy in that moment? The most purely myself?

"Stop it!"

Daniela is standing in the kitchen nook, dressed now.

She looks at Jason2.

She looks at me.

At the Jason with a bullet through his head.

The Jason on the screened-in porch with his throat cut.

And somehow, without so much as a tremor in her voice, she manages to ask, "Where is my husband?"

Jason2 looks momentarily thrown.

I wipe the blood out of my eyes. "Right here."

"What did we do tonight?" she asks.

"We danced to bad country music, came home, and made love." I look at the man who stole my life. "You're the one who kidnapped me?"

He looks at Daniela.

"She knows everything," I say. "There's no point in lying."

Daniela asks, "How could you do this to me? To our family?"

Charlie appears beside his mother, taking in the horror all around us.

Jason2 looks at her.

Then at Charlie.

Jason2 is only six or seven feet away, but I'm sitting on the floor.

I couldn't reach him before he pulled the trigger.

I think, Get him talking.

"How'd you find us?" I ask.

"Charlie's cell has a find-my-phone app."

Charlie says, "I only turned it on for one text late last night. I didn't want Angela to think I'd blown her off."

I look at Jason2. "And the other Jasons?"

"I don't know. I guess they followed me here."

"How many?"

"I have no idea." He turns to Daniela. "I got everything I ever wanted, except you. And you haunted me. What we could've been. That's why—"

"Then you should've stayed with me fifteen years ago when you had the chance."

"Then I wouldn't have built the box."

"And that would be so terrible, why? Look around. Has your life's work caused anything but pain?"

He says, "Every moment, every breath, contains a choice. But life is imperfect. We make the wrong choices. So we end up living in a state of perpetual regret, and is there anything worse? I built something that could actually eradicate regret. Let you find worlds where you made the right choice."

Daniela says, "Life doesn't work that way. You live with your choices and learn. You don't cheat the system."

So slowly, I transfer my weight onto my feet.

But he catches me, says, "Don't even."

"You going to kill me in front of them?" I ask. "Really?"

"You had such enormous dreams," he says to me. "You could've stayed in my world, in the life I built, and actually lived them."

"Oh, is that how you justify what you did?"

"I know how your mind works. The horror you face every day walking to the train to go teach, thinking, *Is this really it?* Maybe you're brave enough to admit it. Maybe you're not."

I say, "You don't get to—"

"Actually, I do get to judge you, Jason, because I *am* you. Maybe we branched into different worlds fifteen years ago, but we're wired the same. You weren't born to teach undergrad physics. To watch people like Ryan Holder win the acclaim that should've been yours. There is *nothing* you can't do. I know, because I've done it all. Look at what I built. I could wake up in your brownstone every morning and look myself in the mirror because I achieved everything I ever wanted. Can you say the same? What have you done?"

"I made a life with them."

"I handed you, handed both of us, what everyone secretly wants. The chance to live two lives. Our best two lives."

"I don't want two lives. I want them."

I look at Daniela. I look at my son.

Daniela says to Jason2, "And I want him. Please. Let us have our life. You don't have to do this."

His face hardens.

His eyes narrow.

He moves toward me.

Charlie screams, "No!"

The gun is inches from my face.

I stare up into my doppelgänger's eyes, ask, "So you kill me and then what? What does it get you? It won't make her want you."

His hand is trembling.

Charlie starts toward Jason2.

"Don't you touch him."

"Stay put, son." I stare down the barrel of the gun. "You've lost, Jason."

Charlie is still coming, Daniela trying to hold him back, but he rips his arm away.

As Charlie closes in, Jason2's eyes cut away from me for a split second.

I slap the gun out of his hand, grab the knife off the floor, and bury it in his stomach, the blade sliding in with almost no resistance.

Standing, I jerk the knife out, and as Jason2 falls into me, grasping my shoulders, I stick him again with the blade.

Over and over and over.

So much blood pouring through his shirt and onto my hands, and the rusted smell of it filling the room.

He's clutching me, the knife still embedded in his gut.

I think about him with Daniela as I twist the blade and rip it out and shove him away from me.

He teeters.

Grimacing.

Holding his stomach.

Blood leaking through his fingers.

His legs fail him.

He sits, and then, with a groan, stretches out on his side and lets his head rest against the floor.

I lock eyes with Daniela and Charlie. Then I go to Jason2 and search his pockets as he moans, finally emerging with my set of car keys.

"Where's the Suburban?" I ask.

When he answers, I have to lean in close to hear his voice: "A quarter mile past the turnoff. On the shoulder."

I rush over to the clothes I stripped out of just moments ago, dressing quickly.

When I finish buttoning my shirt, I bend down to tie my boots, glancing over at Jason2, bleeding out on the floorboards of this old cabin.

I lift the gun from the floor and wipe the grip off on my jeans.

We need to leave.

Who knows how many more are coming.

My doppelgänger says my name.

I look over—he's holding my wedding band in his blood-soaked fingers.

I walk to him, and as I take the ring and slide it onto my finger over the ring of thread, Jason2 grabs my arm and pulls me down toward his face.

He's trying to say something.

I say, "I can't hear you."

"Look . . . in . . . the glove box."

Charlie comes over, wrapping his arms fiercely around me, trying to hold back tears, but his shoulders jerk and the sobs break loose. As he cries in my arms like a little boy, I think of the horror he's just witnessed, and it brings tears to my eyes.

I hold his face between my hands.

I say, "You saved my life. If you hadn't tried to stop him, I never would've had a chance."

"Really?"

"Really. Also I'm going to stomp your fucking phone into pieces. Now we have to leave. Back door."

We rush through the living room, sidestepping pools of blood.

I unlock the French doors, and as Charlie and Daniela move out onto the screened-in porch, I glance back at the man who caused all this.

His eyes are still open, blinking slowly, watching us go.

Stepping outside, I pull the doors closed after me.

I have to track through the blood of one more Jason to reach the screen door.

I'm not sure which way to go.

We head down to the shoreline, follow it north through the trees.

The lake as smooth and black as obsidian.

I keep scanning the woods for other Jasons—one could step out from behind a tree and take my life at any second.

After a hundred yards, we turn from the shoreline and move in the general direction of the road.

Four gunshots ring out at the cabin.

We're running now, struggling through the snow, all of us gasping for breath.

The adrenaline tide is keeping the pain of my bruised face at bay, but I wonder for how much longer.

We break out of the forest onto the road.

I stand on the double-yellow line, and for a moment, the woods are silent.

"Which way?" Daniela asks.

"North."

We jog down the middle of the road.

Charlie says, "I see it."

Straight ahead, off the right-side shoulder, I clock the back of our Suburban pulled halfway into the trees.

We pile inside, and as I push the key into the ignition, I catch movement in the side mirror—a shadow sprinting toward us on the road.

I crank the engine, release the emergency brake, and shift into gear.

Whipping the Suburban around, I pin the gas pedal to the floor.

I say, "Get down."

"Why?" Daniela asks.

"Just do it!"

We accelerate into darkness.

I punch on the lights.

They fire straight onto Jason, standing in the middle of the road, aiming a gun at the car.

There's a burst of fire.

A bullet punctures the windshield and rips through the headrest an inch away from my right ear.

Another muzzle flash, another gunshot.

Daniela screams.

How broken must this version of me be to risk hitting Daniela and Charlie?

Jason tries to step out of the way a half second too late.

The right edge of the bumper clips his waist, the contact devastating.

It slings him around hard and fast, his head slamming into the front passenger window with enough force to break the glass.

In the rearview mirror, I watch him tumble across the road as we keep accelerating.

"Anyone hurt?" I ask.

"I'm fine," Charlie says.

Daniela sits back up.

"Daniela?"

"I'm okay," she says, beginning to brush the pebbles of safety glass out of her hair.

We speed down the dark highway.

No one says a word.

It's three in the morning, and we're the only car on the road.

The night air streams through the bullet holes in the windshield, the road noise deafening through the broken window beside Daniela's head.

I ask, "Do you still have your phone with you?"

"Yeah."

"Give it to me. Yours too, Charlie."

They hand them over, and I lower my window several inches and chuck the phones out of the car.

"They're going to keep coming, aren't they?" she asks. "They're never going to stop."

She's right. The other Jasons can't be trusted. I was wrong about the lottery.

I say, "I thought there was a way to fix this."

"So what do we do?"

Exhaustion crushes down on me.

My face hurting more every second.

I look over at Daniela. "Open the glove box."

"What am I looking for?" she asks.

"I'm not sure."

She pulls out the Suburban's owner's manual.

Our insurance and registration paperwork.

A tire-pressure gauge.

A flashlight.

And a small leather bag I know all too well.

FIFTEEN

We're sitting in our shot-up Suburban in the deserted parking lot.

I drove all night.

I study my face in the mirror. My left eye is purple, badly swollen, and the skin over my left cheekbone has turned black from the blood pooling underneath.

It's all agonizing to the touch.

I look back at Charlie, and then over at Daniela.

Reaching across the center console, she runs her fingernails down the back of my neck.

She says, "What other choice do we have?"

"Charlie? This is your decision too."

"I don't want to leave."

"I know."

"But I guess we have to."

The strangest thought passes through my consciousness like a fleeting summer cloud.

We're so clearly at the end. Everything we've built—our house, our jobs, our friends, our collective life—it's all gone. We have nothing left but one another, and yet, in this moment, I'm happier than I've ever been.

*

Morning sun streams through fissures in the roof, lighting patches along the dark, desolate hallway.

"This place is cool," Charlie says.

"You know where you're going?" Daniela asks.

"Unfortunately, I could take us where we need to go blindfolded."

As I guide us through the abandoned passages, I'm beyond tired. Running on caffeine and fear. The gun I took from the cabin is jammed down into the back of my waistband, and Jason2's leather bag is tucked under my arm. It occurs to me that as we drove down to the South Side at dawn, I never even glanced at the skyline as we passed just west of downtown.

One last glimpse would've been nice.

I register a twinge of regret, but immediately push it back.

I think of all the nights I lay in bed, wondering what it might be like if things were different, if I hadn't taken the branch in the road that made me a father and mediocre physics professor instead of a luminary in my field. I suppose it all comes down to wanting what I didn't have. What I perceived might have been mine through a different set of choices.

But the truth is, I did make those different choices.

Because I am not just me.

My understanding of identity has been shattered—I am one facet of an infinitely faceted being called Jason Dessen who *has* made every possible choice and lived every life imaginable.

I can't help thinking that we're more than the sum total of our choices, that all the paths we *might* have taken factor somehow into the math of our identity.

But none of the other Jasons matter.

I don't want their lives.

I want mine.

Because as fucked as everything is, there is no place I'd rather be than with this Daniela, this Charlie. If one tiny thing were different, they wouldn't be the people I love.

We move slowly down the stairs toward the generator room, our footfalls echoing through the vast, open space.

One flight up from the bottom, Daniela says, "There's someone down there."

I stop.

My mouth runs dry as I gaze into the gloom below.

I see a man get up from where he's been sitting on the floor.

Then another beside him.

And another.

All throughout the darkness between the last generator and the box, versions of me are coming to their feet.

Fuck.

They came early for the lottery.

Dozens of them.

All watching us.

I look back up the stairs, the blood rushing in my ears so loud it temporarily blocks out everything in a waterfall of panic-driven white noise.

Daniela says, "We're not running." She pulls the gun out of my waistband and links her arm through mine. "Charlie, grab your father's arm and don't let go no matter what happens."

"You sure about this?" I ask.

"One million percent."

With Charlie and Daniela clinging to me, I slowly descend the last few steps and start across the broken concrete.

My doppelgängers stand between us and the box.

There's no oxygen in the room.

Nothing but the sound of our footsteps and the wind blowing through the glassless window frames high above.

I hear Daniela let out a trembling breath.

Charlie's hand is sweating in mine.

"Just keep walking," I say.

One of them steps forward.

He says to me, "This isn't what you proposed."

I say, "Things have changed. A bunch of us tried to kill me last night, and—"

Daniela interrupts with, "One of you shot at our car with Charlie inside. Over. Done."

She pulls me forward.

We're closing in on them.

They're not getting out of our way.

Someone says, "You're here now. Let's have that lottery."

Daniela squeezes my arm even tighter.

She says, "Charlie and I are going into the box with *this* man." Her voice breaks. "If there were some other way . . . We're all just doing the best we can."

It's unavoidable—I make eye contact with the nearest Jason, his envy and jealousy a living thing. Dressed in tattered clothes, he reeks of homelessness and despair.

Says to me in a low growl, "Why should *you* get her?"

The Jason beside him says, "This isn't about him. It's about what she wants. What our son needs. That's all that matters now. Let them pass. All of you."

The crowd begins to part.

We move slowly through the corridor of Jasons.

Some are crying.

Hot, angry, desperate tears.

I am too.

So is Daniela.

So is Charlie.

Others stand stoic and tense.

Finally, the last one steps out of the way.

The box looms straight ahead.

The door wide open.

Charlie enters first, followed by Daniela.

I keep waiting for something to happen as my heart hammers in my chest.

At this point, nothing would surprise me.

I cross the threshold, put my hand on the door, and catch one last glimpse of my world.

It's an image I will never forget.

Light from the high windows streaming down onto the old generators as fifty versions of me all stare toward the box in a stunned and eerie and devastated silence.

The locking mechanism to the door triggers.

The bolt shoots home.

I turn on the flashlight and look at my family.

For a moment, Daniela looks like she's about to break down, but she holds it together.

I pull out the syringes, the needles, the ampoules.

Set everything up.

Just like old times.

I help Charlie roll his sleeve above his elbow.

"First time's a little intense. You ready?"

He nods.

Holding his arm steady, I slide the needle into the vein, pull back on the plunger, see blood mix into the syringe.

As I fire the full load of Ryan's drug into my son's bloodstream, Charlie's eyes roll back and he slumps against the wall.

I tie the tourniquet around my arm.

"How long does the effect last?" Daniela asks.

"About an hour."

Charlie sits up.

"You all right?" I ask.

"That was weird."

I inject myself. It's been a few days since my last use, and the drug smashes into me harder than usual.

When I've recovered, I lift the last syringe.

"Your turn, my love."

"I hate needles."

"Don't worry. I've gotten pretty good at this."

Soon we're all under the effect of the drug.

Daniela takes the light out of my hand and steps away from the door.

As it illuminates the corridor, I watch her face. I watch my son's face. They look afraid. Awestruck. I think back to the first time I saw the corridor, to the sense of horror and wonder that overwhelmed me.

The sense of being nowhere.

And in between.

"How far does it go?" Charlie asks.

"It never ends."

We walk together down this corridor that runs into infinity.

I can't quite believe I'm here again.

That I'm here with them.

I'm not sure exactly what I'm feeling, but it isn't the raw fear I experienced before.

Charlie says, "So each of these doors . . ."

"Opens into another world."

"Wow."

I look at Daniela, ask, "You okay?"

"Yes. I'm with you."

We've been walking for a while now, and our time is running short.

I say, "The drug will be wearing off soon. We should probably get going."

And so we stop in front of a door that looks like all the rest.

Daniela says, "I was thinking—all these other Jasons found their way back to their world. What's to say one of them won't find their way into wherever we end up? In theory, they all think the same way you do, right?"

"Yeah, but I'm not going to open a door, and neither are you."

I turn to Charlie.

He says, "Me? What if I mess up? What if I take us to some terrible place?"

"I trust you."

"I do too," Daniela says.

I say, "Even though you'll be opening the door, the path to

this next world is actually one we're creating together. The three of us." Charlie looks at the door, tense. "Look," I say, "I've tried to explain to you how the box works, but forget all that for a minute. Here's the thing. The box isn't all that different from life. If you go in with fear, fear is what you'll find."

"But I don't even know where to start," he says.

"It's a blank canvas."

I embrace my son.

I tell him I love him.

Tell him I'm so proud.

Then Daniela and I sit on the floor with our backs against the wall, facing Charlie and the door. She leans her head against my shoulder and holds my hand.

Driving here last night, I assumed that in this moment I'd be terrified of walking into a new world, but I'm not afraid at all.

I'm filled with a childlike excitement to see what comes next.

As long as my people are with me, I'm ready for anything.

Charlie steps toward the door and takes hold of the handle.

Just before he opens it, he draws a breath and glances back at us, as brave and strong as I've ever seen him.

A man.

I nod.

He turns the handle, and I hear the latch bolt slide from its housing.

A blade of light shears into the corridor, so brilliant I have to shield my eyes for a moment. When they finally adjust, I see Charlie silhouetted in the open doorway of the box.

Rising, I pull Daniela onto her feet, and we walk over to

our son as the cold, sterile vacuum of the corridor fills with warmth and light.

A wind through the door carries the scent of wet earth and unknown flowers.

A world just after a storm.

I put my hand on Charlie's shoulder.

"You ready?" he asks.

"We're right behind you."

ACKNOWLEDGMENTS

Dark Matter was the hardest work of my career, and I couldn't have pushed it across the finish line without the help and support of the constellation of generous, talented, and amazing people who brightened my sky during its writing.

My agent and friend David Hale Smith worked some serious magic this time out, and the entire team at Inkwell Management has had my back every step of the way. Thanks to Richard Pine for wise counsel when we needed it most, to Alexis Hurley for her brilliance and determination to sell my work internationally, and to Nathaniel Jacks, deal-paperer extraordinaire.

My film and TV manager, Angela Cheng Caplan, and entertainment attorney, Joel VanderKloot, are exceptional in every way. I've been so fortunate to have them on my side.

The team at Crown are some of the smartest people I've ever worked with. Their passion and dedication to this book have been nothing short of astounding. Thank you Molly Stern, Julian Pavia, Maya Mavjee, David Drake, Dyana Messina, Danielle Crabtree, Sarah Bedingfield, Chris Brand, Cindy Berman, and everyone at Penguin Random House for getting behind this book.

And a second thank you to my genius editor, Julian Pavia,

who pushed me as hard as I've ever been pushed and made this book better on every page.

I couldn't ask for a stronger group trying to make *Dark Matter*, the movie, a reality. Huge thanks to Matt Tolmach, Brad Zimmerman, David Manpearl, Ryan Doherty, and Ange Giannetti at Sony. And also to Michael De Luca and Rachel O'Connor, who were wonderful champions for the book early on.

Jacque Ben-Zekry edited all my Wayward Pines novels, and even though this wasn't her book, she gave it the same care and attention as if it were. *Dark Matter* would be a shadow of itself without her insight.

The physics and astronomy professor Clifford Johnson, Ph.D., helped me to not look like a total idiot in discussing the broad-stroke concepts of quantum mechanics. If I've said anything wrong, it's my bad.

I could not have written *Dark Matter* without the work of many physicists, astronomers, and cosmologists who have dedicated their lives to seeking fundamental truths about the nature of our existence. Stephen Hawking, Carl Sagan, Neil deGrasse Tyson, Michio Kaku, Rob Bryanton, and Amanda Gefter were instrumental in helping me begin to understand all things quantum. In particular, Michio Kaku's elegant analogy of a pond, carp, and hyperspace informed my understanding of dimensionality and became the basis of Jason2's explanation of the multiverse to Daniela.

My early readers suffered through multiple drafts and gave me indispensable feedback along the way. Special thanks to my writing partner and great friend, Chad Hodge; my brother from the same mother, Jordan Crouch; my brothers from different mothers, Joe Konrath and Barry Eisler; the lovely Ann Voss Peterson; and my big-idea soul mate Marcus Sakey, who, while I was visiting Chicago two years ago, helped me spot the potential of this book in a sea of foundering ideas, and encouraged me to write it in spite of how much it scared me. *Because of* how much it scared me. And a fond shout-out to the bar at the stellar Longman & Eagle in Logan Square (Chicago), where the shape and identity of *Dark Matter* literally emerged from the fog.

And saving-the-best-for-last thanks to my family: Rebecca, Aidan, Annslee, and Adeline. For everything. I love you.

extracts reading groups

competitions books new

discounts extracts extracts

competitions extracts

books new extracts discounts

events books

extracts new titles reading groups

interviews

events extracts

discounts

new books events

events new

discounts extracts discounts

www.panmacmillan.com

extracts events reading groups

competitions books extracts new